Creating Memories

A Medieval Romance

The Sword of Glastonbury Series

Book 6

Lisa Shea

Cover design by Lisa Shea
Book design by Lisa Shea

Visit my website at LisaShea.com

First Printing: February 2012

~ 13 ~

Print ISBN-13 978-0-9798377-2-2
Amazon Kindle ASIN: B00791A3DW

We can create a world
Where women act with honor,
Where men stand loyally by their side,
Where truth is all-important.
All we have to do
Is believe.

Creating Memories

Chapter 1

Laura spun smoothly through her counter-block, swinging her short sword in a high arc, relishing the bone-jarring frisson of contact as her opponent's weapon skittered down the length of her own and barely missed her left shoulder. She lunged forward at once, pressing her advantage to lay a hail of blows that her opponent, a lanky, brown-haired teen, blocked with effort. The echoes of the strikes reverberated hollowly on his worn wooden shield. The lad grinned as he stepped back, and she flashed a smile in return as she swung again, immersed in bliss from the exertions of the autumn afternoon.

The blue skies seemed a cavernous dome above them, traces of white clouds dancing with the sounds of training which rang out from all sides. Laura breathed in the crisp air, taking in the scents of her well-oiled leather gear, the freshly turned dirt beneath their feet, and the musky stables nearby. She pursued her attack for a few more minutes, testing his weaknesses, smiling in appreciation as he reacted to her twists and jabs. Satisfied, she eased off, allowing him to take the lead.

Her opponent sensed the shift and dove in with vigor, using his greater strength to his advantage. Still, his blows rarely found their mark. Laura deftly twisted under one sweep, then jumped nimbly to dodge a move aimed at her ankle.

A church bell rang out strong and clear from the chapel down the hill, the sound echoing around the courtyard. Laura drew to a stop, and the teen lowered his own sword, resting it point down in the deeply churned dirt.

"Stuart, that was excellent," praised Laura with a smile, looking up fondly at the lad before her. He might be a few years younger than her, but this past year's sunshine had exuberantly shot him up several inches over her height.

She continued, "Your shield skills are improving at an impressive rate. We can pick this up again tomorrow, after -"

She glanced behind her as a scrawny, eggshell-blond boy of twelve dashed through the pairs of fighting men, wending his way deftly to her side. In a raspy voice which spoke of approaching manhood he called out in sharp staccato, "Your father demands your presence immediately. See to him."

Laura slid her sword into her scabbard, pushing the escaped strands of auburn hair from her face with a distracted grimace. Her eyes automatically went to the large, three story stone keep which lined one side of the courtyard, to the bank of windows on the second floor which gave a commanding view of the bustling activity below. The warm afternoon sun came from behind it, leaving the courtyard in the shadow of the keep. The windows were dark, unfathomable depths, but she knew he was there. Watching. Judging.

She took in a deep breath to marshal her energies, then turned to follow the lad toward the heavy, wooden doors banded with iron strips. As she strode across the courtyard, a few of the men she passed gave her a fortifying look, their knowing gazes helping to steel her for whatever new punishment her father might have in store. She acknowledged their concern with a nod, but her step never faltered. She had faced his rages and tempers before and had survived. One more would do no worse.

The messenger abandoned her when she reached the main doors; her footsteps echoed hollowly as she crossed the deserted central hall alone. Reaching the narrow spiral staircase at the far end, Laura took the stone steps two at a time. She had just reached the top when the door to her father's study burst open and a slim, red-haired girl came racing down the hall toward her, tears streaming from her swollen eyes.

Laura's heart dropped. Sally had been a sweet maid, friendly and helpful, and now undoubtedly her father had used and discarded her as one more casualty in his line of conquests. The girl did not slow as she passed Laura, racing down the stairs and out of sight.

Laura let out a long breath. *So it was going to be one of those days.* She ran her left thumb idly along the silver circle which had been on her ring finger since she hit puberty. The blue enameled forget-me-nots were half worn away from her constant rubbing, but she did not need to see them to know what they signified to her. She had vowed to herself, having watched her father work his way through every female within reach, that she would never give her heart to any man. She would not allow herself to end up in the heartbroken, miserable state she had seen far too often. Life held enough pain without inviting more.

Her hand fell to the fine sword at her hip; the one presented to her by Sarah just about a year ago. Laura smiled. This was what she could rely on. The strength of steel and the discipline in her muscles.

She forced herself into motion, taking the length of the hall in a few strides, resisting the urge to slow as she stepped through the open doorway and into the shadowed room beyond.

Like most of her father's chambers the room was a precise combination of Spartan efficiency and high quality craftsmanship. She glanced around at the plain stone walls, at the one sword which hung on the back wall, encrusted with rubies. The desk at the center of the room was intricately carved out of oak and ebony. The rug beneath had been imported from Persia.

Laura knew her father was a man of intriguing contrasts. The youngest son of an impoverished noble family, it had been something of a local scandal when her well-to-do mother had consented to marry him. Since their union, he had poured most of the family's money and resources into expanding his properties.

Her eyes scanned the room, but she knew where he would be. Her father was standing by the windows, looking out over the soldiers training in the courtyard. He was a muscular, stocky man, handsome in a bullish sort of way. His dark hair was short cropped and starting to fade to grey on the sides. His sense of simplicity did not extend to his own dress; today's outfit was an ornate tunic with red and gold embroidery.

He turned as she entered the room, then nodded at the two guards who stood by the door. In a moment they closed the door behind her with a soft click. A shiver ran down her spine at the familiar sound, but she steeled herself so no flicker of emotion showed on her face. She walked forward to stand at parade rest before the desk.

Her father ran a steady eye up and down her frame as she stood before him. Laura glanced down at herself self-consciously. She was wearing doe-brown leather armor and pants with high leather boots, the uniform worn by all of his guards. The outfit was in good repair and only slightly dusty from the afternoon's activities.

She brought her eyes back up to her father, meeting his gaze with a steady look. He would hardly be upset at her gear. He had treated her more as a guard-in-training than a daughter for as long as she could remember.

He nodded. "You have done well for yourself," he commented frankly, done with his perusal. "The regimen agrees with you."

Laura shrugged. "It was the path you set me on as a child," she responded evenly, reciting her words as if by rote. "If I was going to wield a sword, I might as well learn to do it well."

A smile creased her father's face, and he chuckled quietly as he stepped forward. "Indeed you did. Barely twenty-one, and you are one of our lieutenants. The men respect your talents." His grin widened. "You may not be strong, but you certainly are quick."

Laura shrugged, watching her father with a sharp eye. She felt a nagging suspicion at his unusual praise. He was manipulating her for some reason ... but why?

She had little patience for games. Despite her control, she found herself snapping at his unusual posturing.

"What is it you want?"

He frowned slightly, then strode to loom in front of her.

"You are going to marry James Falcon."

Laura's composure threatened to burst; waves of shock and appalled fury overtook her. She had been prepared for blows and insults, but this? A defensive strength infused her muscles, her hackles rose in alert, her spine shimmered into steel. She had complied with her father's every wish, had endured grueling labor for years. This was the final straw.

"No!" she shot back, resistance flaming within her. She relished the sound of the challenge in her own voice.

Her father's face roiled like a thunderstorm preparing to unleash hellish torrents. "You dare to countermand me?" he raged, his face flushing crimson, his jaw clenching.

In the next moment, his hand shot out in a well-aimed punch at her chin. Even though Laura knew it was coming, a part of her marveled at how quickly he moved. Her years of training served her well. She automatically ducked beneath the blow, rolling to the right and coming up in a defensive crouch.

The nearby guards, men she had sparred and drank with for many years, watched the activity with a neutral gaze. She would find no assistance there. She might be a valued comrade in arms, but her father was lord of the land and not to be gainsaid.

Her father took another step toward her, and Laura tensed for action. If he thought she was going to go down without a fight …

Apparently her father had no desire to injure goods which he was preparing for sale. A tic at the side of his jaw twitched as he reined himself in, staring down at his daughter. Without turning, he barked an order to his guards. "Take her to her room. Now."

The two men rolled off of the wall, complying instantly. Laura did not resist as they each took an arm and led her from the study. Within moments they had hauled her up the stone stairs to her room, gently but firmly tossing her within. It was her father who then personally slammed the door on her. The solid *thwak* of the bar driving home was clearly audible in the silence.

Her father's voice thundered through the thick door, his anger resonating through the oaken beams. "You will stay in there until you are prepared to comply with my wishes!" There was a pause, and then his footsteps echoed as they retreated down the stairs.

Laura stared at the door for a few moments, taking in long, shuddering, deep breaths. To force her to marry that monster! She was deluged by the temptation to rail, to scream, to cry in exasperated futility. The power of her frustrations threatened to overwhelm her.

She closed her eyes and focused on her breathing. With a control built on years of experience, she let her emotions flow through her and away. Slowly, ever so slowly, her shoulders eased of their tension. Her father had finally crossed a line which her sense of self-preservation utterly refused to accept. She found to her surprise that rather than fear, she felt only a growing sense of peace.

He had a right to choose her husband, of course. Had it been any other man, she would have fought down dislike and disdain to do her duty.

But not James Falcon.

She would not – she *could* not – allow herself to be partnered with that ruthless barbarian. That her father would even suggest such a match was the final proof that he cared little if she lived or died.

Opening her eyes again, she took a long look around her. Her room's only item of decoration was a small, carved oak chest, about two feet long. Within were her most prized possessions. There was the periwinkle-blue shawl of her mother's. Next to it lay a small codex of poetry from her maternal grandmother; she had memorized the contents long ago. Finally, there was a sapphire-fronted locket. Her mother had given the necklace to her when she was young, to adorn her on her wedding day.

It would be too risky to carry those items with her now and chance losing them in the woods. Her father would storm and rage once she had gone, but then he would settle down to practicalities. It was a pattern she knew all too well. In a few weeks she would come back and reason with him. Together they would find another husband who suited both of their needs.

Her thumb went to her ring, spinning it gently on her finger, and her breathing eased. She would find a husband she could tolerate, and life would flow on.

Laura sat patiently on her meager bed, pulling aside the thick curtains by the lone window and waiting for the sun to set. The hours came and went in steady progression. Laura maintained her vigil patiently, gathering her strength. The rosy orb slipped lower, sliding down to meet the horizon, and darkness spread across the realm.

It was time.

She stood and turned, pulling hard on the lumpy mattress to bring it away from the wall. Lifting a loose floor board in one corner, she pulled out a small wooden token. She reset the room to its proper state.

Carefully tucking the coin into the leather belt at her waist, she gave one last glance at her small cell before swinging her legs over the window ledge. She steadied herself for a moment before beginning the three story descent to the ground below.

Inch by inch she worked her way down the outer stone wall, her strong fingers and leather boots finding the ledges and nooks to ease her way. She had learned the handholds and footholds of that wall over many years of nighttime escapades.

Once on the ground, she breathed a sigh of relief. The hardest part of the escape was behind her. She worked her way through the shadows to reach the stables. She slipped through the main door slowly, careful to lift as she pushed to avoid the squeaky hinge's usual protests. She took her time in coaxing her favorite mount out of his stall as quietly as she could. Her thick cloak was hanging, as always, on a peg by the door.

No stable boy or servant stirred as she made her way through the courtyard to the main gates.

Once she reached the guards, she showed her wooden token without a word, keeping her face hidden in the shadows. The guards barely glanced at her cloaked form before allowing her to pass. Lord Walker was infamous for his after-hours traffic; horses were often coming in and out of the compound at odd hours. As long as the bearer carried a token, they were passed through without comment. Laura had learned that trick long ago, and had made good use of the knowledge many times.

And then ... freedom.

Chapter 2

Laura rode her mount hard through the moonlit night, her auburn tresses streaming out like a victorious knight's banner over her heavy, black woolen cloak. Fall foliage had come early this year; although it was barely the end of September, the richly colored autumnal landscape was spread before her, brightly lit by the full, orange moon. Her breath released in sparkling billows as she thundered along the meadow path.

She urged her horse to even faster strides, riding with breathtaking speed across the gently undulating landscape. She needed to put as much distance as she could between her and North Walsham, the only home she had ever known.

The forest covering the southwestern part of her father's domain soon enveloped her in a shadowy embrace. The vibrant colors of the leaves faded into a muted blur. The musky aroma of moss and peat filled her nostrils.

As she moved into the darker recesses of the woods, she pulled her horse in to a trot, then slowed to a walk. She finally allowed herself the luxury to brush the tears from her eyes with one long sleeve, taking in several deep, steadying breaths to calm herself.

Laura had known for years that her father had marriage plans for her. He had brusquely denied the proposal offerings of several local nobles. Most notably, he had turned down his ne'er-do-well merchant partner, Much, who had been lecherously eyeing her since she was twelve. Much had been quite persistent in presenting his suit the moment she had come of age.

Her father's constant refusals of his friend's requests confirmed her fears. He planned to use her maidenhead as a bargaining tool, to be sold whenever he felt it would be most valuably played. She had confronted him on the topic several times, but her father would not tell her his thoughts. He would only remind her with stern admonition that it was her duty to abide by his wishes.

Still, to marry her to James Falcon!

Laura was amazed at her father's outright audacity. The Falcons and the Walkers had been fighting, as far as she could tell, since time began. The western border of her father's land had slid back and forth at least ten times in the past few years alone.

Lord Falcon was known as a ruthless adversary; a bloodthirsty warrior with a heart of cold marble. It was said he took on large and small groups of enemies with equal fervor. It was not simply his border rivals he pursued with this level of passion. His ferocity toward even the most mild wrong-doers was legendary.

Did her father really believe for a minute that Falcon would be willing to negotiate with his lifelong enemy? If Falcon did agree to accept her, would it be for any reason other than to humiliate and abuse her? Laura knew her father was capable of sacrificing her happiness for his monetary gain. She took that as a given. However, this went beyond even her single-minded father's usual mercenary actions.

There was no question about it. Her father was scheming, and was somehow planning to use her to end the rivalry once and for all. She doubted the marriage was his end game. It was just one part of some larger, darker plot. Laura was sure he did not care if she was broken – or slain – as long as his goal was achieved.

Laura spun her ring again, her lips pressed together with determination. Whatever her father's twisted machinations, she would have no part of them.

She walked her horse slowly along the quiet path, the oaks waving leaves of gold as she went. She deliberately ignored the natural beauty, instead focusing her eyes on the road ahead, her mind resolute. Her father manipulated friends and foes alike with the skill of an experienced chess player. She would not allow herself to become yet another pawn in his expansionist schemes.

With a steady hand she directed her horse to carefully pick its way down the darkened forest path for a long while, her mind churning over the events of the past few days. What was her father plotting this time? There had always been idle talk of a truce with the Falcons. Usually her father bandied the idea around just before the latest, most devastating attack was launched. How would he use the marriage plans to rain a final destruction down on his enemy's head?

A glint ahead caught her attention, and she looked up. The forest opened up ahead of her, the moonlight streaming in to light her way. A small pool lay silent, the dark water surrounded by a ring of swaying brown reeds. The trees encircling the oasis waved their branches sleepily in the quiet wind, the low, whooshing sound gently soothing to her ears.

Laura wearily dismounted and tied her horse to an ancient oak, then stooped with cupped hands to drink some of the cool water. The night's crisp air provided a chill reminder of the approaching winter season, but after her long, hard ridden journey, it felt refreshingly brisk.

As she stood from the water's edge she threw her heavy cloak back and dusted down her body to release the road debris. She wore the simplest of cotton shirts and pants for her escape; her guard outfit would have made her far too easy to spot. Her weapons were of far higher quality than her clothes. On her left hip hung the finely-made long sword, sheathed in a sturdy, well-cared for leather scabbard. The precious, treasured gift from Sarah. On the opposite hip was a bare, short dagger, one she kept on her person at all times.

Feeling slightly refreshed, Laura slowly scanned the clearing, her hand falling automatically to rest on the sword's hilt as she did so. Her eyes lit on the horse, noting with a sigh that he carried only a small pouch of emergency rations hanging to one side of the saddle. She had taken next to nothing with her on her flight from home.

The meagerness of her situation made her again ponder how this had all come to pass.

In a way, it was funny that her father should expect her to give in so easily to his marriage demands after he had ruthlessly trained her for her entire life to fight and challenge. There had been nobody else for her to turn to for support or comfort as she grew from child to adult. Her mother had died when she was young; she barely remembered the day of that tragic riding accident. Her father had chosen not to remarry, instead focusing his energies on building up his wealth and land holdings through carefully planned border skirmishes.

Her mouth twisted into a sour grimace. And, of course, he made ample time for deflowering any female who entered his field of vision.

Given her father's debauchery she supposed she was lucky not to be surrounded by bastard sisters and brothers. For better or for worse, despite his lechery, she remained an only child. There had been no sisters to confide in, no baby brothers to coddle. She knew it was a tiny consolation to the women he had abused.

She rolled her shoulder, seeking to release the strain that had settled there. Her position as sole heir had not made her special in the eyes of her father. Quite the opposite. She was currently dressed in clothes that even a typical farmer might find unkempt. She had put on the worst she owned to help with her escape, but none of her clothes were of luxurious material or design. Her father believed in frugality in most things related to her care.

Laura shook herself from her memories, glancing around. Here she was. Perhaps she was a bit hungry, but she was free and clear from her father's influence for the first time in her life.

"Now what do I do?" she asked her chestnut bay with a thoughtful tone, giving him a pat on the neck as he nibbled the grass. She felt no trepidation at her lonely plight. Her newfound liberty was almost overwhelmingly refreshing - and her prospects were far from grim. She was a skilled swordswoman with a reputation for hard work and honesty. With the current problems with bandits she had no doubt she could find employment for the weeks ahead. Even a woman fighter was better than nothing in these rough times.

She had often considered that the nunnery in the far northeast of her father's lands would gladly take her in as a highly appropriate guard. She had even spoken of it with a few of her soldier companions. Maybe she would turn in that direction once she had put more distance between herself and the keep.

Laura nodded to herself, a plan forming in her mind. She slid her hand gently down her steed's mane, drawing from his calm. Her horse was weary; it would take him a while to be ready for another leg of the journey. Still, it was wise to be prepared. She cinched the well-worn saddle with an easy motion, then put one hand on the pommel, reaching for her provisions.

A dull clunk of metal on leather echoed from a distance behind her. She froze in place, automatically closing her eyes. Her world narrowed to a pinpoint focus on the sounds around her. A long moment passed with only the gentle rasp of her horse's breath and the quiet chirp of a cricket breaking the night's silence. Still, she waited.

There it was again – the softest of footfalls from the other side of the pond. As they grew closer, she could pick out the individual noises the men made. There were four of them, slowly closing in.

She opened her eyes again, looking with weary resignation into the large, liquid-brown gaze of her steed. Fleeing was not an option – the men undoubtedly had mounts of their own nearby and would overtake her in moments. It would be better to stand and fight where she had room to maneuver.

She turned and drew her sword in one smooth movement, then tossed the weapon into her left hand as she plucked one of her three throwing knives from her leather belt. Across the pond, four shapes separated themselves from the dark forest. The men were rough, bearded, dressed in tattered leather tunics. All four carried a short sword at the ready.

Laura steeled herself. Bandits. It would not be pleasant if she allowed herself to fall prey to them. She had fought bandit groups since her first days on patrol, but never on her own, and never with these odds.

She forced her voice to be strong and sharp. "Leave now and I shall allow you to live," she commanded, tossing her head back in challenge.

The men let out a low chuckle. "You are a feisty one," spat out a balding, heavy-set ruffian as they continued to approach. "We will be sure to leave your dead body somewhere it can be found, once we are through with you."

That was enough for Laura. Taking in a deep breath, she slowly let it out and sent her right arm forward with a sharp movement. The throwing knife sped unerringly across the distance, burying itself in the open triangle at the man's throat. He fell back in shock, gurgling his dying breath.

The remaining three men let loose with a howl of fury and descended on her. She threw the remaining blades as they closed, but although the knives hit their targets, the men did not slow their rush. She barely had time to swap her sword into her right hand before the blows were raining down on her. She acted without thinking, moving by instinct.

Block high left, letting the blade slide.

Swing sharply toward the exposed waist.

Leap back to avoid the hissing blade tip.

Stay on balance. Stay on balance.

Laura had no shield to protect her left side. Blocking attacks from three directions was quickly becoming a losing proposition. She knew she could not keep up her frantic efforts for very long.

She glanced behind her to see where her mount was. The steed, battle trained and hardened, was standing wild-eyed but ready about ten feet behind her. If she could make that distance, then even if she could not flee, perhaps the horse's hooves could take down one of the men and even the odds to something more manageable.

It was a risky move – it would leave her vulnerable while she mounted. Her arm flagged as the blows continued to rain down on her from all sides. She had little choice.

Making up her mind, she grit her teeth and poured her energy into a sweeping spin, driving the three men back a pace. Turning, she sprinted desperately for her mount, reaching his side with a thrill of triumph. She put her foot into the stirrup -

A blow landed solidly on the back of her skull. She lost her footing, flinging her arms wide as she fell back toward the soft ground. Distantly, she knew her sword was leaving her hand, thrown by the impact to some far off location. Then the ground struck her and her world spun to pitch black.

* * *

Laura groggily awoke to the slow swaying and jerking of a covered horse–drawn cart. She could plainly hear the squeak of the wheels, and by the rough movement she knew the wagon was not one of her father's. If he was anything, he was a stickler for well-maintained equipment. No carpenter in his realm would risk the beating that would result from less than fully functional gear.

Exhaustion soaked into her bones, but she opened her eyes with weary deliberation. Above her, the cart was covered with a tattered canvas ceiling. She was lying amongst small wooden boxes and piles of roughly woven black cloth. The place reeked of dust and sweat.

A sharp, throbbing pain in her neck reminded her how she had come to be in this predicament, and she reached to massage the bruise. She stopped short in surprise. Her hands were bound behind her back! With a quick tug she ascertained that the rope holding them in place was strong and secure. She struggled to get herself into a sitting position.

A nasal voice came from behind her. "Feeling better, eh?" She turned to find a thin–haired, reedy, sallow man watching her with eager interest. His clothing was torn in several places. His leer widened as he ran his eyes over her body, idly flipping a small coin in one hand as he did so.

A shiver wracked her, although she maintained a stony face for her captor's benefit. The recent events flooded back in a rush. She had been taken by the bandits. Countless villages had blazed into hellacious infernos due to this vicious group of lawbreakers. If the wolves' heads did not plan a ransom for her, her death would be long in coming and deeply seasoned with humiliation.

Would they know enough to bargain for her, though? She had been far from the keep when she was caught. From the morning sun shining through the slit in the back of the wagon she could tell they were heading west, further away from home. Her clothes, old and worn from rough use, hardly spoke of a highly valued prize.

By the way her guard was eyeing her, Laura realized she had better speak up quickly. Her vow of chastity had kept her own experiences pure, but her father's exploits ensured she was quite aware of what could happen between an innocent woman and an unprincipled man.

Laura had no desire to end up under some bandit's legs. She needed to convince them she was of noble birth, of an elegant class. She had not actually lived that life of luxury, but she could do a fair turn at troupe-quality acting, to present the proper appearance to her captors. She drew herself up with a stiffened spine, pitching her voice into a nasal, clipped tone.

"I am a young woman of great renown," she proclaimed imperiously. "I demand that you allow me to speak with your leader immediately." She was gratified when the guard, though suspicious, poked his head out of the wagon to call to one of the riders.

Laura tried to get a glimpse of her escort group, but as she moved toward the half-open curtain she was roughly dragged back inside by the guard. She shook him off, then settled against the opposite wall.

It was hard to tell by the hoofbeats, but it seemed there were five or six horses accompanying the cart. Perhaps this was a small raiding party, heading back to camp to join with the main group. She wondered with sadness which small village had borne the brunt of the assault this time. How many more had perished?

In a moment the cart staggered to a groaning stop and the curtain across the rear was thrown open. A shaggy bear of a man took up the opening, blocking out the sunlight. His voice boomed into the small wagon, gravelly and loud.

"What is this I hear of you being worth some easy cash? Speak up, girl. Keep in mind that, if you are lying, we can make you thoroughly regret your mistake." His twisted grin provided evidence that he would enjoy personally being in on the punishment.

Laura was not about to provide him with that chance.

She filled her expression with haughty disdain. "I am Laura Walker, sole heir of the lands of the Walker clan," she announced with a richly pitched voice. "My father will pay handsomely to have me returned." She focused her stare, wiping all trepidation from her mind. "However, if you harm one hair on my head, my father will spare no expense to have every one of you run down, drawn, and quartered." She eyed him with bravado; she knew better than to let her enemy sense her fear.

The horseman stroked his grizzled beard thoughtfully. "You might well be her," he growled slowly, considering. "I have heard tell the wench is loud and obnoxious, and sadly lacking in all womanly charms."

At Laura's outraged look he threw back his head and laughed heartily. "You will need to learn patience, missy. This discussion will wait until we join the main party tomorrow night. However, Grimes," he added to the pale guard who perched on a box behind Laura, "if she is being truthful, we want to make sure she has no complaints when we return her to her father. If you lay a hand on her -"

"Oh, I would not sir, you can be sure of that," stuttered Grimes. "Never you worry." He flipped his coin with more alacrity, watching the spinning object with furious focus.

Satisfied, the larger man turned his back. The curtain was thrown into place and the group rolled in motion again down the wooded trail.

Laura sunk in exhaustion against the side of the wagon. Hopefully she could trust that she would not have to worry about Grimes bothering her. Still, two days travel … that would bring her deep into Falcon territory. Were the Falcons somehow involved with the bandits? Who was it that this group had to discuss her fate with?

A more chilling thought suddenly occurred to her. After her recent behavior, what if her father told the bandits that he did not want her back?

Laura put that idea quickly out of her mind. Cold as he might be, her father would never abandon a strong position. Laura sensed that he had been working on her marriage plans for months. As long as he could get her back untouched, he would certainly have a use for her.

Laura sighed. It was just as well she would soon part ways with her father. He had ruled her life with an iron fist, and in the past few years his sole point of conversation with her had been the most profitable way in which to be rid of her.

His dismissive attitude was not a new one. Thinking back over her childhood, Laura felt a sense of regret. There were few good memories there. If she had been a boy, perhaps her father would have been more proud of her, but ...

She shook her head, dispelling the notion. There were too many "what ifs" in life to become swept up in them. She had to play the board as it lay. Her father cared little for her well-being, and was quite deliberate in frequently letting her know this. She was naught but a brood mare and game piece to him. She understood that.

Once she got out of this current mess, then she could begin to plan anew for a future free from his influence.

Laura settled herself into a more comfortable position. Well, she thought wearily as the cart bumped along the forest road, it could be worse. She was warm, reasonably clothed, and had a fair amount of assurance that she would get out of this unharmed. Now she simply had to wait out the two days until she could speak with the leader of the bandits.

If she stayed alert, she might actually find out enough to help her father or others against these scum. They would little suspect that she could perform reconnaissance, noting what she heard and saw.

It was time to play the foolish girl. She smiled up at Grimes and motioned to the ties on her wrists. "My head is awfully sore," she purred in her sweetest voice. "Could I have the ropes loosened a little bit to rub the bruise?" She fluttered her eyes and put on a vapid smile. "I would be *very* thankful."

Nodding, Grimes scurried down from his post to slightly release the knots in the ropes. Laura held in her relief as the bonds loosened. She gingerly reached up to probe at the injury to her neck. There was a little swelling, but nothing life threatening. She'd had worse in the courtyard practicing sword work with the guards. Still, drowsiness eased over her as the swaying cart rumbled its way down the path.

She knew she should try to stay awake, but her eyelids would simply not stay open, despite her best attempts. She lay back against the wagon side and drifted off to sleep.

* * *

Laura woke to darkness. She glanced around in surprise, taking a moment to remember where she was. The wagon was stationary and silent, and her guard snored in one corner.

Fuzzy confusion swept over her. She was a valuable hostage – by all rights they should be hurrying her back to the safety of their camp. Why would they have stopped so soon? Had she slept through the next day entirely?

She felt for the bump on her head, and was relieved to find the swelling had begun to subside. She knew from experience that head injuries made one sleepy. If she had slept through a full day unharmed, then perhaps she would have healed that much more as a result. She would endeavor to find out in the morning how much time had passed.

She ran her gaze carefully around the wagon's interior, seeking anything which might help her situation. To one side her captor tossed softly on a pile of rags. She inched herself forward, testing to ensure he was truly sound asleep. He muttered once at her motion, then slouched over and began snoring even louder.

Laura saw a glint near his hand, and leaned forward, intrigued. It was not a coin he had been flipping so determinedly, but a wooden token, painted with a golden rooster's head. Her eyes focused on the item, and she gave a quiet gasp. She knew that token. She carried a brother to it in her own belt.

To see that token in the hands of a bandit ...

She would have to confront her father about this later on. For now, she had more pressing issues. With effort, she pulled her eyes away from the token and wiggled clear of the grime-covered guard. She leaned back against the side of the wagon, settled herself into a shadowed corner, and began pulling methodically on her bonds one by one.

After over an hour of deliberate work, she was able to wriggle one hand loose from its loop. She glanced about the area sharply, pulling back further into the depths of the cart. Suddenly thoughts of talking with the chief were replaced with thoughts of her escaping on her own. Why wait to see if her father would be willing to pay a ransom?

She quickly slid the other hand free, then looked up to see if Grimes had noticed. He was still fast asleep. Laura exhaled in relief. If it came down to it, she was prepared to kill him. However, she only wanted to take that step if it was absolutely necessary. Even if they were bandits, she felt uneasy at the thought of slaying a man while he slept.

Laura reached automatically down to her hip – her dagger and sword were both missing. Laura's heart skipped a beat. The weapons were so much a part of her; without them she suddenly felt vulnerable. If they were somewhere in the wagon, she did not have the luxury of time to search for them. She needed to focus on her escape. Hopefully she could get to a horse without being noticed. She moved toward the back of the wagon to take a look around.

Suddenly there was shouting from a short distance away. An alarm was raised and quickly echoed from all around her. Laura shrunk back in surprise. Who would be attacking the bandits? Had her father discovered her missing and come after her? Was it a Falcon force? She shivered – by all accounts a rescue by them would be worse than staying with the bandits.

Laura cautiously poked her head through the rear curtain to evaluate her situation. Mounted swordsmen were racing into camp, pursued by other riders. With the darkness it was hard to see any distinguishing characteristics on the pursuer or pursued.

She scanned the area with sharp appraisal. None of the combatants appeared to be looking toward the wagon. Laura did not hesitate - this was her opportunity. She moved over to the opening and prepared to jump down to freedom.

A hand grabbed her long, thick hair and yanked her backwards. "Not so fast, missy," a reedy voice called to her in a sing-song fashion. She was pulled sharply down onto her back, and a leering face pressed close over her own. "God only knows what is happening out there, but I know what is gonna happen in here," Grimes hissed with a grin.

The stench coming from his mouth was like an open sewer with decaying sludge. Laura reacted on instinct; she fought and clawed to get free. Grimes reached to his belt and brought up a sturdy cudgel. He hit her twice, solidly, in the side of the head. Laura's world shimmered in and out of focus, but she willed herself to remain conscious. She had to escape!

Grimes' slimy hands were now struggling with her pants. Laura's training triggered instantly; she twisted, coiled, then landed a strong kick against his kneecap. Grimes howled in fury, then staggered, swinging his right arm back.

Lashing in rage, the bandit brought down his cudgel in a shattering blow against her temple. Laura's world exploded into bursts of fiery lava. She cried out in agony, then slipped down a dark tunnel to unconsciousness.

Chapter 3

The world swam into fuzzy focus. It seemed that every part of her body ached with throbbing pain. Her eyes, barely open, closed again of their own accord. Her lids seemed impossibly heavy. Gathering her energy, she forced them to reopen.

The scene was completely unfamiliar. She lay in a large, four poster bed covered by a heavy robin's egg blue quilt. One wall boasted two large windows, currently closed off by thick wooden shutters. She could hear the rain steadily hammering on them. Tapestries with pastoral scenes decorated the remaining stone walls. A fire blazed brightly in the large fieldstone fireplace.

The quality of the decorations and fabric were luxurious to her eyes; she had never seen creations like these before. This was nothing like her own bedroom, back home.

She tried to bring an image of her room to mind, but to her surprise she could remember nothing. There was a complete blank when she thought back to her room, her home ...

What was her name?

A sudden wave of panic threatened to overwhelm her, and she took a few deep breaths to regain her balance. It would not help matters any to lose control. She needed to think.

Despite the pain, she pushed off the covers and crawled to the end of the bed. She shakily swung her legs around to touch the ground. From there it was a short step or two to reach the polished oak dresser against one wall. Hands trembling, she picked up a silver-backed mirror which lay on the dresser's top and critically gazed at her reflection.

Dark brown eyes, full mouth, long auburn hair.

She raised one hand to trace the curve of her face. It was so familiar and yet so strange. She smiled tenuously, and the reflection seemed to smile back.

Replacing the mirror on the dresser, she next looked down at her body. She was wearing a floor-length, intricately embroidered ivory-colored gown. She ran one hand along the length of the fabric, marveling at its smooth texture. It seemed so unusual that she knew this could not be hers. Perhaps that meant she wasn't where she was supposed to be. If so, then where was she?

The door opened, and she started back against the wall, her hand dropping automatically to her hip, finding nothing there. The grey–haired woman entering looked first to the bed, and, finding it empty, swept her eyes around the room in surprise. She clucked disapprovingly when she spotted the figure huddled in the corner.

"This will not do at all, miss!" the middle-aged woman scolded as she came over to help. "Please get back into bed where you will stay warm!"

The older woman assisted her as she stumbled the few steps back to the bed. Her voice was creaky but warm. "I am amazed they got you back in one piece, what with that thunderstorm coming on and the fighting and all," she continued as she tucked the quilt back into place.

This was all too much coming in at once. Struggling against the weariness which threatened to overwhelm her, she pressed the woman for answers. "What happened to me – who am I?"

A deep voice came from the doorway. "We were hoping you could tell us," he countered. Turning her gaze, she saw the door's opening was now filled by a tall, lean man. The figure wore finely crafted dark brown leather armor, well worn with use. A simple but well-made sword hung at his side in a quick release scabbard. The man's face was rugged and clean shaven; he wore his dark hair in a shaggy mane down to his shoulders.

The man's height and broad shoulders blocked the doorway. For some reason that image frightened her, and she shrunk back into the bed, pulling the covers up to her neck.

He seemed to immediately sense the reason for her reaction. He walked closer and stood at the foot of the bed, leaving her path to the door clear. "You are safe now," he added in a softer voice, soothing her. "You have been through a lot."

He paused for a moment, considering what she had asked. His brown eyes sharpened slightly as he looked her over.

"Do you remember anything of the battle?"

She slowly shook her head, fighting off the swell of miasma which accompanied the movement, trying to think back. "Nothing. I do not remember a battle or anything before this morning." She paused, then pressed forward, figuring honesty would do her the most good. "I do not even remember who I am," she admitted weakly.

It occurred to her that these two people seemed as curious about her as she was about them. Was she not a local to these parts, then? The thought made her more willing to ask further questions.

"Where am I? What town is this?" She glanced at the shutters, wondering what landscape lay beyond them. She paused a moment, looking back at the man's face. He seemed so steady, his eyes full of concern and intelligence. Did she know him? "Who are you?" she asked with growing curiosity.

"My name is Lord James Falcon, and I am the owner of this keep," he replied without inflection, giving a short bow. His sharp eyes stayed on her face, watching for a reaction. Finding none, he explained, "We found you in a wagon while pursuing a small group of bandits on the border of our land. They are a constant scourge in these parts, and we met up with this group near one of our outlying villages."

He allowed a silence to drift for a few moments before asking, casually, "Were you with them?"

She sensed a change in the way he looked at her, and she retreated a little into herself. She tried as well as she could to remember, but she could find nothing in her mind to indicate one way or another. She slowly shook her head, her thoughts muddled and slow. "I am sorry, I honestly do not know," she quietly admitted. "I would fervently hope that I was not."

Falcon looked her up and down, his eyes critically scanning her. He thought for a few moments before responding. "The border you were on is with the Walker family," he stated at last. "It may yet be that you are from their lands and were taken captive."

His gaze slowly moved down her body, and she could almost hear him compiling her attributes, making the list to distribute to his messengers. Long, thick auburn hair. Deep brown, wide eyes. Barely in her twenties. Her face in the mirror did not have the emaciated strain she associated with the poorest of peasants, but she did not feel like nobility either. She ran her right hand in consideration along her left bicep. There was definition there. Whoever she was, she apparently led an extremely active lifestyle.

Falcon's eyes came back up to meet hers, and he muttered softly to himself. "Neither noble nor peasant, and found with bandits." It looked as if the thought bothered him.

He took in a deep breath, his voice becoming firm. "Let us start with the basics. If your memory does not return of its own accord in a few days, then I will send Thom to North Walsham. Thom has relayed messages there several times for me and knows the way well." He glanced up at the shuttered windows before continuing. "It may be just as well to delay his departure for a week or so, with the storm that is wailing out there."

He seemed to consider the situation for a moment, then added, "Walker's response will at least help us determine if you are from their stock."

A weary look came upon Falcon's face. "As cynical as it may sound, if you were indeed a new captive of the outlaws, this situation could help our standing in the upcoming truce negotiation. We could show that we are helping to save their womenfolk from the bandits' camp. Yes, the Walkers have been our enemy - but their people have suffered from the predations of the bandits as much as ours have."

She felt even more confused, and the throbbing in her head grew more insistent. "If you do not know who I am, and I was a captive of the bandits, why did you come after me?"

Falcon nodded and patiently explained. "We did not set out to find you; you were simply a bonus. Bandits are a constant plague on our lands. They kill the menfolk in our villages, abducting the women and children for slave labor."

He gave a wry smile. "We were lucky in many ways last night. I was with a patrol to the far west when we got word that the mother of one of my men had fallen ill. Having no urgent plans, we rode eastward to check on her. Once we arrived in that area, we were alerted that a small group of bandits had been spotted heading toward a nearby town. We happened to be in the right place at the right time."

His hand dropped casually on his hilt as he thought back to the previous night's events. "We had killed or captured all of the bandits we could find. We were just about to head out when I heard your cry from the wagon. I went inside and found one of the bandits on top of you, trying to –"

At her pained look he held off, his eyebrow rising. "Do you remember now?" he asked neutrally.

"I remember struggling," she slowly responded, recalling the feeling of the situation more than any visual image. Her body tensed as the sensations came back to her. "Someone was on top of me, and I was trying to get free. Then, I remember that he hit me -"

She broke off and looked away in shame, the pressure of the filthy pair of hands touching her becoming more real.

The older woman, who had been watching the exchange in patient silence, patted her on the shoulder. "Well, that is all over now, missus," she soothed reassuringly, sparing a scolding glance for Falcon. Her voice became more firm as she turned to speak to him. "Perhaps you can continue this later?"

"Perhaps you are right," responded Falcon reasonably, untouched by her tone. "She will not be going anywhere any time soon. This weather is going to keep us shut in for a while." He brought his gaze down to the bed. "We will have to call you something, until you get your memory back," he mused with a wry smile. "Any suggestions?"

Her mind was an absolute blank. No images, no visions, no glimmer at all appeared. Finally she sighed. "You saved my honor and undoubtedly my life as well. You can decide what name I go by until my own returns to me."

His smile gentled, and he nodded. "As you wish," he agreed. He looked her over slowly, carefully, a distant look coming to his eyes. A gust of wind hammered at the shutters, giving them a rusty rattle, and he turned to gaze at them for a long moment. His face stilled in focus.

"When we found you," he commented, half under his breath, "the man assaulting you had cheeks furrowed with fresh scratch marks. You had apparently fought him like a wildcat before he knocked you unconscious. What do you think of the name *Storm*, to symbolize both this torrential downpour we found you in, as well as the fiery strength you hold within you?"

She rolled the name around in her mind, and it connected with something deep within her. She nodded, her shoulders easing. It was something, at least, to have a name. It was the first step.

He paused for a long moment, looking her over, his gaze somber. "Rest well, Storm." Turning on his heel, he headed out of the room, gently closing the door behind him.

The grey-haired woman bustled around the bed, her simple brown dress swaying as she moved. "Do not mind him, missus," she clucked as she tidied up the room. "Lord Falcon means well, even though he sometimes has the manners of a goatherd. After all, they did bring you back here to safety. We will take care of you now, and help you heal up.

She finished settling the covers in place, then nodded. "Rest is what you need. There is a mug of cider on the table if you get thirsty. Are you feeling hungry at all?"

Storm shook her head no, wincing at the pain that the motion brought. Suddenly it seemed as if her energy had drained out of her, leaving only a limp shell behind. The woman sensed her mood and headed toward the door.

"I will leave you to rest now. Call out if you need me; my room is right down the hall." She closed the door quietly behind her as she left. Storm was abandoned with her swirling thoughts.

Storm sighed deeply, stretching her hands out in front of her. They were strong, well worn, not thin and delicate. Her arms were smoothly toned, firm, and tanned. She was a working girl, then. Perhaps she was the daughter of an innkeeper?

Her eyes lingered on her hands, on the small silver ring circled with blue forget-me-not flowers. She twirled the ring with her thumb, contemplating it. Was she married? Engaged? She could not remember the faces of any loved ones, but that meant little right now.

She snuggled more deeply into the covers as her eyes closed. Outside her windows she could hear the fierce thrumming of the wind, but within these walls she was safe. She slid her hand idly under the pillow, then stopped as exhaustion overtook her. Whoever she was, she was warm right now, and tired ... oh so tired ...

Chapter 4

The wind was howling outside her windows when Storm awoke again. She felt slightly better, and after taking her time to fully awaken, she swiveled to sit at the side of her bed. From where she sat she could lean forward and push one of the shutters open part way. She ran her hand along the stone sill for a moment. The window base and wall were slightly curved, as if the keep she was in was rounded. The thought intrigued her.

She turned her attention back to the window. A steady stream of heavy rain blew diagonally across her field of vision. The sky was dark grey and layered with thick, billowing clouds. She could see through the dense rain that her room was on the second floor and faced the inside walls of an enclosed courtyard. A large two-story wooden building was across to the right, and a series of small huts and structures were scattered to the left. A pair of enclosed watchtowers marked the two forward corners of the surrounding stone wall.

Beyond the front wall, a small town spread neatly along a stream, nestled among gently rolling hills and fields. The far end of the fields met a thick forest. Everything appeared peaceful and quiet in its blanket of grey fog; steady streams of black smoke rose from the scattering of homes.

Storm spotted movement below; a group of soldiers emerged from one of the larger buildings on the left and began drilling in the rain, using sword and spear in a well-coordinated attack. Storm watched them for a while, enjoying the give and take, admiring the form and skill of some of the men. It was hard to distinguish faces from here, but she thought she recognized Falcon's build at one end, providing instruction to one of the other men. His movements were quick and sure, and his demeanor was, at least from this distance, a patient and encouraging one.

A knock sounded on her door, and Storm spun to look, her hand falling to her hip. She looked down absently, wondering what it was she sought there. The middle-aged woman poked her head around the slowly opening door, then smiled as she saw Storm was awake.

Storm took a better look at her new friend. The woman was perhaps forty-five, well fed, showing smile lines that reflected a cheerful disposition. Today she was wearing a simple but finely woven burgundy dress.

The woman spoke in a friendly tone. "I have brought a tub for a bath here; do you feel up to it?"

Storm nodded her approval cheerfully; her hands were coated with dirt, and she imagined the rest of her body was in similar shape. Looking up at the woman, a thought suddenly entered Storm's head, and her face reddened in embarrassment. "You know, I do not even know your name! I had never thought to ask!" Storm's face fell in consternation.

"Mary is my name, and I am the head maid for the keep," responded the woman agreeably, walking over to her side. "Please, do not worry yourself about that. Many of the ladies who stay here do not even consider asking." She patted Storm's hand.

Storm glanced at up at that comment, her heart twisting in dismay at the image of woman after woman passing through this room. She wondered why she felt so strongly upset by the idea. She gave herself a small shake and forced her tone to reflect light curiosity.

"So Falcon has a steady stream of female visitors, does he?"

Mary shook her head. "Oh, nothing like that, missus. The wives of his allies come sometimes, when the menfolk are discussing a treaty or addressing the bandit situation. Lord

Falcon has not had any women here to visit him, in a courting sense, for many years. Not since –"

Her face reddened, and she took in a breath. "Here I am prattling on, when you wanted that bath drawn." She turned and helped to supervise the male servants who first brought in a large, wooden tub, and then ferried in a series of buckets of warm water.

Storm held her tongue, unwilling to press a servant about the doings of her master. In short order the bath was ready, and once the men had left, Storm gently shooed Mary out as well, insisting that she would be fine on her own.

When the door was firmly shut and bolted, Storm carefully stripped off her clothing, acutely aware of her weakness and lack of balance. She placed a towel to one side where it would be within easy reach, and then gently eased herself into the warm water.

Storm stretched her head back in relaxation, moving slowly to minimize the throbbing. The room was blissfully quiet, with only the crackling of the fire and the softly calling wind outside to ruffle her thoughts. She wondered how she used to live if she found this to be so peaceful.

Languorously, she gazed at the richness of her surroundings. The bed's frame and posts were created with finely carved oak. The side table was also fine wood, and held a grey marble washbasin and pewter tankard. The dresser with its silver mirror and brush had been polished until it shone.

Storm knew she was not used to this, but she also sensed that she had been in a keep before. She could recognize the style of construction of the stone and understood the function of the keystone above the door. The open courtyard, defensive walls, and efficient layout below had seemed quite natural. Perhaps she was a steward's daughter? A cook's assistant? Anything was possible. She only hoped that she was not associated with the bandits.

Storm sighed and stretched to submerge herself further beneath the waters. She would need to be patient. If nothing else, when the messenger returned from North Walsham she would – hopefully - know for sure. In the meantime, she would try to see what she could remember on her own.

She looked again at her arms. They were definitely not those of any noble woman she could imagine. The muscles of her forearms and the calluses on her hands were plain to see. Small dents and bruises told of an active life. Perhaps her legs would give a hint; she raised them up out of the water to examine them.

Turning her right leg, she stopped in surprise. A long, twisting scar showed along the right calf – not fresh, but perhaps three or four years old. She knew at once that it was a sword cut. She ran one finger down it, lost in thought. Had her family been attacked by bandits?

She pressed away the thought that perhaps this was further proof that she, herself, was a bandit wench, skilled with the sword and aiding in attacks. She could not allow herself to believe that.

She deliberately went about the task of rinsing the thick layers of dirt and sweat from her body, using the wood ash soap held in a small pottery jar. She paid special attention to her hands, to the deep brown material caked beneath her fingernails. Again she found herself examining the ring, giving it a gentle spin, looking at the small blue flowers with a mixture of interest and frustration. Why could she not remember the tiniest thing about this ring?

She brought it closer to her face. She tried to imagine an adoring husband holding her hand in his, sliding the ring on her finger, and gazing into her eyes.

Nothing. There was not even the slightest indication that any such man lurked in her walled-off memories.

She ran a finger along the silver circle. Perhaps a distant knight, off in the Holy Land, had given this to her to remember him by?

Again, despite her best efforts, not even a hint of feeling tickled her heart.

She sighed, laying back against the wall of the tub. She would have to be patient with herself, to give her mind time to heal.

When the water finally began to cool, Storm mustered her strength to climb out of the tub. She slowly toweled herself off, lost in thought. She prayed with every ounce of her being that she wasn't involved with the bandits. With all Falcon and Mary had done for her, she did not want them to have inadvertently rescued one of the enemy. It seemed a foul way to repay their kindness.

Storm went to the bed where Mary had laid out three new dressing gowns from which to choose. She ran her hands over the fabrics in awe. She knew she had never felt anything like this before. The softness and quality were mesmerizing. Then there were the colors – vibrant and rich. There was a twilight blue, a moss green, and a deep burgundy dress, all in a fitting size. Storm donned the blue one, then, feeling weary, crawled back over to the bed.

Mary came in a short while later, and after supervising the removal of the bath gear, went to fetch some chicken soup on a wooden tray. She helped Storm move into a sitting position, then sat patiently by the window on a small wooden stool. Storm eagerly drank up the warm broth, lifting the small wooden bowl to her mouth with both hands.

Steady footsteps sounded in the hall, and in a moment Falcon walked into the room, brushing the rain off his hair. "So you are up and about, Storm?" he asked, reviewing her appearance. "You look more alert – the soup and sleep seem to have done you some good."

Storm put the bowl down and wiped her mouth on the nearby napkin. "That was delicious. Thank you very much for your hospitality," she responded with careful politeness. "I still feel worn down, but I am not as exhausted as I was before."

Storm was comfortable in this room, and did not want to leave her oasis. However, looking up at her rescuer, she could read the open hesitation in his eyes. She made her decision. "I am sure I am ready to move, if you wish it. Maybe there is an inn in town -"

"No!" called out both Falcon and Mary in unison. Falcon took a step forward, his face suddenly apologetic. "I am sorry if I am a bit rough in manner. I am unused to having female visitors here. With the bandits -"

Storm shook her head even as he was speaking. "There is no need to apologize, Lord Falcon. You have already gone out of your way to rescue me and nurse me back to health. I do not wish to be a burden in any way. It does not feel right, lying around idle like this."

Falcon gave a short laugh. "Maybe you cannot see the lump on your head, but believe me, that is an injury well worth tending. Stay put and heal up. That is your task for now. Do not waste the effort we have put into having you mend properly." He softened this last line with a wry grin, and Storm found herself smiling in return.

"As you wish," she replied, nodding in acquiescence. "Still, there must be something I can do while I lie here." She cast around in her mind for a task that could be done while sitting stationary, without the benefit of good light. "I could polish some silver -"

A shadow crossed over Falcon's face, and he shook his head. "You just rest, and we will take it from there," he responded curtly. He nodded, then turned and left. His footsteps faded as he moved down the hall.

Storm realized belatedly that, with Falcon harboring the thought that she was in league with the bandits, asking to get her hands on the silver was probably not the wisest move she could have made. She looked up at Mary, contrite. "I only meant -"

Mary patted her hands before leaning over to take the tray from the bed. "I know, dearie," she chuckled soothingly. "Never you mind him. Just lay back and get some more rest now. Your body needs to heal."

Storm did feel sleepy again, now that she was clean and full of warm soup. She nodded in agreement. Mary moved to the window and settled the shutter back in its secure position. The room was bathed in darkness, with only the fireplace emitting a soft glow. Storm slid one hand beneath her pillow, and in short order she was fast asleep.

Chapter 5

The gentle tolling of a church bell woke Storm from her restless dreams. Was it Sunday? She wearily moved her way to the window, pressing open the shutter and gazing through the heavy rain down at the small chapel below. Indeed, the keep's inhabitants were slowly making their way through large puddles toward the stone building. Storm had pushed herself halfway into dressing before Mary came in and shooed her back to bed.

"I am sure the priest will not mind at all coming up to pray with you later," she reassured Storm with a smile, tucking her back in under the covers. "God would want you to heal up quickly, not to waste his miracle of rescue by dying of a cold."

Storm allowed herself to drift along with Mary's intentions, and, true to her word, the elderly priest arrived only a few hours later. Storm tried her best to stay awake during the mass he gently gave to her, but sleep overtook her partway through his reading.

* * *

When she awoke, she basked in the deep contentment of a long night's sleep. Storm sat up, pleased to find she felt a little stronger. Moving to the bed's edge, it seemed her balance was slightly askew, and her legs wobbled when she put weight on them. She pushed open one of the shutters. The sun poked feebly through the thick grey clouds – morning had come around again. She moved carefully around her room, building up her strength, watching the soldiers train from her window.

Curiosity got the better of her, and while she waited for Mary to arrive she rummaged through the drawers of the dresser. The top two drawers held clothing, but the bottom drawer held a few items apparently brought in from the bandit's wagon. There was a finely balanced dagger, a well-cared-for sword in a leather scabbard, and a few grubby odds and ends.

The dagger and sword seemed familiar to her. Maybe someone had been guarding her, and these had been taken from him? Did they belong to the bandits?

As much as Storm willed herself to believe the weapons were owned by someone else, she thought back to the times that she had been startled, when her hand had flown to her hip for defense. She sat on the stool by the window for quite a while, watching the guards drill. While she followed their moves with her eyes, she turned the dagger over in her hands. Finally, without knowing why, she stood and put it beneath her pillow. She trusted Mary and Falcon, but still … it made her feel better, knowing the dagger was there.

Weariness overtook her, and soon she was asleep again.

* * *

By the next morning Storm was feeling much more energetic. She was ravenous and itching to leave her room. As nice as it was, she was beginning to feel claustrophobic. The brief visits from Mary and Falcon could not assuage her restlessness.

She found a simple but well-made dress of sapphire blue linen in the top drawer and carefully put it on over her chemise. She brushed her hair out, working out the many snarls that had developed during her bed rest. Finally she felt more human and ready to explore.

Emboldened, she peeked out of her door to see what lay beyond her little world.

This hallway was short, with only a few doors which opened out on either side. To the right the corridor vanished at a ninety degree turn, but to the left it came to a dead end. A young page was at the far left end of the hall, polishing a small wooden table. He looked up and briefly smiled when he saw her emerge, then went back to his work.

Storm slowly headed to the right. At the turn of the hallway, the floor opened into a wide staircase down. Still feeling a bit weak, she held firmly onto the polished railing as she descended, heading into a large hall.

It was apparently the lunch hour. Two tables, one down each side of the hall, held a collection of soldiers and workers scattered down their lengths. The head table was sturdy oak laden with platters of roast turkey, bowls of fresh bread, and pitchers of wine. Behind it, Falcon sat in a simple but finely carved chair featuring a bird of prey in diving descent. To his right sat a grizzled veteran, and to his left sat two young, burly-looking soldiers in their late teens.

The room grew quiet as she walked in, and she blushed, a self-conscious panic causing her to slow with each step. Falcon's eyes widened in surprise at her approach and he quickly moved around the table to come by her side.

When he touched her on the arm, before she could think, Storm's body violently flinched back. It seemed his fingers had seared with the red hot of a blacksmith's tongs.

Eyes wide, she clenched her arm against herself in a turmoil of surprise and fear. She struggled to bring her pounding heart and sharp breaths under control. Certainly he had not done anything to deserve such a reaction.

Falcon drew back at once, holding his hands to the side in a gesture of peace. He stood quietly, watching her, his gaze serious.

Storm breathed in deeply. She had no idea where her reaction had come from. Surely he only meant to help, and she was indeed worn down. She let out a long, steadying exhale, gathering her resolve.

She carefully put her arm on his, slightly leaning against him. She drew in the warmth of his body, the steadiness of his frame, and let out another shuddering breath. Surely life should be easier than this. Perhaps she had pushed herself too hard by coming down to take a look around.

Falcon echoed her thoughts, saying softly in her ear, "I think you might have waited another day or two." He led her to a seat beside him, making sure she was comfortable before regaining his own.

"I know," she replied apologetically. "I just wanted to get out. The four walls were closing in on me."

Falcon nodded in understanding. "I would feel the same way." He turned to the other men at the table. "This is our mysterious rescue from the bandit camp, as I am sure you have guessed. For now, we are calling her Storm." He looked back to her and gestured to his companions. "Storm, this is my captain – John – along with two new arrivals, David and Shawn."

Storm greeted each man in turn, then her attention was drawn to the bowl of steaming stew placed in front of her by a smiling young girl. The aroma was heavenly! She focused on the broth, gratefully drinking in the warm liquid, taking bites of the fresh bread in between sips. A delicious warm cider was presented in a tall pewter tankard.

After a short while her bowl was empty and she was pleasantly full. She sat back to look around her. The hall was amply furnished with numerous wrought iron sconces providing a dapple of soft light. In between those hung embroidered tapestries depicting a variety of scenes.

The table before her was crafted of a fine wood, gleaming from daily polish and carved with images of apples and pears. The chair where she sat on had a comfortable cushion both below and behind her.

Bowls of grapes were brought around to the tables, and Storm eagerly reached forward to take a handful. Watching her, Falcon burst out laughing.

"If we keep you for much longer, we will have to bring in more items for the larder!" he commented, chuckling. "Truly, though, I am glad you are feeling better." He looked her up and down, his sharp eyes missing nothing. "It appears that the clothes are a good fit; that was convenient. We do not have many women's outfits here for you to have chosen from."

Storm smoothed the bodice of the blue dress, again admiring the fine stitching. "It does fit well," she agreed. A thought occurred to her, and she glanced around the room with curiosity. "Does this belong to your wife?"

Falcon's smile faded, and he looked out into the room, not meeting her eyes. "My wife to be," he responded flatly. "That is, if this truce ever gets signed."

Storm wondered at his reaction. "What truce is that?"

Falcon sat back, taking a long pull on his ale as he thought. The room began to empty out as the keep community returned to their duties. John and the two soldiers who shared their table nodded a farewell, then took their leave.

Storm began to wonder if Falcon had forgotten her question. She was searching around in her mind for another topic of conversation when Falcon sighed deeply, returning from his musings.

"The proposed truce is with the Walkers – our neighbors to the east. They have been sending wave after wave of assault on us for years. Lord Walker has finally agreed to a truce, but it requires me to marry his only daughter."

Storm was curious at Falcon's reticence. "What is she like?"

Falcon shrugged and took another drink. "I have never met her. She is not present during any of our talks." He looked down into his mug, pursing his lips.

Storm's interest was piqued. "Surely you have asked after her, if you are preparing to attach yourself to her for life?"

Falcon sighed, then continued with obvious reluctance. "Yes, I have. Rumor is that she is obstinate and willful. Most of the positive traits I know are what her father chooses to tell me." He began ticking qualities off on his fingers. "He insists that she is trained to obey. He promises that she will be a good breeder. He provided her measurements for the clothing, saying that they prove she is in fine and healthy shape. He swears that she can read and write. Of course as nobility she can speak French, to well educate our children personally."

He chuckled softly. "There are other skills that the father does not mention quite as readily. I hear from my men that she can defend herself with a sword and has actually won a few knife throwing tournaments."

Storm kept her face carefully neutral. "She sounds like the perfect woman."

Falcon glanced up at her, his eyes narrowed, then relaxed into a smile when he saw the sparkle hidden in her eyes. "It is all very surreal," he agreed, his tension easing. "I had no thought of marriage, least of all right now." He stretched out, rolling his shoulders. "Sometimes life puts you into a situation, and you have little you can do but accept it. None of us choose the world we are born into. We can only choose how we react to it."

Storm's heart resounded with an echoing call at his words, and it brought with it a sense of exhaustion. She sagged back against her chair. Falcon's sharp eyes followed the movement, and he rose easily to a standing position, offering his arm to her without a word. Storm realized she was more tired than she had thought as she pushed herself to stand. She paused for a long moment, then cautiously took his arm, a nervous shiver running through her as she leant against him. He glanced down at her, but did not comment. Together they slowly walked back up to her room.

He pressed open the door, then escorted her in. "You should rest now," Falcon suggested with quiet concern. "Do not push yourself to heal too quickly. It will come with time."

"I am sure you are right," agreed Storm, sitting on the bed with a weary sigh. "It is just hard for me. I feel idle, useless."

Falcon's mouth quirked. "Then make it your focus to heal and regain strength."

Storm nodded, realizing there was not much more she could do at the moment.

Falcon's brow creased as he gazed at her. "If your memory has not returned by now, then it is time we take action. I will have Thom leave immediately for North Walsham, to see what he can learn there. I imagine, with the bad weather, that he would be back in a week – two at the most – with whatever he can learn from that area."

Storm hesitantly smiled. "It would be wonderful to know who I am," she agreed. "I thank you for your efforts."

"It is nothing," he absently responded. He turned and walked through the door, closing it behind him.

Within moments of his departure Storm was crawling wearily under the thick covers. She slid her hand beneath the pillow. Calm swept over her when her fingers wrapped around the hilt of the dagger.

Feeling secure for the first time since her arrival, she curled up in bed and slept.

Chapter 6

Storm stretched back in her chair by the window, the courtyard empty beneath her, the late morning sun barely filtering through the heavy clouds and drenching rains. It was nearly time for lunch, but she could not bring herself to get up and moving. She held the sword in her lap, the blade nestled in its scabbard, the weight comfortably reassuring.

There was a noise to her left, and the door swung open. Falcon stepped in, instantly stopping in surprise. His eyes sharpened for a moment as he looked between the open drawer of the dresser and the sword on her lap. Then his face became quietly neutral.

"Do you recognize that weapon?" he asked smoothly.

Storm shook her head no, running her hand slowly down the leatherwork on the scabbard. There was a pattern of ivy and leaves along the edge of the sheath which she found beautiful.

"No, it does not bring up any specific memories," she responded distractedly, lost in thought. "I found it in the lower drawer. Was it from the bandit camp?"

Falcon nodded in agreement, walking over to stand beside her. "Yes, it was in the wagon near you. We thought perhaps the weapon was taken when you were. The style seems much finer than the bandits usually have." He paused for a moment, then added casually, "There was a dagger in there as well."

Storm's eyes flashed instinctively to the pillow, and her face flushed crimson. Falcon instantly interpreted her motion and froze in place, a look of concern clouding his eyes. His voice was steely and low when he spoke. "Has any person here -"

Storm immediately shook her head. "Everybody here has been more than kind, and only you and Mary have been in my room." She paused, her eyes dropping. "It is just -" she looked out the window, unable to explain it in words. "It seems right," she finally whispered. "It makes me feel safe."

Falcon sat quietly on the bed beside her, looking thoughtfully at her profile. "What kind of a life must you have led?" he mused, half to himself.

Storm felt as if she owed him full honesty, with all the trust he had put in her. Without saying anything, she reached down and pulled the side of her dress upward, revealing the cut on her calf.

Falcon dropped to one knee at her side to inspect the scar. Storm was surprised that she did not feel embarrassed at all by his perusal; oddly, after so few days, she already felt that she could trust him.

His eyes met hers. "A sword cut, maybe four years old?"

She held his gaze and nodded. "That is what I thought. I ..." She hesitated, then turned and looked out the window. "I want to be as honest with you as I can be. I do not remember anything at all. Still, with this cut ... for all I know ..."

Falcon gently turned her face to his. His voice was low and soft. "I know I have not been the best of hosts," he admitted. "I appreciate your letting me know of this. Whatever your past has been, you are our guest, and you deserve our hospitality."

Storm looked down; she could not meet his eyes. She wanted to face the issue, but her heart pounded in her chest as she spoke. "What if I was with the bandits? What if my memory returns, and I am horrified by the things I have done?"

Falcon was silent for a moment. He looked as if the thought had occurred to him as well, and his answer was ready. "Storm, each of us makes a decision, every day, about how we lead our lives. Every day is a chance to forge a new path." His eyes drew hers with serious calm. "Whatever course you were on previously – for whatever reason – you have the opportunity to renew yourself."

Falcon absently ran a finger down the scar on her leg, and a nervous tremor followed his movement, but it was melded with a new feeling, one she could not easily name. He was not upset about the scar, not denigrating her for it – he was accepting it. A thrill rippled down her spine, and her cheeks flushed. She turned away as he gently pulled the dress down to conceal the wound again.

His eyes drew up to her face. "Your past is just that, the past," he quietly stated. "You are the master of your future."

She took in a deep breath. The thought of being in control infused her with a sense of elation. Could it be true?

Falcon glanced again at the pillow, at the knife concealed beneath, then stood and offered his arm. "Are you ready to head down to lunch?"

Storm looked up, caught in the depths of his eyes. It took a moment before she rose, tentatively putting her fingers on his arm.

Her voice was low.

"Yes, I am ready."

* * *

The lunch – a meat pie with fresh bread – was just as delicious as yesterday's meal, and Storm found herself eating seconds, much to the amusement of the men who sat with her. The young, heavyset maid with apple cheeks who took her bowl blushed pink with pleasure when Storm asked her to please convey her compliments to the cook.

It seemed only a short while later when she and Falcon were the only two left at the table. Falcon waited until the servant had brought them both fresh mugs of cider, then he leaned back in his chair.

"I cannot ask anything of you," he considered, his voice holding a hint of a teasing smile. "Apparently that will have to wait until your memory returns. On the other hand, you must be full of questions," he added placidly. "What would you like to know?"

Storm thought for a while, her eyes running down his strong shoulders, his broad chest. He seemed to be nearly thirty years old, intelligent, kind, with ample land holdings. Why had he remained single for so long? She pushed her curiosity aside and found a more neutral query to start. "Well, tell me about yourself. What is your family like?" She nibbled at a biscuit.

Falcon took a drink from his stoneware mug, then set it down and turned to look at her. "The Falcons have ruled this land for generations," he explained, his brown eyes lost in thought. "My grandfather built this keep, and my father tended it as well. It is not an easy place to grow up. This area has always had its share of warfare, both from bandits and acquisitive neighbors. I imagine it is because there are no natural boundaries to delineate the boundaries, to discourage land–grabbing. There are just rolling hills and forest."

He paused for a moment, then plowed ahead. "My father was killed seventeen years ago in a battle with a bandit group. I was barely eleven at the time. My two younger brothers had already been sent away to become novices in a nearby monastery, for their own safety.

"I did what I could to help out and to console my mother." He took a pull on his cider. "Only a few months later, my mother ... passed away. From heartache, it was said."

"I am so sorry," offered Storm, covering his hand with her own. "That must have been very hard on you, being so young."

"It seems a very long time ago," replied Falcon softly, but his eyes were shadowed. "Since then, I have built up our defenses with the help of my compatriot John, who you met yesterday. The bandits have remained a constant thorn in our side. Somehow they seem to remain well funded even when we press them hard for months on end."

He slowly spun his mug with one hand. "We now have secure borders on all sides except our eastern line. Only the Walkers, and the bandits, remain problems."

Storm quietly nodded. "That explains the truce you are working on."

Falcon took in a deep breath, then let it out in a stream, rolling his shoulders to release the tension. "Yes. I have worked out treaties with all of the other local lords, but Walker has always refused. Only recently has he sent me an offer – and it requires his daughter's hand in marriage."

Falcon looked away for a moment. "It is not a generous offer. The dowry is slight, and she -" he shook his head. "Whatever the father says, rumor has it that she is a rough and difficult woman. With a father like that, one could expect no less." He sat back in his chair, lost in thought. "Still, political weddings are not made for the comfort of the parties involved. They are arrangements designed to keep a population safe."

He finished his drink in a long swallow, then stood. "Shall we head upstairs, My Lady? You should rest, and I have riding to do with David and Shawn."

Storm chuckled at his courtly manner of address. She stood and dipped to an elaborate curtsey before laying her hand on his proffered arm. A tingling flush spread through her at the warmth, and she blushed, lowering her eyes. She walked slowly with him back to her room.

He nodded as they came to a halt by her bed. "Rest well, Storm," he offered. Then he turned and strode off.

Storm found she was twisted by an odd sensation. Could she be missing him already, after only knowing him a few days? She pushed the thought from her mind and looked around the room for something to do.

Well, she could not do much, but she could certainly walk. She stepped in slow circles around the room, taking her time, building up her strength. She knew the exercise would help to heal her.

As her feet made the circuit, she ran her thumb over the ring, exploring different scenarios for its presence. Perhaps a childhood friend had given her the ring - a girl she had giggled with over ghost stories on playful afternoons.

Nothing.

Perhaps a loving father gave her the ring as a token of his fond affection for her.

Emptiness.

Her eyes glanced at the dresser drawer which held the sword. She tenuously poked at an idea. Perhaps this ring was a stolen item, taken from an innocent victim by the bandits.

She rolled the idea around in her head, summoning it as willfully as she could, but to her relief not even the slightest echo of truth returned. She gave a soft smile. Maybe she was not part of the bandit group after all.

Her mind drifted to Falcon, and she found herself thinking about his upcoming marriage. Her thumb ran along the ring again. Maybe she was about to be married to someone against her will as well, and she was resisting the engagement with all her heart.

To her surprise, there was the slightest flicker of answering emotion at that, and she pulled up to a staggering halt. Her eyes went down to the ring, and she poured all her focus into the thought, into a vision of a man forcing the ring on her finger, requiring her to wear it.

The feeling dissipated like mist on a sunny day, evaporating as quickly as it had come. No matter how hard she tried, she could not bring even a hint of it back again.

Finally, exhausted, she climbed into bed, tossing and turning as the grey day faded into a deeper gloom. When darkness came she fell into a restless sleep. Her dreams were of a thick forest with dense foliage, a hedgerow that she relentlessly but unsuccessfully tried to breach.

Chapter 7

Storm shook off her grogginess the following morning, tentatively pleased to find that her strength was returning. She was able to walk around the room with only glimmers of pain.

It was well past breakfast, but she decided to head down to the main hall to spend an hour there before lunch, learning more about her surroundings. She dressed, then tucked the dagger into her belt. It seemed a natural thing to do, and she hoped that following her instincts might lead her to more clues to her identity.

The hall seemed quiet as she came down the large flight of stairs, but it was not deserted. To the right, by a large tapestry, Falcon was talking with a young, attractive blonde woman. Storm paused for a moment to look over the pair.

Storm guessed that Falcon was just over six feet tall, and he towered over the woman by a good eight inches or more. She was slender and delicate, with long, straight hair which fell like golden rain down her back. She wore an elegantly embroidered dress of pale lavender. Her movements were refined and graceful as she spoke softly to him.

Falcon wore the light leather armor Storm had seen him in every day, with a sword at his hip and black leather boots. He was not talking much, but appeared content to listen to the blonde's discussion with quiet patience.

Storm had no interest in interrupting the couple; she turned to retreat to her room. Her movement caught Falcon's eye, and he called after her in a friendly voice.

"Storm? I did not think you would be up so early. Come down and meet a friend of mine, Jessica."

Reluctantly, Storm turned and made her way down the stairs, acutely aware of Jessica's eyes following her clumsy movement. She thought that a piercing sharpness lay behind the friendly smile, but as she approached the two, Jessica's voice was sweetness and light.

"Why, Storm! I have heard so much about you. It is wonderful to meet you at last." The blonde stepped forward to stand by Falcon's side before continuing. "What an interesting name, Storm. I do not believe I have met anyone with that name before. It sounds a bit rough!"

Falcon spoke up before Storm could phrase a reply. "I am afraid that is my fault, Jessica," he interjected evenly. "She was found during the thunderstorms, and we needed a name by which to call her."

Jessica pouted prettily, then gave a light, tinkling laugh. "Why of course you had to call her something!" she merrily agreed. "You could hardly refer to her as 'it' while she heals!" Her eyes swiveled to look Storm up and down. Storm felt like a gangly calf on market day being evaluated for a Sunday dinner.

Jessica pursed her lips. "No, I do not believe I have seen you before at any social events," she drawled with much consideration, "and you seem a sturdy enough lass." She turned to look up at Falcon with bright cheerfulness. "Have you asked around with the local farmers? Maybe one of them has misplaced their daughter."

Falcon's eyes flickered to peruse Jessica's face; she returned his gaze with a blissful, serene smile. "Yes," he confirmed after a moment. "We have sent out messengers and are making all appropriate inquiries. We will undoubtedly discover who Storm is in a matter of weeks."

Jessica slid her arm smoothly through Falcon's, and her smile grew more toothy. "Why, then, we will have to entertain her until she heads back to where she belongs!" she declared with enthusiasm. "We would not want her wandering the keep lonely, now would we?" She looked up at Falcon and fluttered her eyelashes gently. "I am sure you could not refuse to provide me and Storm with a personal tour of your home?"

* * *

Storm found the next two hours to be an odd combination of unexpected emotions and awkward situations. Falcon was a congenial host, escorting the two women through every corner of the motte and bailey, from the central keep to the buildings which lay within the protective curtain wall.

He thanked Jessica patiently for her profuse, gushing praise over each silver pitcher and embroidered tapestry. He assisted her when her dress became mysteriously caught on the corner of a fireplace. He helped her up and down stairs where she requested his assistance.

Falcon equally took time to answer Storm's questions about the items which caught her attention – the unusually narrow arrow slits in one outer wall and the extra thickness around the doors in some parts of the building. Storm found the defensive constructions fascinating.

Storm was careful to conceal any feelings of weariness or pain that she felt. Despite Jessica's prattling conversation, she was really enjoying the tour and learning about the keep. She did not want to give either of her companions an excuse to draw it short.

Storm was especially touched by how well Falcon knew his staff, and how much he cared for them. He stopped to introduce each person, no matter what their station, and asked after their family and situation.

When they reached the kitchen buildings, the heavy-set serving girl was in one corner, helping a large woman stir an iron cauldron hanging over the crackling fire. They wore a matching set of green surcoats over a white under-chemise. Both looked up with a smile as their master entered the room.

Falcon's voice was warm. "Molly! Heather! Here is the woman who has been praising your cooking." He turned with a grin and motioned to Storm. "Storm, Molly has been our cook here for as long as I can remember. Heather is her daughter, and she does a wonderful job helping out with any task you can imagine."

Jessica gave a slight nod, turning to move on, but Storm stepped forward with a wide smile. "I know it might not mean much from a person with no memory," she teased, her eyes twinkling, "but your food is delicious, and I cannot believe I have had any finer before. You are to be commended for your talents."

Molly blushed crimson under the praise, and Heather's eyes shone as she looked up at her mother.

Molly's voice was friendly and low when she responded. "You just tell me what dishes you like best, mum, and I will make sure they are always available for you."

Storm's smile grew into a grin. "See, you have it easy," she joked merrily. "Since I cannot remember any previous foods, every dish you make will of course become my new favorite. I trust in your judgment completely."

Molly laughed, a low, rich sound. "Then we shall see if I cannot exceed myself each day, and you just let me know what you think!"

Storm curtseyed in agreement, then turned with Falcon to follow Jessica, who was already heading out of the room.

They moved from the inner keep area toward the outer courtyard. Jessica was less enthusiastic about this part of the tour, staying safely on the clean grass as Storm roamed with interest in the dusty interiors of the brewhouse, the armory, and the other small buildings.

Jessica's unwillingness to brave grime suddenly vanished as they headed into the stables. Both women looked around the long, wooden building with interest. There was a row of stalls down each side of the lower level. The upper level only stretched across the back half of the length, stopping midway near the main doors. A wooden ladder on one side of the main floor led up to this storage area, which was stacked with hay and extra equipment.

A tall, reedy man with sallow skin walked over to meet them. He looked about thirty years in age, dour and thin-lipped. Falcon turned with a smile. "Women, let me introduce Harold. He became part of our household when he was just a lad." Harold nodded sourly to the women, then continued forward to climb up the ladder toward the loft.

Jessica walked down the row of stalls, looking over the half door of each one to examine the steed within. "Your collection of beasts is amazing, Falcon!" she gushed with pleasure, looking over the horses. "We really should go riding sometime. Look at the legs on this one! He must have been bred from champion stock. Look at that line, that form!" She moved from one to the next, staying well back from each as she passed.

Storm had scanned the horses, then walked over to a specific one on the left side. The horse was a soft brown color, and while Jessica had barely glanced at him, to Storm it was as if she were being drawn in by a beacon.

Storm swung open the half-height door with ease, stepping in slowly toward the horse. She held out her hand to allow the horse to smell her, then moved closer, running her hand down his neck.

"What a beautiful boy you are," she murmured, her eyes shining. "I bet you love to run."

She glanced at Falcon, who stood watching the pair of women from the stable's entrance. "What is his name?" she asked with interest.

A fond smile infused his face. "That is Mercury," he explained with warmth. "I found him at a local county fair. He was presented as an average colt, coming from a quiet farmer family – but I could see the potential in his eyes. He is one of my favorite horses."

There was a cry of surprise from the back of the stables, and both turned to look. Jessica had stopped by the back wall and was peering down at a young lad. Storm recognized him as the page who had been working around the keep. The boy was looking up at Jessica with focused interest.

Jessica's eyes were cold. "You startled me," she snapped with irritation. She turned her back with a huff and began walking up the length of the stables. The boy followed along behind her, staring at the back of her head, his gaze full of curiosity.

She spun as she reached the ladder leading to the loft, looking down at the boy in irritation. "What is it?" she growled.

He shied back, but continued to gaze at her face. "It is just … you seem familiar for some reason," he explained hesitantly in a soft voice.

Storm's world suddenly shuddered to a halt. There was a sharp, whistling, immediately familiar noise, and her eyes tracked upwards to automatically latch onto the source. A shining, spinning shape was descending from the balcony above. It was a short-handled scythe, the blade's edge gleaming with a razor's sharpness. The tool was falling directly toward the pair, yet they remained oblivious in their conversation.

There was no hesitation – she burst forward at an all-out sprint, her eyes focused on the spinning form. Time slowed, and she could see each cycle, each lazy turn as the wooden handle rotated around the finger-slicing blade. One … two … three turns …

Her fingers closed around the handle only inches above the lad's head, then she tucked in her body, allowing the momentum to carry her somersaulting into a pile of blankets against the back wall. She landed with a loud thud which knocked the wind out of her. She lay there, dazed.

The world spun back up to normal speed. The lad fell backwards, his face as white as a sheet. Jessica began shrieking in alarm, wrapping her arms around herself and leaning back against the stable wall. Falcon was at Storm's side in an instant, taking the scythe from her firmly but gently, putting it down behind him in a smooth movement as he scanned her for injuries.

"Are you hurt?" he asked in a quiet hush.

Storm took in a few deep breaths, pressing herself up to a sitting position. There was a sharp pain in her right hip where she had landed, but it did not seem serious. She held her arms out before her and flexed her fingers, counting to ensure she still had ten.

"Nothing that will not mend," she offered with a wry chuckle. She automatically put out a hand to him, and Falcon hesitated for a moment, checking her again for injuries before taking it and pulling her to her feet.

Jessica was between them in an instant, pressing herself hard against Falcon, her face bright with emotion. "Did you *see* that?" she cried out. "I could have been *killed*!" She clung to Falcon, looking up into his eyes with wild panic.

Storm moved over to the shaken boy, leaning down to be at his eye level. "Are you all right?" she asked, her voice tender.

He nodded his head yes, gazing at her with thankful eyes. "You saved my life," he whispered. "I could not move."

She smiled, patting him gently on the shoulder. "It happens to the best of us," she soothed. "If you are untrained, you freeze in surprise when the attack comes. I am just glad you are unharmed." She stood up straight, taking in a deep breath of relief. "My name is Storm, or at least that is what I am called. What is your name?"

"I am Zach," he responded with a hesitant smile, glancing briefly at Falcon. "My uncle is one of the guards here."

She returned his smile warmly. "Nice to meet you, Zach," she offered, taking his hand and giving it a gentle squeeze.

Falcon directed his gaze upward, to where Harold was looking over the edge. "What in God's teeth are you doing up there?" he called, his voice sharp with anger. "You almost killed this boy!"

Harold moved his way slowly down the ladder, and, when he turned, his face was emotionless. "I am so sorry, M'lord," he stated in a monotone voice. "My foot … it must have slipped."

Falcon leant to the hay, picking up the scythe and hanging it on a nearby hook. He swept back to hold Harold with his gaze. "Make sure all your equipment is better stored in the future," he ordered. "I do not want to see this happen again. Ever."

Harold nodded acceptance, his face dour.

A clanging bell rang out from the main building. Jessica immediately turned to Falcon with a wide smile. "Lunchtime!" she chimed brightly. "I am famished!" She hooked her arm into Falcon's, drawing him out of the stables. He took one last appraising look at Zach before allowing himself to be pulled along. Storm gave Zach a friendly pat on the arm, then walked out behind the pair.

As they entered the main hall, Jessica disentangled herself from Falcon, then took Storm by the hand.

"Here, you must sit by my right, so that we can talk more," she gushed, pulling Storm forward into the furthest seat. Jessica now sat between Storm and Falcon. The blonde arranged herself in her wooden seat with a smug grin, then called sharply for some mead.

Storm's mouth quirked, but she took her assigned seat without protest. It had become quite clear to her in the past few hours that Jessica did not appreciate Falcon's upcoming marriage plans, and that the dainty woman was quite anxious to insinuate herself into his life and stop them.

Storm wondered why Falcon was moving forward with a marriage he did not wish. Was there truly no other way to bring an end to the fighting? He apparently had at least one enthusiastic partner ready to share his bed. Surely there must have been another way to negotiate the truce. She wondered if Jessica was at least part of the reason why there were few other women around the building.

Heather moved past the table, filling their mugs from a pitcher of warm cider. Storm gave her a grateful smile, and the girl blushed softly.

Jessica's eyes blazed. "Wake up girl, I said mead!" she barked, moving her mug away from Heather's outstretched pitcher. Storm winced in sympathy as the young girl turned beet red and ran off toward the kitchens, calling out her apologies.

Jessica barely noticed the serving girl's flight, instead making a show of straightening out the intricate embroidery of her lavender sleeves.

Storm buttered some bread, then turned with what she hoped was a look of innocent curiosity. She wanted to learn more about this woman by her side. "So tell me, Jessica, how long have you lived here at the keep?"

The sour look that flashed through Jessica's eyes warned Storm that she had begun on the wrong foot. "Unlike you, I was not fortunate enough to become entangled with the bandits and need rescue," came the snappish reply.

Falcon, who had been conversing with John at his other side, turned his head at the tone of her comment.

Jessica quickly rearranged her features into a more friendly pose, laughing cheerfully to take the sting out of her words. "I am sure Falcon has rescued many people over the years; he is such a kind-hearted man. He will take in any lost stray he comes across! No, I have a home in the village. I am staying with my aunt Carol, the seamstress. I am looking to open a new branch of our family business here in town. My father owns and operates Wilson's Sundries."

She paused with a satisfied smile, waiting for a reaction.

Storm felt no recognition of the name. "Oh, is that some sort of a store?"

Jessica's look soured for a moment, then she brightened with a sharp grin. "Of course, I had completely forgotten that your mind was not working properly." Storm bit her tongue as Jessica continued without taking a breath, her voice taking on a more expansive quality. "It is not just *a store*. It is the finest of shopping experiences. We have branches in several towns and are looking to expand our presence here. We bring in only the highest quality house wares, cutlery, and, of course, jewelry." She fingered the necklace she wore – a brilliant opal surrounded by a sea of citrine. "This was made in Persia," she boasted with pride.

"It is quite lovely," responded Storm with what she hoped sounded like appreciation. She found the design a bit gaudy for her own taste and realized she did not have much of a craving for shiny trinkets. She mused that this might indicate she came from a poor family, unused to such extravagance.

She thought back to the curving ivy leaves which traced along the leather scabbard in her room. Someone had spent days intricately carving out those leaves, and the effect was breathtaking. They enhanced the natural beauty of the scabbard, which was itself a carefully crafted, highly functional item. Now there was a combination she could appreciate.

Jessica tossed her flaxen hair and turned to talk with Falcon, leaving Storm to finish her meal in silence. Storm listened idly while the blonde kept up a running commentary praising Falcon's fine collection of silver, the elegantly carved furniture, and the collection of steeds in the stable.

The meal was barely over when Falcon pushed back from the table, apologizing to the two women. "I am afraid that duty calls," he explained. "I have business with David and Shawn." Indeed, the two young men stood behind him, their burly faces alight in eager anticipation of some activity. Falcon slowly stood, looking from one woman to the other. "Perhaps you will find a way to spend the afternoon together? I bid you good day." He bowed, then turned and left through the main doors, trailed by his two soldiers.

He was barely out of the room when Jessica also rose. "I am afraid I must go as well," she sighed with sadness. "There are so many things to attend to in setting up the new shop here. I imagine you must want to rest up, so you can heal and leave as quickly as possible." She spun on her heel and followed Falcon out of the room.

Storm shook her head, sipping at her cider. In a short while the other diners had moved on to their daily tasks, and she was left alone with her musings. Now that the hall had emptied, she appreciated the peace and quiet. Only Zach remained, working his way around the room, cleaning and polishing.

After a while she stood, mug in hand, and wandered along the walls, admiring the tapestries which adorned them. Each told a story in warp and weft, recounting battles, marriages, births, and deaths. She found the works fascinating and spent a long while contemplating them.

Eventually her aches caught up with her, and she retreated upstairs to her room. The afternoon sun gave a soft glow to the polished wood floors, and she found it a pleasant oasis. She left the door open, bringing some fresh air into the room. For a long time she stood quietly by the window, lost in thought.

A noise from behind her caused her to spin quickly, her hand dropping to her left hip, finding nothing.

Falcon stood in her doorway, his eyes narrowing as he watched her. He took a step forward.

"You made it back to your room all right, I see," he commented. "No ill effects from the incident in the stables?"

Storm shook her head, although she was sure her face reflected her weariness. "I am fine. I am feeling better every day, thank you," she responded. "I am sure I will be as good as new in no time."

Falcon's eyes were sharp on her. "It is a good thing that your reflexes were so quick."

Storm flushed, looking down. The same thoughts had been running through her head all afternoon – was this a sign she had lived with the bandits? Was it simply an indication that she worked with her hands, maybe in a field or a kitchen?

"Perhaps my father is a butcher," she offered quietly, hoping against hope that it was true. Even the most menial of jobs would be better in her mind than an association with the bandits.

To her surprise, she heard a low chuckle escape from Falcon's lips. She looked up to see the hint of a smile drawing across his face. "That is probably true," he agreed with a nod. "There are many probable explanations for your background, before we go seeking the unusual ones."

Storm felt caught in a sea of emotions. She did not want him to go – but between his engagement and the attentions of Jessica, she did not want to entangle herself with him, either. He seemed to have enough on his plate without her interfering.

She put some of her thoughts into words. "Jessica seems a nice woman," she commented without inflection. "Is she an old family acquaintance?"

Falcon's mouth quirked into a wry grin. "Jessica's aunt, Carol, has been a loyal friend over the years. She has done much of the fabric work for my staff. When Carol pleaded with me to be a good influence on her niece, I felt it important to do my best."

Storm's interest was piqued. "Oh? Does Jessica need a guiding hand in her life?"

Falcon nodded. "Her father is a merchant, but some question how legal his operations are. I imagine Carol is nervous about that and is hoping that Jessica does not follow in her father's footsteps. Jessica's mother – Carol's younger sister – died many years ago. Jessica has only her father to guide her in life."

Storm felt caught by this idea for some reason. "Just because her father is a rotten apple, that is no reason to assume the daughter is damaged fruit as well." She found it ironic that she was defending Jessica, but it seemed that the issue mattered to her. "Maybe she has had a difficult childhood, with a father like that, and found it hard to escape his influence."

Falcon tilted his head to one side. "Indeed, that is what Carol feels. She hopes that by sheltering Jessica here, and allowing her to set up business on her own, that she will prove her own character's worth, without her father's heavy hand."

Storm sat on the edge of the bed, lost in thought. "I wish Jessica luck then, truly. I imagine escaping from a harmful parent's influence can be challenging."

Falcon chuckled softly. "Not all women would be as charitable as you are, given how Jessica acts toward most females in her vicinity."

Storm gave a wry smile. "I can hardly tell what influences there have been on me, to say why I am the way I am. At least with Jessica, we know what has helped to shape her. If she manages to free herself from that influence, then good for her."

Falcon was silent at this. He stood staring at Storm for a long while, lost in thought. She did not feel uncomfortable at his perusal; her own musings drifted over Jessica's petty jealousies. She wondered just how Jessica had grown up; how her father had treated her.

Storm's frustration at her own empty memory gnawed at her. What type of parents had raised her? If her own childhood had been full of anger and harsh treatment, would she have turned out any differently?

Falcon gave himself a gentle shake, returning from his thoughts. "It is getting late, and I imagine you wish to rest. Sleep well, Storm," he offered with a pensive look. He paused for a long moment to gaze at her before turning and heading back down the hallway.

Storm watched him go, hollowness descending on her. She pushed it away, standing to prepare for bed.

Footsteps drew closer to her room, and she turned eagerly toward them. To her disappointment it was Mary who entered the room.

"There you are, Missus," she warmly greeted Storm, bringing in another blanket. "It looks like a cold one tonight. I was wondering where you had gotten to. The master gave you the full tour, then? That was kind of him, with all he has to do right now."

Storm smiled and nodded. "Falcon is quite a gentleman," she agreed, a warm sensation curling around her. "I imagine he is a skilled fighter as well." She wondered why that mattered to her. She sat on the edge of the bed, waiting to see if any memories floated by. She knew that she was impressed by Falcon. Her smile deepened as she remembered how kind he had been with the staff.

The maid puffed up with pride. "Lord Falcon is indeed the best of masters. In fact, I would say -"

Suddenly she stopped short. She gazed closer at Storm's face, then walked over next to her, concerned.

"My dear, I know you've lost your memory. You feel new and shiny, like a girl at her first harvest dance. And it's certainly normal enough for a master of a household to enjoy the company of any single women who are interested. Many would say it's critically important for his health, as much as eating and drinking is. It doesn't do for a man's energies to be pent up for long. Especially not a man of power and responsibility, like Lord Falcon."

She ran a gentle hand along Storm's cheek. Her eyes shone for a moment. "And were it any other way, I would say you were just the one to bring health back to him. He has shied away from a woman's touch for far too long. It has taken a toll on him. He needs that back in his life again."

She let out a sigh, her gaze holding Storm's. "But, dear Storm, we do not know of your past. It could be that you are married to another man. It could be that you have vowed yourself to God. You could always regret what happened here, once your memory returned. I would not see you endure that heartache. And I know that Lord Falcon would not wish that either."

Storm sighed, trying to push the image of Falcon's intelligent, deep eyes from her mind. "You are right, of course," she admitted to the older woman. "I do not know anything of my obligations. I would not want to inadvertently do something to cause Lord Falcon trouble, or to hurt those who might care for me."

Her eyes went again to the ring on her finger. "It is just, when I search my heart, I do not find even the smallest glimmer of the joy I feel when I am with him. What if I am all alone in life and this is my one chance at happiness? What if this time I have with him is my brief glimpse of contentment in a life of despair?"

Mary's eyes shadowed. "You are not the only one who could be caught in that situation," she sighed. "Lord Falcon is a remarkable man. I have known him since he was born; I was the maid to his mother. I have always wished the best for him." She gave a sad smile. "Unfortunately, with what we know of this upcoming wedding, it does not seem that he was meant to find someone who would bring him peace."

Mary gave herself a shake, as if to release the gloom, and then came around to brush out Storm's hair. Storm's thoughts drifted away as the sunlight faded slowly from the room.

Why was she so taken with Falcon? After all, she had only just met him. Surely she must have known men like him before. She sensed it wasn't his title that interested her – she couldn't care less that he was a Lord. It was his intelligence, his easy grace, his warm eyes ...

Was her real life that bleak, that Falcon's gentle touch was a stream of sunlight in a darkened room?

Chapter 8

Storm awoke the next morning full of energy, eager to get moving. The previous day's walk around the keep's grounds had given her the confidence to explore even further. She now knew the layout of the building well enough that she felt ready to take advantage of her newfound strength.

After dressing, she nodded to Zach as she headed down the hallway, then moved out into the main hall. The wall hangings held a fascination for her; she moved from one to the next examining them.

A noise sounded from one of the hallways. Falcon came in from the courtyard, fresh from practice and drenched to the bone. He smiled with surprise to find Storm there and walked over to stand beside her in front of a row of intricate tapestries.

"Do you like them?" he asked with curiosity, looking sideways at her face as she studied the images. "Those tapestries are a Falcon tradition. The women record all major events in cloth, to be remembered by all future generations."

He pointed to the newest one, only partially finished. His voice became somber. "My mother was working on this one when she fell," he quietly added. "Now, by all accounts, our tradition may be lost."

Storm's eyes flicked over to his in surprise. A new picture began to form in her mind. "Your mother did not pass away from an illness?"

Falcon was blunt. "They claim it was a suicide," he replied flatly. "However, I knew her well. I had spent every day with her. She was not despairing. She was making plans; talking to neighbors about how to design a truce. I saw that strength in her."

Storm turned to face him more fully. "Maybe it was an accident then," she quietly offered.

Falcon shook his head. He turned and looked up at the ceiling, as if he could see through the walls. "She fell from the top tower of the keep, which we use as a watchtower. The window there is over waist high for safety reasons. Her fall does not make sense."

"The tower?" asked Storm, not remembering the room from their tour.

"We have that closed off now," responded Falcon somberly. "Ever since that incident happened, the room has been left empty." His eyes became distant. "I was down in the courtyard, training, when it happened. I saw her fall." He clenched his hand unconsciously.

Storm shivered. "That must have been awful," she consoled him, knowing her words were woefully inadequate. "I cannot even imagine how you felt."

Falcon shook himself and looked back at the tapestry. "That was a long time ago," he mused, half to himself. "It took me a while, but I have moved on. I have to build on the legacy my parents left me."

A small group of soldiers began to filter into the room, and without speaking further, the two moved over to the main table. They had barely sat down when Jessica came gliding into the room. She spotted the pair in an instant and swooped down to position herself in between the two, dragging over a chair.

Storm ate patiently while Jessica kept a running commentary aimed at Falcon for the next hour. To Falcon's other side, John and the two young men joked and talked amongst themselves. The meal was delicious, as always, and Storm was sure to pass her compliments along to a delighted Heather.

Jessica declared the meal passable, but complained about the mead she was served. "This is only normal mead," she sniffed in indignation. She turned to Falcon. "Your staff is mistreating you," she coyly purred at him. "You should allow me to bring in some cyser for you. The apples add such a great crispness to the drink. Once you try it, you'll never be satisfied by this basic mead again."

Storm guessed from the occasional darts of sharp glances Jessica threw in her direction that Jessica was deliberately excluding her from the conversation and feeling quite smug about this. Storm wondered if she should tell Jessica that she was enjoying the quiet and the food far better than she would have appreciated the inane chatter, and her mouth twitched in a smile. Perhaps some things were best left unsaid.

After lunch was complete, Falcon apologized to the pair as he stood. "I am afraid I have some business in town which needs tending to," he explained as he prepared to go. He looked across at both women. "Feel free to enjoy the hospitality of my home during my absence."

Jessica looked as if she would speak up with an idea to hold back Falcon. Looking at the tense distraction on his face, Storm suddenly felt the desire to help out.

She put on a grateful smile. "I am sure we will be fine," she responded with a light voice. She looked at Jessica to encompass her with the offer. "You go and do what you have to. We will find something to keep ourselves busy."

Once he had left the room, Storm was not surprised to watch as Jessica left in short order, barely attempting to create an excuse for her departure. Still, she had done the best she could to let Falcon get about his business.

Storm finished off her mead, then headed out into the main courtyard, turning left toward the kitchen building. She smiled as she deposited the mug into the large tub holding the dirty dishes.

Molly's eyes went wide with surprise. "What a lamb you are!" she praised. "There are not many people like you in the world, young lass."

Storm shook her head with a wry grin. "I do not know what type of person I am," she reminded the cook. "For all I know, I am a serving wench at a riverside tavern. This could be my life, tidying up for others."

Heather spoke up impishly. "For sure, your manners are far too fine to be related to many of the nobles we have seen visit here!"

Molly playfully swatted her daughter, but her twinkling eyes showed that she felt much the same way.

Mary strolled into the room, her face lighting up with pleasure when she spotted Storm casually chatting with the cook and help. "Maybe you would like to take a seat in the sitting room, by the fire? We could bring you some freshly baked biscuits."

Storm shook her head. "I am tired of being idle," she admitted. "I want to help. What will you three be doing for the afternoon?"

Mary held her gaze, and a wicked grin spread on her face. "Well, actually, we were going to be polishing the silver."

Storm burst out in peals of laughter, and Mary explained to the other two women how Storm had asked to help with the silver on her first day at the castle. Soon the four were positioned around the large oak table, passing cutlery, platters, and candelabras to each other. The large, sunny room was warm with cheer, and the rich smell of herbs and baking bread filled the room.

Storm found the task soothing, moving the cloth in small circles to wear away the tarnish spots. It brought her a deep sense of relaxation and contentment.

She could tell by their easy smiles how happy the three women were with their lives here, and the idea intrigued her. "How long have you been working with the Falcon family, Mary?" she asked, looking up at the woman's smiling face.

"Oh, now, my entire life, I suppose," answered the older woman genially. "I was a personal maid to Lord Falcon's mother, back when she was younger. When the young lad was born, he was the most darling child you ever saw. Soon he was my charge. I enjoyed every day I spent caring for him."

Molly leaned over with a teasing grin. "Mary became a nun for him," she added with mock solemnity.

"Oh, pshaw," waved Mary, a laugh rolling through her. "I have had my share of lovers. I simply never found any man who suited me well enough to tie myself for life. Yes, I am still single. I do not regret it. I have made my family here, and I am very pleased with the results."

Storm rotated her silver platter to reach a new section. "Do you not have any brothers and sisters?"

"Oh, yes, one younger sister," responded Mary with a nod. "I see her when I can. She lives on the far borders of Lord Falcon's land, so the travel can be challenging."

Her face shadowed. "It is not safe where she chooses to make her home. Several years ago, she lost one of her sons in a bandit raid. The lad was only eight." She dropped her head in sorrow. "He was a strong child – undoubtedly they wanted him as a slave and would not have hurt him. Poor thing, he panicked and tried to escape. He was accidentally trampled by one of the bandit's horses, and died instantly."

Storm shook her head. "You never can tell what life has in store for you," she commented somberly. "Sometimes I suppose it is best to choose your battles, and to wait it out until the moment is right to act. He was far too young to understand that."

Heather's soft voice spoke into the silence. "My father was hurt during action against the bandits," she stated with a tone of pride. "He is one of the soldiers here. He does his best to help keep the villages safe. I am sure that soon the outlaws will be rounded up and brought to justice."

Molly patted her hand, her eyes dark with worry. "The sooner, the better," she agreed, bringing the wooden crucifix around her neck to her lips for a kiss. "The bandits seem better equipped each year, and I am nervous each time he heads out after them."

Storm thought again of the scar on her leg. Was she the victim of a past attack as well? She hoped fervently that she was not a bandit herself, part of a group that brought nothing but pain.

She focused on her cloth making small circles on the bowled side of a silver pitcher. "Do you think someone can change, mid-life, and become a different person?" she asked, keeping her tone light.

Heather looked confused, but Mary's shrewd eyes met with Molly's. Mary reached over to put her hand over Storm's, causing her to look up.

"Now see here, Storm," instructed Mary with gentle firmness. "Each of us has a type of character deep within us. We might go through rough times and we might have awful situations inflicted on us. I am sure if you talk to any person in this building, you will find they have faced pain and heartache. It is part of life. Sometimes you end up in situations you never could have imagined."

Mary gave Storm's hand a squeeze, then went back to polishing the platter before her. "Whatever life you had, before you came here, it is clear that your nature is an honest and good hearted one. Whatever environment you were in before does not matter. What matters is how you act, now that you are in our world. You must never move backwards – you must always move forwards."

Storm lapsed into quiet, and spent the afternoon in somber reflection. Sensing her mood, the other three began to talk of casual goings-on about the village, keeping the conversation open for her to join, but allowing her to reflect inwardly, lost in her own thoughts.

Eventually the silver was buffed and gleaming, and Storm thanked the women for their company. Worn, she headed back up to her room to rest. She thought of how content and well cared for the staff at the keep was, and reflected that this was directly due to Falcon's gentle and heart-felt attention.

Despite her best intentions, Storm knew she was growing even fonder of her host. She prayed that Thom brought news of her home soon, before she fell completely in love. Before she was wholly lost.

Chapter 9

Storm was delighted to find golden shafts of sunshine drifting into her room when she woke the next morning. The world glowed with fresh brilliance, and her spirit buoyed. She slid her stool over to the window, resting there for a while, relishing the block and strike of the guards' practice. Falcon moved amongst them, steady, sure. Warmth spiraled within her, drawing itself around her in a tender embrace.

Her thoughts moved again to the wall hangings - the visual tale of his life. She decided to head down early, while the hall was deserted, to take a closer look at what they portrayed.

Apparently someone else had also thought of early rising. As she descended, Storm spotted Jessica lurking in the hall.

Storm paused on the stairway, torn. She knew she should continue down and attempt to be polite, to spend time getting to know Jessica. However, she admitted to herself that she would much rather head back to her room, biding the next hour in quiet thought rather than facing Jessica's double-edged barbs.

Sighing, Storm scolded herself for her uncharitable attitude and began to move down the stairs.

She suddenly spotted movement to her left, and Falcon came striding into the room, pulling up short when he saw Jessica standing there. He seemed almost ready to turn when the blonde woman spotted him, coming forward in an enthusiastic rush.

"Oh, Falcon, I am so glad I caught you," she purred in thrilled glee. "It is critical that we have a talk. Alone."

Falcon glanced around the empty hall, and Storm pulled even further back into the shadows, making sure she was shielded from their view. She could hear Falcon's low voice come up in a murmur. "Well, here we are, then. What did you want to talk with me about?"

Jessica dropped her voice down to a lower pitch, and Storm had to slide down a few steps to hear what she said. "It is about ... that *woman*," stated Jessica with concern.

Falcon's response was short. "You mean Storm," he sharply clarified. "What about her?"

Storm peeked around the corner and saw that he was standing a few feet away from Jessica, staring at her coldly.

Jessica was nonplussed by this chilly reception, and pushed forward with her suit. "I have been asking my customers," she divulged with a conspiratorial whisper, "and none of the reputable families have heard of a missing girl. Not. One. Word."

Falcon's face did not change. "We found her on the border. She could be from one of Walker's villages, not one of mine."

Jessica was shaking her head before he finished. Her voice gained a harsh edge. "Have you gone completely daft; completely forgotten the lessons you learned the last time a stray woman appeared on your doorstep?"

Falcon's eyes flashed with a sharpness that Storm had not seen before, and Jessica took a half step back before regaining her composure.

"I am only looking out for you, Falcon," she insisted, moving toward him again. "Someone needs to take care of you, to watch for danger. You are simply too trusting." She waved a hand toward the front of the keep. "Look at how you divulged every little detail about our defenses to that stranger. She wanted to know about *arrow slits*. What kind of a woman is fascinated by arrow slits?"

A look of doubt flickered across Falcon's brow. "We cannot assume -"

Jessica launched into the breach. "Can we afford *not* to assume?" she pressed, her eyes shining. "The bandits were barely thwarted the last time they tried this tactic. Here we are again, and it seems you are missing the clear warning signs." Her eyes flicked toward the stairs, then back to hold Falcon's eyes with focused attention. "I have no doubt in my mind. She is in full control of her memories, she is one of the bandit's leaders, and she is playing you for a fool. You not only allow her free access to your home, but you enthusiastically provide her exactly the details she needs in order to invade and destroy it!"

Falcon's voice was low. "You have no proof," he pointed out.

Jessica's voice rang with certainty. "You cannot prove I am wrong," she retorted. "You have a solemn obligation to protect the lives of the innocent people in your home. What about your maid, what's-her-name, the one you like so much? Would you want her brutally murdered in her sleep by a bandit whore?"

Falcon made to speak, but Jessica was not done. "A fanged viper is loose in your home. You owe it to the people who rely on you for their very lives. She needs to be sent away. Now. Immediately. Before it is too late."

Falcon took in a long, deep breath, his face becoming a mask. "I have heard your opinion, and I understand your concerns," he stated at last, his shoulders tense. "I am not ignorant of the potential danger here. She is being watched, and I have taken precautions." His face became steely. "As to the rest, she stays where she is. That is not open to discussion."

Jessica's mouth pressed into a thin line. "Do not be blind to the warning signs this time," she urged him. "Consider what she says. Evaluate what she does. Be ever vigilant for even the slightest indication that she is deceiving you."

"I am," he answered sharply, then turned and stalked out of the room. Jessica stared after him for a long moment, her eyes brightening with a glow of triumph. Then she spun and strode out a side door, leaving the room in empty silence.

Storm staggered back against the wall. She knew that her current lack of memories was authentic, but so much else of what they had said had echoed her own fears. Why had she been so taken with the defensive fortifications of the keep? How was she so adept at catching the spinning blade? Was she indeed a member of the bandit group; had they been planning to use her as a way to seduce and deceive him? It seemed that Falcon had considered this possibility – he said he had her under watch.

She glanced around, her heart thumping. Watched? By who?

Her eyes lit on Zach. He was dusting cobwebs out of the corner of one of the hallway windows. He caught her eye and shyly smiled, then went back to his work.

Storm eyed the lad in consideration, realizing that she had never thought about him before; he had simply blended in with the servants moving about the grounds. The lad seemed about fourteen and was in admirable shape. He had said he was a relative of one of the soldiers; he certainly seemed as if he would be fleet of foot. One wrong step by her and a group of guards would be after her in moments.

Storm sat back against the wall, her mind whirling. Could she be a threat to Mary, Molly, and Heather? As much as she hated to agree with Jessica, she knew she could not deny that she might be.

The knife, the scabbard, the defenses of the keep - the interests she possessed were none that a farm girl would enjoy. The way she had grabbed the whirling scythe had surprised her. Her build belied the thought that she was a quiet noblewoman. What else could she be?

Her mind skipped forward with lightning speed. What if she were indeed a bandit leader, responsible for a trail of death and destruction? What if this plan had been her own idea, a way to finally bring down Falcon's resistance?

She shook her head, but she could not prove the charge was false. Falcon could easily be forced to lock her up once he discovered her true nature. Perhaps that is why he wished to keep her here, where she would be easy to move from bedroom to dungeon as soon as that news was revealed.

Storm sighed as she began to accept the bandit link as a possibility. She wondered if her personality would change once her memory returned. Mary had been so kind and sweet to her.

Storm wondered if she would suddenly be capable of bringing harm to the gentle maid if it became necessary in order to escape.

She sharply shook her head, praying that would not happen. She knew her mind. She knew how much she wanted to protect people from harm.

Desolation wrapped around her. Maybe that strong sensation was solely because her memory was currently blank? When the pieces were filled in, would she feel differently? Could she become a different person? If she had been raised to despise the noble folk, would that way of life settle over her as easily as a cloak settles around a chill body?

Storm stumbled back to her room, sick to her stomach at the thought. She resolved to do her best to heal quickly, to give her mind every possible chance to recover.

She also swore to herself not to betray the trust of those who had cared for her. No matter what happened, she would find some way to keep that much of her current self intact.

* * *

Storm barely heard the conversations swirling around her. She forced herself to pick at her chicken pie. The meal was delicious, but she just could not bring herself to eat.

She looked down again at the ring on her finger, at the delicate blue flowers. She wished fervently that she could have some glimmer of her memory back. Something – anything - to help her know for certain that she was not part of the bandit crew.

Jessica's voice suddenly sliced into her musings. It sounded honestly curious. "What an interesting ring! Perhaps if I took a look at it, I could help figure out where you are from, so we could return you there promptly!"

Storm found her heart lifting, and she looked at the item in surprise. It had never occurred to her to enlist Jessica's help. The woman was interested in jewelry and apparently knew many of the local craftsmen. Why had she not thought of this earlier?

She gave a few tugs on the ring before convincing it to slide from her finger. The dent left behind seemed to indicate that she had rarely removed the band. She rotated it around once or twice in her hand before turning to place it into Jessica's outstretched palm.

Jessica examined the ring, her eyes aglow with interest, taking a careful look at the shape of the flowers and the construction of the ring. Storm noticed that Falcon had turned and was watching the proceedings attentively.

Jessica nodded. "Fine craftsmanship," she murmured, "and the forget-me-not, certainly a sign of a loved one. Probably a husband, I would guess," she added sweetly, looking up at Falcon. "This means it is even more important that we return her to her home as quickly as possible. Think of the agonizing torment the poor man is going through, with his wife missing!"

Falcon's eyes were shuttered, and he quietly nodded.

Jessica turned the ring around in her fingers again, her voice brightening. "Her husband will certainly be appreciative of your honor, Falcon, that you ensured Storm was treated with the utmost respect while under your protective care!"

Tightness wrapped at Storm's chest. "I have tried remembering any loved one," she pointed out, "but I do not get any sense at all that -"

"Of course you do not," interrupted Jessica with a laugh. "Your mind has been completely wiped clean! I am sure your husband will forgive you. He will be quite happy to begin his courtship anew once you are safely home again."

Falcon's voice was low when he spoke. "Jessica, do you recognize the ring?"

Jessica pursed her lips, looking back at the ring with focus, apparently enjoying being the center of attention. "As I said, forget-me-nots are a sign of remembering a vow." She chuckled. "A little ironic, in this case." She gave a final look, then nodded in triumph. "I have seen work like this done in

Mundesley. That is a port town fairly near to North Walsham, the Walker stronghold."

She smiled in satisfaction. "So I would have to guess that our lost soul is indeed from the Walker area, and that you, Lord Falcon, have done quite well to send your messenger there. I am sure he will return soon with news of Storm's family, and we can send her back into her husband's loving embrace." Her grin widened, and her eyes twinkled. "Who knows, maybe she has a litter of young ones waiting for her as well!"

Storm flushed crimson, looking down, It had never occurred to her that she might have borne children, and the thought felt utterly alien to her. Had she forgotten so completely her intimate encounters with a man, forgotten the long nights of him holding her?

She found her eyes moving up to meet Falcon's, and they also held a sense of shock. He pressed his lips into a tight line. "We will find out soon enough," he commented in a low voice. "In the meantime, I imagine Storm would want her ring back."

Jessica's eyes brightened. "Of course! We would not want her to be parted from her token of love for a moment longer than necessary!" She turned and placed the ring on the table back in front of Storm.

Storm stared at the ring, focusing on its shape, searching for even the hint of a memory. Surely she should have some faint recollection about the man who had given this to her. Even a tiny emotion or feeling should bubble up.

But there was nothing at all.

She lifted the ring up with a sigh, then closed her eyes. She slowly, carefully slid the ring on her finger. She settled it down into its groove, placing it back where it obviously belonged.

A crystal clear vision suddenly came to her. She was young, perhaps twelve, and sitting by a window overlooking a treed landscape from somewhere high up. She was completely alone. She had a blue shawl wrapped around her shoulders, and she was sliding the ring on her finger, gently spinning it, transfixed by it, repeating a vow to herself.

She tried to focus on the words, to hear what was being said. But the more she tried, the more the vision slipped away from her, dissolving, evaporating like birds scattering from the tree in which they'd sheltered.

Frustration welled up within her, and her voice was rough as the words slipped out. "What was the vow?"

Jessica's bright, bubbling laughter caused Storm to open her eyes, to remember where she was. Jessica was nudging Falcon in the side, her mirth spilling over. "She cannot even remember the vow she gave to him," she chortled.

Storm found herself shaking her head. "Not to *him*," she absently stated, still grabbing desperately at the tails of the visions, finding each one eluded her with ease. "It was me. I gave myself the ring. It was when I was younger, and it signified something extremely important." She let out a frustrated sigh. "I cannot remember why, though."

Falcon's voice was low and steady. "So you do remember *something*?"

Storm looked down at the ring on her finger. "I thought I did," she quietly responded. "I could sense a window, a shawl, and a feeling … but it is all gone now."

Jessica gave her a gentle nudge. "I am sure your husband will be disappointed when he hears he did not even make a small appearance in your memory," she chuckled.

Falcon's voice came smoothly across to Storm. "In any case, we should know soon enough when Thom returns if Storm's memory is a true one." He gave an encouraging smile. "In the meantime, let us enjoy this delicious meal while it is still warm."

Storm gave herself a shake, refocusing her attention on the food before her, taking a bite of the chicken pie. In a short while she had finished it, and any remnants of her memory had drifted far from reach. A melancholy fog settled over her afresh. If she were not a part of a family, then maybe this was proof that she was a loner amidst the bandits. Perhaps when her memory returned to her fully she would find the vow was simply one to stay away from all men, to focus solely on herself and her own self-interest.

To her surprise, an echo of affirmation sounded deep within her.

She blanched. A deep hole opened up beneath her; she was teetering on the edge.

Maybe she did not want her memory to return. Maybe it would be best if she remained as she were, starting from the beginning, forging a new path with her life. Her past was looming like a bottomless pit, one which would only suck her down into its depths, grab at her with black fingers and taint her … taint her …

There was a bone left in her bowl, and one of the house dogs nudged against her leg, his tail wagging. Storm absently dropped her hand to pet him, scratching idly between his ears, struggling to shake off the mood that had overcome her.

Falcon's voice came to her as if from far away. "Storm, are you all right?"

Storm let out a deep breath. Part of her wanted to run back to her room, to hide and prevent even the smallest memory from intruding on her world. But she knew she could not take that path. She needed to share with them her thoughts, to find a way to integrate her past and present into a whole that she could accept.

She mustered her strength, then let her eyes move upwards to encompass both Falcon and Jessica.

How could she put this turmoil in her heart into words? Her previous self could be a bandit wench whose frame of reference was completely different than her current one. How might she explain how utterly alien her world view might be?

She struggled to put her thoughts into the simplest terms she could imagine.

"We are brought up to consider chickens as food and dogs as pets. Both groups exist in their distinct roles. That is our norm in life, and one we do not even consider questioning."

She took in a long breath, glancing at her bowl. "What if we grew up in a family where we were taught that a chicken was a beloved family member, never to be harmed? What if we adored our pet chickens?"

She looked down at the contented dog nestled at her side. "Even further, what if our parents raised us to despise dogs, to think of them as dumb, smelly, and worthless? What if, to our society, dogs were dirty pen animals used for stew? Say we were raised with *that* as a normal fact of life, and never had reason to doubt it."

She rubbed the dog's head idly, running a hand down his back. "How might we react if brought to a place where our beloved chickens were mindlessly slaughtered? What if the remains of our beautiful chickens were fed to those 'dirty, worthless' dogs? Would we change? Would we strike out at what we now saw as injustice?"

Storm shook her head in confusion, looking into the large brown eyes of the canine, lost in thought.

Jessica's laughter came loud and high, and the blonde fought to control it, to answer. "Are you saying that you are drinking the blood of your best friend in that stew?" She chortled in earnest, her mirth carrying across the hall.

Storm's voice was low, almost lost in the peals. "The blood of a best friend ..." she echoed, her look haunted.

Jessica turned to Falcon with a wolfish grin, giving him a conspiratorial nudge. "If I came across such a family of chicken-lovers, Falcon," she confided with a wink, "I would immediately contract for as many chickens as I could. They would raise the chickens with great care. I would promise to send the feathered pets to fine new homes. We would have the best chicken soups and chicken pies that these lands have seen."

This sent Jessica into a new round of merriment. After she caught her breath, she launched a litany of recipes and improvements she felt would benefit the keep.

Storm let Jessica prattle without interruption, and finally she built up the strength to look across at Falcon, to see how he had reacted. He appeared to be completely oblivious of Jessica's stream of commentary, instead lost in serious thought. She wondered if he was considering her possible involvement in the bandit activities. Perhaps he was wondering if she would change, once her memories had returned. She knew the concern was always with her, always pressing at her.

Falcon suddenly shook his head, then stood, causing Jessica to stop mid-sentence in surprise.

"I am sorry, but my duties call to me," he curtly offered to the two women, nodding to them, his mind clearly elsewhere. He turned, calling out, "David! Shawn!"

In a moment the two young soldiers had come to his side, and the trio was heading out the door toward the courtyard.

Jessica's lips pressed to form a tight line. Her voice came in a low mutter. "Well, the sooner they finish checking every village, the sooner we can get Storm back to where she belongs," she mused. Then she stood and strode out herself, not making even a small effort to offer a farewell to Storm.

Deep exhaustion settled down onto Storm's shoulders like a wet, sodden wool cloak. She barely had the strength to rise from her chair, and she made her way up to her room at a slow pace. There she tumbled into bed and wearily closed her eyes.

Chapter 10

A modicum of peace settled over Storm when she awoke to the sound of church bells ringing. She would not have to hide out today. None would question her when she chose to spend the day praying in the chapel. She quickly dressed and made her way down to the small stone building, finding a quiet pew in the back corner.

When the others stood and left the chapel after the mass, she remained behind, relishing the serenity that settled over her as the rows of well-worn benches slowly emptied.

The rain was still pattering down on the roof, although its ferocity had abated somewhat over the past week. It was more of a friendly sound now, the fresh autumn smells of moss and wet ground permeating the stone walls.

A large stained glass window sent patchwork colors down the stone floor, scattering light across the polished wooden pews. A small table to one side held several beeswax candles in front of a small statue of Mary. Storm did not give in to the extravagance of lighting one; the light grey sky provided ample illumination for her quiet thoughts.

She did not know if she was devout or passive in her faith. She wore no cross, but indeed had few possessions at all when she came, beaten, bedraggled, and spent, to the steps of this keep. Who knew what the bandits had taken from her? All that mattered was that she felt a great sense of peace in this chapel, and that while she was here, she was not causing any further harm to her friends.

As she sat pondering her state, and considering the possible futures which spread before her, she was well aware that her mind and memories of her time here could be used against her. If she was with the bandits, and they somehow regained possession of her, they could then force her to reveal everything she had learned about the security here, the location of valuables, even the skills and weaknesses of the guards.

Storm was ruthlessly realistic. Try as she might, even if she set herself heart and soul against cooperating with the bandits, she knew that every person had her breaking point. She would not fool herself. A determined torturer would eventually cause her to reveal all important details she knew.

The sun was setting before she finally allowed herself to return to her room. Mary was waiting there with a small platter of cheese and bread, as well as a cup of wine.

"Thank you," smiled Storm in gratitude. She ate the fare eagerly, realizing that she had become quite hungry.

Mary banked down the fire, then removed the remnants of food as Storm wearily climbed into bed, falling asleep almost instantly.

* * *

Storm spent the next morning watching the men work out in the fog and drizzle. She alternated between sitting by the window and moving around the room to build up her arm and leg strength. Weakness still trembled through each limb, but pressed herself to walk, to move, to swing her arms.

The thought hammered at her with growing intensity. She had to take her potential ties with the bandits more seriously. The less she learned about the keep and Falcon, the better. Hollowness gnawed at her at the thought of staying away from Falcon, but she resolved herself to her path with determination.

She resisted going down for lunch, and about an hour later there was a knock at the door. Pulling the wooden door ajar, she found Heather waiting for her in the hall, carrying a platter of chicken, cheese, and bread along with a mug of cider.

"Mum thought you might be getting hungry, and sent me up with some food for you," she greeted with a smile.

Storm returned the grin, drawing the girl into the room with a sweeping motion. She sat down on the side of her bed, with Heather plunking herself down on the bench by the window.

Storm nibbled on the chicken leg. "This is delicious, as always," she praised. "Your mother is a wonderful cook, and you are a darling help. You will make someone a fantastic wife someday."

Heather's eyes dropped, her face tight. "Someone would have to like me first, for that to happen," she commented under her breath.

Storm looked up with real surprise. True, Heather was on the heavy side, but she was so sweet ... Storm looked Heather up and down with a studied glance. The girl had her hair tightly pulled back from her face, giving her face a puffy, strained look. The bright green dress she wore made her skin seem faded and dull. Mostly, though, it was her expression. Her eyes seemed listless and sad, and her mood seemed grim.

Storm smiled with a fresh wind of energy. If she was going to sit in her room for the next few days anyway, she might as well be useful if only in a small fashion.

"Do you think your mother could spare you for a few hours each afternoon, to help me with something?" she asked casually.

Heather absently nodded. "Yes - with the ongoing rain, many of the harvest tasks must wait for better weather. I am sure I can help with whatever it is you have planned."

"Well then, tomorrow after lunch it is," agreed Storm. "I will see you then."

* * *

Rays from the morning sun streamed through her windows, and Storm stretched in their warmth, watching as the remaining soldiers headed into the keep, their practice complete. Soon Heather would arrive with her lunch, and then they could get started on Storm's project. She looked forward to the afternoon, her face glowing with anticipation.

There was a knock on the door, and she turned with a bright smile. To her surprise, Falcon stepped in. He drew to a stop, his eyes caught on hers, and it was a long moment before he gave a gentle bow.

"We missed you at lunch yesterday," he commented in a rough voice. "I came up to escort you down, so we would not be deprived of your presence yet again."

Storm's throat tightened. She craved the warmth emanating from him; it drew around her center and held her close. She knew she should turn him away and ask him to leave. And yet she found herself rising, walking to him, and laying a hand on his offered arm. Together they headed down into the main hall side by side.

Jessica beamed at them as they approached the head table. "It has been three days since I have seen you," she teased Storm with a bright smile. "I was beginning to think you had run off with the chickens!" She giggled merrily to herself.

Storm settled herself down on Jessica's right, nodding in greeting. "I have taken on a small project," she demurred. Heather came over to fill their mugs, and Storm stopped abruptly, nodding her thanks to Heather.

"Well, do tell, what is it?" prodded Jessica, her interest piqued. "What will you be up to in that room of yours?"

Storm hesitated, but looked over Jessica's intricate braids and well-tended look. If anyone could offer advice, Jessica would be the one. She nodded her head toward Heather, who was now serving the other end of their table. Jessica turned her head, and together they watched the young maid. The two teen soldiers, David and Shawn, were teasingly harassing the maid with sharp tongues, and Heather retreated with a crimson face toward the kitchen.

Storm hesitated before speaking. "Maybe if she braided her hair along her brow line …?" She stopped, wondering at the wisdom of involving Jessica in this discussion.

To her pleasure, Jessica's face immediately lit up. "Oh yes," she answered, her eyes sparkling. "That would be *much* better than that tight look she has now. Full, soft braids, so that it creates an oval frame for her face. It will draw attention to the beauty of her hair, instead of the sallow texture of her skin."

Her eyes followed Heather with critical attention when the girl came back into the room, and she nodded. "I have a number of old ribbons I no longer use in my baggage. I will send them up to you as soon as we finish with lunch."

Storm looked over to Jessica with a warm look. "That is very sweet of you."

Jessica appeared lost in thought for a moment. "My mother died in childbirth with my younger brother," she quietly replied. "I never had anyone to guide me in these matters. I spent hours by myself, trying and experimenting. If this young girl can avoid the harsh tongue of snide boys, then so much the better for her."

True to her word, Storm was barely back in her room when a messenger arrived, bringing a small collection of ribbons. It was only a short while later that Heather appeared, standing at attention within the door.

"So, what shall you have me do?" she asked with resolute readiness.

"We are going to plait your hair today," replied Storm with a grin. "Take a seat on the bench by the window, where we have some good light."

Heather blushed pink when she realized what Storm's intentions were, and noted with pleasure the array of ribbons.

"Are these really from Jessica?" she wondered in surprise. "Maybe she is hoping you will stay up here forever, leaving Falcon completely at her mercy!"

Storm chuckled as she brushed out Heather's long hair. "If you feel someone has a bad nature then you will look at everything they do through that lens," she pointed out amiably. "However, I think you will find that most people have a mix of motivations. They are neither all good, nor all bad. It is better to take each action as they come, and hope for the best with each new move."

"I suppose," responded Heather doubtfully, holding up a rose colored ribbon. "This is a beautiful color, whatever the reason she has for giving them to me."

Storm held the ribbon up against Heather's cheek. The rosy red of the ribbon brought out the natural color in her cheek, and was a far better match for her than the bright green of her outfit.

"Do you have any dresses of this color?" she asked, going back to her brushing.

Heather blushed. "I have just this one. Every year we get a new dress, and each time it is the same as the previous year."

"Why is that? Are you required to wear this color?" asked Storm with curiosity.

Heather shook her head. "I guess it has just always been that way, and I never thought to change it," she replied pensively.

"When do you get your new dress?"

"Just a week or two from now. It comes with the fall harvest, so that we have fresh, warm clothes for the winter season."

Storm nodded, done with the brushing. "I am sure we can get your dress in rose this year, and you will find it suits you far better."

Storm moved around to sit in front of Heather and began softly braiding the hair along her brow line. She took her time, doing and undoing the work until she created an even fall of hair along both sides. She brought the braids back to meet at the nape of her neck, then used the rose ribbon to join them.

She found the small silver mirror and handed it to Heather. "Well, what do you think?"

Heather's mouth formed a perfect O as she looked at her reflection. "It is lovely!" she gushed, looking at herself from several angles. "It is almost pretty!"

"You *are* pretty," retorted Storm with a chuckle. "We just have to coax you into letting it show!"

They spent the afternoon braiding and unbraiding the hair until Storm was sure that Heather had gotten the hang of the style and could do it on her own. By then the light had begun to fade and Storm's energy was flagging. She sent Heather off eager to show her mother, and climbed into bed.

* * *

Storm considered avoiding lunch again, but it was the one time when she left her room, and she found she could not resist heading down the stairs to join the others. It was only an hour, after all. Besides, she could ask Jessica's opinion on Heather's new hair style.

Jessica nodded in proud approval as she saw Heather approach, and even called the maid over to scrutinize the braids from close up. Heather blushed profusely, and listened attentively as Jessica suggested a gentler weave along the top brow.

Falcon waited until Heather had moved out of earshot to turn an intrigued eye on his female companions. "I assume you two had something to do with the new look of our young maid?"

"Why yes," interjected Jessica smoothly. "It is the role of the mistress of a keep to ensure that all of her minions – no matter how lowly – look their best. As you are currently single, I felt it was the least I could do, to repay you for your kind hospitality." She raised her glass of wine to him in a salute.

Falcon's mouth quirked at the answer, but he nodded, raising his own mug in return to the two women before him.

Jessica took a swallow, then turned back to Storm to comment in a low voice. "Next, you have to do something about that skin," she firmly instructed Storm. "It is puffy and sickly looking. Go out walking with her, outside but in the shade. You two should spend all afternoon together, I would think. It will be necessary so that you develop some skin tone on that girl!"

Storm suspected Jessica mainly wanted her outside, but Storm knew that she needed more exercise as well to rebuild the strength in her legs, and took the advice to heart. As soon as Heather showed up in her room, she led the girl downstairs and out the front door. The drizzle had held off for the afternoon, and together the two made their way around the outside of the keep. Heather was unaccustomed to long walks, and Storm was still weak from her injuries, so they found they made a companionable pair, moving past the geese and chickens of the keep's environs.

Storm had many questions about the falcon roost they passed, as well as several other buildings, but she held her tongue. She forced herself to focus on the path ahead, tamping down her curiosity with an iron will. The less she knew, the less of a threat she posed to her friends.

By Thursday, Jessica pronounced Heather's braids well done, and was happy to hear that the pair had begun going for long walks. When Heather had moved out of earshot, Jessica murmured to Storm, "The walks are one thing, but she needs to cut back on sweets as well. She has crossed the line between healthily plump and unhealthily stout."

Storm looked down at the table, where an apple pie and a peach pie had just been brought out. "Maybe if there were not so many desserts with leftovers?"

Jessica's eyes lit up and she spun to face Falcon. "Falcon, my dear, do you like cheese?" she asked with hearty interest.

Falcon broke off his conversation with John and glanced between the two women, his eyes glinting with curiosity. "Well, certainly. Our last master cheese-maker moved away and we have not found someone to replace him yet."

Jessica put her hand on his arm, leaning forward. "Well, then, I have just the thing for you! My shops bring in the finest cheese from all corners of England! We have a number of varieties. You can have a plate of cheese for dessert, rather than these baked pies. What do you think?"

Falcon slowly nodded. "Certainly, I enjoy cheese very much. If that would appeal to you, then I would be quite happy with the variety."

"It is done!" cried out Jessica, delighted. "I will have it all arranged right away. You will not be disappointed!"

Storm found herself growing stronger as she and Heather walked their circuit later that afternoon, her legs more sure and steady. Heather also seemed to be moving more easily, and she tucked a loose strand into her braid with practiced ease as they came around into the wind.

As Heather walked beside her, the girl began humming a country tune in time with her step. The melody was light and gay, and when Heather eased into words, her voice was clear and strong.

When Heather had finished her song, Storm turned to her with a smile. "You have a beautiful voice!" she praised with delight. "Do you sing at the local festivals?"

Heather flushed a rich shade of crimson under the compliment. "I would never do such a thing," she insisted, looking away. "I could not sing in front of people."

"Well, for now, I am happy for you to sing for me," replied Storm. "It is quite delightful."

Heather blushed an even deeper color, but she continued to sing as they walked, and the two stayed out until the setting sun painted the sky in burgundy and gold.

* * *

Storm's stomach rolled somersaults Friday morning as she ticked another day off her stay at the keep. Thom had been gone for over a week – surely he should be back by now? She did not know how long she could remain in the keep, trying to stay blind to everything she saw, trying to avoid Falcon's presence. She was striving to live her life with blinders on, and the attempt was driving her to distraction.

Part of it, she sensed, was the lack of activity her daily routine provided. Yes, she enjoyed her walks with Heather, and the girl had the voice of an angel. Still, she longed for something more. Her arms and legs craved motion of some kind, but she could not tell what.

Most of all, it was the incessant spinning of her mind which wore at her. Storm longed to know, for once and for all, who she was. Billowing frustration grew with every hour that ticked by in ignorance.

When Saturday dawned sunny and bright, Storm resolved to get out of the keep's walls for even a few hours. Despite her concerns about gaining knowledge which the bandits might misuse, she knew she would go stir-crazy if she did not stretch her legs further than her strolls around the building. Perhaps she could find a quiet corner of the village where she could safely relax and walk about without learning anything useful to the enemies.

To her surprise, she discovered the hall Jessica-free when she descended for lunch. She had come to expect Jessica as a fixture of the room, always positioned between her and Falcon, always controlling the conversation.

Falcon strolled into the hall, moving to sit by her side with a contented smile. Storm automatically began to pull her chair away from his, to make room for Jessica, and he put a hand on top of hers, forestalling her motion.

"No need to be distant today, Storm," he smiled at her with a chuckle. "Jessica will not be joining us for lunch. It seems that she had to meet with some buyers about a new shipment of some sort for her store."

Storm had steeled herself against Falcon's charms. It had been easy enough to do with the barrier of Jessica between them. Suddenly, though, his smile hit her full force, and she blushed beneath his attentive regard.

She lowered her eyes and searched for an appropriate response. "I am very happy for her – it sounds like her new project is launching quite nicely."

Falcon was silent until she looked up again, then he held her eyes with his gaze. She was drawn into the depths of his focus. "Yes," he agreed. "It is very good news."

Blushing, Storm looked down again at her hands, relieved when Heather came by shortly with steaming bowls of vegetable soup.

Their meal time was spent in quiet conversation. Despite her decision to avoid any interactions, Storm's reserve eased with Falcon's gentle questioning, and enjoyed the discussion as much as the wonderful food.

When lunch was over, Falcon showed none of his usual rush to leave for business. He sent John out with David and Shawn to do a patrol of the nearby villages, and the room slowly emptied. He leant back in his chair, taking a long sip of his ale. His eyes held hers with quiet interest.

"So, Storm, what would you like for us to do this afternoon?"

Storm hesitated for a long while, weighing the wisdom of her plan. "I find that I am in the mood for a ride," Storm finally admitted to her host. At the surprised look on Falcon's face, she quickly added, "Maybe just around town, of course. I promise not to endanger the horse."

She realized suddenly that perhaps he did not trust her yet with one of his steeds, and wished she had not made such a foolhardy request.

Falcon gave a reassuring smile. "It is not the horse I am concerned for," he responded. He glanced toward the main door, one eyebrow raised in a question. "Surely, though, it is a little cold for a lady to be out riding for enjoyment?"

Storm thought for a while about this concern. She wondered again at her past. It seemed quite natural for her to want to be on horseback, even while a crisp autumn wind was blowing. Light to see by was all she craved. She shook her head, finding herself as intrigued as Falcon apparently was.

"It seems I enjoy riding, and the thought of cold weather does not trouble me at all. I am curious to see how well I can manage it."

Falcon considered this for a moment, then nodded. "We will take it slowly, and see how you do. You are still healing from the attack, and regardless of your past level of skill, we should be cautious. I know where the quiet trails lie."

Falcon offered his arm, and Storm found herself accepting it without hesitation, feeling as if it was natural to be beside him, to lean on him for support. Falcon's eyes moved silently to her hand, and he smiled quietly as he led her through the keep proper out into the cobblestone courtyard. The wooden stables were to the right, and the pair headed in that direction.

Harold was standing at the stable's doors as they approached. As they entered, Harold nodded his head at Falcon, then turned without speaking to lead the two into the main stall clearing. Storm glanced up uneasily at the loft area, then put the image out of her mind and focused on the present.

She slowly walked up and down the paddocks, eyeing each mount with careful precision before returning back to Mercury's stall. She smiled, opening the door and moving in to stand beside the steed, patting him with tender gentleness. Falcon said nothing, only watching with a quiet eye.

"I think I will try him," she decided at last.

Storm waited anxiously as Harold silently bridled and saddled the horse. Was she sure she could ride such a powerful mount? In what seemed too short a period of time, Harold had the steed ready and was holding the reins, indicating that she should climb up.

Taking a deep breath, she put her foot in the stirrup and lifted herself onto the horse, tucking her dress underneath her legs. She settled herself astride the horse.

She ran her hand down his mane and was filled with a feeling of deep satisfaction. She smiled over at Falcon, who was keeping a steady eye on her progress. When he saw that she was comfortably settled, he quickly mounted his own steed and drew up alongside her.

Feeling more confident, she gathered the reins in her hands, motioning to Falcon that she was ready.

Falcon nodded his thanks to Harold, then turned to Storm. "We can begin slowly, to see how you do," he offered. He gently clucked his horse into motion.

Falcon walked his grey stallion next to Storm's bay across the courtyard and through the main gates. The rolling landscape opened up in a foggy sweep before them, and Storm sighed at the beauty of the realm. The chill October wind was sharp, and it whistled past the thick black cloak wrapped around her.

The curtain walls stretched greyly behind her; to her right the town spread in a patchwork of lanes and buildings. The left was open – the fields empty and coated with a layer of crisp frost. At the far end of the fields stretched a line of trees.

Falcon turned to her. "Let me take you through town today," he suggested solicitously. "That will be an easy ride, and will let you learn more about these lands."

Storm's smile was genuine. "That sounds delightful," she readily agreed. "I would love that."

The two walked their horses side by side through the quiet streets, with Falcon providing a running commentary on the history of the area. As they came by a low building with brightly colored curtains, he pulled to a stop, motioning for her to do the same. In a moment they had dismounted and pushed open the wooden door. Storm only needed one glance inside the shop to realize that this was the seamstress' shop. Carol, the heavy-set proprietor, was thrilled to see Falcon.

"My Lord, how good of you to stop in," she bubbled effusively, her blonde curls bouncing with her energetic movements. "How did you like the dresses I made you for your new wife?"

Her eyes popped round in surprise when Storm stepped into the doorway after Falcon, her cloak pulling to the side momentarily to reveal a flash of blue.

"Carol, this is Storm, the woman I rescued from the bandit camp," explained Falcon. "We had to borrow one or two of your dresses in order to clothe her. She came from the area of North Walsham."

Carol clucked her tongue in understanding. "If she came from the North Walsham area, she would be lucky to have a stitch of decent clothing on her, even before the bandits took her. That Lord Walker is the most frugal man in the realm, from what I have heard. Villagers who see even my most simple outfits are often in awe of what I offer." She shook her head. "Did you want me to put together a new dress or two, then?"

"If you would," asked Falcon with a smile. "Of course, it completely depends on your schedule -"

Carol grinned and waved his concerns aside. "Do not worry at all, my Lord! I can start working on that right away." She turned to Storm, looking her up and down. "Would you mind removing your cloak for a moment, miss?"

Storm obliged, blushing under the scrutiny. She looked around with curiosity at the ribbons and outfits hanging from the walls; all seemed quite foreign and fascinating to her.

Carol examined the fit of the clothing with a careful eye. "It looks as if these clothes fit well enough with the measurements I had for your future wife, my Lord. I can make some fresh clothes with this same fitting and they should do fine." She turned again to Storm. "Did you have a color or style you preferred, miss?"

Storm looked down at the blue dress she was wearing, again admiring the embroidery and texture of the dress. "I think this is simply beautiful," she praised the seamstress with quiet enthusiasm. She ran her hand down the fine cloth, then looked up.

"If you had anything more plain, I would be quite content with that. I do not need anything this fancy; this quality befits the wife of a Lord and -"

Carol burst out into peals of laughter, and Falcon looked abashed. When her laughter had subsided, Carol was able to explain.

"Actually, my dear, these are only casual house coats. Falcon had expected his new wife to come with full sets of clothing, and only had me make these as emergency outfits, in case something disastrous happed to his wife's trunks along the way. This is about as simple as it gets around here."

Storm hesitantly smiled. "Then I would be quite pleased to have a dress or two in this style, in blue. If you can, of course," she added in concern. "Any color will do, really."

Carol clapped her hands with pleasure. "Blue it is," she agreed. "It goes very well with your coloring. I will send them to the keep as soon as they are ready."

"I have one more question, if you would," added Storm. "Is rose dye any more expensive than green dye to make?"

Carol shook her head no. "The two are just about the same. Why?"

Storm hesitated for a moment. "When you make your dress for Heather, the maid at the keep, would you be able to make it in rose instead of green? She is seeking a change."

Carol smiled in understanding. "Of course I can," she agreed. "I think that will look quite lovely on her. Consider it done."

Falcon's eyes brightened with interest, but he only added, "Thank you again, Carol. I look forward to your next trip to my home."

The group made their farewells, and soon Storm and Falcon were again riding slowly through the quiet village streets.

Storm shyly glanced over at Falcon. "I appreciate your offer of clothing very much, Falcon. I will of course repay you for the effort as soon as I get home again."

Falcon waved her off. "Do not worry about it," he commented. "Carol's mother is having a hard time with a wounded leg. The money Carol gets from this commission will go to a good cause."

Storm rode in silence for a few moments, considering this. That Falcon would be so well informed about the inhabitants of his village, and care about their finances … it seemed both unusual and heartwarming to her. She wondered what other surprises this ride would bring.

The horses turned a corner in the street, and Storm spotted the sign for a leatherworker on the opposite side. Her spirits immediately rose. "Oh, can we go in there?" she eagerly called out.

Falcon's eyebrow lifted in curiosity, but he said nothing and nodded. He pulled his horse to the side, dismounting and tying up the steeds at the railing which stood before the shop. The two entered through the heavy wooden door.

The middle-aged, rough-hewn leatherworker looked up with pleased surprise when he spotted Falcon entering the shop. "My Lord, welcome!" he cried, putting down his tools and walking over with a broad grin. "I had not thought to see you back here so soon."

"Theodore," greeted Falcon with ease.

A blonde girl, maybe eight, suddenly stood from behind a table and looked between them shyly before racing off into the back room.

"Never mind my Caroline, she is at that age," chuckled Theodore. He looked down Falcon with careful attention. "Is your new armor serving you well? Any rips or pulls that need mending?" He examined the full leather jerkin and pants which Falcon wore with a practiced eye, seeking any problems or pulls.

Falcon shook his head, then looked over with interest at Storm, who was moving slowly along the walls, staring with open fascination at the collection of scabbards, greaves, vests, and other items on display. She ran her fingers with awe-struck admiration over the carved designs worked into some of the pieces.

She finally stopped at a dagger scabbard which was decorated with an intricate tracing of leaves and ivy.

"This is amazing," she pronounced in a quiet whisper, holding it up to the light to get a better look at the detail work.

The shop owner smiled with pride. "You have a fine eye, M'lady," he agreed. "That took me two months of work. It was a commissioned piece, but the buyer changed his mind."

Storm turned it over in her hands, entranced by the design. Over her shoulder, she heard Falcon talking quietly with the man. The two stood by his counter on the far side of the room, and she missed most of the conversation.

Then the volume grew. "We will take it, Theodore," came Falcon's voice.

Storm whirled in alarm. "Oh no," she protested quickly. "I could not possibly -"

Falcon waved his hand, dismissing her concerns. "Consider it a gift from me, in thanks for your company," he quietly insisted. "There is no need to pay me back for this."

Storm was going to protest further, but something in Falcon's eyes had her bite her tongue.

She brought her attention back to the beautiful leatherwork in her hands, immersed in its artistry, lost in the moment. She wondered faintly that she had found this emotion in an armor shop, of all places.

"Hold this for a moment?" she absently called out to Falcon, staring down at her new scabbard with joy while pulling her dagger free from her belt with her right hand. She idly flipped it across the room to him, sending the hilt in a sure, straight line toward him. He caught it easily, but she barely noticed; she was transfixed with her new present. To think it was now hers ...

She sensed vaguely that Falcon was staring at the dagger in his hand, looking between it and her with a sharp gaze. She chuckled, dismissing his surprise. It was hardly a throw at all, barely a distance of fifteen feet. Child's play.

She pulled her belt loose, then slid the scabbard along its length, settling it on her right hip. As she finished buckling the belt, she automatically put her right hand up in the air, signaling that she was ready for the dagger's return. Her eyes caressed the scabbard - the intricate design; the delicate workings along the leaf.

She could almost feel Falcon's stare as he narrowed his eyes. Surely the man was not nervous about a little knife toss.

Finally. She sensed the motion as he flipped the dagger around in his grip, then with a quick movement he sent it spinning in the air, aiming past her head. She grinned at his over-abundance of care. He was playing it safe; at that angle, if she did not catch it, it would land harmlessly embedded in the side wall.

The dagger never made it that far. As it spun past her head, without moving her gaze from her scabbard, Storm reached up and plucked the moving weapon out of the air. She heard the whistle of admiration come from the shop-keep at his side, but Falcon's eyes remained cool and shuttered.

Everything else faded from her mind as she nimbly flipped the weapon around in her grasp and eagerly slid the dagger into her elegant new scabbard. She turned, her eyes bright, to move forward to Theodore and take both of his hands in hers.

"It is simply amazing," she praised him, her heart full of joy. "I have never seen its equal. I will treasure it forever. You are truly an artisan."

The man blushed to the roots of his hair, the smile nearly reaching his ears. Then Falcon was taking her by the arm, guiding her from the shop and bringing them back to their mounts.

* * *

Falcon seemed more reserved than usual as they rode slowly away from the shop, and she glanced over at his impassive face. He was lost in thought. She wondered if perhaps there was a story behind the leatherworker's financial situation as well. She shrugged, gently rolling her shoulders. If so, there was no need for her to press. She would allow him to tell her in his own time.

She patted the scabbard at her side; it truly was a work of art. She would count it amongst her most valued treasures. Her mood bright, she gazed around the quiet town as they passed, admiring the quiet gardens and the flocks of chickens contentedly scratching in front yards.

When the two had ridden a ways from the shop, Falcon shook himself, looking over to meet Storm's eyes. His voice was serious. "So you like the scabbard? You were not just being polite to humor Theodore?"

Storm's smile brightened her entire face. "Very much so," she promised. "It is the loveliest thing I have ever seen."

Falcon considered this for a moment, then nodded, gently returning the smile. "I am glad, then. That scabbard has been in Theodore's shop for several months now. It is out of the price range of the locals here, and I think he had despaired of ever making back what he put into that piece."

He paused for a moment, watching her eyes. "It pleases me that you were so taken with it; the scabbard deserves to be somewhere it is appreciated."

Storm looked down at the beautiful workmanship which now hung at her hip. "Who ordered it, and then abandoned it like that? It is simply gorgeous."

Falcon's lips compressed, and he looked away. "It was Lord Walker," he admitted in a cold voice. "He was visiting a while ago for preliminary talks. He had admired the workmanship of my armor and asked about having a scabbard made with this design. He settled with Theodore on a price, and Theodore promptly went to work. Theodore knew how important this treaty was to me and put more time into it than on any other project I have seen."

Falcon's voice became brittle. "When the finished piece was presented, Lord Walker demanded that he pay only one quarter the original price. Theodore simply could not do it; he has a family to feed, and he had put aside many other projects in order to complete this one. Lord Walker stalked out and refused to pay."

Storm did not know what to say. It seemed that the Walkers were not people that Falcon should be dealing with, but she was not in any position to advise him. She held her tongue, riding quietly through the leaf-filled streets.

They moved into more residential areas of town. Occasionally the two would stop by a house as the occupant came out to talk for a while, pleasantly passing the time. Every home showed a measure of pride and care which shone even through the layers of fallen leaves.

By the time the light began to fade and the two had returned to the stables, Storm was exhausted but glowing with pleasure. Harold was across the courtyard as they rode in, and slowly began to make his way across to the pair.

They stopped deep within the stable building. Falcon was on his feet in a moment and came around to help her dismount from her horse. She found she appreciated his steadying arm as she lowered herself from the saddle.

When she gained her feet, she turned, putting her back to the steed to regain her balance. Falcon was close before her. She could smell the rich aroma of the leather of his armor, the musk of his body in a heady blend of scents. She looked up into his eyes and felt lost in their depths.

Her voice came soft and deep. "Thank you, for everything."

Falcon's voice, when he responded, had a husky quality which made her heart ache. "It was my pleasure."

Storm was caught by his gaze; her heart thundered within her ribs. With an effort she made herself turn, to move away from that tempting closeness and head into the open courtyard. Falcon was practically an engaged man. She had no proof she herself was unattached. She had no place encouraging him or indulging in her own dreams.

She practically ran up the steps, heading back to her own room. Once there, however, sleep was a luxury that was long denied her. It seemed that everywhere she looked, Falcon's understanding eyes were gazing back at her.

Chapter 11

Sunday dawned with rainy dreariness, but Storm felt the draw to Falcon as if a magnet was pulling her in. She dressed quickly and headed downstairs with a light step, hoping against hope that Jessica would be absent again.

To her delight she found Falcon alone, waiting for her in the main hall. He was freshly washed, dressed in a quietly elegant tunic of rich blue. He escorted her with a smile into the small chapel, sitting beside her on the polished wooden pew.

Storm was swept away by the beauty of the morning. The rain gently thrumming on the wooden roof overhead, the melodic chanting of the priest as he gave the mass, the comfortable presence of Falcon at her side. She wondered at how easy everything felt and considered what it might be like to have this routine laid out before her for her entire life. She was suddenly wistful that this was only a tiny snapshot of life – one which could be whisked away at any moment.

When the pair had finished with lunch, Falcon glanced out the windows, then turned to Storm. "It does not look like today is a good day for riding," he commented wryly. "However, I have another idea. Come with me."

He led Storm through a side door into a richly appointed study. The floor had two thick fur rugs; a pair of comfortable leather chairs flanked a large fireplace with a marble mantle. Rows of shelves lined the wall around the fireplace.

Falcon brought a small table over to sit between the two chairs and lay a chessboard on top of it. He began placing the pieces down one by one.

"This seems a perfect way to spend a long, rainy day," he commented as he finished putting the board in order. "Have a seat, and let me explain to you how these pawns work."

Heather brought them in mugs of mead, and Storm bit her lip in concealed mischievous delight as Falcon patiently explained each piece to her in careful detail.

It was a relatively short while later when Storm pressed her castle forward, coming up alongside his king.

"I believe this is checkmate?" she offered, a twinkle shining in her eye.

Falcon sat back for a moment, a suspicious look coming onto his face. "You have played this before," he finally growled out, tipping over his king in defeat.

Storm took a long drink from her mug, her face shining with delight. "It does seem familiar to me, yes," she agreed with glee.

Falcon shook his head, a smile growing on his face. "Well then, the next time you will not find me quite such an easy victim," he promised, and the challenge was on.

The two played long into the night, until the fire had faded down to quiet embers. They had tied at two games apiece before Storm's exhaustion brought her to call it a night. Falcon walked her up to her room, coercing from her a promise to play fresh matches in the coming days.

* * *

Storm drifted awake to motes of dust dancing in the sunbeams streaming through her open windows. She smiled and nestled into the blankets for a while, allowing herself to bask in the warmth. She knew it could not last forever. At some point soon Thom would return, and she would have to leave the keep. If she only had a few days left, then perhaps it was not so bad to relish the beauty, the serenity that life was presenting to her.

A golden glow drew through her. Perhaps the afternoon would unroll with a delightful ride through the quiet village. Perhaps the evening would glisten with candles as she slid her queen along the ebony board.

She brushed her hair out until it glowed, and her feet barely touched the stairs as she descended down to the main hall … and pulled up short. Despite the early hour, the room was laid out as if for a county fair.

A pair of burly servants had positioned a series of elegant looking blue and white pottery items along the length of the main table. There were tall, twisting vases, sprawling serving bowls, elegant small plates, and a plethora of other assorted accessories.

Jessica was standing regally behind the selection of her wares, carefully adjusting the position of each item. Falcon and Mary waited to one side, quietly conferring together. He looked up as he heard her soft footsteps on the stairs and nodded a quiet greeting to her.

Storm came down to stand beside the two, offering good mornings to each in turn. She found herself intrigued by the items set out on the table. Jessica had frequently discussed the luxurious nature of her wares, and Storm had assumed that she would find Jessica's offerings similar to her jewelry – pretentious and gaudy.

Instead, these mugs and platters made Storm feel comfortable and relaxed. The patterns were of flowers and vines; the lines traced the shapes of the objects with a gentle balance. That Jessica's store stocked items that Storm found appealing and beautiful brought her up short. She reminded herself not to make assumptions about other peoples' lives.

Jessica finished arranging the last bowl, then came around to stand in front of her products. She completely ignored Mary and Storm, instead speaking directly to Falcon. All of her friendly demeanor of previous days seemed lost, subsumed by her professional arrogance.

"This collection of fine artwork has just been imported from southern France," she explained to Falcon with practiced verve.

"There is a small commune there, an artist's enclave, which has perfected their craft over hundreds of years. These are not ordinary items, but master crafted works of art which will become beloved heirlooms for your family."

Falcon listened to her sales pitch with casual attention, then, when Jessica swept him forward, he strolled down the row of items with Mary and Storm on either side of him. Jessica attempted to interject herself into each conversation, but Falcon made sure that Mary and Storm were consulted on each piece.

Mary passed over most of the items, but she found a trio of serving dishes which she said would do nicely for vegetable recipes. Falcon nodded with agreement, deferring to her in the selection. Jessica bubbled with delight and assured Falcon that they were a wise investment.

Storm found that she was transfixed by one of the vases set at the center of the table. The vase began with a low, bulbous base, then narrowed and sprouted into a thin cylinder at the top. The vase would hold perhaps four or five stems, no more. A delicate tracing of blue vines spiraled around the tube.

She reached forward to pick it up, only to start back when Jessica snapped at her. "Careful, there!" came her harsh scold. Storm looked up guiltily, bringing her hand back.

Jessica walked forward to pick up the vase and hold it in front of Storm. "This vase is probably worth more than your family makes in six months," she estimated in clipped tones. "Please do be careful."

Falcon's voice came quietly from behind her. "Add that in to my order," he stated calmly.

Jessica's eyes burned with a combination of avarice and jealousy, but she turned with a sweet smile on her lips. "Of course, Lord Falcon," she purred. "Anything you wish."

The rest of the items were packed off and the room was cleared for the noon meal. Despite Jessica's endless prattle, Storm could feel Falcon's eyes on her, and she blushed despite herself. She found herself remembering in detail how he knew each person along their ride through the village. How he had gently teased the newly handfasted young couple, asking if they were getting enough sleep. How he'd helped the elderly farmer with his sticky gate.

She was not surprised when he left with his men shortly after the meal – and when Jessica followed only moments after him. Storm headed back to her room, lost in thought. An afternoon rain shower had moved in, and she distracted herself by doing arm and leg exercises for several hours, slowly but surely rebuilding her strength slowly.

It was late in the evening when a knock sounded at her door. She looked up in surprise, then smiled in greeting when Falcon came into the room. He had one hand behind his back and drew it out to present her with the blue vase, filled with a harmony of colorful reeds.

"I am sorry I could not bring you flowers," he offered with a wry grin. "I am afraid this is not the season for roses or daisies."

Storm came forward to stand before him. She carefully took the vase from his hands, looking down to admire it. "The reeds are beautiful, perhaps more beautiful than the vase itself," she thanked him with a smile. "They remind me …"

Falcon's eyes sharpened. He watched as her gaze lost focus, and did not speak or interrupt her musings. He stood stock still, waiting in attentive quiet.

The moments slipped by.

Storm's world shifted around her. There were no visual images, only feelings. She ran one hand across the tops of the reeds, feeling their willowy texture. "There was a clearing by a pond … a horse … a circle of reeds. I was safe. I was finally safe."

The feeling blew away, dissipating as a morning fog in the growing dawn. She shook her head, realizing that Falcon was watching her closely. "I am sorry," she softly apologized. "I cannot remember much at all, just the emotion."

Falcon was standing quite near to her, and he half reached toward her before stopping. His voice was low and husky. "How do you feel now? Do you feel safe?"

Storm did not need to ponder the question at all. She knew immediately the sensation she felt. She looked up into Falcon's eyes, losing herself in his gaze.

"Yes," she breathed. "Yes."

He was quiet for a long time, and Storm was drowning in his eyes, joined in the depths of their emotion. Time seemed to stand still, and she almost held her breath rather than break the spell.

Then, with a deep sigh he dropped his eyes to the ground. "That is good," he bit out huskily. His eyes flickered back up to her hip for a moment, then he turned away. He strode out of the room, closing the door firmly behind him.

Storm stood still, watching the door for many moments before she accepted the fact that he was not going to return. She went to the window and placed the vase on the sill.

She sat on the edge of the bed, staring at the reeds for a long while. Over time, the fading dusk muted the colors into shades of grey. Finally only flickering shadows from the fireplace lit their profile.

Chapter 12

Storm spent the next morning perched on the wooden stool by the window, watching the men practicing sword moves down in the courtyard below. Her heart ached with conflicting emotions. She knew that she was becoming drawn in by Falcon's charm, his compassion, and his skill with a blade. It would be incredibly easy to fall in love with him.

She also knew that this was not meant to be.

In an ideal world, she would be the fairy tale princess, a perfect match for Falcon. She would be told that her father was a king and that their wealth would ensure the safety of the kingdom for all time. She and Falcon could be together, happily ever after.

She knew in her heart that the reality would be far from a storybook plot. Reality never worked out perfectly like that. For all she knew, she was a serving wench, and this very day could see her sent back to a harsh master. Her future could be comprised of long days of rough labor and lonely nights in a cold cell.

Storm both longed for the messenger's return, to free her from this torment, while at the same time wishing that this waiting could go on forever. She was suspended between two worlds; neither offered her what she wanted from life.

Tense with frustration, she grabbed the sword from the bottom drawer and began swinging it around. The sharpness of the blade slicing through the air seemed to match her mood, and she slashed at imaginary enemies for a few moments. Then, as if on their own accord, her movements began to fall into a pattern. Swing the blade forward and down, until the tip rested above her right toe. Pull the blade up, hilt by her cheek, pointing the tip toward the eyes of the enemy. Slash the sword down and across, resting to the lower left. Her feet moved to match, steady and balanced.

The tensions of the morning melted away from her. She was moving without thinking, without evaluating. Her legs were a little stiff, but that would fade. Snap the blade up to hold it straight before her. Drop the hilt to her left hip, tip high. The moments spun on into a relaxing litany. The fluid turns stretched one after another; the minutes rolled on as she lost herself in her actions. Another spin, and she turned toward the door ...

Storm found herself staring straight into Falcon's eyes. They were shuttered and unreadable, and by his posture he had stood there for some time. His hand rested easily on the hilt of his sword.

Storm's face flushed, and she brought her own sword slowly down to her side. The hilt felt so familiar in her hand, as if she knew every curve, every twist. There was no question in her mind. The sword was hers.

Leaning over, she retrieved the leather scabbard from the bed and slid the blade smoothly into its place. She laid both gently down on the covers, avoiding Falcon's eyes.

Falcon's voice was smooth and even. "I suppose you just now remembered how to use that."

Storm was at a loss for words. "I ..."

She turned and stared out the window at the now empty courtyard. "I do not remember the look of the sword at all," she explained in confusion, trying to put the sensations into a context that Falcon could understand. "When it is in my hand, when I feel it move ... that, I remember."

She paused, laying her forehead against the cold stone at the side of the window. She knew her sword skills seemed a sure indication of her guilt, of her association with bandits. Even so, at her core, she knew more than ever that it could not be true.

Storm took in a deep breath, searching for a way to put the feeling into words for Falcon. "It is not that I feel aggressive when I hold the sword, or powerful. It is different than that. I feel … secure. I feel I hold the strength to protect myself … to protect others. I know I would put my life on the line to shield a family from harm."

She shook her head, realizing this was small proof that she was not a member of the bandits. She had now shown she had some skill with the sword. Just what did her past really hold? What did Falcon believe about her character or her background?

Frustration grew within her, and she bit back tears. "I know you need to know about my past," she grated, her voice hoarse. "I swear to you, if I only knew, I would tell you everything. I do not. I do not know what you want to know."

Falcon was silent for a long while, then he quietly walked up close behind her. She could feel his presence, feel the power of him there. She forced herself to stand in place, to not turn and see the expression on his face. Did he despise her? Did he imagine her standing with fellow bandits, preparing to cause harm to others?

He stood near her for several minutes, not speaking. Then suddenly he turned her around to face him, almost roughly, and she was stunned by the desire she saw in his eyes.

He took her hands in his, holding them gently. "I believe in you," he insisted, sounding as if he was trying to convince himself as much as her. "There could be a thousand reasons you know how to defend yourself. A thousand valid reasons."

"I want you to be proud of me," Storm bit out hoarsely, caught by his gaze, the words slipping out before she gave them thought.

"Oh, Storm," he ground out, moving closer to her, looking down at her in torment. His attention moved from her eyes to her lips and he almost leant down before reining himself in, taking in a deep breath.

"If there is anything I need to know, the only thing important to me …" He held her gaze for a long moment. "If you remember through touch, maybe there is a chance." He brought up her hands, gently pressing them against his cheeks. His voice was thick with longing and jealousy.

"Does this feel familiar in any way?"

It took only a moment for Storm to realize what he was saying. He was asking her if she remembered touching another man; remembered being with another man. The knowledge swept over her like a raging flood. She realized that he was as worried of violating an existing relationship or commitment of hers as she was.

The thought hit Storm with blazing clarity. If they did discover that Storm was a married woman, and the loyal husband arrived here to claim her, might the marriage be forever tainted by Storm's unwitting adultery? And if she were married to a high-ranking town official, how would that disruption affect the other villagers' estimation of Falcon?

Storm knew that many Lords shared in the bounty of their female tenants. Those women often sought out the relationship and considered themselves lucky to raise the resulting child. Their allowance might be a boon for their entire extended family.

But from what Mary had said, Falcon had, until now, chosen a life of celibacy, at least until his upcoming wedding. Storm had a sense that something had happened to Falcon in the past – something he had not fully healed from.

And yet, here he was before her, his eyes deep with emotion. His mind was clearly torn between a longing for her and a concern of hurting her.

He wanted to know if she was free.

She shook her head in frustration. How could she answer his question, when she had no memory of her past?

Storm closed her eyes and concentrated, running her hands along the lines of his cheek, down his neck to the strong muscles of his shoulders. She could feel him tremble beneath her touch, could sense the force of will it took him to stand still beneath her gentle caress. Her own body flushed with the sensation, became faint from the desire flowing throughout her.

Moving with deliberate slowness, she slid her hands down his well-muscled arms, recognizing without looking the different muscle groups that were in evidence beneath his leather. What would it be like to have those arms wrapped around her, holding her tightly against his chest ...

Her breathing was constricted; her heart hammered against her chest. She took in a deep, shuddering breath. She was enveloped with his scent - of musk, of leather, with the barest hint of sweet woodruff.

Her hands once again met his, and she interlaced her fingers into his before opening her eyes. It was as clear as day to her.

"No, never," she whispered throatily, her eyes open and wide before him. "There is no man in my life. I swear it."

Falcon uttered a low curse and, twining his fingers more tightly into hers, pulled his hands behind him, drawing her in to him. Storm's heart pounded against her ribs. Her body tingled as if it was aflame as she pressed against him. She wanted nothing more than to wrap her arms tightly around him, to kiss him ...

She struggled to retain control over herself. She knew in her heart that this could not be allowed to continue. Something deep inside her shouted, screamed, thundered that this was wrong, that she had to stop, that it was an absolute imperative.

Desperately, she turned her head to the side, breaking the eye contact which threatened to engulf her.

"We cannot," she rasped brokenly. She grasped to find some logic to cling to. "So much depends on your truce. If I were to distract you now, when you are so close -"

Storm could not bring herself to continue; her voice was near breaking. It took every ounce of strength to keep from giving in, from looking up into his eyes and losing herself.

She brought the truce into the center of her mind, focusing on it, her breathing at last coming more under control. This was bigger than her, bigger than any man or woman. After all, if this had been just an arranged marriage between two people, and the match seemed poorly suited, perhaps she would be as active as Jessica was in advising Falcon to call it off.

But it was not just a simple marriage. This tie was joining more than two individuals. The arrangement was a truce – an end to the wars. It held in its power the fate of his people, a people who so loyally supported him. This was the fate of Heather's father, of Mary's sister …

The innocent villagers of this region desperately needed the marriage – and its attached treaty - for a much longed for peace. They deserved it.

The strident claxon of alarm within her settled and quieted, and she knew she had made the right decision. Even so, she could not bring herself to pull her hands free of Falcon's tender grasp, to take even a small step back from his warmth.

It was a long minute before Falcon let out a deep breath and released her hands. He stood in the center of the room for a moment, then leant over to pick up the sword and scabbard from the bed, to place them back in the lower drawer.

He turned away for several long moments, regaining his composure. Finally he turned back to Storm and offered his arm with a resigned smile. "Let me at least escort you to lunch, my Bandit Queen."

Storm's eyes flew up to meet his. "Please, do not even joke about that," she pleaded. "I do not know who I am. I have no idea why I can use that sword. If I am truly a part of the bandit group -"

Her voice broke at the thought that she could be the cause of so much unhappiness.

Falcon's face was immediately somber. "You are right, of course," he agreed. "We will find out soon enough, when the messenger returns." He paused, then continued in a quieter tone. "Still, remember my words. Whatever you were in the past, you do not need to be that woman any more, going forward. You control your destiny from this day onward."

* * *

Jessica was away on a delivery, and it seemed to Storm as if she and Falcon participated in a delicate duet for the rest of the day. Almost every topic they discussed seemed to relate to the truce and impending marriage, but they danced around addressing the subject directly.

After a delicious lunch of fried pork, they headed out to the stables. Harold was there to saddle up their mounts. He looked dourly at Storm as she waited, then commented to Falcon, "It will not be long, sir, before you have a new bride here at the keep. Shall I look into getting a fresh horse selected for her? She might appreciate having a mount of her own, to go riding with you."

Falcon's face stilled, but after a moment he nodded. "Yes, of course you are right, Harold. Please see to it."

Harold gave a soft grunt, adding, "It will be nice to have the Walkers and Falcons finally merged. Things will be better then."

Storm's face blazed, feeling that her presence here was inappropriate. She could not bring herself to look at Falcon, to see his reaction. Instead she watched as Harold went about his work. He soon brought the two horses over for the couple.

Distraught, Storm gave her steed a firm nudge, and soon they were out the gates. She only began to relax as they meandered on a long, quiet ride through the village.

Storm found herself looking thoughtfully at each friendly face they stopped to talk with, reminding herself that these innocent people were why Falcon needed to wed.

It seemed far too soon when they had arrived back at the stables. Despite her intentions, Storm was loathe to part from Falcon when they approached the keep doorway, and she could see in his eyes that he was caught in the same feeling. With the light fading from the sky, instead of escorting Storm back to her room, Falcon guided her to his study.

She felt welcomed by the surrounding ring of dark oak shelves. She peeled off her socks and shoes, curling her toes into the thick rug on the floor.

By the light of the fireplace and several beeswax candles on the marble mantle, they sat opposite one another in high leather chairs for their deciding match. In short order they were playing chess on the finely inlaid wooden chessboard. A large mug of mead sat by each chair.

The game had gone on for about an hour, and the room had settled into a comfortable silence. Storm took a drink of her mead, relaxing back into her seat. Falcon was calculating his next move, while Storm watched with interest, curled up in her chair.

Falcon's eyes, always so expressive, moved over the pieces on the board with careful consideration. Storm held her breath. She had laid an elaborate trap for his queen and was eager to see if he would spot it.

Storm's gaze moved up from the wooden chessboard to the man who sat across from her. The firelight flickered over his focused face; the stubble showing on his chin. His skin was firm and muscular, exposed as his white cotton shirt lay open halfway down his chest.

Storm was suddenly struck by how perfectly he seemed to match her. He was a martial man, skilled with weapons, as apparently she was. He enjoyed the long horseback rides as much as she did. He truly cared about the household members. She felt secure when she was with him – safe, happy, and alive.

She realized that she did not want the game to end. She did not want to be sent back to her room. Not yet.

Storm gently caught his hand as he reached for his Queen. Her voice came softly. "No ..."

Falcon's eyes flicked up to catch hers, and immediately the distraction of the game was lost to them both. She had forgotten how firm his grasp was, as he folded her hand in his and pulled her toward him. The hungry look in his eyes showed her he had been fighting the same emotions, and that his hold on his self-control had been tenuous at best.

She knew she should resist, and the warning bells within her head were almost deafening. She put her hands up instinctively against his chest. He was so close ....

A knock sounded loudly on the door. Storm sprang back, alarmed, spilling the board and pieces across the floor. She moved away toward the window, grabbing her cloak and wrapping it tightly around her.

Falcon stood more slowly, glancing dismissively at the scattered pieces, then swore under his breath.

"Come in," he ordered, his voice short.

The door instantly opened. Thom strode in, his breath heaving in deep draws. He moved straight to his master, bowed to Falcon, and handed him a small, wrapped parcel.

"My Lord," he murmured in salutation, his eyes downcast. Slowly his breathing slowed to a more normal pace. He did not turn his head, but his eyes skipped between Storm's turned back and the overturned table without comment.

Falcon examined the package in his hands, then he put it aside on the table. He smiled and dropped a grateful hand onto Thom's shoulder. "Thank you for returning so quickly," he offered in a low voice. "I know the weather has been rough, and clearly you rode hard. You must be exhausted; go get yourself some hot food and drink."

Thom smiled at the offer and nodded his thanks. He bowed again, then turned and left, closing the door gently behind him.

Storm pulled her cloak even tighter about her, staring bleakly out the dark window. Once that package was opened, she would know who she was. A paralyzing fear swept over her. She had been so happy these past few days. Above all, she did not want to lose Falcon's respect for her.

She did not turn as Falcon came to stand alongside her. He held the parcel in both hands, looking down at it, then spoke softly.

"Storm, it is always best to know the truth. Let us learn, together, what the core of this matter is. We can move on from there, whatever it is. The news held here will not change in any way my feelings for you."

Storm held her breath as he broke apart the package and found the letter within. He quickly scanned the contents.

"Well," he began with an even voice. "Lord Walker sends his regards. He seems a man of few words and gets right to the point. He says that, according to his research, you are a local young woman named Doris."

"Doris?" replied Storm with uncertain confusion. The name did not sound familiar at all. "I think I like the name Storm better," she confessed after a moment.

"Storm it is," confirmed Falcon. "Still, at least it means we have an identity to connect with you, after all this time. Let us see …"

His eyes scanned the words. "You were reported missing from the nearby … nunnery."

Storm's mouth flew open in surprise. "I am a *nun*?" she burst out in shock, looking down at herself in confusion.

Falcon chuckled softly, shaking his head. "No, no. Apparently you took work there as a civilian – you were a protective guard for the sisters, one they felt comfortable with." His brow wrinkled in thought. "I suppose that explains several things about the skills you have exhibited so far."

Storm leant back against the wall, thinking about this. "That does seem a *little* familiar," she admitted at last. "At least, it seems much more natural to me than the thought of being a nun."

Falcon was silent, looking down to read further. Storm saw his face relax suddenly, a tension release from his shoulders.

"He says you are unattached," he offered quietly.

A burst of joy streamed through her body, and immediately a flush of guilt followed in a wave. While she might be free, Falcon was about to be married. Would it make it even harder on her to rein in her feelings, now that she knew she was not beholden to any other man? She reminded herself fiercely that she owed it to her host to support him in his chosen path, no matter what her own desires might be.

Falcon had finished reading, and looked up to gaze at her in the flickering shadows. "Lord Walker explains that he was going to visit in just under a month, to finalize the treaty in person. He asks that you remain here until he does. He will provide you with an escort home then, if you wish."

"If I wish..." echoed Storm, returning Falcon's gaze. She could imagine no better way to spend her time – and no more dangerous.

She gave herself a gentle shake. There were no more wishes to be granted her. She had already been given the greatest news she could hope for.

"I am *not* a bandit," she sighed in overwhelming relief. "I am not a threat to you or your people. They cannot force me to betray your trust in me." She was shaky and incredibly light as the overwhelming worries of the past days were finally swept away.

Falcon's eyes shone, and his voice came deep and hoarse. "That your sole concern would be our safety ..." With a low groan he wrapped her beneath him in a firm embrace.

They stood that way for a long time, Storm pressing her head against his chest.

Finally, Storm gathered up her last remnants of strength. She gently separated herself from Falcon's arms, making her way up the long, quiet stairs alone, pressing the door shut with a firm, regretful hand.

Chapter 13

Storm sat on the end of her bed the following morning, gently brushing out her hair, awash with almost overwhelming relief. Everything was as she had barely hoped to dream. She was not associated with the bandits. There was an honorable reason for her possessing the skills she did.

She glanced out the window, watching the men below, her eyes automatically seeking out Falcon's form. Her heart beat a little more quickly when she spotted him moving amongst his men. She had not realized it before, but the news that she was single raised a great shadow from her heart as well. It was not immoral or unworthy of her to have been so drawn to her host. She had not been violating any sacred vow with her desires.

She drew the brush through her long waves. Not only was she unmarried, but the letter had not even spoken of a fiancé or boyfriend waiting at home for her. She imagined if she had been involved with somebody that the letter would have mentioned a man coming to fetch her sooner than this planned visit by Lord Walker.

Storm stood with a sigh, moving to put the brush down on top of the dresser. She dropped to her knees to pull out the bottom drawer and retrieve the sword nestled there. She ran her hand slowly down the length of the decorated scabbard before pulling the sword free.

She looked along the blade's sharp edge, and regret seeped into her soul. Single she might be, but it did not change the greater problem. Falcon had a duty to perform, and he deserved a chance at happiness with his new wife. Storm recognized that her presence here long term could only serve to jeopardize that relationship. It was just as well that she had a job to return to, far from this keep.

She turned her back on the window, holding her sword out before her. She knew now that there was no way that she could remain here, in the area, while Laura and Falcon settled down to a long married life together. Even beyond her wish to leave Falcon to his marital happiness, she knew that watching him in Laura's arms would be a daily torment for her.

Now that she had a reason for owning and using the sword, Storm felt no twinge of discomfort as she began doing gentle thrusts and parries around the central part of her room. The movements felt rusty and slow, but they were there, flowing easily one after the other. Once again she found herself lost in the movements, relaxing with the remembered motions. Once again she pulled herself up short when she found that Falcon was there at the door, watching her.

This time when he spoke his voice had more tone in it and his eyes sparkled with intrigued curiosity. "Do that last part again, the part with the circling motion."

Storm shook her head. "I do not think I can," she explained. "I do not really know what I am doing. It just sort of happens. I think I have to start from the beginning."

Falcon nodded. "Well then, that is fine. I will watch from here."

He stood quietly, his eyes keen on each movement she made, watching as she transitioned from a defensive to offensive posture. When she moved into the section that he had been asking about, he drew his own sword, smoothly injecting it into her motions. His voice reflected his confusion. "I am not sure I understand - I can simply do this ..." He gently lunged forward against the attack she had begun, aiming for her exposed side.

Storm turned on instinct, dropping to one knee under the attack, firmly using his momentum to smoothly roll him over onto his back.

Falcon's initial impact was soft, but his roll took him into the dresser, tipping it against the wall with a loud thud. The impact caused his sword to skitter out of his hand.

A few moments passed, then Mary burst into the room with a cry of alarm. Her mouth made a large O shape when she looked between Falcon sitting against the far wall and Storm standing over him, sword in hand.

"Everything is fine," called out Falcon, calming his startled maid. "I was just explaining to Storm how you fall safely if you are attacked. There is nothing to worry about."

Mary did not look as if she believed this explanation, but she backed out of the room, closing the door after her. Storm waited until the door clicked shut before breaking into a wide smile, putting her arm down to Falcon. He took it, but used most of his own arm strength to push himself back up to a standing position.

"Ah yes, I see now," he commented complacently, brushing the dust off of his pants. "It makes much more sense to me when you put it like that."

Storm chuckled. "Teaching me to fall indeed," she snorted. "As if that is a skill I need to learn. Judging by my fading bruises, I imagine I am quite good at that particular activity."

Falcon innocently shrugged his shoulders. "You never know when a new variant on a skill might come in handy," he dryly replied.

He bent down to retrieve his sword, and when he stood his face was a mask of concentration. "Still, there are things we can learn from your moves. I assume they are the standard sword moves for the Walkers?"

Storm rolled her eyes. "As if I know!" she cried out in exasperation. "I barely know what I am doing, never mind whose style I am doing it in."

Falcon smiled and shushed her. "Right, right, that is fine," he soothed, half to himself. "I imagine they probably are." He thought for a moment more, then continued briskly. "If you start joining us in our morning practice, that would give us an even better advantage. That way, if this truce falls through -"

Storm looked up at him sharply. "You cannot be serious!"

Falcon's brows came together in concern. "You would feel uncomfortable about practicing out in front of others? We can do it in private, then."

Storm shook her head distractedly. "No, of course I do not mind practicing in front of the guards. We can practice in the courtyard, or in the hall, that does not matter to me one whit. What matters is you giving up on the truce when it is so important to your people and your land's stability."

Falcon's eyes caught hers, and she was swept up by the attraction between them, the heat in his eyes as he looked down at her. Time seemed to slow. She forced herself to remember the impact of just how much could be lost if she inadvertently turned Falcon from his chosen course.

She swallowed and willed herself to speak. Her voice came out in a hoarse whisper. "Falcon ... if my presence here is going to end up compromising the safety of the townsfolk, then I will move to the inn immediately. I can remain there until Lord Walker can send an escort to take me home."

Falcon's response was immediate and guttural. "Please, no ..." He held her gaze and took a long, deep breath before replying. "We are both adults. We can acknowledge that we enjoy each other's company – and it will stay at that. Please do not deny me these few days of pleasure in the meantime."

He paused for a moment, then nodded, his voice more somber. "You are right, of course. This truce must go forward. It must be signed for the sake of everyone I care for. I have tried other solutions for too many years without success. There is no other choice."

Storm looked away, her heart heavy, but her mind in full agreement. She gave her blade a quick wipe down, then put the sword and scabbard away in their drawer.

Steeled for what lay ahead, she turned and preceded Falcon out the door to head down for lunch.

Jessica was waiting for them at the table, her eyes bright with interest as Falcon and Storm sat on either side of her. "I hear the messenger has returned," she called out with a smile.

"So you have figured out where to send Storm back to? Is she a farmer's daughter? A fisherman's wife? I want to hear every last detail!"

Falcon turned to her, the corner of his mouth quirking. "Actually, Storm is a well-trained protector at a nunnery, keeping the women safe from harm," he told Jessica, his eyes twinkling. "She is unattached, so she will stay with us for at least another month or so until Lord Walker arrives. We will see at that point what we choose to do."

Jessica's eyes flashed with sharp annoyance, her lips flattening for a moment. She took in a long, deep breath, resetting herself.

"Nuns, they take a vow of chastity, do they not?" she asked with a bright smile, buttering a roll with a vicious swipe of her knife. "I imagine the guards must too, so they do not corrupt the pure souls within the walls."

Falcon shook his head, his eyes glinting with mischief. "I believe the nuns like to live vicariously through those with whom they work," he commented with a soft chuckle. "It is why they like to take in the most wayward souls, to hear about their exuberant lives in the lusty world of the flesh."

Jessica did not like this answer much, and showed her simmering anger with her renewed knife stabs at her chicken filet lunch. Storm knew that she should be charitable, but the urge to laugh grew when she glanced up and met Falcon's twinkling eyes. She bit back her mirth with an effort.

Jessica looked up and down the table with a steely eye, then commented with a snap, "What did the maids do with that vase? I had wanted it to be here for us to enjoy for our lunches, to add beauty to our afternoon. After all, it was brought back from the sunny Mediterranean, where it undoubtedly held roses, irises, and lilies." Her voice took on a lilting quality, and she waved her hands in time with her words. "To me it symbolizes the tumultuous seas, traversed by elegant two-mast ships. It reflects the joy of life's travels that two people can share. The blue vines symbolize the binding ties of matrimony, never to be released."

Storm leaned back to take a sip of her of mead. Jessica's description brought to mind a vivid mental image of the slim, white pottery vase, the blue tracings of ivy swirling up its fluted center. The mead washing down her throat, the vines on the vase …

"Not the sea," she mused almost to herself. She had spoken softly, but Jessica immediately stopped her gesturing and turned to look at her, mouth half open at the interruption. Beyond her, Falcon put his mug down and watched her with interest.

"No, not the sea," Storm continued, the feeling growing stronger. "A stream. A mill stream, with a rolling mill wheel. So peaceful, so rhythmic. The vase sat in a window." She chuckled softly to herself, her eyes turning to meet Falcon's. "With reeds in them, from the local pond."

Jessica scoffed in open disbelief. "These vases were made by artisans in the south of France," she sniffed. "They were meant to hold the highest quality roses, not pond reeds."

Falcon ignored her outburst and held Storm's gaze steadily. "A window," he gently encouraged. "A big window?"

Storm shook her head, remembering the feeling more than the visual image. "A small window, perfect for curling up near. I would drink mead as I nestled there. I would watch the wheel turn; I can still smell the wet clay."

Falcon leant forward, his stare intense. "Beyond, out the window? Past the mill wheel?"

Storm did not concentrate – by now she realized that she had to relax, to sense faint glimpses of feelings and emotions. "Church bells," she responded after a few moments, closing her eyes. "Four of them, four descending notes pealing out."

Jessica was indignant and angrily launched to her feet. "These wares are from France!"

A hush fell over the room, and all eyes turned toward the commotion.

Falcon's voice was low and smooth, talking up to the rigidly set blonde. "It should be easy enough to find out," he replied in a conciliatory fashion. "There's a well-known church which fits that description in Walker's lands. If a potter is not at that church, maybe Storm did indeed take a trip to France, near your artist colony. A similar church could easily exist there."

He motioned to Thom, who sat at a nearby table and was, with most of the occupants of the room, watching the scene with undisguised interest. Thom came over at once.

"I realize you are just returned from a trip," offered Falcon by way of apology, "However, you know the Walker territory better than anybody else here. I would like you to go on a bit of a scouting mission."

Thom dropped to one knee immediately, with no hesitation at all in his movements. "Where would you like me to go, my Lord?"

Falcon nodded. "There is a church near the town of Dilham," he explained. "They are famous for their bells. Ask around the region; see if any know of a millhouse which has a potter in residence. If you find that location, describe Storm to them and see what you can learn of her past.

Thom nodded in understanding and promptly stood, heading out the door on his mission.

The room began humming with conversation again, and Jessica regally regained her seat, leaning forward to maintain Falcon's focus on her. A fresh smile brightened her features.

"I hear from my servants that you have been out riding recently, Falcon," she purred, drawing his eyes down to her. "I am a fine rider and would love to spend the afternoon on a trail with you! Shall we get our horses ready to go? I have my own, of course, and will not need to trouble you for a loan."

Falcon's eyes turned automatically to Storm. "What do you think? Does that sound of interest to you?"

Jessica gave a cry, interrupting before Storm could draw a breath. "Oh, but I wanted to go at a fast rate, to canter or perhaps even gallop! Surely Storm is not up to such exertions just yet in her fragile condition." Her smile widened. "After all, we would not want to risk the health of our guest, would we?"

Storm saw at once the possessive look in Jessica's eyes and hastened to soothe the woman's prickly pride. It would do no good to exacerbate the problems between them, if they were to share the keep's environs for another month.

"You are quite right, of course," she agreed with the blonde woman, her voice low and accepting. "I do need to heal. I will stay here. You two go on ahead and enjoy yourselves." She turned back to the food before her.

Falcon's eyes shuttered, and the trio finished their meal in silence. Storm forced herself to smile a farewell when Falcon graciously offered an arm to Jessica, escorting her out toward the stables. It was only when they were both safely out of sight that she sat back, sighing deeply, her thoughts muddled.

Storm turned her mug in her hands. She felt unchivalrous about abandoning Falcon to Jessica's clutches. However, perhaps Jessica's forward behavior would help him to be more content with the relative quiet of what Laura offered.

Storm shook her head. It was as bad imagining Falcon with Laura as it was thinking of him out riding with Jessica. One thing was clear to her, though. She was uncertain of her own ability to keep Falcon at arm's length, now that she knew she was not promised. She could not afford to become fonder of him, to test her own limits.

Resolved, she headed out through the courtyards and into the kitchen building. She was pleased to find her three women friends sitting around the sunlit table in cheerful conversation. The trio welcomed her with bright cheer.

There were carrots and turnips to slice, and Storm eagerly sat down to join in the task. The women had already heard of the message's contents, and shared their appreciation with her that she was not a member of the bandits, but had an honorable profession.

Storm reflected, as the conversation wended its way through the afternoon hours, that this time seemed so unique, so special. She would have imagined that she would have many female friends around her if she worked in a nunnery. For whatever reason, this time with the three women seemed a fantastic treat, one to be savored.

The time spun by, and she was relieved when evening came that she had made it through the afternoon without thinking about Falcon and his outing with Jessica. Maybe these remaining weeks would also fly by, if things were planned properly.

* * *

The next morning, true to his word, Falcon showed up in her room early to take her down to the courtyard for practice. The soldiers had all heard by now who she was and were curious to see what she was capable of. John, David, and Shawn stood to one side, their attention keen.

Storm had strapped her sword and dagger to her hips and stood, relaxed, in the cleared courtyard. To her surprise she did not feel uncomfortable at all standing in the center of the group of soldiers. She accepted their interest with ease.

She considered that, even if she was currently a guard at a nunnery, she must have learned her skills somewhere. Maybe she had grown up around a soldier's camp with a military family. That could explain many things about her personality.

Falcon's voice pulled her from her musings. "Now, keep in mind," he cautioned, "she still has amnesia. She does not remember specific things about what she has learned or why she does them. We cannot ask her to explain what she is doing. All we can do for now is watch and make guesses. Still, I believe we can learn a lot from observing her style of movement."

He turned to Storm and gave a nod. "All right then, whenever you are ready."

Storm took a deep breath and closed her eyes. The weight of the sword and dagger on her side were comfortable; it seemed as if they were a part of her. She reached down to draw the sword out smoothly from the scabbard, giving a flourish bow as she did so, bringing the sword up to her forehead and then swinging away to the right.

The movements began on their own. Her hilt dropped to her left hip, and she took a quick step forward. She thrust forward, her sword outstretched, then swung it down sharply, bringing it to rest just above the ground. She pivoted smoothly, facing in the opposite direction. The blade came up and through an imaginary opponent, resting for a moment over her shoulder, preparing for the next attack.

The movements seemed an instinctive part of her, as she turned, ducked, and retreated. She was no longer aware of the men watching her or the surrounding walls. She became lost in the movements, a part of the sequence of events.

Suddenly she realized she was kneeling on the cobblestone ground, her blade wide to the right, her head bowed at the end of the routine.

There was a loud clapping noise around her. She opened her eyes to see the soldiers sincerely applauding her efforts, showing great interest in what she had done.

Falcon's eyes sparkled inquisitively, his face alive with interest. "I know you are still healing up, but could you do that once more? I just want to see -"

Storm chuckled and nodded. She knew that feeling only too well. She closed her eyes and set herself into the initial stance. In a moment she was in motion again.

When the workout was complete, she returned to her room to clean up for lunch. By the time she reached the bottom of the stairs, Jessica had already joined Falcon at the table and was in close conversation with him.

"Of *course* you were right in sending Thom off to the Walker territory, after that 'memory' of hers conveniently appeared," insisted Jessica with serious intensity, her eyes held on his. "Who would not check up on such a story? After all, you only have Lord Walker's word for it that she is associated with a nunnery. You must admit, that hardly seems likely."

Falcon's face was neutral as he sipped his drink, but Jessica leaned forward, her gaze intense. "Walker could easily be lying about her, for who knows what reason. From what I hear, his daughter is equally untrustworthy, which is why I keep warning you to turn your back on this marriage. It will not bring the peace you seek." She took a long pull on her wine, then plowed ahead with force.

"If Lord Walker is claiming something, it is best to get a second opinion to know what the truth is. You *cannot* trust any statement that family makes."

Falcon's voice remained even as he asked quietly, "Speaking of second opinions, what is your thought about the vases you brought in?"

Jessica flushed, leaning back in her seat. "As far as the wares go, I was told those pottery items were from France. Perhaps I was lied to as well. Believe me, I am making my own inquiries into the situation." Her brow creased, and she looked up, realizing that Storm was approaching.

"My dear, there you are," Jessica purred effusively, patting the seat next to her. "Here, come sit with me." She made room by pulling her own chair closer to Falcon's. "I hear you are now cavorting with the guards. Do tell, is that fun?"

Storm moved toward the seat, settling herself into it. To her surprise, a calm acceptance settled over her. In a way, Jessica's manipulations and pointed darts were a type of game.

One that two could play.

"Oh yes, my morning exertions were very enjoyable," she responded, bringing a mug of mead to her lips for a long sip. She put the drink down and turned to look at the woman by her side. "The guards are quite friendly and appreciative of my talents. I hear they want me to stay here full time, they are so enamored of my skill."

Jessica's wide-mouthed stare and long silence were all Storm could have hoped for. Storm was even able to talk with Falcon during their breakfast, to discuss the practice routines and plans for the next day.

Jessica did not break her silence until the meal had come to an end. To Storm's surprise, Jessica stood suddenly, her normal attempt to insinuate her way into Falcon's afternoon apparently put aside.

"I have just remembered, Falcon, my dear, that I should be able to reach my main suppliers in the next town over today. I want to go talk with them right away about this pottery issue. I hope you understand."

Falcon stood and smiled politely. "By all means, take as long as you need. Your shop's reputation is, of course, its most important asset."

A frown crossed Jessica's face, but she regained her smile quickly. "I will be back by sundown, never you fear. Until then!" She took Falcon's hand and gave it a warm squeeze, then turned and strode out toward the stables. She stopped at the entryway to the hall, turning quickly to look back.

"Be sure to behave as the nuns would wish you to," she reminded Storm with a sweet grin, her eyes flashing with a different emotion.

Storm's mouth quirked, but she nodded demurely. "Of course, Jessica. I will do them credit. Have a safe journey."

Jessica looked as if she did not quite believe Storm's intentions, but after yet another fond farewell to Falcon, she turned and headed out.

A wave of peace washed over her as Jessica left the room, and she stretched out in her chair in languorous relaxation. She looked up with a smile as Falcon lowered his hand to her.

His voice held a gentle tease. "Shall we go for a ride?"

Storm did not need to be asked twice. She stood with him, walking down the hallway and out across the courtyard to the stables. He moved to one stall, drawing out his stallion, and she walked over to Mercury's stall, standing before the horse with contentment. He was such a beautiful creature. His large, brown eyes held hers with wisdom and calm. She ran a hand tenderly down his mane, drawing from his strength.

There was a grasp on her arm.

She reacted by instinct, spinning hard, drawing her knife from her belt. She brought it up and across, pressing its razor-sharp edge against the soft flesh of his throat. Her heart pounded against her chest as she stared up into his eyes.

Falcon stood stock still, not moving, his gaze locked on hers.

Storm blinked in shock, motionless for a moment, then she realized the position she was in. She drew in a long, shuddering breath, then took a step back, lowering her blade and resheathing it.

"I am sorry," she offered hoarsely, almost at the point of shaking. "I have no idea -"

Falcon's mouth quirked into a half smile. "I think, with that display, that we have proven beyond a doubt that there is no tender man in your life," he chuckled.

"There *was* none," Storm found herself saying before she could stop the words from escaping. She flushed, her mouth going dry, lost in the warmth of his gaze.

He took a step toward her before reining himself in with a visible effort. His eyes held hers with a regretful acceptance. "If I only have a month with you, then it will be enough," he vowed. "I would not lose one day of it. In the years to come, I will treasure my memory of our time together."

Storm forced herself to smile. "Well then, let us get out of these stables and be on our way."

In a few moments they had their steeds saddled and were moving side by side through the autumn sun, walking their horses quietly down the lanes and meadows of the village.

* * *

A drifting fog whirled playfully across the dawn courtyard, moving among the soldiers with easy grace. Storm danced and blocked through her routine, all watchers fading from her attention as she became caught up in the focus of her actions. Time seemed to suspend as she moved; before she knew it she had done the full sequence twice and was quite worn out. She rolled her shoulders in weary relief. Falcon nodded at her in thanks, then turned to start working individually with his troops.

Storm ran a hand through her thick hair, drawing it back. A pair of heavy stone benches sat against the encompassing wall, and she walked over to rest. She stretched out her legs with pleasure, then began wiping down her blade with long, steady strokes.

A soft squealing noise rose up from behind her. Her eyes lit up with curiosity, and she turned to look. A female hunting dog was lying in the shade, five newborn pups nuzzling at her teats. Their small eyes were barely open. She imagined each could fit within her cupped hands.

"Oh, how precious!" she cooed, dropping to her knees beside the mother.

A familiar boy's voice sounded beside her. "Her name is Bethany; she belongs to me," offered Zach with pride. "She is one of the best hunters in the land, my uncle has said so!"

Storm smiled up at him while running one hand down the dog's head, scratching behind her ears. "I am sure the pups will do just as well," she promised the lad. "Look at how active and alert they are already!"

A clatter of hoofbeats sounded and Jessica trotted into the center of the courtyard on a proud, high-strung horse of jet black. She slid off the steed, careful to hold her skirts above the dirt of the ground, then tossed the reins at a passing servant. Her eyes swept the area, and her face lit up with delight as she spotted Storm kneeling beside the dog.

"Oh look! You have found your best friend!" she called out, her eyes flashing with mirth as she slowly moved forward, avoiding a muddy puddle. "Wait, I forget – was the dog your meal for tonight?"

Zack's face went white with shock, and Storm patted his arm. "It is what passes for a joke with her," she reassured the boy under her breath. "Pay her no mind." More loudly, she responded, "How did your talks go with the suppliers about your French pottery?"

Jessica's face turned a flaming shade of crimson, but her mouth froze mid-retort. Her eyes moved up behind Storm, and a smile appeared on her face as if by magic. Instinctively, Storm turned to follow their gaze and found Falcon coming up behind her. He looked down at the pups with a fond smile, then brought his gaze back up to encompass the group.

Jessica's voice took on a contrite tone. "I am afraid we have not yet tracked down the bill of lading for the pottery," she admitted tightly. "I will be heading myself to the main shipping office later today, to get to the heart of the matter. I am sorry to say I might be gone for a week or more, if I have to go to the docks or even to France to track down where the paperwork has gotten to."

"It is always worth it, to find the truth," commented Falcon, moving up to stand beside Zack and Storm.

Jessica's brow creased, and she spun to head inside.

Storm cast a long glance at the dog family, lost in thought.

Chapter 14

True to her word, Jessica left abruptly after the meal was over, promising to return as soon as she was able to. Storm admitted to herself that she was not sad to see the woman go. It was only moments after her departure that Falcon's warm eyes had turned to her.

Storm knew that she should stay away from Falcon, not allow herself to grow fonder of him. But she could not bring herself to refuse his company. It was only for a month, after all. She could allow herself this one month of pleasure.

They walked side by side to the stables, saddling up their horses together. Falcon moved past her as he reached for his bridle, and his arm brushed hers. She flinched; with effort she reined in the reaction, taking a deep breath. He glanced over at her, his eyes warm, holding still, and she leaned against him, allowing herself to relax before stepping forward and continuing with her task.

A gentle breeze rustled the leaves on the trees as their horses walked side by side down the quiet lanes. They stopped in to talk with Carol, then moved further down the street to where it turned at the stream. Falcon glanced over at Storm for a moment, then his eyes drifted ahead, his gaze losing focus.

Contentment eased over Storm as she moved alongside him, simply being with him. They had reached a thick hedge, and she noticed a small, quiet dirt road which wended its way down toward the far edge of the woods. She was intrigued that she had not spotted it before.

As the pair passed the turn-off, their horses moving at a gentle walk, Storm stopped and gave the reins a slight tug.

"How about we try that way this afternoon?" she asked with a casual glance down its dusty length.

She was unprepared for Falcon's reaction. His face became like marble; he did not even look down the path she had indicated. "No," he barked. "There is nothing down there."

Storm could clearly see the edge of a house's eaves beyond the trees, but she did not respond, wondering at his sharp reaction.

Confused, Storm took a deep breath, then prodded her horse to follow him as he continued in silence down the path. She did not bring up the subject of the house again as they rode, and Falcon seemed content to let the quiet follow them back to the keep.

* * *

The next morning, Storm was playing with the young pups after the morning workout when Zach came over to stand near her, watching his dog with a troubled eye. His left hand continually strayed to his right arm, scratching at it through his linen shirt.

Storm watched for a few minutes without commenting, but finally felt compelled to say something. "Did you do something to your arm, Zach?"

Zach looked down in misery. "I do not dare tell my uncle," he quietly admitted. "He would most likely whip the hide off of me if he knew."

Storm turned to face the boy, taking a gentle hold of his arm. "Come on, let me see," she insisted. He did not resist as she slid the sleeve up, but to her surprise there was no welt or mark on the skin beyond the scratches Zach had made himself.

"It had been tingling furiously for a while," he commented sheepishly, "but now it feels almost numb, and I do not like that at all."

Storm immediately released his arm, her eyes flashing to his. "Were you touching a bushy plant? One with tall, violet flowers?"

At his hesitant nod, she grabbed a hold of his other arm, dragging him toward the stables. "Just what did you think you were doing?" she sighed in exasperation as they rounded the corner of the building.

Zach did not meet her eyes. "It was those two new soldiers," he grumbled. "They have been hounding me since they arrived. This time they threw one of Falcon's boots into the patch. They threatened, if I did not fetch it out, that they would tell Falcon I had stolen it." He gave a long sigh. "What choice did I have?"

Storm shook her head. "I will never understand what boys think passes as funny," she muttered. She drew to a stop beside a half-barrel nearly full of rain water. She plunged her hands into the water, then turned to dig her fingers into the fist-sized jar of wood ash soap which rested on a nearby ledge.

She nodded at him while she carefully worked the froth between each finger. "Remove all your clothes. Be quick about it."

Zach's mouth opened in shock. "All of them? Now?"

Storm shook her hands through the water, thoroughly rinsing them. "You have got the oils from the monkshood all over your clothes, no doubt. Unless we get rid of it now, your entire body could soon be absorbing the toxins."

Zach blanched at this, then hurriedly began stripping off his items of clothing. Storm did not feel uncomfortable with the lad; she felt as if this was a common scene for her. She wondered if she had younger brothers who she cared for, back home.

Wherever that might be.

He left his clothes in a small pile, then clambered into the half-barrel. The water came up over his waist, and she handed him a large metal cup to pour water over himself with. She scooped some of the soap out onto a cloth, presenting it to the lad with a stern look. "Every corner," she reminded him. "You do not want to leave one speck of that oil behind."

A thought came to her. "Which boot style was it, that was in the patch?"

"It was his one of his dark black boots, the ones with the coiled rim," responded Zach, scrubbing furiously at his neck. "He rarely wears those; I was able to get it back into place without him noticing."

A deep voice came from behind them. "Actually, I did notice," commented Falcon.

Zach jumped guiltily, splashing water out from his tub. Falcon smiled, waving for him to continue on with his task. Falcon then looked over to Storm, raising an eyebrow.

Storm relaxed into a smile. "You might want to send those boots to Mary, who will need to thoroughly clean them along with these clothes," she advised.

"Yes, I am quite familiar with monkshood, unlike our young friend here," agreed Falcon with a chuckle. "Now that I am warned, it will be done this afternoon."

"The numbness is beginning to wear off, but now my scratches are all itchy," moaned Zach in desperation, continuing to scrub. "How long is this going to last?"

"Here you wanted to not be numb, and now you grouse about having feeling again," responded Storm with gentle smile. "I imagine it will be back to normal in a few hours."

Zach's face fell. "A few hours?"

Storm shrugged elaborately. "That will teach you to give in to those bullies the next time around. Come tell one of us, and we will set things right for you instead."

Falcon's brows knit. "Bullies? Do you mean David and Shawn?"

Zach shifted uncomfortably, but he silently nodded.

Falcon sighed. "I am trying my best to get those two to learn the ways of our keep, but they are indeed the wild souls my brothers warned me about."

Storm looked up in surprise. "Your brothers sent them to you? You mentioned them before – they are at a monastery?"

Falcon nodded. "Yes, both of my brothers are younger than I am. They were sent to be novices before my father died, for their own safety. The elder of the two took to it immediately, and the youngest dotes on him and would go wherever he did."

Storm thought back to her own recent musings about brothers. "Do you get to see them often?"

Falcon shook his head no. "I have not seen them in many years; their monastery is quite far from here. Between the bandits and their duties … well, they are quite content where they are."

Storm looked back down at the lad by her side. "What about the two young men?"

Falcon wearily shook his head, his eyes running down the marks on Zach's arm. "David and Shawn were orphans who were taken in by the church. Their rambunctious nature did not fit well with the novices, and after a few years it became clear that they were not suited for the clergy. My brothers wrote me and pleaded with me to take them in, to train them as soldiers."

His voice became quiet. "My siblings ask so little of me, I could hardly refuse them in this request. I have done my best with the lads, spending time with them, going riding with them. Still, I begin to wonder if their wildness is beyond taming."

Falcon looked down into Zach's eyes. "Whatever their childhood, I will not allow those two to run helter-skelter over the other residents of the keep. If they trouble you again, please come to me."

Zach's eyes fell, and he jutted his lower lip out. "That would probably only make things worse," he muttered to himself morosely.

Storm's eyes lost their focus for a moment. "Well then … perhaps another option …" she mused quietly. With an effort she snapped back to the present. "For your itching, at least, there is something we can do to help you directly."

She glanced back at Falcon. "Do you think we could get some oatmeal and a pot of hot water?"

Zach's voice trembled with nervousness. "What are you going to do?"

Falcon looked over the page huddled in the barrel. "I believe she is going to boil the infected skin off your bones," he offered dryly.

Zach shrieked in terror, wrapping his arms tightly around him, glancing in panic between the two adults.

Storm threw a wet rag at Falcon, hitting him squarely in the face. "That was *not* nice," she scolded him, although her eyes were dancing. She smiled down at the frightened boy. "No, no," she soothingly promised him. "The oatmeal will help the scratched-up skin gentle, so it heals quicker. The hot water will overwhelm the itching for a short while, so you do not feel it any more."

A short while later, Zach was in fresh, clean clothes, and his face looked relaxed for the first time all day. Storm was still shaking her head at Falcon's comments as they headed in together to lunch.

When Falcon headed out for the afternoon with the two young men for a ride through several of the villages, Storm stood in the gateway for a long time, lost in thought. She began formulating a plan for how to help Zach become more self-sufficient.

If only she had time to see it through.

* * *

Sunday dawned sunny and crisp. Storm found a freshly made blue dress laid out for her; Carol had finished the new outfit. It was beautiful. Storm ran her fingers down it in appreciation before putting it on and braiding her hair down the sides of her face.

She was glad she spent the extra time. Falcon's eyes glowed as she walked into the room. He held out a hand to her, and she placed hers gently into his. With a smile he brought his lips down to press against her hand in a courtly kiss. She found herself dropping to a curtsey automatically, falling into the routine as naturally as if they had known one another for years.

Heather and Molly joined them from the kitchen, and Storm gasped in surprise. Heather was wearing the rose dress, and the difference was stunning. Her cheeks now blushed in harmony with the dress, and the braids highlighted the glow of her face. Since they started serving fruit and cheese for dessert, Heather's skin had become lustrous and smooth, and her figure one of lush curves.

Falcon bowed in greeting to the young girl. "At this rate, my keep will be known throughout the area for its beautiful women," he commented with a smile to Heather. She blushed pink straight down to her toes, and the glow did not leave her until long after the mass was complete.

Lunch was a delicious meal of stew and fresh bread; Storm had two large mugs of mead and was quite warm by the time the trenchers were being cleared away. Falcon leaned over, pressing a hand tenderly on her arm, and to her surprise she did not flinch, but rather leaned in to his touch in response. Warm currents ran through her from where his fingers lay.

"Shall we try a game of backgammon?" he asked her in a low voice. "We can see if that awakens any fresh memories for you."

A tremor of desire thrilled through her, she was nearly overwhelmed with longing to be alone with him for the afternoon. She was all too aware of the danger in that situation. Her eyes glanced over to Heather who was moving past the table with a pitcher of mead.

"Heather, come sing for me," she asked in a friendly voice. "It would be the perfect way to pass a Sunday afternoon."

"Just for you?" asked Heather nervously.

"Well, Falcon would be in the room, but I promise he will not listen," teased Storm gently.

Heather blushed, her eyes going between the two, but she nodded. "If you wish, I would be happy to provide some songs."

The three moved into the study and Falcon set up the board by the fireplace. Storm sat across from him, and Heather curled up in the window seat, gazing out at the quiet landscape. Heather's voice was pure and sweet, and with her presence

Storm relaxed. She almost convinced herself that the friendly backgammon game was a quiet pastime, nothing more. The afternoon passed in tranquil contentment.

* * *

The next morning Storm dutifully ran through her workout routine with the soldiers, allowing them to watch and comment as she moved. However, it was when that phase of her morning was over that her eyes sparked with interest and her step quickened. She walked over to where Zach was kneeling with his puppies, playing gently with the brood.

"Well then, my lad, are you ready for your lesson?" she asked with a smile, resting her hand lightly on the sword at her hip.

Zach looked up at her in confusion, then stood uncertainly. "My lesson in what?" he asked, idly scratching at his arm.

"Let us call it self-defense," offered Storm, taking a step forward so she stood squarely in front of him.

Zach nervously licked his lips. "They are both much bigger than I am," he offered, glancing around him. "I really think it is much better if I just let things be."

The smile on Storm's face spread. "Look at me," she responded. "I am certainly smaller than just about any man I meet. Would you want me to simply give in to any bandit who accosted me on my travels, or would you want me to at least try to defend myself?"

Zach looked Storm up and down, a glimmer of hope sparkling into life. "What can we do, if we are smaller and weaker?" he finally asked.

"Well, let me show you ..."

* * *

To her delight, Storm found that Zach was an apt pupil, quickly picking up on the sweeping leg moves, side steps, and other grappling actions she practiced with him.

"I am about their size," she pointed out to him as they set themselves up in an arm lock. "They are not yet fully grown, but for now I am the perfect model for you. So if you just do this ..."

Zach's eyes lit up with pleasure as he realized the techniques they were practicing were of practical value, that he just might be able to hold his own against the tormenters. He threw himself into the practice with fervor, and in a short while they were both drenched with sweat and mud.

The lunch bell rang, and Storm gave Zack a fond pat on the back. "Shall we say tomorrow, at the same time?" she asked him with a grin.

"Absolutely!" he returned, and then scampered off around the corner of the stable, a spring in his step that Storm had not seen previously.

She smiled with pleasure, heading around toward the stairs, pulling up when she realized Falcon was standing there waiting for her, his eyes on hers, holding a look of pride.

She looked down her body, realizing that she was completely caked with mud and grime. She chuckled, shaking her head. The man clearly needed to eat more carrots and have his vision improved.

Falcon's voice was warm as she drew up close to him. "There you are, Storm. Ready for lunch?"

"I am famished," responded Storm heartily, her stomach rumbling loudly at the thought of food. Her eyes drew down across her dress again, and she chuckled. "Just let me get changed, and I will be right down."

Falcon stood back to let her past, but she could feel his warmth as she moved by him. Her step slowed. Then her stomach rumbled again and she took the stairs two at a time, changing quickly to return to his side.

The luncheon meal seemed to drift by with ease, the surrounding babble fading from her awareness. It was just him and her, with an easy comfort she was delighted to wrap around herself as a warm blanket on a chill winter's night. It was so soothing to talk with Falcon. She felt that she could share anything with him without being judged, without being evaluated.

Then they were finishing their meal, moving to the stables, and heading out into the serene afternoon.

Her eyes drifted over his profile as the faint scent of sweet woodruff drifted in the breeze. She was struck again with how well he handled his horse. With how skilled with sword he was; with his tender care for his people and the attentive focus to their needs.

It suddenly seemed almost impossible that he had made it to this age in life without having a bevy of women desperately in love with him. Surely more than Jessica had tried. How had he avoided the other single ladies in the region; side-stepped succumbing to one's charms and having a trio of smiling children running to be in his arms? How was he even free to contemplate this truce?

He glanced over at her as they rode their horses side by side through the familiar village lanes, walking at a slow pace beneath the fluffy autumn clouds.

"What is on your mind?" he asked with interest. "Those seem to be deep thoughts in which you swim."

Storm glanced up guiltily, a flush pinkening her cheeks. "I have no right to ask," she demurred, looking down from his intense focus.

Falcon sharpened his gaze, intrigued. "Now you have me curious. What do you want to know?"

She paused for a long moment. A sparrow flew overhead, undulating in its path before darting back into a nearby barn.

"How is it that you are still single, to be available for this marriage and truce?" she asked at last. "Surely *some* girl has caught your eye before now."

Tension settled over Falcon's face and shoulders, and it seemed to be an effort for him to hold her gaze, not to look away. His voice was tight when he spoke. "I suppose that is a fair enough question." He chuckled wryly. "I would want to know the same thing about you, if you had the memory to answer it. How could such a beautiful, intelligent woman not have a husband to care for her?"

Storm flushed at the praise, not responding. After a moment Falcon seemed to uncoil a bit, taking in a deep breath.

"After my parents' deaths, for many years I felt lost," he quietly explained. "I worked on my training, I talked with the neighboring leaders, and I built up my reputation. I achieved a great deal in that period of time - but I was haunted by loneliness."

His hand ran absently down the mane of his horse. "As I turned sixteen, then seventeen, many of the neighbors offered their daughters and nieces for me to talk with." He shrugged. "I am afraid that none interested me at all."

He looked off down the road, his gaze unfocusing. "Then, one day, a young woman came to town. Her name was Sheila; she was a red-head with a wide smile and quick wit. When she met me a few days later at the local faire, her eyes grew wide with recognition. She said that she had spent her early youth at the keep, and that we had been playmates. That we had hidden our friendship from the adults, because they would have found it inappropriate."

He shook his head. "She knew so many things about me. She knew the tree I loved to climb; the spot in the stream where I swam and fished. She knew the song I enjoyed belting out at the top of my lungs. I began to believe it. No, more than that, I began to actually remember that she was there, in my past. I figured I had forgotten about her, somehow, due to the ensuing trauma."

Storm rode along in silence, letting him talk. He hesitated for a long moment, his gaze moving to meet hers with a mixture of unsure emotions and trust. She smiled gently, allowing him to unfold his story at his own pace.

Falcon took in a long breath. "The clincher – the part when I was swept away by overwhelming love – was when she told me how upset she had been when my favorite hunting dog had died. I was ten years old when that happened. I had been desolate for months, mourning the loss of my pet."

His eyes shadowed. "I still remember every detail of the afternoon she recounted her memories to me. We discussed my beloved pet's death on a bench by the tower window. Suddenly, Sheila was overcome by grief of the memory of my suffering. Here she was, a grown woman, and she sobbed as if her heart would break. I held her close, and I was lost. It touched me to my very core that she could care so much, after so long."

He paused for a moment, lost in thought. "We parted ways over ten years ago, and even now I still remember how it felt to have this brave woman crying in my arms, desperately sad, needing my concern and care."

"She must have been quite a woman," commented Storm neutrally in a low voice.

Falcon rolled his shoulders. His voice became brisk. "Well, that was a long time ago. We went our separate ways, and there has been nobody since. I got used to being alone, and the longer you settle into a routine, the easier it is to simply stay with it."

Storm quietly nodded. They rode on together through the fading light, both lost in thought.

* * *

The courtyard echoed with a chill breeze; the late October sun was pale as it rose slowly into the sky. Storm carefully stepped through her routine, trying to insert pauses into her actions for the sake of those watching. Falcon moved around her, working with his soldiers, guiding them as they strove to mimic her guards and strikes.

Storm enjoyed the workout, and was equally delighted that Zach eagerly joined her afterwards, diving into his training with a zest she found quite admirable. By the time the lunch bell had rung they were again coated with dirt and glowing with satisfaction. Again Falcon was waiting for her on the front steps, a look of relaxed pride on his face. She wondered if he knew what she had been up to. If so, she was glad that he seemed inclined to let her continue with it.

A true sense of contentment flowed over her as she sat at Falcon's side at lunch, discussing the progress of the guards, embarking on a long discussion over the benefits of a high versus medium block with dagger. She found herself laughing, enjoying the gentle debate greatly. Suddenly she was immersed in the waking dream that this could last forever; that Falcon could remain at her side, be forever a part of her world.

She wondered if Falcon had become caught in the same spell, for he stopped speaking, simply gazing at her, his eyes becoming tender.

She knew it was a fantasy she could not indulge in for long – but only for a moment she allowed herself to become lost in it. A cascade of emotions built within her soul, an intense longing swelling in her heart. It could so easily overwhelm her …

She wrenched her gaze from his, dropping her eyes to her hands folded in her lap, to the ring of blue forget-me-nots on her finger.

A lightning bolt of warning flared through her chest, catching her off guard, drenching her with an icy cold alertness. She could not lose control of her emotions. She had to break free of the spell, to remember her vow.

What vow?

She shook her head, but the near-panic feeling remained. She drew to her feet, her legs shaking beneath her.

"I need some air," she murmured. "If we could head out now?" She turned without waiting on a response, and it seemed the flutter of a leaf before they were mounted on their horses, heading beneath the main gates. She urged Mercury into a trot, needing to be in motion. She drew in deep, long breaths, desperate to shake loose the feeling of fear and danger which had burrowed into her.

Falcon was close at her side, his eyes on her with concern. She felt an almost overwhelming desire to turn, to lose herself in his gaze. She forced herself to maintain focus on the road ahead, on the path that lay before her. She urged her mount again, stretching him out into a canter, moving in a thrumming flow across the field beside the town. Finally the tension eased, her heart gentled its pounding, and she could lose herself in the fresh air and rich aromas of turf and meadow.

A structure moved into view. They were heading toward the millhouse which sat alone at the far end of the village, nestled against the winding stream.

A waving figure caught her attention; a blonde girl was on the far side of the stream, standing near the base of the woods. Something boot-sized was caught up in her arms. The child smiled merrily as Storm and Falcon approached the stream. It was Caroline, the leather worker's daughter. She held in her arms something pinkish brown and wriggling.

"Look at the cute piggy I found!" she cheerfully called out across the water. Her high pitched voice carried easily across the rushing stream.

Storm had been reining in; her blood suddenly ran cold in shock. She took a closer look at the animal in Caroline's arms, then urged Mercury into motion, driving him into the river. "Put that down!" she cried out at the top of her lungs, plowing hard into the current. Her horse reached the middle, swam for a few long strokes, then clambered up the other side of the river bank.

She heard the loud squeal from the woods.

She saw the charging shape of the mother boar.

Caroline shrieked in fright, dropping the piglet and turning in horror. The piglet froze in panic.

The mother catapulted in braying fury toward the blonde thief.

Storm drove Mercury in hard, drawing her knife from her belt. She launched the blade at a midpoint between the boar and its target. The flash of silver startled the mother, turning her left, and the piglet bolted into action, fleeing toward her mother with a long, drawn out squeal.

In seconds the two were swallowed up by the woods, lost into the shadows.

Falcon thundered into the center of the clearing, sword drawn, his eyes sharp on the forest's edge. Storm slid from her mount. She ran toward the girl, dropped to one knee, and quickly checked her over.

"Are you all right? Did you get hurt?"

Caroline burst into frantic tears, and Storm pulled the girl close, gently holding her. "It is all right," she soothed her, her heart racing. "Everything is all right now."

Falcon was at their side in a moment. "Is she injured?"

"No, just frightened," reassured Storm, drawing Caroline into her arms and standing.

"Thank God," he sighed in relief. "We should get her back to her father." He took Caroline and hefted her up onto his saddle, then mounted behind her.

"Wait a moment," requested Storm. She moved over to the glint of silver, pulling her dagger out from where it had embedded itself in the soft dirt. She wiped the blade before settling it into her sheath. In a moment she was back on her horse and the two were riding at a canter back up the river bank, heading toward the low stone bridge.

It was only minutes before they pulled up at the leather shop. Theodore came running at the sound of his child's wails, taking the still-sobbing Caroline down from the horse into his arms. He looked up at Falcon with wide eyes.

"What happened? Is she all right?" he cried, drawing his daughter into a tight hug.

"She is fine," promised Falcon, "if only thanks to Storm's fast action. Your daughter decided to play with a boar piglet."

"Oh, Caroline," ground out Theodore, his voice caught between exasperation and concern. "You know better than that!"

"She was so cute," sobbed Caroline, clinging tightly to her father. "I just wanted to hold her!"

Theodore turned to look up between the two. "How can I ever repay you?" he asked, his voice tight with concern and relief.

Storm smiled. "I am just glad she is all right," she murmured, looking over the young girl. "We all make mistakes in life. She will learn from this one."

Theodore nodded, then turned, pushing his way into his shop. The sobbing noises faded as he moved further back into the building.

Falcon turned his horse to come alongside Storm. He shook his head, looking her over. "I doubt any bandit woman would have flown across the stream the way you did to save a young girl from harm," he pointed out, his voice gentle.

Storm smiled. "I imagine you are right," she agreed. "When I saw her there, the little boar in her arms, I did not think. I just acted."

"Actions speak far louder than words," mused Falcon. "You gave no thought to yourself – you raced to her side."

"As did you," pointed out Storm, her eyes held on his. "You were barely three seconds behind me."

"Caroline did not have three seconds," countered Falcon. "She was lucky to have you."

"I was lucky to have the dagger made by her father," returned Storm. "That blade is balanced like a work of art. It flew true."

Falcon's voice became serious. "That throw was skill, not luck." His eyes shadowed, and he looked away.

Storm shivered at his change in mood. She looked down at the dagger on her hip. It had felt so right in her hand, so easily thrown to exactly the spot she wished. She wondered what that meant. Perhaps it would come to her in time.

Falcon nudged his horse into motion. They slowly began walking their steeds back up toward the keep.

* * *

Storm did a full run through of her sword routine in the dawn mist, but by now it was for her own relaxation. Falcon's soldiers had become familiar with her moves. They were already experimenting with integrated routines on all sides of her. When she finished with her pass-through, Falcon came up before her, his eyes holding hers with quiet curiosity.

"Do you feel up to an actual sparring run?" he asked, his eyes scanning her body. "How are your wounds doing?"

Storm gave her sword arm a spin. "I think I should be fine," she assured him. "I would enjoy the opportunity immensely."

"Well then," offered Falcon, taking a step back and holding his sword in a high guard. "Let us see how you do."

Storm swept her sword down and away, holding his eyes for a long moment. She had been watching him for almost a month now. She was familiar with his style of action, his preferred motions. He led with his shoulder. He tended to move his right foot ahead of any strike. The corner of her mouth quirked up. This would be interesting indeed.

She started slow, circling him, probing low to the left, then to the right. He blocked her easily, letting her come, his eyes sharp on her. She feinted left, stepped left again then spun hard right. He twisted, sliding barely in time to dodge the flat of her blade. His eyes brightened with amusement.

"So that is how we are going to play?" he asked, his eyes twinkling. Then he drove in, and they were off. He attacked high, and she turned beneath the blow, sweeping right. He deflected the move, pushing in, and she bent back, moving into a new attack. Every time she drove in, he managed to find an opening; every time he came toward her, she slipped away.

Her foot skidded; one of the dog's bones skittered away across the dust and she sprawled hard on her back, her sword flying from her hand. Falcon's sword came down against her chest, and she found herself staring into his eyes.

"I yield," she called out in cheerful resignation, and the courtyard filled with applause. Falcon drew back his sword, then offered a hand down to her. She took the sturdy arm, allowing him to swing her up at his side.

Zach trotted up with her sword in his hand. "Sorry about that, Storm," he apologized brusquely. "I should have cleaned those up before we began."

She fondly tousled his hair. "It is my own fault for not keeping an eye out," she grinned. "I could hardly expect my fields of battle to be lawns of perfection."

Falcon swept her with an appraising glance. "That was
nicely done," he congratulated her. "The nuns must be quite
grateful to have your arm protecting them."

"I would hope I was more than just a figurehead," agreed
Storm. "If I am to do something, I should want to do it as well
as I could."

The soldiers turned, chattering in conversation, and headed
off to the barracks. Zach remained at her side, eager, alight with
anticipation. Storm smiled, nodding to Falcon.

"If you do not mind, I need to spend some time with Zach
now."

"Of course," agreed Falcon, stepping back. "I will see you at
lunch."

* * *

Zach was even more enthusiastic than usual after having
seen her in action, and the two grappled and sparred with high
energy. She was coated with dirt and sweat by the time they
were through. She grinned as Falcon fell in step alongside her,
as she moved her way through the great hall, heading back up to
her room.

She brushed the loose hair out of her face as they reached her
door. "I am afraid I am not quite the elegant lady one would
normally find in a well-maintained keep such as yours," she
joked merrily. "I am sure that I am more fit for the stables, the
way I am coated in grime."

Falcon swept his eyes down her lean frame, and a distant
look came into his eyes. She wondered what he was thinking,
but pushed it out of her mind. She stepped into her room,
moving to kneel before the dresser. She gave a hard yank on the
lower drawer, preparing to store her sword.

"You still keep the sword down there?" came Falcon's voice
from behind her, low and musing.

Storm glanced up. "This is where I found it."

Falcon looked consideringly around the room. "The weapon
seems so much a part of you. Maybe if we arranged things

differently, it will trigger some memories of yours. I cannot imagine you kept it in a drawer like that in whatever home you lived in before. After all, your dagger ..." he glanced at the pillow meaningfully.

Storm flushed, but stood again, her sword still in her hand.

Falcon held out his hand. "Here, give that to me." Storm dutifully placed her sword in his grasp.

Falcon stepped back toward the door. "Now climb into bed, and close your eyes."

Storm's brow wrinkled in confusion, but she complied without a word. In a moment she was stretched out on the bed, her lids shut.

Falcon's voice came soft but sure. "Imagine your home is surrounded by enemies. You know that they will attack soon. You will need your sword to defend yourself. Your knife would be too small. It would be your sword you would go for. You are resting ... it is night ... and then ..."

There was a burst of sound as Falcon slammed the main door of the room open so it rebounded against the side wall. Storm acted instinctively; she rolled off the bed in a flash, her hand outstretched to a spot beneath the window, grasping. Her eyes flew open in surprise when her fingers closed on empty air.

Falcon was beside her in a moment, looking into her eyes. "The sword – where was it?"

Storm looked down to her hand still held in its desperate reach for a weapon. She spoke without thinking, the vision coming in a flash. "It is always under my window. It rests there, lying on a low box. They are my only possessions, in my empty stone cell." The vision faded, and she strained to see in the mists. "The box ... I know it has all I hold dear in it."

"How big was the box?" asked Falcon, his voice low.

"As long as my forearm, and perhaps six inches high and deep," recited Storm, trying to hold on to the faint memory. "There is something carved in it ... but ..." She sighed in frustration. "I do not know, it is gone. I have no idea what is in it. I just know it is all I have."

Falcon handed her back her sword, and she carefully put it down in the spot beneath the window. She looked at it for a long while.

Falcon's murmur eased into her thoughts. "If you lived in a nunnery, what you say makes sense," he commented half to himself. "A bare room; a small box of personal belongings." He stood slowly, still looking down. "I will have one made for you, to sit in that spot. Who knows, maybe more memories will follow once your surroundings become more familiar."

Storm stood to stand beside him, looking into his eyes. "Thank you so much for helping me with this. Even the smallest memories mean so much to me."

Falcon looked away, and when he spoke, his voice was gruff. "You had best get changed now, so we can head down for lunch," he instructed. He turned and left the room, closing the door gently behind him.

Lunch moved by in quiet conversation; when the table was cleared they rose without a word and walked over toward the stables. Soon they were walking their steeds side by side down the sunny pathways of the village.

* * *

The next morning's practice went smoothly, with Storm spending even more time doing one-on-one combat with Falcon. She found her strength returning, and her quick reflexes allowed her to dodge and roll out of the way of many of Falcon's strikes. She even landed a few blows with lightning-fast hits, drawing enthusiastic cheers from nearby soldiers.

Zach's mastery of the basic blocks and throws was improving day by day, but Storm was more impressed with the change in his demeanor. Rather than looking at the ground when he walked, he was holding his head high and moving with purpose. The thought pleased her greatly, that he was finding his self-respect.

Falcon was waiting for her when she approached the keep, and he grinned as they headed up the stairs toward her room.

When Storm pushed open her door, she immediately saw the new item. A simple but well-made box lay beneath the window, an ivy design woven along its top.

Storm moved over to it, dropping to one knee to run a finger along the carving. She lay down the sword on top of the box, and a swell of emotion overcame her.

This was right. It was just right.

"Well?" asked Falcon behind her, his voice warm with curiosity.

"Yes," replied Storm simply. "Yes."

She stood looking down at the sword and box, her world feeling more and more natural to her. It was almost unsettling to raise her eyes and look around at the rest of the room, with its sumptuous curtains and elegant tapestries.

Falcon followed her gaze. "I could always have the rest of the room stripped ..." he mused with a quiet grin.

Storm shook her head, chuckling. "No, that is quite all right," she reassured him. "I am sure memories will return to me in time without having to ask your staff to rearrange the entire place for my pleasure."

Falcon gave her a gracious bow. "As you wish, my lady," he agreed with a smile.

Their lunch and afternoon ride sailed by in a blur of quiet, contented motion, and Falcon drew her into a game of chess when they returned. The day seemed perfect.

As she lay in bed ready for sleep, nestled deep within the blankets, Storm thought back over the calm of the past few days. She was truly at peace. Yes, she still cherished fond thoughts about Falcon – but to her surprise she found she was able to put her feelings into perspective. He was a wonderful man, and he was betrothed to the lady of her land. The marriage would bring a lasting peace which would benefit the entire countryside.

Storm only hoped that the lady was worthy of this sacrifice ... worthy of Falcon's love.

Still, Storm felt blessed beyond measure. Even if she left with Lord Walker never to return again, she would always treasure the memory of these weeks with Falcon. The memories would have to be enough.

* * *

Friday morning offered bright sunshine and a warming heat. Storm was finishing up her lunch and looking forward to the afternoon ride with Falcon when there was a noise in the entryway. Thom came trotting into the main hall, his eyes sweeping the room, seeking out those of his master.

Storm's throat tightened, and she could barely breathe. Falcon rose without a word and drew Thom and Storm into his study. He shut the door firmly, then turned to face the pair.

"Out with it," he barked, his face tense. "Was Storm's memory of the vase a true one? Was Jessica deceiving us?"

"What Storm says is true," replied Thom with an exhausted but pleased smile. "The potter who makes those wares does indeed live near the church. His work is well respected in the neighborhood. He is a high quality craftsman, but he is definitely not French."

Relief swept over Storm when she heard this, and she sagged back against the bookcase. Her memories had not been false.

Thom's eyes flicked toward Storm in concern for a moment, but on seeing her regain her footing, he continued his report. "The potter's studio is as she described it. The structure is laid out with small windows overlooking a mill stream."

"Yes, yes, and what did he have to say about Storm?" asked Falcon with tight impatience.

Thom's face fell. "I am afraid I could not find the potter to speak with him directly," the messenger admitted in chagrin. "Apparently he had just been called to go in to court, at Walker's request. The man's neighbors said that he was ordered to make a set of plateware for the upcoming wedding."

Thom paused at that, then continued more slowly. "I did not feel you would want me to chase after him, to question him in Walker's own home."

Falcon patted him on the shoulder. "No, no, you did well," he praised the messenger. He stalked across the room for a moment, lost in thought. "Still, did nobody else in the area have any information on Storm's past or situation?"

Thom shook his head. "None knew of any missing woman matching Storm's description, or of any woman who had become a guard at the nunnery," he admitted. "She is definitely not from the area around the potter's studio. If she visited there, she was a visitor from somewhere else."

Falcon pursed his lips, but nodded. "You have learned a great deal, and I appreciate it. Go rest, you deserve a drink."

Thom saluted him, nodded to Storm, then turned and went through the study door back to the main hall.

When the two were left alone, Falcon turned and gazed with curiosity at the woman before him.

Storm sighed. "I do not know whether I am relieved or frustrated," she admitted at last. "It seems we are stymied at every turn when we seek to know more details. Still, at least the memories I am having are proving to be accurate. It gives me something to hold onto."

Falcon put a hand beneath her chin and raised her eyes to meet his own. "Have faith," he whispered. "The truth will out in the end. Whatever it is, we will face it together."

Chapter 15

Storm dodged left, twisted under Falcon's blade, and came to her feet in a low guard. Her reflexes were returning; she gave a broad smile, breathing in the crisp autumn air. She feinted left, then leapt to the right, laughing out loud as Falcon followed her move and turned with her. They were beginning to learn each other's tactics, to anticipate each other's pivots and thrusts. Falcon's eyes were on her, bright with appreciation, and she basked in the glow of his gaze.

Suddenly Falcon drew up, and she turned, following his attention. Jessica, clothed in an elegant violet riding outfit, trotted into the courtyard. She was flanked by a pair of burly guards in expensive leather armor, mounted on equally fine steeds. The two men dismounted first, then made a great show of helping her down. They walked in escort over to where Falcon and Storm stood watching.

Jessica scanned Storm's dusty outfit with hearty enthusiasm. "There she is," she announced. "Look, she has weapons in her hand, too. Why am I not surprised?"

Falcon took a step forward, his voice calm but steely. "Storm is a guard with a nunnery, to the far northeast of the Walker land," he pointed out. "It would be natural for her to handle weapons in that position."

"For a woman who held that position, yes," agreed Jessica with a sharp grin. "However, my sources tell me that the nunnery in that region does not have a female guard matching Storm's description."

Storm could not help herself. She spoke up with quiet heat. "Would these be the same sources who claimed that your English pottery hailed from the south of France?"

Jessica's eyes shot daggers at her, but her lips curled into an apologetic smile. "I am so sorry about that, Falcon," she agreed demurely. "I am still new at some of these arrangements, and I am afraid I must have misunderstood what my suppliers were telling me about the pottery. It was a different line of pottery – one of the most delicate green – which came from France. That white and blue pottery was definitely of English origin, although of course of the highest quality. We only carry the best items in our shops."

Falcon's voice retained its sharp edge. "This story of yours about the nunnery? You have proof?"

Jessica laughed in merriment. "What kind of proof can you have about a situation that does not exist? If she did work there, we could have asked for a copy of the contract of employment. As they say she is not associated with them, there is no proof for them to offer."

Storm deflated. Why would Walker deliberately lie about her past? She had laid so much hope on the idea that she worked with a nunnery, helping to protect innocent women. It explained her familiarity with swords and weapons.

If it was true that this was not her calling in life, then there were few other honorable situations she could imagine herself in. It suddenly seemed again that she was somehow involved with the bandits. Why else would Walker have tried to deceive Falcon? Her throat went dry.

When she spoke, her voice was hoarse. "I am going to head up to my room to change," she rasped. "I will see you both at lunch."

She turned and walked across the courtyard, not looking at either of their faces.

Behind her, Jessica did not even wait for her to move out of earshot before pressing her conversation with Falcon. "You see, she *is* a member of the bandits, as I warned you," she extolled with fierce energy. "You need to keep a close eye on her.

Bandits often know the wares of an area, so that they can fence goods for the highest price. Undoubtedly she was sent into this potter's home to learn what was most valuable. Notice how she picked that vase from the collection right away."

The voice faded away as Storm moved inside, and she was grateful for the silence. After she washed up, she stood by the window, staring at the beautiful vines twining around the vase, the gentle colors of the reeds within. She could not bring herself to go down to lunch, to face Jessica and Falcon.

It was best that she remained alone.

Her thumb instinctively fell to rub at her silver ring, turning it with gentle familiarity. She dropped her eyes to the small item, the delicate forget-me-nots tracing around its edge. Deep despair swept through her. If only the tiny trickles of memory would open up, turn into a deluge, and remove all the guessing from her world.

She drew in a shaky breath. Even if she were with the bandits before, it would be better to know the truth, to accept that past and to move on. Being caught in a state of unknowing, of sorting out lies and deceptions, was tearing her apart.

The ring seemed to symbolize her standing alone. It echoed most firmly within her when her thoughts tended in that direction. Maybe that had been why she had set her path toward the nunnery? To be protected, alone, and safe?

A wave of warmth washed through her, and she eased back onto the stool, letting her breath out in a long, grateful heave. Thom had proven that her past memory fragments were truthful. She would trust completely in them. She would trust that they were providing a path – no matter how faintly lit – back toward her true nature. She would follow those clues, one small step at a time, until they helped her become whole again.

A knock sounded at her door, and Storm turned to find Falcon pushing it open, carrying a platter of cheese and bread. Behind him, Mary brought in a mug of mead.

"I thought you might be planning to dine alone this afternoon," offered Falcon with a wry smile.

Storm chuckled despite herself, and he placed the platter down at the table by her side. Mary added the mug of mead to her setting, then discreetly left the two together.

Falcon spoke without preamble. "You know, even if you are not from the nunnery, there are many explanations other than your being a bandit," he mused. "Jessica has latched onto that idea; we both know she is hardly unbiased in this matter. I will wait to pass judgment until we know for sure what the situation is. So far, it seems what you remember is honest, and what she presents is less so."

Storm took a long drink of the mead before gazing at Falcon. "I realize my faint memories are ethereal at best, but they also feel as if they come from my very core," she explained. "When I hold my sword, it is as if I am ready to protect Heather, Zack, or little Caroline from harm. When I climb onto Mercury's back, I thrill with the gentle movement, not the fury of the chase."

She looked down at the silvered ring. "And this, it echoes the most strongly of all. The images have been soft, but clear. I wrapped myself in a vow as a young teenager. It had to do with remaining alone." She closed her eyes, her thumb moving to the metal band. "And when I think of thundering off toward the nunnery to seek shelter, safety, and security ..." The waves of warmth rose again, encompassing her, and she wrapped her arms around herself, drinking in the sensation. She opened her eyes, and Falcon's were on her. He seemed lost in her gaze, nodding in understanding.

"You look more at peace, just now, than I have ever seen you," he murmured, his voice hoarse.

Storm dropped her eyes. "I just wish I knew more, that the sluice gates would open and my memory would finally release its floods." She twined her fingers together. "I do not know how to even explain what it feels like. I have lost myself. I have no sense of who I am, or why."

She drew her eyes up to meet his again. "Let us take Jessica, for example. Perhaps she is jealous because, in the past, another girl ran off with her beau. Maybe she swore to never let that happen again. Perhaps she is proud because over the years she has struggled and worked hard to build her trade, and she feels those years of effort have finally paid off. Perhaps she is sharp because her father was a harsh man, and maintaining that edge was the only way to survive in her household."

She let out a long breath. "Jessica has a rounded sense of herself, based on all of those memories and experiences. She can think of herself as talented or efficient or driven. She can plan out her actions based on who she is."

She ran a hand distractedly through her hair. "I have no grounding at all. I have no events to lean on. I have no sense of a foundation. It feels as if I am lost in a whirlwind, without the slightest hint of where I came from."

Her eyes moved again to the ring. "Even if I did flee to this nunnery for safety – where had I been before that? Had I been with the bandits and then repented? Perhaps both stories are true."

Falcon dropped to one knee in front of her. "I am telling you, it does not matter to me," he swore. "Whatever you were before you came to our door, that is not what you are now."

He took a deep breath, then continued more quietly, "I cannot believe that, when your memories return, your personality will suddenly change you into a different person. It seems much more likely that you will be as you always have been – but with more awareness of what you have escaped by coming here."

Storm looked up, caught by his words. "Escaped?"

Falcon's eyes took on a haunted look. "A dagger beneath your pillow. The ability to defend yourself with a sword. Scars on your legs." He paused, then pressed on. "There is more. I see the way you look when I walk into the room – you are suddenly a rabbit, desperate for a hole to hide in."

He gently laid a hand alongside her cheek. A wry smile ghosted his face as she resisted the urge to flinch and relaxed into his touch. "Whatever life you led until now, I believe it was dense with pain and suffering. You may not wish to remember it." His voice dropped down to become quiet. "You may not wish to return to it."

Storm was silent. She had spent so much time worrying about what her past would reveal to her that it had not fully sunk in that she could simply choose not to return to that way of life. Whatever she had been, she could choose an entirely new direction for her future.

She took in a long breath. Maybe, even if she had been with the bandits in the past, she could indeed turn over a new leaf and pledge herself fully to the nunnery. She could dedicate her life to redeeming her actions, whatever they had been.

Falcon relaxed as he saw her mood lighten, and then smiled himself. He moved to sit again on the bed. "That choice lies in the future. For now, finish up your lunch. Then let us enjoy the sunny day we have before us. Come riding with me."

A smile played on Storm's lips. "What about Jessica?"

Falcon's smile matched her own. "She has gone up to her father's, to replenish her supplies. Those men with her were from her father's force. She only stopped in to … warn me."

Storm kept her face neutral. "They seemed able enough men."

Falcon's bark was harsh. "Able enough – they are hired mercenaries. Jessica's father has a small army to move his wares, and I have always half suspected that legitimate goods did not make up the bulk of his business. I have never found proof of it, and I had great hopes that Jessica was turning over a new leaf, free from her father's taint. Only time will tell … but for now, it is just you and me."

Chapter 16

Storm woke early the next morning and sat by the window for a long time, lost in thought. It was October thirty-first, Samhain. The harvest had been brought in; the year had come to an end. It was time for the long, cold dreariness of winter to begin. The spring celebrations of reawakening seemed a long time off.

She moved through the preparations and morning mass with distraction. She was halfway through lunch before Falcon drew her from her thoughts.

"Will you be joining us for the festivities tonight?" he asked for what apparently was the third time.

Storm shook away the cobwebs in her mind, nodding in agreement. "Certainly. What do you have planned?"

"Drinking, singing, perhaps some dancing. We put out all the candles, everywhere, to indicate that the harvest is done and the year is over. Then tomorrow morning we light them afresh, as we begin anew."

Storm looked up at this, becoming caught by Falcon's eyes. "Begin anew," she echoed, her heart calming.

Could it really be so easy?

Falcon tenderly took her hand in his and nodded encouragingly. "Every day you have the ability to start on a new path, to chart a fresh course for yourself. Tonight, of all nights, that is natural and proper. It is what Samhain is all about."

The room was decorated with sheaves of wheat and a rainbow assortment of gourds. Soon Molly and Heather were bringing out roast goose, steamed turnips, fish stew, and pitchers of wine. Villagers streamed in, bringing in samples of their own ales and viands to complement the already groaning tables.

The volume of noise in the room grew steadily as more people arrived. Storm spotted Carol across the room, and moved across to greet her, thanking her profusely for both her own dress and the lovely rose dress she had made for Heather.

"There she is now," added Storm with a smile. "Look how pretty she is in it!"

As Storm watched, David and Shawn came up behind Heather, pinching her on the bottom. Heather spun, half pleased at having attracted such attention, half shocked at their outrageous behavior. Her look quickly lost its smile as the pair leant in more aggressively, pressuring her backwards.

Storm furrowed her brow. If those miscreants thought they were going to abuse her Heather … she dropped her hand to her knife and began striding forward.

A strong hand caught her on the upper arm, and she whirled in anger. Falcon held her easily in his grasp, his eyes focused on the young maid.

"Let me go," hissed Storm, her voice tight with fury. "Surely you saw -"

Falcon cut her off with a low shushing noise. "Look," he insisted, nodding with his head.

Storm turned against him; he had not relinquished his grip on her arm. To her surprise, Zach was pushing his way through the crowd and interjected himself between Heather and the two boys. Storm could not hear what was being said over the loud hubbub of the room, but she could see clearly in his stance that he was defending her.

The two other boys pressed forward, expecting him to give way – and he stood firm. She saw his eyes flash; saw the surprised look in the two soldiers' eyes as they realized he would not back down.

In a moment it was over. The soldiers turned, moving on to other pursuits, and Zach took Heather's hands in his own. She gazed up at him tenderly, her face aglow.

Storm slowly exhaled, becoming aware that she had been holding her breath. "I had not realized …" she sighed, looking between the two young people.

"Nor had I," admitted Falcon, his voice coming close behind her. He still held her arm, and she was flooded with the knowledge that his fingers had become more of a gentle embrace, that his chest was pressed up against her back. She could smell the rich muskiness of him, and that elusive hint of sweet woodruff.

She drew herself away, fighting the emotions rising within her. Shaking loose his hand, she moved forward to the couple. They smiled up at her as she approached them.

"Zach, do you play any instrument?" she asked without preamble as she drew to a stop before them.

Zach blushed but nodded. "I play the lute. My uncle does not think it a proper instrument for a soldier, but my mother used to enjoy it, before she died. It made me happy to bring some joy into her world."

Storm added a gentle prod to her tone. "Maybe you could accompany Heather in playing some background music for us, then?"

Heather looked around the large room full of people with fright. "Here? With everyone staring at me?"

Storm chuckled, patting her on the arm. "Listen to the noise," she pointed out sagely. "They will barely hear you. It will just be a quiet background that perhaps one or two will make out. It would make me happy, to sit in a corner listening to you and taking a break from this babbling."

Heather's face regained some of its color. "Well, if you put it like that, that would be fine, I guess." She looked up at Zach. "If you would play with me?"

Zach beamed. "It would be my honor. I will return in just a moment." He turned and raced out a side door.

Storm guided Heather over to a relatively quiet corner. She set up a pair of stools for Heather and Zach to sit on, then a bench for herself nearby. She was not surprised when Falcon came over to sit beside her in a moment, bringing a pair of mugs of mead.

Zach returned promptly and strummed a few bars to tune his lute. Then he turned to look at Heather.

Storm was touched by how sweetly the pair gazed at each other; how completely lost in each other's faces they became. All of Heather's nervousness melted away, and she sang her song directly to him, his melodies twining around her soaring voice. At first the tune was almost lost in the surrounding hubbub, but minute by minute the conversation faded away as all eyes turned to watch the young couple. By the time the two musicians finished the song, the hall was spellbound. As the last notes faded away, the hall erupted into thunderous applause.

Heather and Zach looked up in surprise, then took hands and stood, bowing to the group. The evening became a series of songs – some quiet and somber, others loud and boisterous, with the entire village joining in to sing.

The evening flew by in cascades of music and conversation. A festive mood imbued the night. To her surprise, even David and Shawn came over to congratulate the young singer and musician on their talents, and played along on a few songs with a pair of small drums.

Soon it had reached midnight. All voices dropped to a murmur as the church bells chimed. People slowly moved around the rooms. Storm watched as the candles were extinguished one by one.

The dark of the castle, filled with so many people, pressed in on her. She wended her way out into the courtyard to stand in the starlight, breathing in the peace of the night air.

She was staring at the constellations when a familiar voice sounded by her ear. "Lost in the stars?" Falcon asked with a teasing grin.

"Just wondering if it really is a new day tomorrow. A new year; a new start on life." She blinked at the vastness of the universe above her. "How easy is it to start afresh?"

Falcon looked down at her, his eyes twinkling. "Probably far more easy for you than for anyone else," he pointed out. "You do not have years of history weighing you down. You can simply set your feet on a new path and head down it."

"Ah, but what path would I choose?" considered Storm. "What path *can* I choose?"

There was a sharp whinny from the stables, and both turned their heads, dropping their hands to the knives at their side. Storm headed toward the noise without a second thought, and she heard Falcon curse under his breath as he moved alongside her. She knew he would rather she stayed behind; she also knew that was not going to happen.

She eased cautiously through the main door, allowing her eyes to adjust to the darkness. There was movement in the back of the stables. Slowly she crept toward it, feeling Falcon mirror her every move.

A shaft of moonlight streamed across the hay at the back of the stable, and Storm saw motion … saw …

She froze in place so quickly that Falcon ran into her; he put an arm around her, steadying himself. It was suddenly clear to both of them that there was no cause to worry. Zach and Heather were curled up together in the fragrant hay, tenderly kissing each other.

Storm moved sideways, into the shadows, ensuring she was not seen. Falcon's strong arm was around her waist, his breath eased warmly against her neck.

It was Samhain.

The day for new beginnings.

Storm felt sure that she was a free woman. Falcon was, as yet, an unclaimed man. There were many in the keep who were concerned with his chastity; concerned that he was damaging his health with the needless restriction. Storm had a sense that Mary, Molly, and the others would shower her with appreciation should she and Falcon become a couple for the long months until the wedding.

She knew the ache in her own heart. She knew the heat which glowed in his eyes.

The aromas of the leather saddles, the fresh hay, the musk of the horses surrounded her and permeated her. She could feel every rise and fall of Falcon's chest against her body. She leant her head back against him, closing her eyes.

Her thumb pressed down on the circle of flowers on her finger, and to her surprise a firm resolve spread throughout her being. As much as her body craved his touch, she could not abandon herself to the desire. It went against something at her very core.

She caressed the ring's cool metal, and a dawning realization came that perhaps her vow had to do with releasing herself to a man. An answering strength coursed through her, and the certainty grew with a steely firmness. But could it simply be a job requirement for her position at the nunnery? She dismissed the thought; she had a sense that it was deeper than that. It was something fundamental to her soul.

His warmth was still around her, the richness of his scent sending tendrils to her heart, and she knew she had to resist the almost overpowering allure. It was not only this vow which held her in place. There was also an equally compelling torment in her soul. Her whole being was already filled with anguish at the thought of leaving him. If she allowed herself to grow even closer to him – to fall completely in love with him – what level of pain would she have to endure each day she was apart from him? How would she wake up each morning, knowing he was married to another woman, that he was always just beyond her reach?

She forced herself to take a step, to separate herself from the warmth, moving silently across the stables. She strode quickly across the darkened hall, almost running up the stairs to her room. She waited there, alone, staring out her window until the misty haze of morning dusted the sky. As the first glimmerings of dawn began to stretch across the cobblestones, she lit the fresh candle, signifying her start ... her new start.

* * *

Despite her lack of sleep, Storm was refreshed as she prepared for the first day of November. The workouts in the morning and riding in the afternoon had brought strength and vigor back into her world.

As she stood and brushed out her hair, Storm deliberately put aside her worries about her past. Falcon was right. Whatever it had involved, it was now her old life. She had control of her new life, of what she chose to do with this day, and each day in her future. She could choose not to be bound by past mistakes or experiences, and to create a new world – a better world – for her future.

She paused by her window, gazing out for a moment, a sense of resignation descending over her thoughts. Her new world, while certainly more open than most could hope for, was not limitless. She had to accept the chasm between herself and Falcon. She had to shield her heart against him, and look on him only as a friend. It was best for her future contentment. It was best for everyone.

Resolved, she headed down the stairs to walk out to the courtyard.

She was surprised when the normally silent, truculent Harold called to her as she emerged into the morning sunlight. Curious, she walked over to where he stood in the shadow of the stables.

He hefted a saddle onto his shoulder. "I hear from the cook that you are worried about being a bandit," he stated without preamble. He carried the saddle over to a small table, dropping it down next to a worn rag.

Before Storm could think of a reply, he sharply shook his head. "It is not so," he stated with firm knowledge. "You would not survive a day in the bandit's camp. They are cold, determined, and ruthless. You are too soft, too caring." He looked her up and down, then dismissed the idea with a glance.

"Not one day," he muttered to himself, looking down at his work.

Storm looked at Harold's downturned head, surprised at his outburst, but oddly relieved. It occurred to her that Harold was undoubtedly right – that anyone associated with the bandits would have become selfish and self-absorbed if only for self-preservation. It was yet another building block for her new path, her fresh new view of the world.

"Thank you," she offered with fervent feeling.

He gave a grunt, rubbing the oil in circles into the leather.

Storm smiled, then headed out to the waiting ring of soldiers. Many of the men seemed to have taken the new year to heart and put a greater than usual effort into their strokes and parries. Storm went through her routine, then found herself working with David and Shawn, who showed a fresh interest in her stance and arm motions. Mindful of what Falcon had said of their troubled past, Storm patiently worked through the movements with them and was rewarded with a focused attention by the pair. They kept her busy right up until it was time to break for lunch.

The boys' enthusiasm did not abate during lunch. Sitting on Falcon's left, they talked with him at length about the latest movements of the bandits and ideas for setting up a series of alert stations between the larger villages. Storm did not mind that she was left out of the discussion; she enjoyed the delicious meal of roast pork and looked forward to the afternoon ride. It seemed the flight of a swallow before they had saddled their horses and headed out into the fresh fall sunshine.

Falcon looked over as they rode side by side along the quiet lane. "It is a day of new beginnings," he observed. His face gentled into a smile. "As always, you have the advantage here. Some of us have a much harder time releasing our old ways; the histories we have built up."

"I may not have memories, but I do still have histories," pointed out Storm. "My body remembered the past. I would flinch in panic any time you touched me."

Falcon's gaze grew serious. "That is true," he mused. He reached out a hand to her.

She gently took it, giving it a squeeze.

His eyes became tender. "You seem to be over that reaction, at least."

Their horses came along a hedge. He glanced to the left, at the small house hidden away down the lane. She felt the stiffening in his posture, the tension in his fingers.

Her eyes went up to his, holding them.

He almost turned away, but instead laced his fingers into hers. He drew in a long, deep breath and then let it out.

His voice was low. "That was Sheila's house."

Storm looked back at it again. There was no smoke coming from the fireplace. The road seemed neglected and unused. She did not want to pry, but she could not help herself. "What happened between you two? It seemed that you were fated to be together. You were long lost childhood friends which life had reunited."

Falcon nodded. "It did seem that way, did it not?" He let the silence go on for a long moment before shaking his head. "We had been innocent playmates, or so she had said. Even as an adult, Sheila had always been very proper in how we interacted with each other. She did not brook any kissing; any intimacy of any kind. She had vowed to remain chaste until her wedding night. I respected that vow and respected her wishes. I was no innocent, but if she wanted to wait I was more than willing to as well."

Falcon withdrew his fingers from Storm's, looking down the road before them. He ran a hand idly down his steed's mane.

"Then, one night, it seemed that she got quite drunk after dinner. We ended up in my room. She was very willing, pressing herself on me. It was clear what she was offering. I admit, I was quite tempted. It took every ounce of my self-control to hold back."

His eyes were shadowed. "Still, I *did* hold back. I did not want her maidenhead taken in such a way, with how clearly she had made her wishes known. I did not want our first time together to be something she later regretted."

He looked down. "Sheila stormed out of the room, raging about my restraint."

Falcon looked off into the woods. The silence stretched on for five minutes, then ten. Storm rode beside him without saying a word, offering her presence as silent comfort. She would hear as much or as little as he wished to share.

Finally, Falcon spoke again, his voice now bitter. "I felt distress for having treated her so. I went to find her, to explain myself and to apologize. I hoped that she would understand things more clearly after she had sobered up." His fingers gripped his reins. "I could not find her anywhere in the keep. At last, I came out to her house."

He took a deep breath, then let it out again. "She was there, all right, naked and wrapped in the arms of a spindly young man named Ryan. I saw them clearly through the window as I approached the house. I moved to the side of the house to hear what they were saying."

It was a long moment before he could speak again, his voice tight. "Apparently they were part of the bandit group and had been lovers for years. They were plotting to acquire a rich husband for her; Ryan would still remain in her life as her secret companion. Their real goal was a steady supply of loot – silver candlesticks, and silver platters."

Falcon's hand dropped to the hilt of his sword, and his face grew tense. "It was all a lie. She had never known me as a child. An ongoing friendship with one of my servants had provided the details they needed for their deception. Every story she had told was a fabrication."

Falcon gave a short, harsh laugh. "Best of all - the reason for the sudden seduction? Sheila was pregnant with Ryan's child, and they were hoping to pass it off as my own. They figured if they could get her to sleep with me, they could then press for a quick marriage and simply claim the child was a few weeks early."

Storm looked over at Falcon with sadness, thinking of all the pain life had put in his path. "What did you do once you knew the truth?"

Falcon ran a hand through his thick hair. "I opened the door and told the two to be gone by dawn. I told them that I did not care where they went, as long as neither set foot within my borders again."

He rolled his shoulders, looking out into the distant forest. "I heard a few weeks later that she had married an elderly gentleman a few towns over. Eventually word came that he was thrilled to be a new father. Who knows, maybe she did give that man a few years of happiness in his life."

Falcon pulled his horse to a stop and looked over at Storm. "The irony of it is that, if she had been truthful about being a poor girl, it would not have bothered me. She was vivacious and intelligent. Her parentage and income did not matter to me. If she had truly chosen me over Ryan, and wanted to marry me even though pregnant with another man's child, I would have raised it as my own."

He shook his head. "However, for her to continually lie to me ... and to plan to base our entire relationship and marriage on a lie ... it was more than I could fathom. The oily taint of those lies ... I feel that is with me, even now."

Storm quietly nodded. "I understand completely," she responded somberly. "If you do not have truth – if you do not have full trust – then you really do not have anything at all."

Falcon's face grew steely. "I was so close to being drawn into her trap, and I have berated myself ever since for missing the clear warning signs. A woman shows up out of nowhere and seems such a good match? She plays coy and demure for weeks on end – and then suddenly she wants to give herself fully to me?" His shoulders hunched.

"Even the moment when I was overcome by love for her – when she sobbed, heartbroken, in my arms over a long-past death. I now see how contrived that moment was. Time may not heal all wounds, but it does temper them. I should have seen that outpouring of grief for what it was – a play-acting of the highest level. A clear sign that she was manipulating me."

Storm's heart went out to him. He had been through so much; his faith and trust had been shattered almost to the point of never mending again.

"Somewhere out there is a woman who deserves you," she murmured. "Someone you can rely on fully; someone who is deserving of your absolute faith."

Falcon looked at Storm for a long time, as the cold autumn air swirled around them in gentle spirals. The horses released their breath in short, frosty huffs, swishing their tails through the browning leaves.

There was no need for words.

After a while, he nudged his horse. The two moved side by side, heading back to the keep.

Chapter 17

The next morning Storm woke early, her body coursing with restless energy. She put on her clothes and headed out into the courtyard, walking around it and stretching her legs. She looked up at the high wall that surrounded the area, thinking of the fine view it afforded. Intrigued, she headed toward the wall, to climb up the ladder and take a stroll along its parapets.

She was halfway up the ladder when she heard a voice call to her from below. "Going for a little walk?" came a deeply voiced query. Storm looked down to see John staring up at her, his hand resting on his sword hilt. At his side stood Zach. Zach looked down at her glance, his face blushing crimson, unwilling to meet her eyes.

Storm's face fell, but she nodded in quiet understanding. Carefully, she began to make her way back down the ladder, holding her skirts out of the way with one hand.

Falcon's voice was a blending of casual tone edged with flint. "What is going on here?"

As Storm found her footing on the dusty ground, she turned to find Falcon had joined the group, looking between the three.

Falcon's eyes were serious. "John?"

The captain bowed to him. "My nephew let me know that your guest was heading up onto the parapets, Sir." He motioned with his hand to the ladder which Storm still held with one hand. "As we had discussed before -"

Falcon cut him off with the wave of a hand. "That was before, in the past," he countered with quiet determination. He looked up at Storm for a long moment, then stated clearly, "Storm is to have the full run of the castle. You can reassign your nephew to other duties."

John blanched, and his grizzled face clearly showed his internal struggle. "My Lord, perhaps we can talk of this later when -"

Falcon sharply interrupted him. "I am decided, and this is final," he instructed. His eyes held Storm's for a long moment. "There comes a time when you must decide to trust."

His eyes on hers, he walked forward and gently patted Storm's hand which still rested on the ladder rung. "If you are in the mood, shall we take a stroll together on the curtain wall?"

Storm only nodded her agreement, not trusting herself to speak. Her eyes shone in happiness, and she prayed that she was indeed worthy of his faith in her.

* * *

Wednesday morning dawned with bright sunlight and a soothing warmth, bringing a fresh clarity and brilliance to the world. Storm flew through her practice and lunch, looking forward eagerly to the afternoon ride. Falcon apparently felt the same electric energy and soon the two headed out the main gates at a fast trot.

He looked over with a curious smile. "Where to today, oh riding companion of mine?"

Storm's eyes twinkled.

"Well, Falcon, I think a nice, leisurely ride is in order." Her smile deepened as a mischievous instinct swept over her. "A race, if you will." His eyebrows arched in surprise, but before he could comment, she had leaned over to secure her grip on her reins. "Ha! To the tree line!" She urged her mount; in seconds she was breathless with the sure, strong stride as her horse eagerly stretched into a gallop through the afternoon air.

Storm's hair streamed behind her; she whooped in pleasure, her heart pounding in excitement. What a beautiful day nature had provided to them. This is where she belonged; this is what she was. The world was glorious and sun-streaked. Autumn leaves swirled around her in great whirls of motion. The thundering of hooves filled her world.

A form moved next to her, and she turned her head to find Falcon pulling alongside her on her right. He laughed at her surprised gaze, then leant into his horse to urge it on. Storm crouched low and called to her bay with excitement. Mercury's legs became a blur; he stretched his neck to reach alongside the grey's.

They flew across the meadow as one, side by side, soaring across the fields of soft grass.

Storm's smile grew as the forest approached – victory was within reach!

A sharp pain shot through her left side, and without thinking she bent her body against the pain to lessen it. The action immediately unbalanced her, and she knew instinctively that pulling on the reins could mean great danger for her charging mount. She instead flailed to grab onto the horse's mane, missed, lost her seat, and flipped head over heels onto the meadow. The soft grass gave her a cushioned landing, but the hard layer beneath knocked the wind out of her.

White, puffy clouds drifted across the sky, impossibly high above her. She pressed down with both sprawled arms, trying to stop the world from spinning.

Falcon was kneeling beside her in a flash. His eyes roamed her quickly from head to toe. "Good Lord, Storm, are you all right? Does anything feel broken?" One hand shakily strayed to her face, smoothing her hair away from her eyes.

Storm couldn't help it – peals of laughter erupted from her, bringing tears to her eyes. Realizing she was not seriously hurt, Falcon sat back, a smile growing on his own face.

She called out in the gaps between her gales. "That was glorious! What a horse! I almost won!"

Falcon helped Storm to slowly sit up, and she pressed her hand into her side, working away the ache. "Now *that* was fun," she chuckled, "even with the pulled muscle." She shook her head. "It seems that a little fall from a horse is not much at all for me," she added with a wry grin. "Maybe I was very clumsy in my previous life. I should have won that race."

Falcon rocked back on his heels, shaking his head at her. "You are a wonder, Storm," he commented as she gathered her legs beneath her. "Most women I know would have been abed for weeks after an attack, never mind racing through the meadows. Here you are, barely upset at falling during a horse race." He stood and offered an arm to Storm, who gladly took it.

Storm's eyes glinted with laughter. "So my sparring and riding are inappropriate, then? Shall I restrict myself to sewing in the window and polishing silver in the kitchen for the remainder of my stay?"

Falcon smiled, looking down into her eyes with tender care. "No, Storm, not at all. I quite like you just the way you are."

A warmth of emotions swelled in answer within her. The sun streamed down across the meadow, the crisp scent of autumn grass wafted around them, and it was as if she and Falcon were the only two people in the world. His gaze was everything she could hope for, everything she could dream of.

If only this moment could last forever.

Reluctantly she turned her head, taking a step back and reining in her emotions. She had to maintain a distance or she would be lost. She looked over toward where the horses were slowly walking back in to the pair. Her voice was low but steady.

"Are you in the mood to finish our ride?"

By way of an answer, Falcon strode to bring Mercury to her side and helped her to mount. He then climbed easily astride his own steed and moved up alongside her. "Where to?"

The thought came to Morgan that she could choose any destination, any location in the world, and he would ride by her side, watching over her.

She looked into his eyes.

She was lost.

Chapter 18

Storm found she overslept the next morning – thick clouds hid the sun and kept her room in shadows as she dressed and prepared herself. To her surprise, the courtyard was almost deserted when she went down to join in the daily workout.

Harold looked out from the stables. "All gone," he informed her. "Took all the horses early this morning and lit out."

Storm glanced between him and the open gates in confusion. "Where did they go?"

Harold shrugged his shoulders and went back to sweeping.

Storm wondered if there had been trouble and found it hard to concentrate on her sword work. Falcon could easily be injured … or slain. She imagined him in twenty different desperate situations, fighting for his life, and wished she could be by his side. She thought of all the things she should have said, should have done, when she had the time.

She forced herself to go through the exercises; to keep herself busy. Finally she gave up in frustration. It was no use – every second of her attention was focused on the main gates, listening for the faintest sound of hoofbeat.

Sheathing her blade, she climbed the ladder and stood on the parapets alongside two guards. They nodded at her in greeting, their eyes never leaving the tree line at the far edges of the landscape. Storm joined them in their silent watch.

It was long after noon when they first heard the horses. They quickly glanced at each other to verify the sound. Storm's heart was in her throat, desperate to know what had happened. A group moved into view, and with overwhelming relief she spotted Falcon's form riding within the company.

He glanced up at her as they passed beneath the wall, then he was on the other side. She restrained herself with tense nervousness, slowly climbing down the ladder and giving him time to talk with his men and guards. After what seemed an eternity the group dispersed, and Falcon strode over to her.

Storm's emotions were in a whirlwind. She struggled to keep her voice low and even. "Was it a bandit attack? What happened?"

Falcon shook his head with frustration, stopping a few paces before her with a weary step. "We received an alert that a nearby village was under attack," he sighed. Heather hurried over from the main doors with a large mug of ale, and he took it with a grateful nod, drinking half of it down in one long pull.

"The news came just before dawn. We went out immediately to help, but it was almost as if they knew we were coming. By the time we arrived, the bandits had vanished." He took another drink from his mug, looking into it morosely.

Storm leaned back on the ladder, her heart sinking. "What were the losses?"

"Two dead. Five others injured," he recited in a tense monotone. He turned his face away from hers, his lips tight. "I just cannot understand it. Every time we have them within our reach, they melt away like butter in a hot pan."

Zach came over to stand beside Heather, his shoulders tight and hunched. Without looking up, Heather interlaced her fingers into his.

Zach's voice was low but steady. "We all know you do the best you can, M'lord," he offered. "There are some who die – but there are many others you save."

If anything, Falcon's eyes became more shadowed as he looked over at the young man. "Four years ago I rescued you from the bandits, but you returned to your village to find both of your parents slain." He paused, then added more softly, "That is hardly something for me to be proud of."

He finished the ale in a long gulp, then handed the empty mug to Heather, his movements sharp and angular.

"I am going for a ride," he stated abruptly to nobody in particular. He looked over at Storm, and his gaze softened. "Would you like to come? I could use the company."

Storm nodded without speaking, and together they walked over toward the stables. Harold prepared fresh steeds without a word, his sallow face a mask of dourness.

Once the pair cleared the main gates, Storm followed along quietly as Falcon turned his horse from the town and headed toward the woods. With the dark clouds overhead, they presented a somber, twisted canopy. She was suddenly nervous at the sight of the thick stand of trees.

She pulled her horse to a stop for a moment, watching as Falcon was swallowed up by the darkness. She hesitated a moment, then shook off her trepidation and followed him into the dense gloom.

* * *

Falcon was quiet for a long time as the trees enveloped them, and a silence settled over the pair. It was not until they reached a small clearing that he spoke up.

"I used to spend a lot of time here when I was younger," he commented almost to himself. He pointed to a stream which gurgled under a thin layer of ice. "That was where I swam with my dogs. Not much time for that nowadays."

Storm felt overwhelming compassion for the man who rode beside her, lost in thought. She looked over at Falcon, noticing the slump in his shoulders; the looseness of his hands on the reins.

"Surely, when things are quiet, you can take time whenever you choose," she commented in a low voice. "You can allow yourself time to refresh, to renew your energies."

"It is not just the time, it is the inclination," he countered in somber reflection. "So many borders and bandits, and there is just me." He slowed his mount as they drew atop the crest of the hill. Falcon dismounted and stood in the steady wind, looking out over the valley.

Storm dismounted as well, then came alongside him and gazed at the landscape in contemplation. The ground rolled down away from them, a series of hamlets stretching out to the horizon. She had seen a map back at the castle, but little realized how thin the forest was in this section, that the neighboring provinces were so close. She shivered at the thought, pulling her black woolen cloak close against the wind.

Falcon's voice came as if from a distance. "For so many years this forest served as a battleground, as we pushed their domains back and they came at us again. Every border is like this. I have spent years working on peace for each quarter. Finally, we will have a truce with the Walkers which is going to last. How many of those families have lost loved ones over the years? Much of the fighting in the east was Lord Walker, stirring up trouble." He looked pensively off into the distance.

Storm spoke softly. "Soon he will be your ally."

Falcon turned sharply, his movements angular. His voice ground in harsh tenseness. "Do you think I can believe that?" he countered, his face a mask of torment. "He has got me trapped like a covey in a bush. All evidence I hear from my townsfolk and my allies is that this man cannot be trusted."

He took a step toward her, standing before her. "Yet, I cannot refuse the offer he has presented, after all of these years of my pushing for a treaty. He has pinned me to a peace I cannot believe in." His voice dropped down a key, and became shaky with emotion. "Trapped in a marriage I do not want."

Falcon's hand moved up to trace the side of Storm's face. His eyes smoldered with desire as he memorized every curve of her cheek.

An answering passion swelled fiercely within her. He seemed so lost, so desperate. The desire swept through her, became an overreaching beacon - she wanted to ease his pain. She put her own hands on top of his, then gently slid her fingers up his arms, winding them tenderly into his thick hair.

"Oh, Falcon," she whispered huskily, her heart twisted with the agony that enveloped him.

Storm drew in a shuddering breath. Every instinct in her body was screaming for her to leave. She felt as if she were being torn in two by a pair of wild stallions. Her overwhelming desire for Falcon grappled violently with a promise she knew was central to her being.

Gazing into his agonized eyes, she reached a decision.

With a long, shuddering breath, she set free the ties of her past. Whatever purpose the vow had served for her younger self, its time was done. Perhaps she had been abused, perhaps the vow had been all that had kept her safe. She was now an adult. She would choose to give herself to the man who stood before her, the man she loved with every fiber of her being.

She flushed with passion as the truth of the statement echoed through every corner of her soul.

She loved Falcon.

Warmth infused her, bringing a glow to her face. She would give this gift to him. She would treasure this moment for all time. They were two willing adults. The memory of this day would sustain her through whatever life her future might bring, perhaps as a guard at the nunnery, perhaps a celibate nun herself.

Her childhood vow had served its purpose. It was time for her to create a new vow, one to be with the man she loved, fully and completely, for the time they had left together.

She twined her fingers more fully into his hair, then stretched herself up, brushing her lips against his. A thrill of passion burst through her, causing her to sigh softly in half agony, her body gently molding against his.

Falcon's eyes flashed with confusion. His voice ground out of him, guttural and hoarse, as he whispered, "Storm, are you sure -"

She pressed herself against him more insistently, her mouth seeking his, the desire washing over her in waves. He groaned with desire, gave a low oath, then pulled her in tightly against him, his reserves seemingly swept away by the matching flood of powerful emotions.

Storm was utterly overcome by the rush of passion sweeping through every part of her body. The feeling of Falcon's strong arms wrapping around her waist was more powerful than she could possibly have imagined. Every movement seared into her memory.

She opened her mouth to his kiss, each cell of her body ablaze with desire. There was no doubt in her mind that she had never been held or touched like this before. It could be that she never would be again. If so, she would let this day last her a lifetime.

The kiss seemed to go on for an eternity, and Storm's breath was coming in deep heaves when Falcon finally pulled back. He turned his face into her long hair, nuzzling her neck and holding her close.

"Oh, sweet Storm," he groaned in barely checked agony. "Were that I had met you even two months ago, I could have promised you much." He pressed his head against hers, and she could feel his hands tremble as they swept down the length of her hair.

His voice was hoarse. "These bandits, and Lord Walker, have got me outnumbered. I have got to ally with the Walkers. I cannot be the man you deserve. If we were to become a couple, even for a few weeks, the memory of our time together might hold you back from moving forward." His eyes rose to hers. "From embracing the husband who waits for you."

He deliberately took a step back from her, then tenderly reached forward to brush her hair gently from her face. His face reflected the great torment he was in.

Storm shuddered at his touch on her face and put her hand over his, holding it to her cheek. With her other hand, she reached out for him.

"I know," she murmured, her voice thick with desire. "I know you cannot make any promises. If it is only for one afternoon, then it will be enough."

Her eyes made plain the offer she was making to him.

Falcon's eyes sharpened again, then he turned away, his movements angular. "No!" He strode away from her and with one swift move remounted his horse.

Storm felt as if she had been tossed onto a rocky beach after days in a stormy sea. She fought to bring her breathing back to normal, looking at the tense set of his back as he stared out over the valley.

Her cheeks flared with burning heat. A deep shame coursed through her that she had been so curtly turned down. Was she that undesirable to him, that he would dismiss her out of hand?

She turned her back to him, glaring at the open landscape. How dare he! How dare he judge her, after having almost openly courted her. Her hands open and closed, making tense fists.

Many long, furious minutes passed, and eventually her thoughts released their wild whirling. Her breathing finally slowed, and her considerations took on some semblance of order. She looked down at her hands, at the ring on her finger.

She gave a soft nod, accepting the truth. He was not disrespecting her. If anything, he was showing his high respect for her by acting with honor. He knew how fiercely they cared for each other. He knew, if they consummated their relationship, that she might never recover.

Storm bit her tongue and wiped the tears of frustration from her eyes. She wanted him … but she would not beg him. If that was his decision, then so be it.

Even with that thought, it took Storm a long while before the pent-up emotion eased out of her. The entire time Falcon waited nearby, avoiding her gaze, enveloped in tense silence.

Finally an exhausted weariness took hold of her. She stumbled to her steed, mounting with effort. As soon as she was settled in her saddle, Falcon turned his horse without speaking, heading back up the path. She fell into step just behind him.

The ride back to the keep was cloaked in silence. When they got to the stables, Storm dismounted and headed to her room without looking back. Once there, she sat on the edge of her bed, lost in thought until dusk settled over the town and the moon began rising high into the sky.

Chapter 19

Storm's mind was settled when she awoke the next morning. Hours of introspection had allowed her to reach a decision. She could see the strain that her presence had put on Falcon. She could see the agony in his gaze and the turmoil in his heart.

He deserved better.

It was time for her to take the action she had recommended from the start. She should leave.

When Falcon knocked on her door, she was ready for him. He came in with a haunted look, and she began speaking before he had opened his mouth.

"I realize I have made things very difficult for you," she stated, her voice tight. "Far more difficult than you deserve. You can hardly afford to have these issues in your life right now."

Storm's throat closed up, and she forced herself to continue before she lost the will to say what needed to be said. "I will ready my things and take lodging in a local boarding house; I can pay for my room with hard work. Once Walker arrives with his group, I will leave with them. It is only a week away now."

"No!" cried Falcon, his voice tight with anguish. He took a step toward her. His breath came in a long draw as his eyes held hers. "We have a week left. One week of memories to last us a lifetime."

His jaw tensed, and he took her hand in his own, looking down at it. "Who knows what your life is like at the nunnery. We have seen how you flinched from even the slightest of contact. The world you are returning to could well be harsh and unforgiving."

His eyes rose to hold hers again. "Let this time here in my keep be an oasis – a brief respite from a life of pain. I would not take one day of that from you. You deserve -"

His eyes shadowed, and he looked away.

Storm's throat tightened. She could barely speak. "Falcon … I cannot stay …"

His eyes swept back to hers, and she was enveloped by the desire which glowed in them, by the matching call within her own heart. His voice was hoarse. "Once you see what your previous life had been like, you might indeed choose to stay here with us," he countered. "Mary and the others have spoken to me about how well you fit into our life here." His hand wrapped into hers. "You could help train the younger soldiers, or simply help out around the castle, whatever pleased you. You would be well cared for and offered a quiet, restful life."

Storm was drawn by the strong pull of the idea. She could remain in the keep, remain at his side …

Reality slammed into her.

"And Laura? How would she feel about this?"

He turned away at that, his eyes staring out the window in tense quiet. "You never know. Laura … she might enjoy having you around, to keep her company."

He drew his gaze back to her, tender and haunted. "We are adults, and I will speak plainly. Yes, I crave you with all my soul." He flushed, but with a visible effort pressed himself to continue speaking. "I swear to you that I can keep my desire under control. I would not lose you because we cannot be married. I would treasure you as a valuable member of my household; someone to talk with, to spar with, to ride with." His face went pale, but he continued. "When you find another to love, another man to marry, I would bless the union and wish you the best of joy."

Storm turned away, feeling the impossibility of it. There could never be a man in her life like Falcon; never a man whose presence overwhelmed her senses, whose eyes saw into the core of her being. She knew that remaining in his household would be a daily torment, one she did not know whether she could bear.

Falcon's voice was wound tight with emotion. "We have at least this one week to be together, before any other decisions need to be made," he pointed out. "Please, I have so little to look forward to, between this marriage and the truce which may destroy everything I have struggled for. I only ask for one more week."

Twisting agony ripped at Storm's core. Her love for Falcon warred against her thin layers of self-preservation. She knew there was no way she could remain in the household once he was married. The sight of Falcon holding his wife's hand, riding out with her, would be more than she could bear. Every moment would be agonizing torment.

She drew her eyes up to meet his; matching passion and hopeless pain echoed in his gaze. A shuddering tremor coursed through her, and she slowly nodded. He had this one week left before he consigned himself to a loveless marriage, to a truce which could very well break him.

She would do what she could to make this one last week a memory which would last them both a lifetime.

"I will stay the week."

He was drew her in, holding her against him. She became lost in his embrace; her eyes welled with tears and all outside thoughts vanished. It was only his strong arms around her, his cheek against her forehead, his broad chest sheltering her.

Finally he drew back from her, maintaining her hand within his. He guided her down the stairs and into the main hall.

Storm drew her gaze along the tapestries as she passed them, tracing out the history of Falcon's life. Her eyes were drawn to the last one, the one his mother had been working on when she took her own life. Another woman would take up that thread, would continue on the journey with Falcon.

She would have to let him go. There was no other choice.

Resignation slid over her, and as they came out into the main courtyard, it settled into something firmer, more desolate. She drew her sword, immersing herself in the routine, drowning her pain and loss in the sweeping motions and turning thrusts.

Chapter 20

Storm sat at the lunch table, her eyes downcast, forcing herself to swallow a forkful of steamed turnips. The food was delicious, but her stomach turned at the thought of eating. Only a few days remained, and then she would be gone. Her hours were ticking away, one by one, and there was no way to regain them. There was no way to unscroll the smooth progression of time.

At her side, Falcon was silent. His face was shadowed, lost in his own thoughts.

There was the sound of quick footsteps. A messenger in a roughly-made tunic came striding in through the main gates, accompanied by a guard. The guard glanced at Falcon, who waved them over with a raised eyebrow.

The messenger moved directly to Falcon's side. He reached into a leather pouch at his side and, with a flourish, drew forth a sealed scroll.

His voice rasped. "A note from my master, Lord Walker."

Falcon glanced at Storm with a concerned look before taking the proffered letter. He quickly unrolled and scanned it.

"It appears the Walker contingent will be arriving in five days, as planned – on the feast of St. Martin of Tours," he commented, his voice tight. "They ask for you to be ready to travel home with them once the feast is complete."

Storm dropped her eyes, staring fixedly at her plate. Five days. Less than a week. Bands of iron constricted around her chest, making it hard to breathe.

She thought again of the way she flinched at any touch, of her dagger beneath her pillow. What kind of a world awaited her? Were there harsh circumstances which she could not escape? Was the nunnery the way she had fled a violent childhood?

As if from a far distance Falcon's voice whispered into her musings, as he issued orders to Heather to prepare the necessary cleaning and culinary tasks. She pushed the discussion out of her thoughts. Her world seemed to close down. Five days. After five short days, everything she knew would be lost. Time was slipping away from her.

A fresh clatter of footsteps sounded in the entry hall, and Storm looked up in tense surprise. Was yet another messenger arriving with fresh news?

Jessica swept into the room with wide arms, beaming. Her blonde hair was done up in a glorious, complex braid, decorated with gold ribbons and sparkling pearls. She wore a sumptuous gold and yellow dress which glistened in the sun.

Storm's mouth hung open at the effect. There was no denying it - the woman was stunningly beautiful.

Jessica smiled broadly as she spotted the pair, then moved over to offer her hand to Falcon in greeting. "There you are, my dear. It has been far too long that I have been away! You know how it is to run a business venture, to keep plans moving along properly. Sometimes it takes more time than you expect! I hurried back to you as quickly as I could."

She waved a hand to a page, instructing him to bring a chair over to insert between Falcon and Storm. "I am simply famished!" she insisted as she settled herself down with a smile. "I have brought you a treat! Some cyser mead from my own storehouses. You will see now how sweet life can be when you have a woman with connections in it!"

Storm slumped back into her chair, looking down at her dark blue dress, drab and quiet in the shadow of the glowing apparition. Jessica bubbled merrily along to Falcon, her conversation running at full steam, regaling him with tales of what she had been up to in the intervening days. When Heather brought around the cyser for the table, pouring it into beautiful new pewter goblets which Jessica also supplied, Storm had to admit that the drink was every bit as luscious as promised. It felt like the final nail in the coffin of her remaining days.

She did not wait for Jessica to push her out of the afternoon's ride. The moment lunch was complete, she offered quiet excuses and retired to her room. She drew her stool over to the window, leaning her head against the side, her shoulders slumping.

Long, grey clouds drifted in slow progression across a pale blue sky. Storm's thoughts trailed to the conversation at lunch, and something nagged at the corner of her mind. There had been an oddity in Jessica's ebullient conversation, in the quick, tense movements of her hands. Was Jessica becoming desperate? Surely she was also aware of the approaching visit of Lord Walker and the upcoming marriage.

Storm shook her head. That golden dress had been a clear signal. Undoubtedly Jessica was going to do everything in her power to turn Falcon's purpose in the remaining days. Storm had no desire to become caught up in that struggle. She counted her blessings that Jessica would no longer consider her a threat, since her days here were now so few.

She spent the afternoon working on her sword exercises alone in her room, willing herself to put everything else out of her mind.

* * *

Storm steeled herself before heading down to breakfast. If Jessica were grasping at her final chance to turn Falcon's purpose, the last thing Storm wanted was to get in the middle of that battle. It seemed the woman would be as tenacious as a badger and would let nothing stand in her way.

She moved to the stairs - and stopped in surprise. Angry voices were in tense conversation in the main hall, and it was only a moment before she picked out the speakers' identities.

Jessica and Falcon were almost shouting at each other. Jessica's voice rang out, sharp and clear.

"And if you do not send Storm away immediately -"

Storm turned on her heel, striding back to her room, pulling the door solidly shut behind her. Could she not even have four days of peace? Could Jessica simply not leave her alone for these few remaining days?

She drew her chair by her window, wrapping her arms around her and staring out at the empty courtyard. Jessica's fury made no sense to her. Why in the world would Jessica still feel so threatened by her? Besides, with her days ticking away to nothing, why would Jessica risk Falcon's good graces by starting up an argument about anything at all? Surely she would do better by dripping honey and sweetness, attempting to capture Falcon's affections before Lord Walker arrived.

A soft knock sounded on the door and Storm hesitated for a moment before turning.

"Come in," she offered, her heart pounding.

Would it be Falcon, or perhaps Jessica?

She sighed in relief as Heather poked her face around the door, her braid-ringed face looking lovely and serene.

Storm smiled at her friend. "Zach really is agreeing with you," she teased as Heather slipped in and closed the door behind her. "Are you two doing well together?"

"I cannot even put it into words how content we are," gushed Heather, coming over to sit beside Storm. "If you had told me a month ago how much my life could have changed, I never would have believed you."

Storm sat back against the window ledge. "I am happy for you. You well deserve it."

"And *you* do not deserve the words being said below!" retorted Heather, a frown creasing her brow. "I came to let you know that I would gladly bring your meal up here, if you wished. Jessica has wound herself into a high dudgeon!"

Despite her better judgment, Storm found herself drawn in. "I admit I am at a complete loss as to what that woman is up to. Just what irks her so that she would risk Falcon's ire?"

Heather planted her feet solidly on the floor, leaning forward to talk to Storm. "She is insisting – again – that you are in league with the bandits. She claims that she heard it from a reliable source that an awful event will happen in the coming days. She is demanding that you be sent away today." She flushed and looked down. "She has threatened Falcon that, unless he acts within a few hours, the blood of his slain servants will be on his hands"

Storm blinked her eyes wide. "People will be slain? What, by me?"

Heather shook her head. "I do not think even she would dare to go that far. She seems to imply that you would let the bandits in to do their dirty work. She insists that your friendly actions, in getting to know the staff, have all been part of your plan to become trusted. She swears that within a few days your lies will bring destruction. According to her, Falcon's only option is to have his soldiers immediately take you across the border to North Walsham and deposit you there."

Storm's heart pounded against her chest. Her throat went dry. She took in a long breath, holding Heather's eyes with her own.

"I swear to you, on my honor and my life, that I have no such plot in my mind." She swallowed. "I would never allow bandits, or anyone else, to bring harm to you or anyone else here." She looked down, flushing, as her past fears bubbled to the fore. "Even if, at one time, I had been allied with the bandits, I have had no contact, no recollection, not even the inkling of such a thought since arriving here."

Heather tenderly patted her hand. "I know that. Everyone here knows that. Do not feel that we are taken in for a moment by Jessica's rantings."

Storm shook her head. "But why would she lie? What could she hope to gain by these arguments? She had a chance of wooing Falcon to her cause. If she had planned her seduction carefully, she might even have drawn him away from his plans for a truce." Her eyes glanced to the door, to the hall beyond. "She is undoing her own success. I cannot imagine engaging

Falcon in a public screaming match will bring him into her arms."

Heather nodded, her eyes reflecting her confusion. "Besides, you are leaving in only a few days anyway," she added. "Why should it matter so much that you are here for another day or two? What does she fear?"

Storm's throat closed up, but she made herself ask the question which mattered most to her. "What has Falcon said?"

Heather's mouth quirked up into a smile. "Falcon has sworn he will not send you away, and that he feels Jessica's claims are completely ridiculous," she assured Storm. "He snapped at her, saying she has been consuming belladonna and should take a purgative."

Storm's heart lightened, wondering how Jessica had taken this comment.

Heather drew herself to her feet. "I imagine you would rather avoid the drama, all the same," she mused. "I will bring you up some wine and a platter of roast duck. I will tell the priest you are not feeling well. Later, when they are finished with mass, you can feel free to go down and spend time in the chapel on your own."

"Thank you, Heather," sighed Storm. In a moment the girl was gone.

Soon Storm had her meal laid out on her table. She ate it slowly and in silence. From her window perch she watched as Falcon, Jessica, and the rest of the household headed into the chapel for mass. Falcon headed out shortly after mass was complete, riding hard on his horse, heading north. It was only a few minutes before Jessica was following him, her face set in determination. Storm waited until she was sure neither was returning soon before making her own way down to the chapel.

She slowly walked up the aisle, sliding into the front pew of the quiet stone building. She lowered herself to her knees. Her head dropped in complete submission. She felt lost at sea, without any sight of land.

On one hand, it seemed ignoble to resist the idea of returning to protect a nunnery. Perhaps she was all that stood between the helpless women and the cruel designs of bandits.

And yet, it seemed that a tumult of competing thoughts swarmed at her. They clamored for her attention, tumbling one over the other.

Jessica was acting completely out of character – why?

Falcon needed to marry Laura. The safety of the keep and his lands depended on it.

She loved Falcon with all her heart.

Tears welled in her eyes, and she brushed them away with a rough movement. She desperately wished that her memory would return; that everything would begin to make sense to her. Her world was a turmoil, a spinning whirlpool which was sucking her down into its depths, and she could not find a firm hold to escape.

Her eyes went to the long line of beeswax candles against the wall, and she found herself calming, drawing peace from their gentle flickering. Somehow, life would go on. A path would be found in this twisting, briar-filled forest, and eventually she would emerge on the other side.

The image of Heather's sweet face came to mind, and she smiled, nodding. If nothing else, Heather and Zach had both developed the self-respect they so richly deserved. If no other good came of her time here, she would leave that legacy behind. As for the rest …

Falcon's deep eyes filled her imagination, and a swirl of pain spread out from her center. She would have to let him go. She adored him, craved him, and felt a connection she knew she had never found before. Even so, there was no place for her in his world. It was absolutely necessary for him to marry Laura; for him to seal the truce which would protect his land from danger. He would take Laura by his side. Perhaps in time he would grow to care for her.

Storm bit her lip, flushing. In all of her musings, she had barely given thought to Laura. Did the woman even have a say in any of this? Falcon was the unwilling groom, and Lord

Walker seemed a man not given to much thought about the comfort of others. Maybe Laura was as miserable at the thought of marrying Falcon as he was of being with her.

A slight easing sighed through her shoulders. The staff here at the keep was gentle, friendly, and kind. If Laura had become used to the harsh treatment her father was famous for, a few weeks in this far more gentle climate could do wonders for her. It might be that she would quickly warm to the comforts of her new life, and that Falcon in turn would warm to her.

Storm clasped her hands together in prayer, dropping her head. She released all hope for herself. She knew there was none to be had. She had to let Falcon go. All that remained now was to pray that the life Falcon had awaiting him would be a long and happy one. She could pray that Laura would be a woman he could learn to love. She hoped with all her heart that Laura was worthy of him, and that over time she could come to respect and care for him as well.

A new calm washed over her, and she poured every ounce of her soul into the prayers.

* * *

Storm did not even attempt to leave her room the next morning. She remained by the window, watching the soldiers gather in the courtyard, knowing it would be one of the last times she did so.

Falcon strode out into the center of his men, glanced around, then turned to gaze up at the window. His eyes hooded when he saw her there, watching him, and it was a long minute before he nodded in acceptance. He turned back to the guards, and in a moment they were in action, moving through lunges and low thrusts in a smooth rhythm.

Storm felt the draw, felt the yearning to be down in their midst, but she held it off with rugged determination. Only two more days. Two more days, and she would be back to her proper place in life, whatever it was. Falcon would enter into his truce, and all would be as it was meant to be.

It seemed only minutes later that the men were heading in for lunch. Shortly after that, Heather was slipping in through the door, bringing her stewed turnips, and setting down the glass of thick red wine. The blink of an eye - the empty trencher was being cleared, Falcon was streaming through the gates on his horse, and Jessica only a short distance behind. The courtyard settled down into a dusty silence.

The quiet of the keep gnawed at Storm. Finally she stood, taking the long stairs at a slow pace and making her way into the kitchen building.

Mary's eyes were gentle. "Welcome," she greeted in a low voice. "Come, have a seat. We were just going to work on some mending." Heather and Molly joined them at the table, picking up their supplies and setting to work.

Storm easily fell into the task. She lost herself in the even stitches, in the quiet progression of thread and fabric. The women were subdued, and an ache settled into her heart. They had become friends to her; she would miss them dearly. It would be so comfortable, so restful to simply remain here, to immerse herself in this world. If only she had some reassurance that the life she was heading to held even a portion of this companionship.

Every item which passed through her hands reminded her of Falcon. The table runner with its designs of apple and pear brought to mind their long conversations, his keen insight into the cares and concerns of his staff. The curtain from his study reminded her of their chess games, of what an able companion he was, how he seemed perfectly crafted to stand by her side. Holding one of his tunics in her arms, she could smell his musky scent, the hint of sweet woodruff. It took every ounce of her self-control not to bring it to her face, not to immerse herself in it, to wrap it around her and become embraced …

She tried to drive her longings from her mind, to pay attention to the quiet conversation of the women around her, but with every passing hour it seemed that her desire for Falcon grew. It became an acute ache, permeating every bone in her body.

Finally she placed her mending on the table, murmuring an apology to the women. She practically ran back to her room, closing the door behind her. The tears welled to overflowing, and she let them stream down her face. She climbed into bed, pulled the covers over her head, and lost herself in the heart-rending sobs.

* * *

Tuesday dawned with grey storm clouds. Storm stared out at them for a long while, all hope lost. The Walker contingent was due on Thursday. Her time was ticking down, draining away, moment by moment. Soon she would be taken away from Falcon forever, only memories left to cling to in her darkest nights.

She finally forced herself to dress, to head down the long stairs with slow feet. The main room was bustling with activity; it appeared the cleaning of the keep had begun in earnest. She spotted Heather to one side and strode up to her.

"I need something to do," murmured Storm, her voice tight.

Heather's eyes went to hers in concern, but she nodded in understanding. "What would you like?"

"Something solitary," cut out Storm, an intense ache burrowing into her very soul.

Heather handed her a bucket along with a rag and oil. Soon Storm had found a quiet corner and was burnishing the woodwork, rubbing it gently until it shone. She threw herself into each new item with an absolute focus, willing herself to release the loneliness which haunted her. Despite her best efforts, it only seemed that the torment within her expanded, stretching into every corner of her being.

She worked her way down the hall as evening approached, and it was with surprise that she found herself nearing the door to the tower. Judging by the activity around her, it was the only area that had not yet been cleaned.

Storm hesitated for a moment, then gathered up her supplies. The whole keep needed to be clean. By all accounts the visitors would never be in this part of the keep, but if by happenchance they did end up there by accident, Storm did not want them to think ill of the staff for its state.

She took a candle from her woven basket, lit it, and set to work.

Storm first scrubbed the stairs up to the tower, which were dusty but otherwise easy to clean. Then she reached the landing and the door to the tower's sole room. She hesitantly pushed open the door, gazing within. The room was dense with cobwebs and sparsely furnished. There was only a small wooden bench and an old loom tucked to one side.

She strode across the room in a few long steps and opened the window's shutters to bring some air into the room. The window was fairly high; the ledge was near the level of her chest. She remembered what Falcon had said about his mother falling out of the window, and she was somber as she leant against the ledge. It certainly did not seem as if it could have been an accident. The poor woman must have been inconsolably desolate at the loss of her husband.

She had taken her own life.

Pain wrapped tight bands about her chest, and she stepped back from the window. Falcon's mother had just tragically lost her beloved husband. Storm had some small sense of how the woman had felt, to lose the man you loved, you craved, you adored …

She turned away with a sharp shake of her head. She had to get the room clean and return back to her room. She took the rag and began clearing away the layer of dust on the bench.

A low voice sounded behind her, tight with pain. "Storm …"

Storm turned swiftly in surprise, her heart pounding.

Falcon stood in the doorway, a haunted look on his face.

It was all Storm could do to remain in place, to hold herself from running into his arms and wrapping herself around him. She craved him with every drop of blood in her body, with every ounce of air which drew into her lungs. His face shadowed with answering emotion, and she was almost lost.

At last his breathing slowed, and he looked around the room as if seeing it afresh. He gave himself a shake, his eyes going to the bench she had been cleaning. After a long moment, he nodded. "Yes, it is time," he agreed hoarsely. "The room needs to be cleaned, and life needs to move forward." His throat closed up, but he pressed on. "Soon the keep will have a new mistress, and the loom will be in use again."

Storm shuddered at the painful stab which speared her heart. She craved with all her soul to be the woman he spoke of. The one who would loyally stay at his side; the one to weave a new future with him.

She turned away, moving to the window and looking out across the landscape. Tears welled in her eyes. She willed them away.

In a moment he had moved to stand alongside her. His voice was tight when he spoke. "You can see nearly the whole realm from this location," he murmured. "Every village which depends on this keep for their protection."

Storm breathed in his warm scent, trembling at his nearness. The pain was almost overwhelming, to think that soon she would be gone from this place forever. She wondered how his mother had felt, in those first days, absorbing the news that her husband was dead, that he would never return.

She glanced up at Falcon, taking in his shadowed face, his tense jaw. He had only been a child, and he had lost both his father and his mother. How had that loss been borne?

Her voice was soft when she spoke. "It seems ironic. You have memories which are painful, which you probably wish to forget. I do not have any memories at all. I wish desperately to remember them, even if they are extremely hard ones."

Her eyes dropped to the ring on her finger, and she descended into a hollow emptiness, an ebony frustration that even this powerful symbol was a mere shadow in her mind. "I have lost part of myself. I worry that it will never return."

Falcon shook his head, coming back from whatever distant land his mind had been lost in. "I admit that I would have thought your memories would have returned by now," he agreed in a rough undertone. He glanced down at her with hooded eyes, then continued. "Maybe they will come back when you are home in North Walsham, back in familiar surroundings. It seems that the things you remember now are all based on actions, and on positions. It seems to be some sort of muscle memory, rather than visual memory."

Falcon's eyes sharpened, and he turned. He moved to the bench and dragged it with a sharp tug to sit beneath the window ledge.

"You remember through senses," he mused. "So maybe the key to unlocking the dam would involve ..." He looked between the bench and Storm.

"Earlier you remembered sitting by a window with the vase of reeds. Maybe recreating the scene will help your mind open that door and regain access to your memories." He nodded at the bench. "Take a seat."

Storm stepped forward, settling herself on the bench. Without conscious thought she turned sideways and pulled her feet up to rest on the bench. She did not resist, pulling her knees in close and closing her eyes. She could feel the cool breeze on her cheek; the air drifting in through the open window.

Falcon knelt at her side. "Release all conscious thought," he advised her. "Just relax, and let your mind drift. Let this wall in your mind soften and release." There was a long pause, and when he spoke again his voice was hoarse. "Imagine that you are the happiest you have ever been."

Agonizing pain billowed within her at the thought of all she was about to lose. With effort she pushed it away and searched through her mind for something to replace it with. She went back to the day of their horse race, when she lay in the grass, the clouds drifting by above, Falcon's tender face gazed down at her. Warmth eased through her, and she wrapped the sensation around her, drawing it close. She became lost in the feeling.

Falcon's voice drifted into her consciousness, a bare whisper. "Where are you?"

Storm was at peace. The breeze easing through the window tickled along her cheek. A scene began to paint itself, at first with hesitant, faint brush strokes. As she relaxed into it the colors were added - the rich blues and the warm browns. She let it come at its own pace. She drew in the strength of the memory, basking in the warm pleasure at regaining a piece of her lost self.

"I am in a high tower of my home," she whispered, afraid to dispel the image. "My secret hideaway; my private sanctuary." There was a familiar leather feel in her hands, and she knew at once what it is. "My poetry codex. I practically have it memorized," she murmured, a gentle smile stealing to her lips. "I would come here to read it, to soak in the golden rays. I could lose myself for hours here."

Falcon was still, not saying a word, letting her memory unfold at its own pace.

She glanced down at her hands, and found there was no ring, that her fingers were small, fresh with youth. "I must be young," she mused. "Perhaps eight? It seems I should not be here today. My father insisted I wait downstairs, in the hall. But I could not resist. I could never resist the lure of my tower room. I curled up within the thick draperies and was lost to the world."

It seemed that there was shouting. She turned her head, staring out the window, her eyes not seeing the landscapes that spread there but a long-lost vision. A woman was streaming toward her on a horse, in full gallop.

She rose to her knees, her mouth going round in surprise.

"Mother? Where is her carriage? What is wrong?"

Another movement. Four men in rough leather armor were thundering after the woman, their horses closing.

Storm grabbed a hold of the sill with both hands, her voice rising in panic. "Watch out!" she screamed, her eyes wide, seeing nothing, lost in the past. "Mother! Watch out!"

The bandits engulfed her mother in a flurry of steel, and Storm was screaming, screaming …

Strong arms wrapped tightly around her, drawing her in against a broad chest, and still she screamed, the sound echoing around her. Tears flooded from her eyes, soaking the fabric of Falcon's tunic. The vision of her mother's brutal murder burned into her, the memory vivid and powerful and seared into her soul.

Storm roiled in agony. Sobs wracked her body. Falcon held her in a close embrace.

Time lost all meaning.

Finally, after what seemed an eternity, her voice lost its strength. Her tears ran dry. She lay quiescent, every ounce of her strength spent.

A gentle hand laid beneath her chin, and she obediently raised her eyes to look at his.

Falcon's gaze was rich with compassion and sympathy. "I wonder ..." he mused. "Perhaps you managed to unlock something that had been hidden even from your adult mind. Something your younger self could not cope with."

Suddenly he tensed, and his lips pressed together. He drew his eyes to look out the window, and his voice dropped to a faint whisper.

"Still, the timing ... and how similar this all is to ..."

Storm had no idea what he was referring to and did not care. She was beyond all thought. She lay quietly within his arms.

Another long while passed. At last Falcon gave himself a shake, drawing himself away from Storm and rising to his feet. His face was shadowed, his emotions masked.

"You should probably head to bed to rest," he suggested evenly. "You have been through a lot. We can talk more in the morning if you feel up to it. After all, we still have a day before the Walkers arrive."

He offered a hand, and she took it, shakily moving to her feet. His eyes moved to hold hers. "*J'espere que cela vous convenient, ma chere?*"

Storm nodded, brushing down her dress. She could do with rest; she was completely exhausted. "*D'accord,*" she agreed.

His eyes flicked, and then he was at her side, guiding her down the long stairs and escorting her to her room. The chamber was bathed in shadows, with only a faint glow coming from the embers in the fireplace.

She climbed beneath the covers, her eyes half closing of their own accord. He stepped away from the bed and began heading out of the room. His feet slowed at the doorway, and he turned to gaze at her. He stood there for a long while, watching her with a furrowed brow, his eyes serious and considering. Then he let out a long breath, turned, and closed the door firmly behind him.

Despite her exhaustion, Storm found it took a long while before she could release herself to sleep.

Chapter 21

Storm sat by the window, gazing at the drifting clouds which slid along the sky as if pulled by invisible strings. Her thumb ran along the ring on her finger, and she drew in a long, deep breath. The memory of the bandit attack on her mother remained solid and firm in her mind. It felt like a keystone, a solid base onto which other memories would begin to cling and form. A kindling of hope swelled within her, that she would finally be able to heal, to reintegrate her old past with her new self.

The process had begun.

Falcon stepped out of the stables and moved past the gathered men to the center of the courtyard. He drew his eyes up to meet hers. A glow of warmth washed through her, and she nodded at him. If there were any more pieces of herself to be found on this final day, she wanted to share them with Falcon. This was it; these were her last hours. She would spend them by his side.

She turned, moved from her room, descended the stairs, and entered the quiet hall. Footsteps sounded from the entryway, and in a moment Falcon had strode in to join her. His eyes were shadowed, his face set.

"I have another experiment I would like to try," he stated without preamble. "As last night's efforts were so successful, perhaps we can gain yet more insight into just who you are."

Storm hesitated. Something was off. His voice was almost sharp; his movements tense. Still, she nodded in agreement, following him back out into the main courtyard.

The guards were milling about on the practice ground, waiting in the crisp autumn air for their session to begin. Falcon strode past them, over to one side where a rack of throwing knives was kept. Storm's eyes drew over it with curiosity.

"Target practice?" she asked Falcon. "I wonder how I would have known this style of activity?"

"How indeed," replied Falcon flatly. He led her over to the selection of knives. "Which of these would you like to try?"

Storm looked at the pile and randomly picked up and discarded several. One seemed to feel right to her, and she quickly spun it in her hand with practiced ease. "This one seems quite well balanced," she mused.

The soldier managing the arms spoke up nervously. "That one? But that is -"

Falcon cut him off with a look. Falcon motioned for her to continue. She chose two other similar blades, then turned to him.

Falcon pointed past her to a pair of wooden targets, some twenty feet away. Knives had landed at a wide scattering of locations around the targets, and a few pierced the outer ring of one of the painted bulls-eyes.

"My guards' aim could use improvement," Falcon commented, his shoulders tight. "I am sure if you have had any practice you could at least hit a target. Give it a try."

The other soldiers had put their gear down to watch, and the courtyard suddenly seemed quiet. Storm looked at the targets. If it were so easy, why hadn't his own soldiers done better? She glanced at Falcon, at his shadowed eyes, and she pushed away her questions. He was her host, and she would comply with his request.

She tucked two of the knives in her belt, then hefted the remaining one. The craftsmanship seemed impeccable. She gave it a final spin in her hand, then settled into a stance and drew her arm back. She held the blade gently at its balance point, halfway down the blade's surface.

The world narrowed down to that one target, and she felt as if she moved in slow motion.

The knife seemed to slip through the air, making a clear, soft noise as it rotated through each half turn. With a quiet *thunk* it sank into the center of the target. She reached for the second, and then the third, launching them with the same easy grace.

One of the dogs barked, and Storm nodded in satisfaction. Apparently this was an area she had skill in as well. Was it part of her nunnery training? She turned to Falcon, and the questions suddenly vanished. He was staring at her with a look she could not decipher, his face grim. Then he turned on his heel and strode into the keep.

Storm watched him go, completely at a loss. She had done as he had asked. Was he upset that she had more talents than just sword fighting? Was there something wrong with her begin able to wield a knife as well? It was simply a spinning blade …

Her mind suddenly flew back to the incident in the stables, when she had caught the scythe. Were they somehow related? Was Falcon once again thinking she was involved with the bandits?

The thought sent a jolt of panic into her heart, and she found she was flying to the keep after him. She raced to explain that she was innocent, that she had no plans to harm him, to harm the staff here.

She skittered to a stop in the empty hall. Falcon was nowhere in sight.

She moved from room to room, asking each servant she came across, but the answer was the same in every case. None had seen Falcon; none knew where he was.

A hollow emptiness opened within her, threatening to swallow her whole. Her remaining minutes were ticking away, precious grains of time vanishing forever, and something she had done had upset Falcon. She searched the entire keep, even the tidy tower chamber, but he was gone. He must have somehow gotten to the stables and headed out of the keep.

She stumbled to her room and crawled into bed, burying her face in her pillow. Every breath was one moment closer to when she would leave. It was approaching like a billowing thunderstorm, and she was helpless to stop it.

The light tinted crimson, then faded into an inky blackness. Still she lay there, a twisting whirlpool dragging her down into its depths. All hope was lost.

It took her a long while to fall asleep. Her dreams, when they came, were dark and twisted, of a gnarled wood with no escape.

Chapter 22

Her eyes blinked open. She could hear the frantic sounds of activity outside her door, as servants raced to take care of last minute tasks. There were shouted orders, calls for assistance, and the thud of moving furniture.

Mary eased herself into the room, bringing a tray of scrambled eggs with bacon. Storm ate it without much appetite. This was it. Today she would leave forever, putting her friends into the past. And Falcon …

Tears threatened to come, and she turned her head, struggling to maintain her self-control. She would have to say good bye to Falcon. After today he would only exist in her memories.

She would treasure him there. She knew she would never find another man like him. She would never find someone to replace him in her heart.

Mary took away the barely-touched meal, then had a bath brought up. It seemed only the blink of an eye before Storm was dressed in a fresh, dark blue surcoat with her hair brushed out and braided.

Mary gazed fondly at Storm, offering a fond pat on the cheek. "I know partings are sad, but you are heading home," she murmured with a half-smile. "Think of your friends who wait there for you."

Storm nodded half-heartedly. "Maybe I will remember them, once I see them," she mused.

Mary drew her to her feet. "I am sure you will," she agreed. "I am sure once you see the people from your old life that everything will come flooding back, and you will be as right as rain."

"I will still miss you dearly," offered Storm, drawing Mary into a warm hug.

Mary blushed crimson, and her eyes welled. "As will we. You have been a delightful guest."

She turned and lifted the mirror from the dresser. "And you will be pleased to know that you look gorgeous for your reunion. I think we can declare you fully healed."

Storm looked at her reflection critically, and she had to admit that Mary had done a fantastic job. The dress fit perfectly, and the ocean-blue color brought out the highlights in her auburn hair.

Storm forced herself to smile brightly at her reflection. For the sake of the truce, she must go into this day appearing content and happy. Falcon was returning a lost sheep to Walker's fold, and it was her job to impress Lord Walker with how well Falcon had cared for her during the past few weeks. It could become a crucial part of ensuring the truce was signed with no further delays.

Too soon, a knock sounded at the door. Heather, fresh as a summer's morn in her rose surcoat and braids, peeked her head in the door.

"Oh, Storm, you are lovely," she gushed with pleasure, looking Storm up and down with a smile. "If you are ready, Lord Walker and his group have arrived. They are asking to see you."

Storm felt faint – in minutes she would have her full past revealed. She took a deep breath and smiled at Mary. For better or for worse, she was going to go down and face her destiny.

The walk down the hallway was interminable. Her steps grew slower and slower, until finally she stopped in the archway leading to the main hall.

She drew in a deep breath. There was no turning back now. She would face her past. Whatever it held, she would accept it and move forward with her life.

So determined, she strode into the room.

Her eyes first caught Falcon's, standing at the head of the table. His familiar leather armor, the sword at his side, the strong hands – all so well known to her …

Her breath caught.

Falcon's eyes were flat, cold, and distant.

Storm's heart skipped a beat, and she drew to a stuttering halt.

What was going on?

There was a movement at his side, and Jessica moved to stand next to him. Her face was bright with a wide, sly grin. She looked as if she would be willing to take on Lord Walker's entire army for the right to marry Falcon.

Storm felt as if she were plunging into a bottomless pit; being swallowed by darkness. Not only was Falcon lost to her, but even her memories of their short time together were being tainted and twisted.

She heard the clearing of a throat, and she realized with a shock that there were others in the room. She had been so focused on Falcon that nothing else had entered into her awareness.

The soldiers in the Walker entourage were lined up against the far wall.

Her eyes scanned down the row, and she drew in a long breath. She knew them. To her surprise she realized that she knew them all. Every man was as identifiable to her as her own hands. The device on their shields was as familiar as the ring on her finger.

The men were staring at her in confusion, their eyes drawing down her form. None looked as shocked as the sturdy, elegantly dressed man in front of the group.

Lord Walker.

Her father.

An avalanche of emotions held her in place as his face morphed from pleasured surprise to a look of calculating greed. He shook himself and strode forward to stand before her, evaluating her as if she were a horse on auction.

"Laura, my child, you look wonderful!" he cried in hearty approval. "I do declare that Falcon has worked wonders! I do not know that I have ever seen you so beautiful!" He ran his eyes from her head down to her feet, examining every inch of her.

An overwhelming flood of memories bombarded Storm, fighting for attention, and she found she could not speak. Memories of him beating her, of him denying her food, of him locking her in her room for whatever transgression had struck his whimsy that day. She was staggered by the rich fury which hammered at her, which welled up from every pore of her being.

She turned her eyes away from him, breathing in deeply, struggling to gain a semblance of control. Her eyes went to the line of men again, each holding a shield with her father's crest on it. Two red lines on a white background. The image burned into her mind. Again her emotions roiled with white hot fury.

Her gaze sought Falcon, and he seemed completely unsurprised at the news. His face was stony, almost hostile.

He had known.

The fury at her situation spun to new heights. She turned on her father, feeling humiliated, used, and betrayed.

"You lied in your message," she snarled. "You set me up for your latest game. A guard at a nunnery, father? *Doris*? That was the best you could invent?"

Her father's eyes turned sharp, and his arm tensed. She willed herself to hold her ground, not to retreat back a step. He glanced at Falcon for a moment, then with an effort unclenched his fist.

I knew you were in good hands, my sweet," he finally growled. "I figured with the frame of mind you were in when you fled the keep that a little amnesia might do you some good." He paused for a moment, then leered at her with satisfaction. "Judging by your appearance, I would say it has done you a *lot* of good."

He reached out to possessively take hold of her arm.

His touch on her arm was a red hot poker, and she instantly flinched back from him. Everyone else faded from view except her father. She snarled, "You nearly broke my jaw. You planned to starve me into submission. I refused, point blank, to go through with this marriage. That is why I was fleeing the keep, alone, in the first place."

She thought back to that long night - riding, galloping at top speed, through the pouring rain. The image was replaced by another, of her mother riding furiously, pursued ... pursued ...

The shields!

Her eyes opened wide in shock. For a long moment all thought fled. She took a step backwards, her hand dropping automatically to the dagger at her hip.

It had been her father. Her father must have ordered her mother's death. The men who had taken down her mother had been carrying his shields.

It was as if she had a mosaic in her mind and the pieces merged, slid, and fit together in a new shape. She struggled to hold in her fury as she saw how they connected. Her mother had come from a wealthy family; her dowry had been impressive. He married her solely for her lands and money. The second he was able to, he had slain her mother and never looked back.

Storm took another quick step backwards, drawing her dagger in one smooth movement. She felt both Falcon's and her father's soldiers react instantly around her, drawing their own blades. They held still in alert readiness. A thought distantly whispered to her. Both sets of men had been her allies at one time. Both would dutifully cut her down now if ordered to do so.

Iron bands constricted her chest. She could barely breathe, her lungs drawing in long pulls.

She had to get away.

She spun on her heel, fled the room, and burst out into the courtyard, not stopping. The arch of the main gate streamed over her head. She only drew to a halt when she reached the grass beyond, when there was naught around her but blue sky and distant trees.

There were footsteps behind her. She turned, all hope being for Falcon's warm eyes. She craved for him to understand what she was going through; for him to stand by her side.

It was her father who strode up to her, his gaze surly. "Just what are you playing at, girl?" he snapped. His eyes moved to the dagger in her hands.

Storm had had enough. The rage burst out of her, taking on a life of its own.

"You murderer," she screamed in agony. "It was your men! You killed her!" She rotated the dagger more securely in her grasp. She had half a thought to drive it into him then and there; to plunge the blade deep into his chest.

"Laura, your mind is muddled." snapped her father, dismissing her accusations with a glare. "You clearly do not know what you are saying. You are still ill." He stopped speaking as his soldiers came out behind him. Their blades drawn, they arrayed themselves around him, a protective constellation.

He held her gaze with sharp focus. Storm wondered if, should she press the issue, he would simply have her slain. And, after all, how could she prove his involvement?

More men came to join the circle, and Storm began to feel hemmed in ... trapped. Her hand relished the texture of the hilt in her grasp, the dagger she always kept by her side. Always worn in defense since that day her mother had died.

She took a step forward toward her father. Her world narrowed down until it encompassed just the two of them. The blades of the guards closed in on her, and she knew she would never reach him if she tried for an attack. She would be cut down before her blade could land.

Frustration mounted in her, but she knew the odds were too great. She had to accept a truce, at least temporarily.

She brought her eyes up to hold his. "From this moment forward, I am no longer your daughter," she hissed at him under her breath. Her mind flicked back to the cell of a room, to the precious cargo remaining in the wooden box. "I will return to the keep and gather my few possessions. That done, I will quit myself of you and your life. You will be troubled by me no more. You have my word on that … *father*."

There was the sound of horses moving, and Storm became aware again of the large group which had formed outside the walls. Harold easily moved between the men, pressing them apart with the train of horses he led.

As he reached Storm and her father, Harold nodded to Lord Walker in greeting. "You will be wanting your mounts, I expect," he commented dryly.

Storm spotted her own steed in the group and wondered how her father had reacquired it after her flight. Perhaps it had gotten loose in the struggle and simply returned home of its own accord.

No matter. It was time to get this over with as quickly as possible. Standing tall, she turned toward the ring of her father's soldiers, daring them to stop her.

The men, uncertain, looked to Lord Walker for a signal, then drew aside their swords and let her pass. With one swift move she mounted her horse and sharply wheeled it to point toward the road home. Without a backwards look she urged her steed into a fast gallop, streaming down the path.

She realized, suddenly, that she had left her sword behind. She had not worn it down to the hall – she had felt it would be inappropriate to do so when first meeting the guests. Now it was lost to her. The thing she had loved most, the precious present given to her by Sarah, was now left behind in Falcon's keep.

All was lost …

The tears streamed down her face, and she wiped them away with her sleeve. It was silly to mourn the loss of a sword. It was a piece of metal. She could certainly acquire another one before she headed out to the nunnery. She would gather her small box of belongings, take an extra sword from the armory, and head north.

She would leave her life behind …

The tears cascaded down her face, and she let them come.

* * *

It was several hours before the steam had burnt itself out of her and she allowed herself to draw in to a stop. A pair of her father's guards had matched pace with her through her rounds of canters and trots. When she eventually drew to a stop by a small stream, one stayed nearby, watchfully silent, while the other whirled and rode out back the way they had come. She presumed he was alerting her father, and the following group, to where she was.

Storm washed her face in silence, then tended to her horse. By the time the others had arrived, she had found a mossy corner by a tree and had curled up in it. She feigned sleep, and none bothered her as the men set up camp. The smell of cooking rabbit made her stomach rumble, but she did not stir. If she could make this journey without once speaking to her father, it was worth the hunger pangs.

* * *

Storm's eyes fluttered open in the soft pre-dawn haze of light. The moistness of early morning dew glistened on her cheeks. She must be out on patrol – there was the familiar feel of lumpy moss beneath her; the snores and grumbles of her fellow soldiers sounded nearby. She racked her memory, pushing herself to a sitting position. Where were they off to this time?

Her eyes blinked wider, and she froze in place, her gaze coming across her father's slumbering form. The man never went out on a patrol. He never risked his own skin for the safety of his lands. Why was he here?

The events of the past weeks flooded in on her, and she drew her knees up against her chest, closing her eyes. A longing for Falcon cascaded through every corner of her being. She ached with the desire to have his arms wrap around her; for him to whisper in her ear that everything would be all right.

She pushed the feelings away with harsh effort. The men were stirring to life around her, stretching, grumbling, and she could not indulge herself in longings, not yet. There would be ample time for losing herself in her memories once she was fully free of her father's influence.

There was a movement at her side. Stuart, her young sparring partner, came up next to her, his pale face tense with worry. He glanced hesitantly back toward her father before dropping to one knee. His voice came in a low whisper.

"I thought you might want some food," he murmured, handing her a half loaf of bread along with an apple. His eyes scanned Storm, his face relaxing. "You are not hurt? When I heard you had fallen into Falcon's hands …"

A vivid image of Falcon leaning over her, gazing down at her with longing, swept over Storm, and she turned her head. "I am fine," she reassured the teen, taking the food from him. "You best get back to your duties, before my father sees you."

His eyes retained their concern, but he nodded, rising and returning to the group.

Storm ate quickly, then prepared her horse. The men around her were quick and efficient. The group was ready by the time she gave her horse a nudge and started on the final part of the journey home.

Not home.

Pain coursed through her as the roads became more familiar, as the landscapes brought to mind memories of countless previous patrols, of sultry summer afternoons and snow-laden winter routes. She no longer had a home. She had sought so desperately to regain her memories, to know where she was from, and now she longed to forget them all again. She had been happy when her world was fresh and new. Now she felt adrift, with no anchor to hold her in place.

A small village came into view. Her father made his way to the front of the group, riding proudly at the head of his entourage. A young child stood watching from beneath a birch tree, and his mother scrambled out, glancing fearfully at Lord Walker before sweeping up her child and moving back within their small, ramshackle home. Further along a shutter was carefully eased closed as they moved past. Lord Walker's arrogant gaze swept his domain, his eyes shining.

A weight settled on Storm's shoulders, and suddenly her memories of previous travels with her father were before her. It had always seemed so natural - the fear villagers had of him, the way they shied away, and his casual contempt. She had never had a frame of reference before. But now that she compared her father's actions with those of Falcon ...

Her eyes threatened to well again, and she gave her head a shake, pushing away the sensation. She did not have that luxury. Not now, not when escape was so close. She just had to get through the remaining few hours. She was almost at the keep.

Another twisting path through a dense wood, another series of low rises, and finally the long, grey wall and corner towers of her family's keep began to emerge from the greying twilight. A sense of gloom settled over Storm as the group came in beneath the main arch and circled to a stop in the central courtyard. The area seemed smaller, more neglected than she had remembered it.

She dismounted, tossed her reins at a waiting servant, and strode into the main keep. The quicker she got through her departure, the less chance there was that her father could create impediments for her. She knew, if he had half a chance, that he would attempt to draw her into a fresh set of machinations.

She moved with purpose through the main hall, heading toward the stairs which led up to her room. To her surprise, she spotted a familiar, white-haired figure sitting at a table in one corner.

The elderly man looked up at her approach, beaming with pleasure. "Laura, my dear, it is so good to see you!" He took her with both arms and tenderly kissed her forehead.

"Matthew, what are you doing here? Who is tending to your shop?" Storm gazed with fond warmth at the potter's wrinkled face. She was immediately reminded of his work, of the beautiful blue vase with the bulbous base. She had left it behind. It currently waited for her on a windowsill in Falcon's keep. It held a collection of reeds, gathered by Falcon, placed there with his hands to comfort her.

Storm could again feel the strength of his arms; the powerful depths of his eyes. She drew in a long, deep breath. Only a few more minutes. She had to keep these longings at bay until then.

Matthew was looking at her with concern. She forced a smile back to her face, reassuring her old friend. "I am fine, it has just been a long day," she explained. "Are you here to bring us some fresh supplies?"

Matthew shook his head, his gaze still holding worry as he looked her over. "Your father ordered me out here a few days ago, insisting it was urgent. I am not quite sure what he wanted." He took a long draw on his ale, looking around. "Since then, it is as if he completely forgot about me. I have been waiting to hear his desire. I of course do not want to press him ..."

Storm thought back to Thom's report - how he had found the potter's location but the man himself was absent. The pieces suddenly clicked. "My father probably had heard we were looking for you and wanted to get you out of reach," she mused, looking at her old friend. "If Thom had described me to you, you would have known in an instant who he was talking about."

"Thom? Who is Thom?" asked the lean potter in confusion.

Storm smiled and patted his arm. "It is a long story, and I will tell it all to you later on, when you are able to return home. For now, I need to gather up a few things. I wish you fond travels; I am sure my father will be releasing you soon."

She turned, her heart beating quicker now that she saw what lengths her father had gone through to maintain his deception. She took the stairs to her room two at a time.

Her room was much as she left it. The thick curtains were pulled snugly across her window, and her small bed was neatly made.

She knelt beside her window, laying her hand fondly on the small wooden box that had for so long protected her personal mementos. She lifted the lid. Everything was as she had left it. The delicately woven scarf left to her by her mother. A small sapphire and silver locket that her mother had given to her for her wedding day. A poetry codex wrapped with care. She verified that all was secure, then closed the small chest's lid with a click.

A louder click echoed in her ears, and she looked up in disbelief at her door. The thick oak had bolts on both sides, and she found, as she ran to it, that the outside bolt was now firmly in place.

Her father was trying it yet again.

"You have no right!" she screamed, incredulous that her father would conceive of holding her prisoner after everything she had been through. "Let me out of here *now*!"

She rained her fists on the door, hammering, but to her surprise her father did not even respond to her pleas. There were no taunts. No challenges. The keep echoed in its silence.

Her eyes sparked with fury. If he thought he would keep her in with a mere lock, he would be vastly mistaken. She spun on her heel and strode toward the curtains, tossing them open.

An incredulous shock staggered her. She dropped to her knees, her heart stopping.

Iron bars had been installed in a grate across the entire window. Her escape route had been cut off. She was absolutely trapped. She was completely under the control of her father.

She collapsed into her bed, her mind refusing to work. There was no other way out of her cell. There were none who would care what happened to her here. For all she knew, her father simply planned to starve her to death in punishment for her actions since he had retrieved her. All hope drained out of her, and she closed her eyes in despair.

A warmth filled her, suddenly. The sense of strong arms holding her. The nuzzling of a head against hers. A gentle voice telling her that everything would be all right.

She rolled on her side, wrapping her arms about herself, allowing her to lose herself in the memories - and in the longing.

Chapter 23

A noise snapped Storm to instant wakefulness, and her hand shot beneath her pillow.

It grasped empty air.

Panic swept through her. She pushed herself up, sitting up on her thin mattress and glancing around the darkened room.

The curtains were still open. A scattering of stars was visible in the night sky.

The sound came again; it was from outside her window. She stood and carefully gazed out through the bars. The creaking was coming from above her. To her surprise she saw that a thin wicker basket hung there, dangling from a rope undoubtedly lowered from the roof. The basket was narrow enough to draw through the bars, and she carefully eased it through the tight space.

Opening the lid, she found a skin of mulled cider, a loaf of brown bread, and a hunk of cheese. Storm did not hesitate; she was famished. She eagerly wolfed down the fare. She recognized that she would have to keep her strength up for whatever came. She might have lost her sword, but opportunity might yet present itself.

Only a few minutes after eating, she suddenly felt drowsy. She stared at the skin, rage sweeping through her. God's teeth, the man would resort to any trick he could concoct. Her father had undoubtedly drugged her drink.

The lethargy quickly set in. She dragged herself into the corner of her bed, setting her back up against the wall, but she knew it was no use. In minutes her heavy eyelids had fallen shut, and the world drifted from view.

* * *

A loud slamming noise, of a bar being dropped into place, and she was jolted awake, her hand reaching ... but it jarred against a restraint. Her hands were held together by the tight pull of a rope. The dry fabric of a gag was firmly in her mouth, and it seemed that even her ankles had been tied. She glanced around the dark room in a panic, but there was nobody else in sight.

Myriad thoughts deluged her, and she fought to bring them into a semblance of order. There was nobody else here; why bother to gag her? Her door was sturdy and barred. Her window, solidly blocked. Why in the world would he need to bind her hand and foot?

She wrestled with the ropes at her wrists, attempting to get each one to loosen, if only slightly. Her frustration increased as she found they would not budge even the tiniest fraction of an inch. Apparently they had learned from their previous mistakes. Still, she kept at it, her brow furrowed in determination, as the soft pre-dawn light eased into the room, drifting across the rough wood floor.

There was a fresh sound from outside the window. At first it was a distant rumble, but soon it became the merged thunder of several hoofbeat coming at a canter up the main road to the keep. They turned off before the main gates, circling around the outer walls.

Storm's heart pounded against her ribs, and she pulled herself up to a sitting position. Her waist caught, and she snarled in frustration. The man had even tied her waist to the handle of her door, preventing her from getting any closer to the window. Was this his aim? To keep her from being seen by whoever was approaching?

The hoofbeat came to a clattering stop below her window, and there was a call. It was the voice she heard in her dreams;

the one she craved with all her being. The one she now knew as well as the worn feel of the ring on her finger.

"Storm! Storm, it is Falcon! Are you in there, Storm?"

Tears streamed down her eyes as she flooded with relief, desire, and longing. She screamed against her gag, thrashing against her bonds, but her noises were feeble and lost against the fabric wound to her mouth. Her strongest pulls did not even slightly release the ties around her. Frustration swallowed her, hearing his sharp cries for her, and there was no way to answer. There was no way to let him know how much she needed him.

She flung herself with every ounce of strength against the ropes. The wound material cut into her skin, leaving long, crimson welts against her flesh, but they did not budge an inch. Again and again she screamed until her throat was hoarse and dry.

Finally he stopped calling. The hoofbeat circled beneath her window, and she glanced with frustration at the iron bars. Surely he could see they were a new addition and surmise that she was being held within this cell. There was no way for him to reach her, however. He would need to first surmount the outer curtain wall and then scale the inner tower, all while warding off her father's troops.

The hoofbeat moved at a trot back toward the main gate, and the keep eased into a fresh silence. She lay back against the mat, exhausted. Now it was up to her father. It was up to whatever plans Lord Walker had in mind for her.

She was suddenly flooded with a realization, and the force of it took her breath away.

She had been engaged to Falcon.

Everything had happened so quickly that she had not had time to take stock of the situation.

She was Laura.

She was Falcon's intended bride.

With all her longing and restraint, she was the one who would have been loyally at Falcon's side. She would have been the mistress of his keep. She would have been able to ride with him on springtime afternoons, able to snuggle in his study for a game of chess and a mug of mulled wine ...

The tears came again, and she shook her head at the insanity of it all. She had lived through such torment, and the whole while Falcon had been hers, had been there for her to take, if she had just reached out her hand and claimed him. If she had only realized the full import on that day when her father had arrived.

The clear image of Falcon's eyes on that day came before her, and her chest ached. He had not spoken one word to her on the day she had met her father. He had stood by while she had been deluged by her memories flooding back in on her. His gaze had been cold, dismissive, and untrusting. Jessica had been alight with triumph, and he had built a wall separating them. What could have happened to turn his heart so soundly?

Her mind sought back. The previous day ... that had been the day he asked her to throw the knives at the target.

The images began to snap into a sequence. Her heart sank, a dark understanding wrapping itself in a cold embrace around her.

The day before. He had gazed at her, after her breakthrough in the tower, and he had said something. What had it been?

"*J'espere que cela vous convenient, ma chere?*"

Her heart stopped. The timeline was complete. Falcon must have suspected who she was. He had remembered the list of traits Laura was known to possess. He then laid out a plan of action to prove his suspicions.

She wrapped her arms tightly around herself. No doubt Jessica had encouraged him, claiming that Storm was aware of her past at every moment. Jessica probably warned that Storm was playing Falcon for a fool. She knew how Falcon felt about deceptions. It might have been Jessica's one tactic with a chance for success.

Anger and disappointment swept through Storm in a tumultuous rush. After all they had been through together, Falcon did not trust her enough to give her even one chance to explain? It seemed too hard to take in, but his actions could not be explained in any other manner.

Her mind went again to the meeting with her father. Falcon had been completely shuttered, while Jessica had glowed in triumph. Storm realized ruefully that her own behavior had done little to help her cause. She had been filled with fury, quick to draw a weapon on her own father. If Falcon had fostered concerns about her "true nature," she had proven to him how little like the calm, caring woman he had grown to care for she truly was.

Empty desolation grew beneath her, and she sank into its depths. In Falcon's eyes, she was naught but another deceiver who had taken advantage of his trustworthy nature. She had manipulated him, coerced him, and almost drawn him into her trap. He would undoubtedly be below expressing his fury at Lord Walker for the machinations. He would be utterly refusing any future truce or marriage.

All was lost.

Falcon was lost to her forever.

She closed her eyes, releasing her last remnants of hope.

* * *

Church bells chimed, pulling her awake with their melodious sounds. She blearily opened her eyes. Streaks of golden daylight streamed through the window's bars, setting a striped pattern across the floor of her room. Her bonds had been removed and the gag gone. A mug of wine, a half loaf of bread, and a wedge of cheese were stacked on her box beneath her window.

She crawled weakly out of bed. Ignoring the food, she made her way to the door, giving it a firm tug. It was still securely barred. She next made her way to the bars, gripping the cold metal with her hands and leaning heavily against them.

No savior gazed back up at her with fierce determination.

Falcon had gone.

She collapsed wearily next to the food. Despite her fears, she began eating as much as she could, washing it down with the wine. If they planned on drugging her, so be it. She needed the nourishment more than she could afford to worry about their plots.

When she finished the meal she collapsed back onto the bed, beyond thought. The dark and light shadows drifted across the floor of the room, and she watched them move with utter disinterest. There was nothing left.

Footsteps sounded distantly, grew closer, and then came to a halt outside her door. She looked up with only the smallest sense of interest. It mattered little now.

Her father's voice was sharp, brooking no opposition. "Laura. Are you awake?"

Storm considered playing silent, to lure him in. She shook her head. She could barely stand against the bull of a man at her healthiest; to try him now would be suicide.

She strove to draw her thoughts into cohesion, to consider her options. To begin with, she knew it was always critical to hide any weakness from him. She could not provide him with any opportunity to take advantage. She filled her voice with as much strength as she could muster.

"Yes, I am awake. What do you want?"

Her father's voice was firm and unyielding. "You will be glad to hear I am no longer turning you over to Falcon. You had clearly begun to fall under his spell, and your presence there would now serve his purposes, not mine." He drew in a breath. "In addition, your ... retrieved memory, although flawed, could have caused problems. Therefore, I have accepted your refusal of the offer. When Falcon visited, I made it clear to him that you have been against this alliance from the start, and that the offer is no longer on the table. He has been sent away. You will have nothing to fear from that quarter, ever again."

Waves of blackness coursed over her, and she drew her knees to her chest, utterly lost. Yes, there had been a brief time that the thought of marriage with Falcon had filled her heart with fury. Since then, so much had changed ...

She closed her eyes and lay back on the bed, exhausted with grief.

Her father's voice echoed through the door, harsh with disapproval. "There is still the matter of a match for you. I cannot be expected to feed and clothe you forever – and I deserve some payback for the years I have spent raising you. I can hardly allow you to simply traipse out of this keep without any compensation."

"Therefore, I am handing you over to Much, the leader of our ... associates to the West. He has been quite a loyal ally of ours for many years. He will keep you out of harm's way. He has also got the ability to deal with that fiery nature of yours. I think he is the man to tame you."

Storm could not have thought that her emotions could become more jumbled. It was as if she had been swirling in a darkened whirlpool and suddenly she realized that this was just one small part of a cavernously huge storm.

She was being sent completely into Much's control?

The man would brutalize her. He would make her life a hellacious torment. She would dream of death. She might willingly seek it.

She thought of speaking out, of pleading with her father, but she knew he would not turn from his purpose. He would certainly never let her into Falcon's home again. He undoubtedly knew that, in a heartbeat, she would reveal to Falcon every detail of Lord Walker's castle defenses and guard strengths. She had served with Walker's troops for her entire life. She knew the weaknesses of the men and the keep, inside and out.

Yes, she had no doubt that her father would keep her as far away from Falcon as possible.

The footsteps faded from her door, and she collapsed back against the bed again. The light from the window grew golden, then rosy, then finally faded into an inky darkness.

The quiet sound of hoofbeat approached; a trio of riders. Her hand slid half-heartedly beneath her pillow, closing on nothing. There was no hope. No way to protect herself.

The horses came into the courtyard, and it was only a short time later before footsteps were drawing close within the keep.

They came to a stop before her door. She wearily pulled herself into a seated position.

The door flung open, and her father stood in the doorway, along with a short, tubby man with reddish hair. Storm did not say a word or move. The man slowly smiled, running his eyes lecherously down the full length of her body. His eyes returned to her lips, and he chuckled.

"I am Much. Surely you remember me." He paused, then snapped, "Well, can you speak, girl?" His oily voice gained a sharp edge.

Storm was tempted to stay silent, but she knew this battle was not one she could win. It was best to save her strength for later, when she was free of this room. "Yes," came her short reply. "I have a tongue in my head."

Much's grin widened. "Well that is good for the both of us," he commented slyly.

Satisfied, he turned to her father. "You have yourself a bargain," he stated decisively. "Let us go down and drink to seal it. Have your guards put her in that spare wagon in your stables. There is a chain in there that connects around the axle; I use it for some of my more … excitable purchases."

The two men left, and four guards moved in against her. She took on a pliant, docile posture. She could not hope to win against these strong guards, and even if she did, she was still stuck in this cell. They would help to bring her out closer to escape.

Storm was less sure of herself when a leather ankle cuff was securely fastened to her. A locked chain led down from the restraint into the lower reaches of the wagon. The wagon looked extremely familiar with its piles of rags and assorted boxes. She wondered if it was the exact one she had been kidnapped in, so long ago. Certainly the guard who watched over her could have been a cousin of that man who tried to rape her. His sallow complexion and reedy frame seemed familiar.

This guard seemed to have better control over himself; he barely looked her way. He passed the time whittling at a piece of wood.

Storm hunkered down in a dark corner of the wagon, conserving her strength.

The moon was high in the sky by the time her father and Much came down to the wagon. Her father glanced in at her, placing her small chest and dagger in a far corner of the wagon. "These are yours, after all, girl," he commented with another look in her direction. "Perhaps with these items by your side you will not find it necessary to return to the keep again for any *family visit*."

He glanced her over, then continued. "Who knows, you might actually find happiness with Much. I hear he has tamed many wild beasts. In any case, in a few days their priest will make you man and wife, and we will find out!"

Much seemed to like this jest greatly; his belly shook with his laughter. Then he clasped her father's hand in farewell. The flap on the wagon was closed and the wheels creaked into motion.

Storm steeled herself to be strong. She was out of her prison and out of the keep. There was still hope.

Chapter 24

Apparently Much wanted to take his time with his first attack on her, or maybe her father had felt one small iota of paternal instinct and insisted on this as part of their agreement. Whatever the reason, Storm found herself blessedly alone all night as the wagon slowly creaked and bounced its way down the forest path. She was tied up and gagged, but other than that she was left to her own devices. The wagon's movement was the only sound she heard.

They could not move quickly in the darkness, but apparently they had no desire to stop for any length of time in the woods. They took short breaks every few hours to rest and swap the animals, but other than that the wagon and outriders continued doggedly along their course.

Storm allowed herself to sleep, conserving her energy, but she only got a few hours of restless dreams in before she was awake again. Night warmed into day, and Storm's captors brought her food and drink at regular intervals. She was allowed out to walk around for a short while every few hours, to stretch her legs and relieve herself. She was guarded at all times. The leg chain was kept securely on her, held like a leash by one of the men. Still, she used the time to recover strength in her legs.

While the wagon rolled, she did what exercises she could. She pressed her arms against each other. She pressed her feet against the walls of the wagon. She was going to be as ready as she could be when the moment was right.

Darkness came on again, and exhaustion overcame her. She was nearly at the point of drifting away, lulled to sleep by the rolling wheels, when she heard an odd sound.

Whoo – Whoo - Whoo.

It sounded like an owl … but it was not. Owls did not call out in even, repeated triplicate like that.

Her hopes rose. Could it be …

The back of the wagon's flap drifted open for a moment, and a dark shape slipped into the cart. The sallow guard looked up from his whittling in alarm, preparing to raise a cry – and was immediately silenced by Falcon's sword slicing across his neck. In a heartbeat Falcon was at her side, his eyes gazing into hers, deep with concern and care. He gently pulled free her gag.

Storm was lost in his gaze. Her heart pounding, love and passion cascading over her in waves. "I thought I had lost you," she whispered, her throat tight.

His hand moved shakily to stroke her hair, and he leant his forehead against hers for a long moment.

"I have lost faith in you three times now, and each time I have been proven wrong," he murmured hoarsely. "I swear I shall never doubt you again."

There was a noise from outside, and he turned with a quick motion, raising his sword in a protective move. "We have to go. Are you ready?"

Storm motioned down to her leg which had the thick leather cuff on it. Falcon followed her gaze and started, his eyes flashing in anger. His eyes adjusted more fully to the dark, and they went to the ropes now visible at her arms and legs. He began with those, carefully slicing her free. Then he eyed the tight leather cuff with concern.

Storm scrambled awkwardly over to her chest. The dagger was right on top. She sat back, setting to work with the narrow, sharp blade, cautiously wiggling its thin shape in between her ankle and cuff. She sawed her way through the binding with small movements. It took a few heart-stopping moments, but it finally fell free with only a soft clatter.

Falcon moved toward Storm's small box and nodded with recognition. He grabbed it up with one hand, settling it beneath his arm. Storm slid her knife into her belt. When she was ready, Falcon helped Storm toward the back of the wagon. They peered out. The night was inky black – the moon had set and they could barely see the horsemen who rode guard several paces behind the wagon's tail.

"Can you do this silently?" whispered Falcon in concern. "I have men with me, but it would be better -"

Storm nodded shortly. "I can do it," she promised resolutely. She would manage, even if it meant her legs throbbed in searing agony.

Falcon watched the ground until they came to a patch of dry, barren earth. Then he gently tugged at Storm, and the two let themselves down from the wagon. Storm bit back a cry as her weakened legs landed on the hard ground. Immediately the pair slipped to the side of the path and into the forest. They crouched down there, still as field mice, waiting with held breath while the rest of the wagon train passed them by. Only when the turning wheels and hoofbeat were a faded memory did they relax.

Falcon still did not allow his voice to rise above a faint whisper. "What was their pattern yesterday? Would they ..." he hesitated, then forced himself to continue. "Would he come to you by night?"

Storm shook her head no, and then realized that he might not be able to see the motion in the dark. "They would not disturb me until morning, for breakfast. We have many hours before they realize I am gone."

Falcon exhaled in relief, then stood. He called out with his soft hoot several times. In a moment, five of his men came up to find the pair, trailing enough horses for everyone. Storm recognized John, David, and Shawn in the party, and nodded her grateful thanks to them.

Falcon brought forward a horse for Storm, and she was pleased to see that Mercury was as eager to see her as she was to see him. She mounted in an instant. Soon the group was riding back as quickly as they could through the darkened trail toward the keep.

If Storm had been on the verge of exhaustion before in the wagon, then she was the walking dead by the time they approached the outer walls the next afternoon. Her eyes were having trouble focusing. When the horses came to stop in the courtyard, it was all she could do to stay in her saddle.

Falcon was beside her in a moment, helping her down and then carrying her to her room. She was asleep before her head hit the pillow.

Chapter 25

Storm awoke to the familiar surroundings of her room in Falcon's keep. She lay in bed for a long while, wondering how everything seemed the same, while everything was now so different. She knew her entire past – even parts of her past which had been hidden to her all these years. She knew now that Falcon was free to love her and marry her. He had been betrothed to her this entire time.

She also knew that the truce he was hoping to achieve with this marriage was not worth the paper it was written on.

It seemed a fine mix of ironies.

A soft knocking sounded at the door, and then Falcon came into the room carrying a tray of breakfast food. He closed the door behind him, sliding the bolt in place. Storm looked up in alarm, but he shook his head reassuringly at her.

"No, there is no reason yet to fear any attack," he soothed as he moved around to the side of the bed. "I just would like to have time to talk with you, uninterrupted by any messengers or maids."

He settled down on the stool, sitting by her head, and helped her pull herself up to a seated position. Storm's stomach fluttered with nervousness as she tried to force herself to eat a few items. She knew she should be starving, but having Falcon's serious eyes on her caused all of her old fears to surface.

What was he thinking about? How did he feel?

Falcon waited patiently for her to finish eating, then moved the tray to the foot of the bed before returning to sit by her side. He took her hands in his own and met her gaze with his. His deep, brown eyes seemed bottomless.

"I want you to be honest with me, Storm. I can accept any truthful feeling or deed. We can get through anything life throws at us as long as we have that trust."

He paused, then continued hoarsely, "When you first came here, did you have any memories of your past? Was your amnesia an act?"

Storm exhaled deeply. If what he wanted was honesty, then that was something she would gladly provide. "I swear, on my mother's grave, there was no falsehood on my part" she responded with equal sincerity. "Every word I told you, every memory I shared, was exactly as it occurred to me. I did not have any idea of my true background until my father stood before me in your hall."

Falcon let out his breath and raised her hand to his lips. "I believe in you."

His eyes held hers. "Three times, now, I have doubted your intentions. First, when you arrived at our keep. Your skills with the blade, your interests in our defensive structures, all seemed to support the idea that you were working with the bandits."

He flushed and looked down. "Second, that afternoon in the clearing. When you offered yourself to me, all I could think of was how Sheila had done the same thing. How it had been a deliberate act designed to manipulate me. It took me a long night of soul-searching to accept that you honestly had fallen in love with me as much as I had you."

His eyes drew back up to meet hers. "Finally, that day in the tower, when you cried so heartbreakingly. I knew at that moment how much I adored you – and the strength of my feelings again brought me back to Sheila. I recalled how she had planned her deception so carefully; how she had made that scene the cornerstone of her plot. But Sheila's pivotal scene had hinged on a true event – that is what gave it its power."

His lips pressed. "My mind searched for how yours could be true, and suddenly I remembered that there had been controversy swirling around Laura's mother's death. Laura had been that same age at the time."

He drew Storm's hands within his own. "Suddenly all the pieces had fallen into place. Your skills with the knife. Your interest in the keep. It struck me with full force that you were not with the bandits – you were with Lord Walker. You were planning a final assault from the inside."

Storm gazed at him, fully open to him, holding nothing back. "I swear to you, I am completely innocent of any deceptions. I have always been utterly truthful with you."

He was caught in her eyes, and he slowly nodded. "That is what makes this so amazing. I doubted, and I looked for hidden meanings, and I fought against my heart's desire." He ran a shaking hand down the side of her cheek, and she nuzzled against the warmth. "I hereby release those memories of the past, the ones which held me back, which twisted and filtered what I was seeing. I will start afresh with you, and together we will create our own memories."

His eyes held hers. "Storm, I love you."

Storm's world shimmered into crystal clarity. Her eyes were transfixed by his. Her ears echoed with the words, drawing them deep into her soul and wrapping them around her heart.

He loved her.

Falcon seemed to move in slow motion; he pressed his lips to her hand for a long moment. When he spoke again, his voice was thick with emotion.

"For so long we both struggled against the idea of marrying who we imagined our mate to be. But when we had the reality of one another, I could feel the power of our bond in every glance, in every touch." He gave a wry grin. "Perhaps we owe the bandits, and your father, a debt of gratitude. They helped us to get past our misconceptions."

He slipped down onto one knee, and Storm's heart leapt into her throat. Only a few hours ago she had been desperately hoping for Falcon to forgive her. It was only the faintest of dreams that he …

"Storm, I will not risk your father pulling you away from me again. Will you marry me?"

Storm slid her hand into his thick locks and pulled him down onto her body, murmuring yes against his lips even as he kissed her, even as he pressed himself to her. He loved her. Against all hope, against all wild chance, he was by her side. They would be together forever. Her body glowed with joyous brilliance.

Falcon pulled himself away with a last gasp of self-control, his breath coming in ragged heaves. "We have made it this far; let us get married immediately and do this properly. I will send immediately for the parish priest, if you are willing …?"

A broad smile stretched across Storm's lips. "Oh so willing, My Lord," she breathed, her eyes shining with passion.

Groaning, Falcon nearly gave in to her offer. Instead, with a fierce effort, he turned and strode to the door. Unbarring it and opening it, he called out for a messenger.

Mary came running in when the news spread, bustling Falcon out of the room.

"It is bad luck for the groom to see the bride on her wedding day!" she exclaimed as she closed the door behind him.

Storm burst out in a gale of laughter. After everything else that had happened, that was the least of her worries.

Mary left for a moment, then returned with a gorgeous sapphire-blue dress, rich with fine embroidery. Storm's mouth hung open at the beautiful creation.

"Carol made this for you," explained Mary with a grin. "She never had a chance to present it to you when you left, and when she heard that you had returned yesterday, she immediately brought it over."

"What could I have done to deserve this gift?" asked Storm in shock, looking over the fine construction of the dress. The details were exquisite, more intricate even than many of the dresses that Jessica had worn.

"Ironically enough, it was because of her niece, Jessica," explained Mary with a smile. "Carol had heard from the keep staff how much you tried to be kind to her, even with the way Jessica treated you and the others. Carol appreciated your efforts, even if they were in vain. Not many would have even attempted to be cordial."

Storm looked up at this, a thought crossing her mind. "Is Jessica still in the building?" She wondered with worry if Jessica had yet another trick up her sleeve to cause unpleasantness in the coming hours.

Mary shook her head, her eyes sharpening. "There is a tale to tell there. It turns out Jessica knew who you were – she had known it since she went to visit her father."

Storm turned in shock. "She knew? Why did she not tell me?"

Mary nodded. "You would think so, but instead, she actively pushed Falcon more strongly to have you leave. It seems she figured that you had resisted the marriage so strongly before, that as long as she could keep you out of his reach, you would go home, regain your memory, and renew your resistance there. In the meantime, Falcon might never realize you were the person pledged to him."

Storm thought through the options. "I imagine she was worried that Falcon, who had already resigned himself to marrying Laura Walker, would be more set on doing so once he knew it was me. So she could not just tell him the truth."

Mary sat down beside Storm on the bed. "I agree. When she could not convince Falcon to send you away, she had to risk the truth. She confronted Falcon the evening before you were to go – saying that she had discovered a traitor. She revealed that you were in fact Laura Walker, here explicitly to learn the keep's secrets in preparation for an assault."

Mary paused, then continued more quietly. "Apparently Jessica's tactic was bolstered by his suspicion that you were Laura."

Storm's mind thought back to those days. "That is what he was doing," she agreed softly. "He was testing my skills against those Laura would have."

Mary sat to brush out Storm's hair. "Even when he became convinced that you were Laura, he still believed that you had amnesia. Falcon and Jessica fought fiercely about it the night before the Walkers arrived. Jessica told him the proof would be how you behaved when you were confronted with the group. She stated that your falsehood would never hold up in their presence, and that you would revert to knowing them."

Storm's eyes sharpened in anger. "I did have amnesia," she insisted hotly. "It was seeing them that triggered my memories' return!"

Mary shushed her, gently pulling through the knots. "That is exactly what Falcon said. Jessica insisted that you were a liar and a traitor. Once you left, they got into a huge row which lasted an entire afternoon."

Her eyes shadowed. "Finally, Falcon said that he would go after you, to learn the truth. Jessica claimed that it was too late – that you were to be given to her father to be 'gentled.' You should have seen his face. Once she said that, there was no stopping him. He immediately gathered a group and headed out."

Mary shook her head at the memory. "The moment he was out the gate, Jessica gathered her things and left for her father's. She has not been seen since."

Storm sighed in relief. Whatever machinations Jessica had constructed, she was now gone.

She took pleasure in Mary's primps and attentions, and soon she was fully dressed and prepared. As a final touch, she took out the sapphire locket that her mother had given her so many years ago. She had tears in her eyes as she fastened it around her neck.

A knock sounded on the door – the priest had arrived. Mary and Storm headed down the hall toward the main room.

It seemed that the entire keep had turned out with only an hour or two's notice. Falcon waited in the main hall, his leather armor and scabbard freshly oiled and gleaming. Storm's heart filled with pride. Now that she remembered her own past, her own skill with sword and horse, she was even more sure that

Falcon was the perfect match for her. Together, side by side, they would keep their home and its people safe – no matter what came.

Falcon took her arm, and the group moved en masse toward the small chapel at the side of the main building. Storm's legs trembled as they walked from the sunlight into the shady recesses by the front steps of the small stone building.

Storm was floating on a cloud. The courtyard filled quickly with the residents of the keep and the village. Falcon stood by her side at the steps, his face shining with pride and love.

Everything seemed to move quickly. The priest gave a talk rich with symbolism and meaning, and they recited vows of loyalty and honor. It seemed like only moments before they were pronounced man and wife.

Then Falcon turned to face her, and the world drew to a stop. He bent down to kiss her. The touch was like nothing she had ever felt before. She was his now, and he belonged to her. Nothing could separate them.

Together the group headed in to the chapel for a full mass, and Storm did not hear a single word. It seemed a heartbeat before they were exiting in a noisy, cheering throng, heading back into the main hall. A feast was laid out, hastily put together from the kitchens of every woman in the village. It smelled heavenly – but Storm had eyes only for her husband. The hunger which filled every corner of her being was one only he could satisfy.

Falcon's eyes showed that he was caught up in the same strong emotions. Over the din of toasting and revelry, he called Mary over.

"You and Molly have done wonders here with the food," he praised her, "but we shall be retiring to our room. Feel free to carry on all week if you wish, and send up mead and cheese – but knock first!"

Mary enveloped him in a warm hug, then turned to Storm. Her wrinkled face shone. "You deserve it, my lass. You will make Lord Falcon the happiest man on Earth.".

* * *

Storm had never been to Falcon's room, and she felt shy when he opened the door before her and led her into his private sanctuary. It was clean and neat, with dark burgundy curtains and blankets. The dressers and shelves were of the same fine, oak construction as her own room's furnishings.

A large wall hanging to one side showed a falcon in flight, coming down to roost at a nest which held a female falcon with three eggs.

Storm's eyes were caught by the hanging, and she turned to look at Falcon, her voice hoarse with passion. "Three children? We shall have to get started right away, then."

Falcon groaned with desire, effortlessly sweeping her up in his arms and carrying her over to the bed. He laid her down gently, and stood back a moment to admire her, love and need shining in his eyes.

Storm reached up to draw him down, and their souls merged.

* * *

To Storm the ensuing week was one of soul-lifting pleasures, a week that she could never have imagined in her wildest dreams. Falcon never left her side, and their love for each other grew with each passing day. The finest dishes were ferried in by laughing, knocking servants, along with delicious meads and wines.

Every night they fell asleep, exhausted, entwined in each other's arms. Every morning she awoke in astonished joy to find him stretched out by her side. She felt she would never tire of the simple pleasure of being next to him.

Chapter 26

After a week of honeymoon had drifted by in tumultuous abandon, Storm knew it was time to start behaving like the responsible adults they were.

She gave Falcon a gentle kiss on the nose when he awoke. "Not that I mind lounging around in bed all day ..." she admitted to her handsome husband.

"Or a week," he interjected with a warm smile.

Her eyes twinkled as she continued. "Still, it would hardly do for us to become fat and lazy while our keep fell to ruins around us. Perhaps it was time we began rejoining the world, to see just how the guards' training has fared without us."

Falcon chuckled, tracing his hand along her cheek. "Now that we know you are a Walker, why of course we want to keep training with you. Who knows what insights you will be able to offer about a family which may shortly be at our gates."

Storm's eyes sparkled with glee. "Now that my memory has returned, there is quite a lot of knowledge I can provide for our defense," she agreed readily. "We will be the safest fortification in the entire land once we are through."

The two dressed quickly, and were greeted warmly by the staff when they descended to the main hall. Heather came over promptly with two mugs, then laid out platters of crispy bacon and boiled ham.

Storm and Falcon were just finishing up the meal when Zach ran up to the table, his face solemn.

"There is a messenger from the Walkers waiting at the main gate," he nervously informed his Lord.

Storm's blood ran cold. Was her father planning to force her return? Would he attempt to annul her marriage? She turned to Falcon, her eyes tense.

Falcon put his hand reassuringly over her own, his gaze steady. "Go ahead, Zach. Let the man in," he instructed smoothly. He pulled his chair slightly away from the table, leaving his sword free.

In a few minutes there were footsteps down the main hall. A muscular messenger, dressed in the Walker colors, slowly approached the head table, drawing a sealed note from within his tunic. He held it up to Falcon, then placed it on the table before him. That done, he stood silently, waiting.

Falcon ran a practiced eye down the messenger, then turned his attention to the missive. He picked up the note and broke the seal with the flick of a finger. After one more glance at the man before him he sat back to scan the contents.

When he was done, he turned to Storm, his eyes reassuring.

"Your father has heard about our wedding, of course," he began in a matter-of-fact voice. "Now that our marriage is sealed, your father feels that a truce is in order. He does not want to be warring with the house of his daughter. He says we are all family now."

Storm openly scoffed at this idea. "My father's idea of family is using someone until they can conveniently be killed," she warned with heat. "I would not trust him over far."

Falcon nodded in agreement. He glanced for a moment at the messenger, then continued. "Still, if your father signs something, he might not be willing to break his word openly. That would cause all of his other truces with his neighbors to become suspect, and several of them would love an opportunity to go back on their agreements. It may be worth it, to hear him out."

Storm poked at a piece of bacon with her knife. "I do not trust that man," she repeated with soft fury. She looked up at Falcon, her eyes filling with pain. "If he gets you within his walls, what is to say that you will ever come out again? I could not stand to lose you."

Falcon shook his head. "Lord Walker is suggesting a neutral location – a small church halfway between our two bases. I know the priest there, and trust him. That way there is no threat of an ambush, and if we both take five men, the odds should be even." He paused for a moment, then looked resolved. "If there is even the smallest chance of a truce, even a false one, we would be wise to see what he has to say."

Falcon turned to look up at the messenger, who was waiting at attention, a stony look on his face.

"Tell your master that I will meet him four days hence," he instructed with quiet firmness.

The messenger nodded in agreement, then turned and headed out.

Storm looked up with worry at Falcon. "Are you sure about this?" she asked with trepidation.

He tenderly kissed her on the forehead, smoothing down her long hair. "I will be fine."

* * *

The next few days dragged by anxiously for Storm. The other-worldly beauty of the honeymoon had transformed into a sense of foreboding doom. She treasured every moment she spent with Falcon, worried that it might be her last.

When the morning of the meeting dawned, Storm found herself unable to leave her husband's side. She wanted to be with him every minute before he left. She helped him dress and walked down to the stables with him.

Falcon joined his men there. John, his captain, was in the group, as well as David and Shawn, their eager faces shining. The men waited patiently while Falcon gave a farewell embrace to his bride.

Falcon looked around at the guards who surrounded them. "We should be back by tomorrow evening," he let them know. "You know the spot – come to meet us if we have not returned by then." He looked down to Zach, who stood by his side. "Zach will be stationed halfway at a village, to ferry messages if needed. If we run into trouble sooner, we will light a signal fire, and Zach will be back to you as soon as possible to bring relief."

He nodded reassuringly to the group. "I am sure there will be no trouble. Walker is family now, and the truce is all but assured."

Harold stood to one side as the men mounted and turned their steeds out toward the main gate. His normally dour face held a hint of a smile, and Storm took this as a good sign.

"You think Falcon and his group will be fine, then?" she asked of the normally truculent man.

Harold nodded slowly, a wry grin coming across his features. "Yes, I think that today shall be a very good day," he prophesized. "You just wait and see."

Storm took heart at this and followed the group out to the main gates. She stood in the center of the opening, watching as the men rode into the distance. She dismissed her nagging concerns as she stared after them until they had vanished into the trees.

* * *

There was nothing to do now but wait. She went up to her bedroom and gathered up a pillow and blanket. Then, tracking down Mary, she was able to acquire a collection of sewing implements.

It was only a short period of time later that she had set up her supplies in the tower in order to wait and watch for her husband.

Her location provided a great vantage point; from the window she could see across the entire woods. From here she had the best chance of seeing him first when he returned, however things turned out.

Now that it was cleaned, the room was a pleasant retreat. It was peaceful and quiet, up away from the main keep proper. The views from here were gorgeous.

She pulled a chair next to the window and settled down to her main task – that of starting a new tapestry. She had decided to leave Falcon's mother's tapestry as it was, unfinished. That represented the end of the old life. Her tapestry was for the beginning of a new life; a new family.

Heather brought up ale and platters of cheese as the day progressed, and often sat to talk with Storm as she worked. Storm read to her from the small poetry codex, sharing her favorite passages. The day passed in quiet discussion and delicate needlework. Soon candles twinkled in the window as dusk approached.

There had been no word or sign, but that was to be expected. The men were not due home for another full day. Storm had resigned herself to be patient.

* * *

She had drifted to sleep in the corner when some noise shook her out of her dream. Curious, she moved over to the window and looked out over the sleeping landscape. Only a sliver of the moon lit up the quiet fields and town.

Her eyes strayed along the wall that surrounded the keep proper.

There, was that a movement?

CLINK.

A crisp metallic noise sounded clearly in the night, and Storm's senses became sharply alert. She saw it now – a figure coming up over the wall, probably on a rope. Then there were two figures. They quietly crept over toward the ladder that led down to the main gate.

A man from the stables moved stealthily across the main square to join the two, and Storm's brow wrinkled in confusion, her still-sleepy brain fighting to process what she was seeing.

In only seconds the trio had slid open the main bolts of the gate and were swinging it wide open.

Storm's senses came wide awake and she found her voice.

"BANDITS! BANDITS!" She called out the warning at the top of her lungs. From her perch high in the tower, her voice carried easily across the courtyard and down to the barracks.

Torches flared, and suddenly a stream of bandits poured through the gates at full speed, no longer interested in hiding their numbers. The guards, caught unawares, were fighting at a disadvantage, and most were beaten quickly into unconsciousness as the troupe moved in toward the main keep.

Without a second's hesitation, Storm flew down the steps toward the dining hall. If the bandits wanted a fight, then by God it was a fight they would have. It was only moments before she reached the main hallway.

Her feet had barely touched the floor when a group of roughly dressed men swarmed in from the front door. Storm dodged to the right. There were too many to take in an open fight, and she needed a weapon. She had not thought to ask Falcon what had happened to her own sword, and her dagger was back in her room.

She ran down a hallway, aiming to reach the pantry. There would be plenty of sharp knives there, and the room would be easier to defend. If she was able to face each bandit one at a time, and attack from the shadows, she had a chance.

When she reached the pantry, she pulled up short, drawing herself into the shadows on one side of the room. The main fire was banked low, and only a feeble glow shone on the scene. Molly was being held to one side by a large, burly man with a cudgel. Her face was white with fright.

In the center of the room, Storm was shocked to realize that Jessica stood proudly, holding an all-too-familiar dagger to Heather's throat. Jessica had a wide grin on her face, and seemed to be relishing the moment.

"My father will have this situation under control in no time," she smoothly advised the pair of servants. "I think it will do nicely to implicate Storm in the attack. When Falcon realizes that his new wife has betrayed him, he will hardly mind that she was killed during the ensuing melee. I will be there to help console him and to nurse him back to happiness."

Heather's eyes shone with loyalty. "He will never believe you," she stated with determination. "He would never turn on Storm, after all they have been through together. Why would he believe in your lies?"

Jessica chuckled in merriment. "Why my dear girl, there will be proof of the betrayal! A dead body always does wonders in these situations." She wiggled the dagger at Heather's throat suggestively. "This dagger, which was acquired recently from Storm's belongings, will clearly indicate who did the horrific deed."

Storm glanced quickly around her. A wood block holding a collection of knives lay to her right. She sidled along in the shadows, slipping out a medium sized carving knife with a stealthy pull. Her eyes carefully moved over her target. Jessica was slim, while Heather was curvaceous. With Heather held in front of her, the maid formed almost a complete shield for Jessica's body.

Storm's frustration grew. There was no way she could get around behind Jessica, and time was running short.

Suddenly, Heather's eyes caught her own and opened wide. She pursed her lips tightly, catching herself in a gasp of surprise.

Storm realized she had a chance.

Staying hidden in the shadows, she made a circling motion with her hand. She mimed to Heather that she had to convince Jessica to turn around, putting her back to Storm. It was her only shot.

Heather blinked in understanding, her face becoming resolute. Then she said aloud in a tremulous voice, "If I am to be the sacrificial lamb, can I at least see my mother one last time to say goodbye to her?"

Molly burst out sobbing at this, struggling to get free of the resolute bandit who held her firm. Jessica laughed out loud at the situation. "A lamb, indeed! You are all sheep to the slaughter. Yes, how delightful for you to have one last glimpse of your dear mum before you sacrifice yourself for my upcoming wedding."

With a flourish, she turned Heather around to face her mother, in the process spinning her own back to face Storm. Storm did not hesitate. She flung the knife with pinpoint accuracy into Jessica's back. The strength of her throw buried the blade up to its hilt.

Jessica coughed in surprise, the dagger in her hand dropping with a clatter to the floor. Heather immediately crouched to the ground to pick it up. Jessica was falling backwards in a heap as Heather ran forward to her mother and the bandit, dagger held close to her body.

The bandit raised his cudgel to bash the girl down, but Molly grabbed at his arm with both hands and bit down on it in fury. Before the bandit could react, Heather had driven the knife into his chest. Molly pulled the cudgel free from his grasp as he let out a yell. She drove it with all her might down onto his head.

He dropped like a stone, dead.

Storm skidded to a stop next to Jessica. Storm could see the dying embers of the woman's life fading from her eyes.

Storm knelt by Jessica. "Jessica, it did not have to be like this," she softly grated. "There were other men out there for you. Other choices."

Jessica's eyes went cold. "I do not make choices," she bit out, her breath wheezing. "I make demands, and life provides them to me. I demand … I demand …"

The light faded from her eyes, and she fell back, silenced.

Storm closed Jessica's eyes, then stood and glanced at the other two women. Molly stood protectively by her daughter, cudgel in hand. Heather cringed at the sounds of combat coming from around the keep, but her face was resolute. As Storm approached the two, Heather handed her back the dagger.

Storm automatically wiped the blood off on her dress, then addressed the pair. "Get a pair of knives. Molly, do you have the keys to the pantry?"

Molly turned them over, and in a few moments Storm had locked the two women in behind the thick, stout doors. It would take hours for the bandits to hack their way through there, if they even felt the inclination to do so. She passed the keys beneath the door to Molly, so that they could arrange to be let out once it became safe again.

Storm tucked a few more knives into her belt and, with a quick glance to ensure all was clear, headed back down the hallway. She came across a bandit who was searching behind the curtains of the study; she was able to sneak up on him without much effort. A slice across his neck, and he was dead.

Storm searched his pockets and realized that the bandit had not taken anything, even though the room was full of valuable items. She found this to be quite odd. Apparently the bandits were not on a raiding mission.

She stopped to listen for a moment. There was only the occasional sound of steel on steel – it seemed the fighting was dying down. She poked her head out of the room, looking down the hallway toward the main dining hall.

The bandits were moving around with a purpose, as if they were searching for someone. She spotted a few staff members tied up and realized they were not being slain out of hand. Something unusual was going on.

A familiar face came into view. It was Harold, cautiously peering around the corner of a doorway. He held a long staff in his hand.

Storm relaxed in relief. She waved her hand to catch his eye. "Over here," she softly called.

Harold's eyes swung around, and his sallow face brightened when he spotted her. He stood up tall and gave a bellow. "I have her! She is down by the study!" He headed toward her at a trot.

Storm gasped in surprise, then turned and sprinted down the hall, coming up short as she reached the stairs which led up to the tower. That was a dead end. She turned and put her back to it, watching warily as Harold and two bandits slowly came down the hallway after her.

Storm backed herself into the doorway to the tower, keeping it behind her. If she could force them to take her on one by one, she had a chance.

The hallway was narrow here, and the three bandits conferred for a moment before sending the large, burly one in after her. Storm grimly chuckled to herself. The bigger they came … he certainly seemed very sure of himself. She allowed herself to seem frail and weak, to play upon his feelings.

He reached out a hand to her. "Come on, little girl," he said, in a voice which he undoubtedly meant to be soothing, but only sounded sepulchral. "You can trust me."

Storm moved as if she would take the hand – then spun and stabbed him hard in his upper right arm. Crying out in pain, the bandit immediately dropped his cudgel. Without missing a beat, Storm swooped up the weapon and turned to bash the bandit hard where his legs met.

The man crumpled without a sound.

Harold and the other remaining bandit looked at each other with a smirk before moving in side by side. Storm now had two weapons – but these men would be harder to trick. The men's reach was longer than hers by several inches, and it would only take one swipe for them to force her to drop her dagger. The unknown bandit wielded a sword, while Harold pressed his staff toward her unrelentingly.

She turned her focus on Harold. "Falcon trusted you," she spit at him in anger, holding her dagger before her defensively. "How could you betray him like this?"

Harold chuckled dryly, holding his staff to point forward at her, prodding her backwards up a step. "I was the oldest son," he replied simply, slowly pushing her up the stairs. "Now hush and get moving."

She backed up a step. They pushed forward, and she found herself inching back up into the tower. She knew this was a dead end – but she had no choice. There was no way to get to them past the long reach of the staff. Maybe there would be something helpful up in the tower room.

When she reached the top, and backed into the room, she was surprised that neither of the bandits entered. They simply stood at the entrance, as if on guard, and waited there.

Storm found she dreaded the silence even more than she had the chaotic attack. Something dangerous loomed in her future, and she felt powerless to stop it.

Chapter 27

Footsteps sounded on the stair. Storm backed herself up against the window, holding her dagger out in front of her. Whatever they had planned for her, if it was going to be a hopeless fight, at least she would die trying.

To her great shock, the bandits parted and her father entered the room, accompanied by Much. Her father smiled when he saw the look on her face and nodded with pleasure.

"Oh yes, that truce talk of mine was of course a ruse," he merrily related to his daughter. "I am sure your true love is figuring that out about now, right on time. Everything is in place."

Storm gripped her dagger even tighter. "I will never come back with you," she snarled. "It is too late. I am legally married to Falcon. Nothing can undo that now."

Much chuckled without mirth. "My dear, you put too much stock in your charms. Truth be told, I am quite pleased to be out of that arrangement. It would have put a crimp on my wenching habits. Not that I would have stopped, of course, but some of my regulars would have complained."

Storm looked between the two men in confusion. "If you did not come to kidnap me back …"

To her horror, her father looked suggestively at the window behind her. "Oh come now, my dear. Surely you are still not so blissfully ignorant of the meaning of this tower? Falcon's mother – she was so weak after her husband passed away that she flung herself out of that very window. Is that not how the story went?"

Realization slowly dawned on Storm. Her face drained of all color. "You cannot tell me you ... you pushed a defenseless woman out of the window?"

Much laughed out loud. "Defenseless? Hardly! That woman was a hellcat, and good with a sword to boot. She reminds me a lot of you. We had to get rid of her, to be able to have a few years to regroup while that brat of hers grew into manhood. Maybe one more tragic death would be just what he needs to throw in the towel and become a priest." He paused, then smiled. "My daughter has other plans, though. She figures she can become the next Lady Falcon. God help him if he agrees to that!"

Storm bit her tongue. The men were quiet and relaxed for now, thinking they had the upper hand. If she revealed to Much that she had just slain his daughter, things could become much more challenging to manage.

Storm's mind settled itself into the basic training of her combat years. Her mind sorted quickly through the options available to her. She heard a noise outside on the stair and remembered that the two bandits were still out there. Perhaps Harold could still come to her aid.

"What about your helper, here in the keep," she called out, raising her voice. "What does Harold get in return for the betrayal of his master?"

Much glanced over his shoulder in mirth. "Harold, have you any desire to explain to the lady how thoroughly she has been duped?"

Harold turned to stand in the doorway, resting his staff against the jam. "I drew the short end of the stick," he explained with a dour look. "It was the burden of being the eldest. My two younger brothers stayed with the bandits, living the life of freedom and fun. I had to take the boring job, mucking out horse stables, trapped here in this keep. Believe me, it was not my choice."

Storm shook her head in confusion. "You grew up with the bandits? I thought you had been with the Falcon family for years … if not for decades?"

Harold nodded in agreement. "It has been over twenty years now that I have been handling the stables."

"Falcon has treated you fairly in all that time," insisted Storm, seeking to draw him onto her side. "I have seen how he is with everybody here. You have been well cared for and have a comfortable living. Why would you betray him after all this time?"

Harold's face grew cold. "When I was young, my father was well respected in the bandit group. He led many of the raids. Falcon's father caught them at their work one night, and my father was grievously wounded. My brothers and I tended to his wounds for a week, but he suffered horribly until he finally died. I swore revenge. The very next day I rode to the front gates, offering myself as a stable boy."

Storm shook her head. "This entire time you have been waiting, plotting Falcon's downfall?"

Harold's face broke into a sly grin. "Do you really believe I have been idle this entire time? It was I who let the bandits know when Falcon's father rode out, so they could ambush and slay him. As the son grew to manhood, I would alert the bandits whenever he went on patrol, so they could stay clear of him. For many years the situation was ideal – he was young, inexperienced, and not much of a threat. When he began to amass strength and consolidate his position, Walker let me know that the time had come."

His face became stony. "It was too late for my family, however. In the past few weeks, Falcon has slain both of my younger brothers. I am all that is left of my family. I insisted that I be allowed to watch you die myself, to have some revenge for my loss."

All emotion drained from Storm. Far from being a source of help for her, Harold was an active participant in this night's planning – and much else besides. She prayed desperately that she could survive to relay this information to Falcon. She settled down into a defensive position and prepared herself for what was to come. She knew her chances of success were slim.

She held the dagger out and to the side, watching both men with sharp precision. Her voice was a deep snarl. "If you want me, you will have to come and get me."

Time seemed to slow. She could see every movement, every flexing of a muscle as the men carefully approached ...

Suddenly, Harold gave a sharp cry, and a blade emerged from the center of his chest. A low voice growled from behind him, "That is for my father!" The sword pulled clear with a quick movement, and as Harold collapsed to the ground, Falcon stepped forward, his chest heaving, his body covered with sweat.

"Storm!" he called out in relief. His eyes quickly scanned her body, noting that she was unharmed. He promptly turned in a spin to block the sword stroke that nearly decapitated him. With another twist of his arm, the bandit's sword flew through the air, landing with a thud in the pile of blankets Storm had been using as a temporary bed. Storm scrambled toward the weapon, tossing her dagger into her left hand. Suddenly more secure, she turned to face her enemies.

A pair of bodies now lay outside the doorway, and Falcon strode into the room, his face a mask of cold fury. He worked his way along the wall until he stood side by side with Storm, facing the other two men in the ten by ten stone room.

Much and her father seemed only slightly put out by this new arrangement.

Lord Walker's sword drew lazy circles toward the married couple "Oh look," he commented drolly. "This gets easier and easier. The new wife is so disappointed that she runs back home to her loving father. Despondent, the husband throws himself out the window, just like his mother had. The lands all go, naturally, to the wife, and therefore, to me. I couldn't have planned it better myself."

Falcon settled down into a ready stance, balanced on the balls of his feet. At his side, Storm did the same. He glanced sideways at her and held her gaze for a long moment.

"I love you," he whispered softly, his eyes holding hers.

"You are in my heart forever," she responded tenderly, her gaze steady.

Without another word, both turned and launched into an attack against their foes, using a combination of their two combat styles that they'd been developing over the past weeks. Much and Walker were both experienced fighters and quickly regained their balance, adjusting to this new style of attack. The close quarters made the feints and counter-feints require every ounce of Storm's focus

Much and Walker grinned as they worked their way around the outside of the room, pressing the two lovers' backs into each other. However, as the fight wore on, it quickly became apparent that Storm and Falcon were even more powerful in this position – by guarding each other's backs, they had only one front to focus on.

The pair of assassins turned to taunts instead, to distract their enemies. Much began the verbal assault. "So, Falcon, would you like to hear how your mother died?" he teased slyly. "She did not volunteer to go up over that ledge, you know."

Falcon did not respond. His attacks became more focused, his movements more deliberate.

Much's eyes twinkled, looking to throw his opponent off guard. "Maybe you would like to hear how I will console your grieving widow, once we get her back 'home' again."

Falcon's eyes grew steely, but he held an iron tight control over his emotions.

Storm's mind snapped at Much's cruel tormenting of her husband. "Maybe you will not be in much of a mood to console me, Much, once you learn that your daughter lays dead on the floor below us. I killed her while saving Heather's life."

Much drew back in shock, then roared in anger, renewing his attack on Falcon with wild intensity. Storm prayed that Much's lack of control would turn the fight to Falcon's advantage.

She noticed with pride that Falcon was holding his own against the expert counter-cuts and low sweeps Much threw at him with fierce fury. She knew that Much's reputation as an expert swordsman was richly deserved. Falcon pressed to gain an advantage, but they seemed evenly matched.

Storm faced a similar problem with her father who, for all his years, was extremely skilled in fighting techniques. At least he could not play Much's tricks with her. The converse was true - she knew there was not much she could say to him that would shock him out of his steady assault.

Out of the corner of her eye she realized that Much had moved himself into a position where he was within almost an arm's length of her. She realized that Much was hoping to grab her, to take her hostage against Falcon's sword arm. An idea formed in her head.

"Clumsy," she called under her breath to Falcon as she parried yet another attack from her father.

"Ready," replied Falcon without missing a beat, understanding with a glance what Much was preparing to do.

Storm waited for another pair of swings, then allowed herself to trip, falling to one knee in front of Much. This was too much temptation for Much to pass by. He looked away from Falcon for a moment, reaching down to drag Storm up in front of him as a human shield.

The next moment, Much gasped in shock as Falcon's sword rammed through his chest, pinning him to the back wall. Storm rolled out of the way, coming up to a crouch alongside Falcon. Much looked between the pair in surprise, then his eyelids fluttered closed.

Storm did not hesitate; she had heard too many tales of deception to take anything for granted. She knelt at Much's side, quickly checking his pulse, verifying the threat was indeed past. Then she turned to stand alongside Falcon. Together they faced her father, their slowing breathing the only sound in the small stone room.

Storm's father's eyes flitted from one opponent to another, his face calculating. Before their eyes his body slid easily from an offensive to a defensive posture; his voice became soothing and gentle. "My daughter, I can see now how much I have been misled by this evil bandit chief!" he promised, his voice full of honey. "I cannot believe he has confused me for so many years. Tell me that you forgive a doddering old fool."

He lowered his sword, pleading with his daughter. "Much is the one who killed your mother, not me. I was heartbroken over it! What could I do, though? I had a young child to raise, and a kingdom to keep safe."

Storm's voice was as steady as iron. "You will be brought in for public charges," she stated coldly. "The world will know of your lies and deeds, and your lands will be divided up amongst its neighbors. This killing will come to an end, and your reputation will be ruined."

Her father's voice took on a wheedling note. "Surely you would not do such a thing to me!" he protested. "For all the years I cared for you, raised you as my own -"

Storm's eyes widened in shocked surprise. "*AS* your own? What do you mean ...?"

Walker's eyes held hers with gentle pleading. "It is time you knew the truth, that we were completely honest with each other. It will be a fresh start for us." He drew in a long breath, as if he were opening himself completely to her. "Your dearest mother had been instructed by her family to marry a different man, and she dutifully obeyed. She soon was pregnant by him, but sadly, he met a tragic end before the child was born. She then accepted me as her husband, and we raised you as our own."

A tragic end. Storm had no doubt that Walker had a hand in that outcome, in ensuring that her mother's lands and fortunes ended up under his control.

Storm was suddenly free. Any last vestiges of guilt she felt over how she was going to deal with this man vanished like morning mist. "Your brutalization of all around you is now at an end," she stated with a clear voice. She spun the sword on her wrist, staying alert for any motion from Walker.

To her surprise, Walker nodded in acceptance, his eyes rich with sorrow. He bent down for a moment, laying his sword on the ground. "You are right," he responded with dense sadness. "I should pay for my sins. I have led an immoral life, and it is time to make amends. You may take me in." He held both hands out in front of him, quiet and docile.

Falcon held his sword at Walker's throat as he moved forward to kick Walker's sword out of reach. Storm was already crying out for him to wait when her father flipped up one hand to reveal a small dagger with a wickedly sharp edge. In the next moment he was lunging, slashing sharply at Falcon's arm.

Suddenly Falcon's sleeve was drenched in blood and the pair were locked in a powerful struggle, both trying to push each other toward the window.

Storm kicked the sword far out of reach of her father, but could not find an angle that would enable her to provide any help. The pair was spinning and moving too quickly. Falcon still had his sword in his hand, but the two were too close for him to use it effectively. Storm watched in horror as her father aimed a fierce kick at Falcon's kneecap, causing Falcon to groan in agony and fall back against the sill.

Falcon looked up past his opponent, meeting Storm's eyes, gazing at her with absolute trust. Then he allowed himself to drop to his knees, leaving himself completely open.

Walker cried out in triumph, turning and raising his dagger high for the final blow.

Storm had only a split second of opportunity. She had only the smallest sliver of space between the two men. She gave herself over to the moment. She put all thoughts aside except for this instant of time.

She cocked the knife back.

She aimed.

She released.

The dagger's blade shaved a ribbon of fabric off of Falcon's tunic as it flew past his body.

It implanted itself firmly, fully, in the center of Walker's heart.

Storm's step-father gasped in surprise; he turned in a rush to escape the pain. His momentum carried him up ... over ... and a second later he was tumbling out the window.

There was a long, poignant cry.

Then, a heavy thud.

Storm ran into Falcon's arms, wrapping herself tightly around him. He kissed her forehead, her cheeks, and her lips, reassuring himself that she really was unharmed.

"You are safe … you are safe …" he whispered against her, holding her close.

Time seemed to slow down.

An eternity passed.

Finally, the seconds began to tick past again, and Storm pulled back from Falcon, looking him over. She eyed the long gash in his arm, then led him over to sit on the pile of blankets. She ripped a strip off of one, forming a bandage around the wound.

He glanced down at it, then back up at her. "That will leave a nice scar," he chuckled with a wry smile. "A memento of the day's events."

Storm gave him a gentle kiss. "Now we will match," she reminded him with a grin.

The dawn light was just starting to peek through the room, and Falcon took a look around him. He noticed for the first time the sewing materials and the tapestry loom. A contented smile relaxed into his gaze.

A shout rang from below them. Both perked up, reaching for their weapons. Falcon looked over at his wife with a grin, his eyes twinkling.

"Well then, my darling, shall we head down to regain control of our home?"

Storm gave a sweeping bow with her dagger and nodded. "After you, my love."

Chapter 28

One month later

Storm squeezed Falcon's hand in happiness as they stepped through the main doors and into the Cartwright keep. It was all so new to her, still, the visiting of each neighbor's territory as man and wife. In each location they had been greeted as beloved heroes. She had never realized how widespread the abuses of her father had stretched – and how grateful the countryside would be for his end of power.

Each fresh visit had involved tellings and retellings of the final battle. How, once Lord Walker had been killed, the remaining bandits had surrendered or fled. How Molly and Heather had been celebrated for their brave actions. How the countryside had since experienced a peace like no other in living memory.

But this particular day would not be one of merriment and celebration. They had arrived to the sad news that the Lady of the keep, Lady Cartwright, had just passed away. Indeed, the guests and staff they passed were all in mourning clothes and a somber mood hung over the great room. The head table was empty save for a lone woman, a few years younger than Storm, garbed in a black dress. Her long, dark hair was held back in a plain braid.

Storm and Falcon approached her. Falcon gave a deep bow. "We are Lord and Lady Falcon," he announced. "We are so sorry for your loss."

The woman stood and nodded. "We appreciate your coming and your sentiments. Your efforts with Lord Walker have been a boon for us, even though his lands did not directly adjoin ours. You are most welcome. Please, come sit on my left."

The main chair at the center of the table was empty, as was the chair at its side. Storm wondered if those had been the seats of the Lord and Lady, when they had been alive.

Falcon's eyes went to a small oval frame laid at the center of the table, set in a place of honor. The painting within showed a young, blond man in his late teens. He appeared strong and handsome, with blue-grey eyes and a forest green tunic.

Falcon's face was quiet as he took in the painting. "Is there any word from Erik?"

A shadow of pain flitted through the girl's face. She gave her head a short shake. "No. He is fighting in the Crusades; even the fastest messenger will not reach him for weeks, if not months. And when he hears …" Her lips pressed together tightly. "He may not return home, even so. With the way they parted, I do not know if we shall ever see him again."

Falcon's eyes shadowed. "I am sorry to hear that. He seemed a worthy man, the times I met him."

Mary's voice cracked. "He was the best −" She bit off the sentence and looked down, her lip trembling.

Falcon's voice was low. "You were Lady Cartwright's ward. With her gone, I would be glad to lend what assistance I can."

Mary's eyes shone with pride, and she looked up again. "I have been trained well in the running of this keep. I share my responsibility of its defenses as well." Her hand dropped to a well-worn sword at her hip. "We will stand strong until the day Erik returns to us. I have sworn it."

Storm knew by the fierce glow in Mary's gaze that she meant every word.

A hum vibrated at Storm's hip. At the sword given to her by Sarah almost a full year ago. It seemed a lifetime. At the time she thought she'd never find joy. And now she had Falcon at her side, a community she adored, and absolute peace.

What was it that Sarah had said to her?

Do not become too fond of Andetnes. When you have at last found contentment, there will be another whose fate balances on the point of a pin. You will know when it is right. And the sword will have a new mistress.

Storm looked over at Falcon, and he nodded.

A warm smile drew on Storm's lips.

"Mary, let us come sit with you. Tell us all about Erik and your plans for keeping the Cartwright Keep secure until he returns home to you. For I have every faith that he shall."

* * *

The Sword of Glastonbury series continues with Book 7, *Sworn Loyalty* –

http://www.amazon.com/Sworn-Loyalty-Medieval-Romance-Glastonbury-ebook/dp/B00FBE82O6/

If you enjoyed *Creating Memories*, please leave feedback on Amazon, Goodreads, and any other systems you use. Together we can help make a difference!

https://www.amazon.com/review/create-review?ie=UTF8&asin=B00791A3DW#

Be sure to sign up for my free newsletter! You'll get alerts of free books, discounts, and new releases. I run my own newsletter server – nobody else will ever see your email address. I promise!

http://www.lisashea.com/lisabase/subscribe.html

Join my online groups to get news of free giveaways, upcoming stories, and fascinating trivia!

Facebook
https://www.facebook.com/LisaSheaAuthor

Twitter
https://twitter.com/LisaSheaAuthor

Google+
https://plus.google.com/+LisaSheaAuthor/posts

GoodReads
https://www.goodreads.com/lisashea/

Blog
http://www.lisashea.com/lisabase/blog/

Be sure to download all of my FREE books! Each of these is completely free and available on Kindle.

COCKTAILS

Low Carb Recipes Series

Delicious recipes
perfect for unwinding,
relaxing, and enjoying!

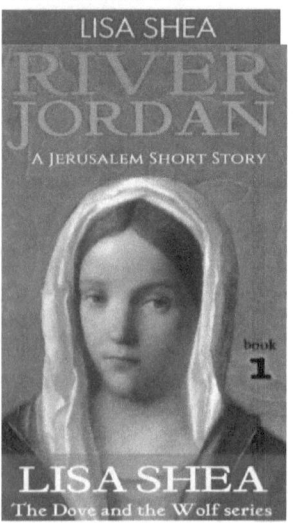

LISA SHEA

RIVER JORDAN

A JERUSALEM SHORT STORY

book 1

LISA SHEA

The Dove and the Wolf series

Destiny Interrupted

1

ETERNAL TIME SHADOWS

LISA SHEA

INTO THE WASTELAND

a dystopian journey

The Ishtato saga
book 1

LISA SHEA

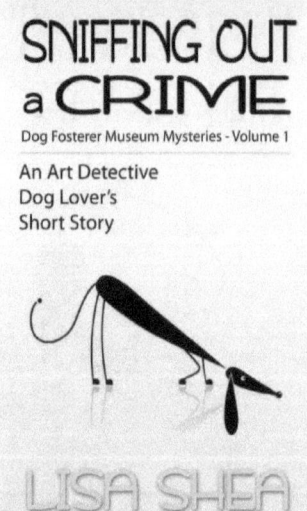

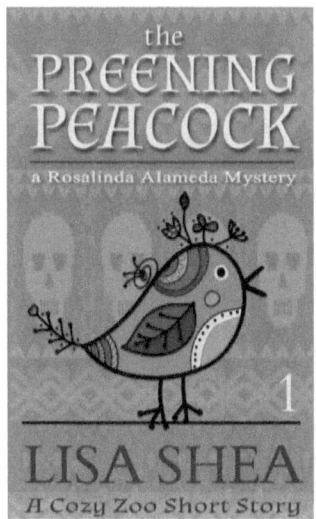

Medieval Dialogue

I've been fascinated by medieval languages since I was quite young. I grew up studying Spanish, English, and Latin, and loved the sound of reading Beowulf and the Canterbury Tales in their original languages. I adore the richness of medieval languages. How did medieval English people speak?

There are three aspects to this. The first is the difference between written records and spoken language. The second is the rich, multi-cultural aspect of medieval life. And the third is how to convey this to a modern-language audience.

Let's take the first. Sometimes modern people equate the way medieval folk would talk, hanging around a rustic tavern, with the way Chaucer wrote his famous *Canterbury Tales*. Something along the lines of this (note this is a modern translation, not the original Middle English version):

"Of weeping and wailing, care and other sorrow
I know enough, at eventide and morrow,"
The merchant said, "and so do many more
Of married folk, I think, who this deplore,
For well I know that it is so with me.
I have a wife, the worst one that can be;
For though the foul Fiend to her wedded were,
She'd overmatch him, this I dare to swear."

Sure, it seems elegant and rich. But did worn-down farmers sitting around a fireplace with mugs of ale really talk like this?

Do we think the London street-dwellers in the 1600s skulked down the dark alleys emoting like Shakespeare –

Two households, both alike in dignity
In fair Verona, where we lay our scene
From ancient grudge break to new mutiny

Where civil blood makes civil hands unclean.

And, in the 1920s in Vermont, did farmers really wander down their snowy lanes murmuring to their farming friends, a la Robert Frost:

Whose woods these are I think I know.
His house is in the village though;
He will not see me stopping here
To watch his woods fill up with snow.

As someone who lives in New England, I can pretty resolutely say "no" to that last one. And, given my research, I'm equally content saying "no" to the previous two. There is a big difference between poetry written with deliberate effort and the way "normal people" talked, flirted, cajoled, and laughed day in and day out. People simply did not talk in iambic pentameter. I'm a poet and even I don't talk in iambic pentameter :).

Modern people sometimes think of the medieval period in terms of the plays we see. We imagine actors on a stage, speaking in formal, stilted language, carefully moving from scene to scene. But medieval life wasn't like that. It was a rich cacophony of people struggling hard to survive amongst plagues and crusades, with strong pagan influences and the church trying to instill order. People fought off robbers and drove away wolves. They laughed and loved in multi-generational homes. It was a time of great flux.

England - A Melting Pot
England wasn't an isolated, walled-off island. It was continually experiencing influxes of new words and sounds. The Romans came and went. The Vikings came and went. The French invaded. Nearly all of the English men headed off to the Crusades, leaving behind women to gain strength and position. The men returned with even more languages. Pilgrims went to Jerusalem. Merchants arrived from all over. This was a true melting pot.

So, in part because of this, Middle English was a rich, fascinating language. People in this time period had a wealth of contractions, nicknames, abbreviations, and combinations of words they used. Often people could speak multiple languages - their old English, the incoming Norman language, Latin from church, and random other words from tinkers, merchants, and pilgrims they encountered. Medieval people had all sorts of words for drinking, for fighting, for prostitutes, you name it. They had slang and shortcuts just like any other language does. After all, these are the people who turned "forecastle" (on a ship) to "foc's'le" and who pronounce the word "Worcester" as "Woostah."

But, here's the trick. With the medieval language being so rich, varied, intricate, and full of fascinating words, how can we bring that to life for a modern audience?

Centuries of Change

Let's start with a basic issue - most modern readers simply cannot understand authentic medieval dialogue. They don't have the grounding in Middle English, French, and Latin that would be required. Even the fairly straightforward, basic Chaucer works look like this:

And Saluces this noble contree highte.

Modern readers generally wouldn't know that "highte" meant "was called" as in "And Saluces this noble country was called."

This happens over and over again. Words change meaning. In the Middle Ages, if you *abandoned* your wife it means you subjugated her. You got her under your thumb. It didn't mean you left her - quite the opposite. Awful meant *awe-ful* - as in stunning and wonderful. It had a positive connotation. Fantastic wasn't great - it was a fantasy; something that didn't exist. Nervous didn't mean worried or agitated - it meant strong and full of energy. Nice meant silly, and so on.

If a book was written with proper medieval words and meanings, first, even if the words are reasonably close to what we use now, modern readers would have to struggle with the spelling -

By that the Maunciple hadde his tale al ended,
The sonne fro the south lyne was descended
So lowe, that he nas nat to my sighte
Degrees nyne and twenty as in highte.

But, again, that is just the tip of the issue with medieval language. The word "bracelet" didn't exist until the 1400s. Necklace wasn't a word until 1590. The word "hug" wasn't around until the mid-1500s. We also didn't have the words tragedy, crisis, area, explain, fact, illicit, rogue, or even disagree! Shakespeare invented the words "baseless" and "dwindle" in the 1600s. Staircase is from 1620. A story written solely with words that existed in the year 1200 - and that still retain their modern meaning so modern readers could understand them - would be fairly basic.

(Speaking of which, the word "basic" didn't exist until the mid 1800s.)

Conversely, some words we might think of as thoroughly modern, like "puke", were also used in Shakespeare's time. "Booze" traces back to the 1500s. And these are just the proofs we have. While "shiner" for a black eye can be traced definitively to the 1700s, it could easily have been used for centuries before then and we just don't happen to have a letter or newspaper article which mentions it.

It's fair to say that people in medieval days did get black eyes and had a wealth of interesting terms for that situation. After all, it could be a rough life back then. Was one of the terms used "shiner"? Maybe, maybe not. Out of the ten fun phrases they used, probably nine of them would make zero sense to a modern reading audience. So authors strive to find phrases that provide meaning to a modern audience without being too *l33t* and techno-speak. It doesn't make sense to completely avoid the word "bracelet" simply because it technically didn't exist in the 1200s. Surely people in the 1200s had several words for "bracelet" and we are simply using the word modern readers understand. Similarly, people in medieval times hugged! They just called that action something else.

Medieval people loved playing with words. They called their kids "dillydowns" and "mitings" (little mites). They called sweethearts "my sweeting" and "my honey. They loved snapping out insults, from "dunce" to "idiot" to "pig filth" and "maggot pie." And, again, these are just the ones that happened to get recorded.

Medieval people loved contractions. There's a phrase "ne woot," meaning *knows not*. They'd simply say "noot". They did this with all sorts of words.

So writing in modern English should have this same sort of loose, fun sense to the writing. It's important to remember that even the kings, in this era, were rough fighters. They were out with soldiers, crossing multiple countries, and experiencing a range of languages. They weren't necessarily concerned about speaking in iambic pentameter. They were more concerned about breaking down their enemy's walls to plunder what lay within and then drinking themselves under the table to celebrate.

So, certainly, treasure the poetry and prose of the time. As a poet, I appreciate that immensely. But also keep in mind that people did not talk in poetry. They did not speak in fantasy-speak of *Lord of the Rings* or *Game of Thrones*. They talked and laughed, flirted and cursed, gossiped and cajoled in a rich, multi-lingual, contraction-filled, sobriquet-laden dialogue which mirrors how we talk in modern times.

About Medieval Life

When many of us think of medieval times, we bring to mind a drab reality-documentary image. We imagine people scrounging around in the mud, eating dirt. The people were under five feet tall and barely survived to age thirty. These poor, unfortunate souls had rotted teeth and never bathed.

Then you have the opposite, Hollywood Technicolor extreme. In the romantic version of medieval times, men were always strong and chivalrous. Women were dainty and sat around staring out the window all day, waiting for their knight to come riding in. Everybody wore purple robes or green tights.

The truth, of course, lies somewhere in the middle.

Living in Medieval Times

The years in the early medieval ages held a warm, pleasant climate. Crops grew exceedingly well, and there was plenty of food. As a result, their average height was on par with modern times. It's amazing how much nutrition influences our health!

The abundance of food also had an effect on the longevity of people. Chaucer (born 1340) lived to be 60. Petrarch (born 1304) died a day shy of 70. Eleanor of Aquitaine (born 1122) was 82 when she died. People could and did lead long lives. The average age of someone who survived childhood was 65.

What about their living conditions? The Romans adored baths and set up many in Britain. When they left, the natives could not keep them going, and it is true they then bathed less. However, by the Middle Ages, with the crusades and interaction with the Muslims, there was a renewed interest both in hygiene and medicine. Returning soldiers and those who took pilgrimages brought back with them an interest in regular bathing and cleanliness. This spread across the culture.

While people during other periods of English history ate poorly, often due to war conditions or climatic changes, the middle ages were a time of relative bounty. Villagers would grow fresh fruit and vegetables behind their homes, and had an array of herbs for seasoning. The local baker would bake bread for the village - most homes did not hold an oven, only an open fire. Villagers had easy access to fish, chicken, geese, and eggs. Pork was enjoyed at special meals like Easter.

Upper classes of course had a much wider range of foods - all game animals (rabbits, deer, and so on) belonged to them. The wealthy ate peacocks, veal, lamb, and even bear. Meals for all classes could be flavorful and well enjoyed.

Medieval Relationships

Some movies present a skewed version of life in the Middle Ages. They make it seem that women were meek, mild, and obediently did whatever their father or husband commanded.

This was *far* from the truth!

Medieval times were times of immense change. Men were off at the Crusades, leaving the women to run things. Christianity was trying to get a foothold, but many areas of Britain were still primarily pagan, with all the Goddess worship and female empowerment which had been tradition for centuries. The vast majority of brewers were female. Most innkeepers were female. Women's knowledge about herbs, health, and food was respected. Healthy women were treasured as the key to a child-rich partnership.

Medieval life was heavily focused on fertility. Farm animals had to be fertile in order to create meat to feed the family. Women had to be fertile to create helpers for the farm and household. Celebration after celebration in medieval times focused on fertility. These people weren't shy about the topic. They watched their horses, cows, and dogs continually engage in these activities. Their festivals focused on the topic with bawdy delight. Their songs lusted about it.

The church tried, again and again, to squelch this behavior so that all aspects of relationships could be regulated by the church. However, half of all medieval couples were together outside of a church marriage and, for those sanctified by the church, a large proportion were "sealing the deal" for a couple already pregnant.

This was the way the medieval people looked at it: they needed to know their partner could create children. This was a key consideration for a relationship.

The Medieval period was far from an era of Victorian prudity. Quite the opposite. People of this era celebrated fertility, felt it was wholly natural, and even felt it was unhealthy for a man or woman to go for too long without sex. The celibacy would block critical flows of the body.

It was considered natural that a male noble might take on mistresses and that unmarried couples might seek out partners. It was the same as someone needing food if they were hungry. It was a bodily function which had to be tended to for the health of the person.

So where does marriage fit in with this mindset?

Medieval Marriage

In medieval times, marriage was primarily about inheritance. It was almost separate from sexuality. Sexuality was an important part of bodily health, like eating well and getting enough exercise. Marriage, on the other hand, was about ensuring one's lands and chattel were cared for from generation to generation. Sex, within a marriage, was focused on creating family-line children to then tend to that wealth.

For this reason, wealthy families would put immense energy into arranging optimal marriages for their children. This was about the transfer of land far more than a love match. Parents wanted to ensure their land went to a family worthy of ownership - one with the resources to defend it from attack. It was not only their own family members they were concerned with. Each block of land had on it both free men and serfs. These people all depended on the nobles – with their skill, connections, and soldiers – to keep them safe from bandits and harm.

That being said, both the woman and man would be consulted about the match. Their input was a critical aspect of the decision. Choices were often made with intricate selection processes. Keep in mind that the woman and her suitors would have been raised from birth to think of this process as natural. They would participate in that choice-making with an eye as to how it would secure the stability of their future family.

Yes, villagers sometimes married for love. Even a few nobles would run off and follow their hearts. Even so, they would have first seriously considered the potentially catastrophic risks which could result from their actions.

Here is a modern example. Imagine you took over the family business which employed a hundred loyal workers. Those workers depend on your careful guidance of the company to ensure the income for their families. You might dream about running off to Bermuda and drinking martinis. But would you just sell your company to any random investor who came along? Would you risk all of those peoples' lives, people who had served you loyally for decades, to satisfy a whim of pleasure? It is more likely that you would research your options, map out a plan, and made a choice with suited both you and your responsibilities.

Medieval Women

In pagan days women held many rights and responsibilities. During the crusades, especially, with many men off at war, women ran the taverns, made the ale, and ran the government. In later years, as men returned home and Christianity rose in power, women were relegated to a more subservient role.

Still, women in medieval times were not meek and mild. That stereotype came in with the Victorian era, many centuries later. Back in medieval days, women had to be hearty and hard working. There were fields to tend, homes to maintain, and children to raise!

Women strove to be as healthy as they could because they faced a serious threat - a fifth of all women died during or just after childbirth. The church said that childbirth was the "pain of Eve" and instructed women to bear it without medicine or follow-up care. Of course, midwives did their best to skirt these rules, but childbirth still took an immense toll.

Childhood was rough in the Middle Ages – only forty percent of children survived the gauntlet of illnesses to adulthood. A woman who reached her marriageable years was a sturdy woman indeed.

You can see why fertility was so important to medieval people!

To summarize, in medieval days a woman could live a long, happy life, even into her eighties – as long as she was of the sturdy stock that made it through the challenges of childhood. She would be expected to be fertile and to have multiple children, which again weeded out the weaker ones. This was very much a time of 'survival of the fittest.' Medieval life quickly separated out the weak and frail. Those women who ran that gauntlet and survived were respected for that strength and for their wisdom in many areas of life.

So medieval women were strong - very strong. They had to be. They were respected. Still, would they fight?

Women and Weapons

Queen Boudicia, from Norwalk, was born around AD60. She personally – and successfully - led her troops against the Roman Empire. She had been flogged - and her daughters raped - spurring her to revenge. She was extremely intelligent and quite strategic. Her daughters rode in her chariot at her side.

Eleanor of Aquitaine, born in 1122, was brilliant and married first to a King of France and then to a King of England. She went on the Second Crusades as the leader of her troops - reportedly riding bare-breasted as an Amazon. At times she marched with her troops far ahead of her husband. When she divorced the King of France, she immediately married Henry II, who she passionately adored. He was eleven years her junior. When things went sour, Eleanor separated from him and actively led revolts against him.

Many historical accounts talk of women taking up arms to defend their villages and towns. Women would not passively let their children be slain or their homes burned. They were able and strong bodied from their daily work. They were well skilled with farm implements and knives, and used them with great talent against invaders.

Many of these defenses were successful, and the victories were celebrated as brave and proper, rather than dismissed as an unusual act for a woman. A mother was expected to defend her brood and to keep her home safe, just as a wolf mother protects her cubs.

Numerous women took their martial skills to a higher level. In 1301 a group of Italian women joined up to fight the crusade against the Turks. In 1348 at a tournament there were at least thirty women who participated, dressed as men.

This is not as unusual as you might think. In medieval times, all adults carried a knife at their belt for daily use in eating, chores, and defense. All knew how to use it. Being strong and safe was a necessary part of daily life.

Here is an interesting comparison. In modern times most women know how to drive, but few choose to invest themselves in the time and training to become race car drivers. In medieval times, most women knew how to defend themselves with a weapon. They had to. Few, though, actively sought the training to be swordswomen. Still, these women did exist, and did thrive as valued members of their communities.

So women in medieval times were far from shrinking violets. They were not mud-encrusted wretches huddling in straw huts. They were not pale damsels locked away in towers. They were strong, sturdy, and well versed in the use of knives. Many ran taverns, and most handled the brewing of ale. Those who made it through childhood and childbirth could expect to enjoy long, rich lives.

I hope you enjoy my tales of authentic, inspiring heroines!

Glossary

Ale - A style of beer which is made from barley and does not use hops. Ale was the common drink in medieval days. In the 1300s, 92% of brewers were female, and the women were known as "alewives". It was common for a tavern to be run by a widow and her children.

Blade - The metal slicing part of the sword.

Chemise - In medieval days, most people had only a few outfits. They would not want to wash their heavy main dress every time they wore it, just as in modern times we don't wash our jackets after each wearing. In order to keep the sweaty skin away from the dress, women wore a light, white under-dress which could then be washed more regularly. This was often slept in as well.

Drinking - In general, medieval sanitation was not great. People who drank milk had to drink it "raw" - pasteurization was not well known before the 1700s. Water was often unsafe to drink. For these reasons, all ages of medieval folk drank liquid with alcohol in it. The alcohol served as a natural sanitizer. This was even true as recently as colonial American times.

God's Teeth / God's Blood – Common oaths in the middle ages.

Grip - The part of the sword one holds, usually wrapped in leather or another substance to keep it firmly in the wielder's hand.

Guard - The crossed top of the sword's hilt which keeps the enemy's sword from sliding down and chopping off the wielder's fingers.

Hilt - The entire handle part of the sword; everything that is not blade.

Mead - A fermented beverage made from honey. Mead has been enjoyed for thousands of years and is mentioned in Beowulf.

Pommel - The bottom end of the sword, where the hilt ends.

Tip - The very end of the sword

Wolf's Head – a term for a bandit. The Latin legal term *caput gerat lupinum* meant they could be hunted and killed as legally as any dangerous wolf or wild animal that threatened the area.

Parts of a Sword

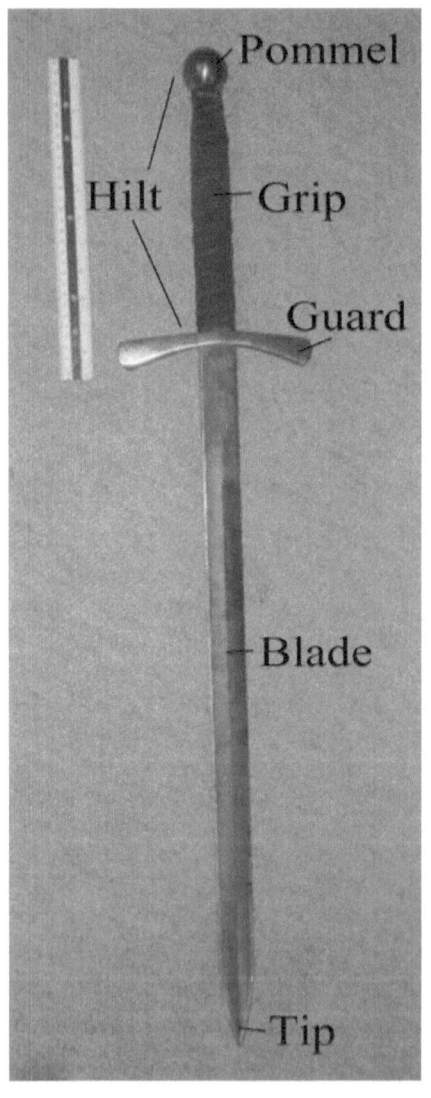

Medieval Clothing

Medieval people - despite modern stereotypes - did have noses and did like to stay clean. Public baths were popular, and people liked to swim as well. However, they did not have the luxury of bathing daily. Also, in medieval times people were often cold. Castles were damp and drafty. Fireplaces were not kept blazingly hot all night long. There is a reason that people wore many heavy layers including cloaks. That way they could add or remove layers as necessary to keep warm.

The basic under-layer was a chemise. This thin nightgown would be worn at night as well as during the day. Because it was against the body it kept the actual clothes clean from sweat. That way you could wash the chemise regularly and not have to wash your actual dress every day. Think of it like when you wear a turtleneck and a wool sweater. At the end of the day you would wash the turtleneck, but you would not wash the wool sweater after every wearing. If you wear a t-shirt under a jacket, you would toss the t-shirt into the washing machine but just hang the jacket on a hook again. The same is true for medieval outfits. The inner layer would be washed, while the other layer would be reused multiple days before it had to be washed.

The chemise was generally not meant to be seen, especially in colder months. It was underwear. There would always be an over-dress with a floor-length hem on top of that. Perhaps a glimpse of the chemise would show at the neckline or at the end-of-sleeve area. In hotter months the chemise might be more visible as the outer dress had short sleeves or no sleeves.

Men would typically wear a tunic over leggings. Men working in summer heat would sometimes wear simple linen "shorts" without anything else. Their chest and lower legs would be bare. This is a stark difference from how covered up women would be.

Both sexes would wear boots or shoes. There was no "left" or "right" - both halves would be made in the same oval shape.

Cloaks would be worn when going out into poor weather, to help keep you warm. These cloaks could be quite heavy if they were full circle cloaks, and incredibly warm.

Monks would wear similar clothing to non-religious men, but the monk's hair would be cut short and have a "tonsure" - or bald spot

- shaved out of its center. The tonsure was a sign of their humility.
This illuminated image is from a 12th century manuscript at the library
at Cambridge University.

Women's Clothing

A number of readers had specific questions about women's medieval clothing so I created this page with those specific details. To illustrate it, I have included a drawing done by Andreas Muller, a famous German artist known for his work restoring ancient paintings. This drawing was published back in 1861, so it's now out of copyright. As you might expect the drawing shows German people, not English, but the fashions are from the 1200s and are quite similar in style.

So, the basics. Women wore at least two layers of long dress. The bottom layer, or "chemise," was often plain white but could be fancier with nobles. This was what was against the skin, got sweaty, and would be washed. The chemise was often slept in, again especially if the person was poor.

The outer layer, what we would call the "dress," was the prettier layer. This would have the nicer stitching and designs. It could have embroidery or different fabrics stitched together to create designs. The outer dress could have long sleeves, short sleeves, or no sleeves, depending on how hot the weather was. In general, though, a woman's arms and legs were covered by the inner chemise and perhaps also by the outer dress as well. Women in medieval times did not tend to show skin from those parts of the body.

You might see images on the web with medieval women wearing long "trumpet" sleeves which made housework impractical. These were sometimes worn by French nobles who were showing off that they did not have to do menial labor. They were not a normal fashion in England or most other areas.

By the same token, women who had to work hard would wear shorter dresses - ending above the ankle rather than dragging on the floor. That was so their dresses did not catch or drag while they went about their work. Noblewomen who had a quiet day planned or a formal event would wear longer, floor-dragging dresses. These subtle differences helped to show off their status.

If it got even colder women would wear cloaks. These range from light, like the woman in the middle is wearing here, to heavy and full-circle, which could be amazingly warm. I have one of those.

Here is an illuminated image done between 1285 and 1292 which shows the famous poet Marie de France. Marie primarily wrote between 1160 to 1190 and was well known by nobility in France and England. Again, you can see how her outer long dress goes to the floor and the inner dress is visible at the arms. This copyright-free image comes via the National Library of France.

Women had an immense array of colorful dyes to choose from, some more expensive, some less expensive. So clothing could be quite bright and cheery. Just as in modern times, practicality had an aspect here. If someone was going to work in the pig pen all day long they'd probably wear something brown and old. If they were going to church they'd wear their best outfit they had.

In modern times we can sometimes think of dresses as "fancy" items we wear to "dress up" that are hard to move in. In medieval times, a dress was normal and natural! These were the outfits they wore every single day. Women made their dresses so they could do all their normal activities in them. To them a dress was like our modern t-shirt and sweatpants. So they're no question about "could they do chores in a dress" or "could they ride a horse in a dress." Of course they could - that's what the clothing was made for. Medieval women didn't generally hide out in tower rooms. Noblewomen would do archery and horseback riding for fun. Working women would scythe hay, ride to the market, and do a myriad of other chores in their dresses. It was what one wore. So those outfits absolutely were made to easily let them do those tasks. Dresses were loose to allow all of that. Women didn't ride side-saddle in medieval days - they simply put their legs on either side for stability. And their clothing was made for that. To ride, a woman could either tuck the skirt beneath her, like when one sits on a chair, or let it flow behind her. Either way works!

In terms of underclothes, most medieval women did not wear a bra. Their simple, straight dresses were meant to keep the body hidden rather than emphasized. A large breasted woman might wear a "binder" to keep the breasts from jiggling around while they tried to work. Current thought is that women didn't wear "underwear" (underpants) either. With their long multi-layer dresses it would be a challenge for underwear-wearing women to go to the bathroom. Instead, they would just move to a section of the field, fluff out their dresses, and go. Then they could get back to work. The same in the outhouses.

Even during the time of their periods, many researchers feel that the philosophy of the time was that binding or constricting a woman's flow would damage her fertility. So she simply bled into her underdress and that was washed. This free-flow practice continued long after medieval times. It was mentioned in doctors' journals in the 1800s. Even as recent as the 1900s there were cotton mills in the United States that had straw-strewn floors to absorb female workers' blood, so again this was not a short-term trend. And given that tampons can cause toxic shock syndrome, maybe those medieval women knew what they were doing :).

Let me know if you have any other questions about medieval women's clothing! I have a library of books here to help with research.

Dedication

To my mom, dad, siblings, and family members who encouraged me to indulge myself in medieval fantasies. I spent many long car rides creating epic tales of sword-wielding heroines and the strong men who stood by their sides. Jenn, Uncle Blake, and Dad were awesome proofers.

To Peter and Elizabeth May, who patiently toured me around England, Scotland, and France on three separate occasions. Elizabeth offered valuable tips on creating authentic scenes. Visiting the Berkhamsted motte and bailey was priceless.

To Jody, Leslie, Liz, Sarah, and Jenny, my friends who enjoy my eclectic ways and provide great suggestions. Becky was my first ever web-fan and her enthusiasm kept me going!

To the editors at BellaOnline, who inspire me daily to reach for my dreams and to aim for the stars. Lisa, Cheryll, Jeanne, Lizzie, Moe, Terrie, Ian, and Jilly provided insightful feedback to help my polishing efforts.

To the Massachusetts Mensa Writing Group for their feedback and enthusiastic support. Lynn, Tom, Ruth, Carmen, Al, and Dean all offered detailed, helpful advice!

To the Geek Girls, with their unflagging support for my expanding list of projects and enterprises. Debi's design talents are amazing. I simply adore the covers she created for me.

To the Academy of Knightly Arts for several years of in-depth training and combat experience with medieval swords and knives. I loved sparring with Nikki and Jo-Ann!

To B&R Stables who renewed my love of horseback riding and quiet forest trails.

To my son, James, whose insights into psychology help ground my characters in authentic behavior.

To Bob See, my partner in love for over 19 years and counting. He enthusiastically supports all of my new projects.

About the Author

Lisa Shea is a fervent fan of honor, loyalty, and chivalry. She brings to life worlds where men and women stand shoulder to shoulder, steady in their desire to make the world a better place for all. While her medieval heroines often wield a sword, they equally value the skilled use of their intelligence, wisdom, courage, and compassion.

Lisa has studied the Middle Ages since she was quite young. She has trained in medieval swordfighting for several years. She studied medieval dance and music with the SCA. She has been to England numerous times and loves exploring old castles and churches.

Please visit Lisa at LisaShea.com to learn more about her background and interests. Feedback is always appreciated!

As a special treat, as a warm thank-you for reading this book and supporting the cause of battered women, here's a sneak peek at the first chapter of *Sworn Loyalty*.

Sworn Loyalty Chapter 1

England,1197

It is not death that a man should fear,
But he should fear never beginning to live.
-- Marcus Aurelius

Mary paused for a long moment before the pockmarked door of the Mangy Cur Tavern. Raucous shouts and harsh laughter made the dilapidated building shudder as if it were groaning in pain. She glanced around in the deepening twilight, her breath puffing crystalline in the biting air. There were no other travelers visible as the meager dirt road twisted into gloomy forest on either side. It was as if this one isolated clearing, with its scum-coated pond, shuttered tavern, and tumbled-down stables, was all that existed in the world.

She took in a deep breath, let it out, then pushed open the door.

A rough cheer of welcome rang in her ears, and it took all her willpower not to tug up on the low-cut bodice of her scarlet dress. She drew her worn tambourine from her hip with a gloved hand and waved it high overhead, sending a shimmer of sound into the crowd. The room was layered with dense, fragrant wood smoke. On all sides burly, scarred men sprawled at tables cluttered with half-empty mugs.

A stumpy, dark-haired man stood at the back of the tavern, his eyes sharp on her. "I knew you'd be back!" he crowed with satisfaction. "Barkeep, a mead for our songbird."

A path cleared for Mary. Her emotions roiled as she approached the stocky man. She was well aware that Caradoc's marked attentions afforded her protection from the rest of the gang. At the same time, the *wolf's head* was dangerous. He had well earned his outlaw status, the designation that he could be slain on sight like a rabid dog. His keen knife had found its way into countless backs throughout the county. His fiery temper could turn on the point of a pin. If she were to survive the next few weeks, and accomplish her mission, she would have to walk a delicate line.

The grimy stool at his side was vacated by one of his many bull-sized henchmen. She took it with a wave of her tambourine, then nodded gratefully to the flame-haired bartender who handed over a mug.

Caradoc thunked his substantial weight back down onto his own stool, then glared at the two other men at the table. "I told you she'd return, so pay up. Even though you're my brothers, you'll hand over what you owe."

Espan and Arbert were cut from the same cloth as their older brother – stocky, dark-haired, sporting heavy brows over brutish faces. They might have been twins, but for the twisted nose Arbert featured and the pair of hairy moles on Espan's left cheek. The men reluctantly dug into the leather pouches at their sides, handing over the coins to the delighted winner.

Mary took a long drink of her mead, her eyes scanning the rough crowd in the guttering torchlight. How long had she been out on her task? Three weeks? Four? The days and nights were running together in one endless, grime-smeared blur. She longed for the solid walls of her keep, the strict but predictable routine she had followed since she was eleven.

She gave a sharp shake of her head. She had known, all those years, that her privileged lifestyle came with an unshakable obligation. She was honor-bound to serve as guardian angel for Erik, whether he wanted it or not; whether he even knew of it or not.

From all reports it seemed she'd finally be able to fulfill her duty.

Caradoc's spittle spewed across the deeply veined table as he laughed, tucking the last coin into the bulging pouch at his side. He drew down a long pull on his ale, then turned to smile at Mary. "They said you might have gone south, to London," he growled, "but I knew better." His eyes took on a crafty look.

"You know, if you joined our band, you wouldn't have to go from tavern to tavern to keep your tips fresh. I could take care of *all* your needs."

Mary forced her smile to stay bright. "I like to be my own master," she stated, holding his gaze. "Just like you. I am sure you understand."

His eyes grew smoky. "Indeed I do," he murmured, leaning forward. "Kindred spirits."

Mary downed the rest of her mead, grabbed up her tambourine with her left hand, and gave it a shimmering rattle as she stood. It had the desired effect – Caradoc sat back, a pleased smile spreading on his lips. The room's roar eased off as well, and a circle of attentive eyes focused on her. She felt uncomfortably like a doe in the center of a pack of wolves, and the image wasn't far off from the truth. Nearly every man here was a member of Caradoc's band; they would follow him without question. She could only hope that the news from her contacts was wrong, that Erik was not being drawn in as a sacrifice to this bloodthirsty crew.

The front door creaked open, and Mary's blood ran cold.

She had only seen Erik in person that one time, a full decade ago, but there was no mistaking the man who stepped across the threshold. He was tall, lean, with short-cropped blond hair and the controlled grace of a stalking panther. He wore a chestnut-colored leather jerkin over matching leggings, and a long sword hung at his hip. She knew through personal experience what the rigorous training regimen at the keep entailed. Michael, the Master at Arms, still spoke of Erik's skill at every turn. Erik's exploits in the Holy Land in the intervening years were nothing short of legendary.

Erik's eyes swept around the room, judging, calculating, and she held in a flinch as his gaze momentarily connected with hers. She needn't have bothered – he was scanning for dangers, nothing more. There was no way for him to connect the lithe, raven-haired gypsy woman in this den of thieves with the young, shy girl he'd once met in a quiet farming village.

Satisfied, he turned, putting a hand behind him to draw in a stunning blonde woman in an elegant forest-green dress. This time Mary knew she did not quite hold back the tremor of anger which coursed through her, but it did not matter. All eyes were focused on the newcomer, on the long, curled ringlets of gold which cascaded down her back and the sensuous curve of her ruby-red lips.

Erik's voice was a low mutter, but in the silence of the tavern Mary had no trouble hearing every word. "Lynessa, are you sure you wish to take your rest here?"

The woman's eyes grew bright, almost predatory, and she nodded, taking a step forward. "Absolutely. My cook said they had the worst mead here she had ever tasted, and I have five pounds on a bet. I can't believe it's more disgusting than that hell-hole in Augustine, but there's only one way to be sure."

A rumbling growl circled around the edges of the room, and Erik's hand eased to the hilt of his sword. His mouth set into a thin line.

"Lynessa, I think –"

She took a step forward, giving a delicate sniff. "Although, judging by the odor here, perhaps my cook was right after all."

Mary shook herself free of the shock which had nearly frozen her. After so long, after the years of training and the weeks of waiting, it was still hard for her to accept just how mercenary Lynessa was, how ruthlessly she was willing to discard Erik now that he no longer served her purposes. Lynessa had even neatly arranged it so Caradoc and his men would be drawn into the chaos, and they themselves would be brought down.

Mary did not mind the latter one bit, but she absolutely had to prevent the former.

There was a movement at her side, and she glanced over. Caradoc rose menacingly to his feet, by all looks a dominant bull preparing to stomp an intruder into a bloody pulp.

She knew she had only seconds in which to act. Mary took a dancing step in front of Caradoc, whirling her tambourine up with a glint of shimmering gold, drawing all eyes to her. Lynessa blinked in astonishment, her mouth hanging open.

Mary's smile grew into an authentic grin. Lynessa hadn't planned for *this* in her intricate schemes and machinations.

Mary pitched her voice to be condescending but patient. "Oh, Lynessa, my dear, is this really the limit of your planning skills? I had hoped for something a little more elegant."

It was another moment before Lynessa was able to close her mouth and pull herself up in an affronted huff. "What in the world are you talking about?"

Mary gave a wave in the air with her tambourine hand, releasing a delicate trill of sound. "I was telling Caradoc just the other day that I'd seen the sheriff's men in the area. Now here you are, and you just happen to be stirring up trouble." She draped Erik with a dismissive glance. His fingers were wrapped around his sword hilt, his eyes carefully sweeping the antagonized group of men. "Let me guess," she continued. "You draw Caradoc's fine band of men into attacking your pet, and when they heroically defend their home, you send the sheriff and his team after them?"

Caradoc was at her side, his greasy hair nearly bristling with anger. His two brothers were close behind. "Maybe it's time we taught that damned Sheriff a lesson," he growled. "Starting with this whelp here."

The mood in the room crackled with energy, and Mary clung desperately to her path. If she could not divert the thieves now, Erik would be slain. All she had worked for would be lost.

Lost forever.

She pitched her voice low, low enough that Caradoc would think it meant for him alone, but she held her body pointed at Erik. She hoped with every ounce of her being that the man contained a shred of instinct for self-preservation.

"Dear Caradoc, you are no man's master," she insisted in a seductive purr. "Least of all that arrogant sheriff. Yes, you want to make them pay. But do it on your *own* terms, on your own schedule. Choose your own location." Her voice became husky.

"Create an epic tale which will ring in the great halls for centuries to come."

Caradoc's eyes lit up at that, and Mary warmed with the slightest kindle of hope. She had studied him carefully for weeks now, preparing for this eventuality, and her research might just pay off. If there was one thing Caradoc craved, it was to build a legacy for his name.

Caradoc puffed up his shoulders, tossing his hair back as he strode forward to stand before Erik. His head only came up to Erik's chin, but with his barrel chest and muscled hands … Mary held in a shiver. It would be an even enough contest just between those two, never mind the twenty rabid men who ringed them.

Caradoc's voice was the soft growl of a wolf. "*I am* the master here," he stated, "and I will not have our sanctuary disturbed by the likes of you. Go, and take that pale trollop along with you." Lynessa gave a soft cry of outrage, but bit it back when Caradoc's amber gleam swung around to pin her. After a moment Caradoc returned his gaze back to Erik. "Do not think this is the end," he warned, his voice deceptively quiet. "No matter where you hide, no matter who you hide behind, we are everywhere. We will find you, and we will have our fun. On our own terms. In a place of our own choosing."

Mary had no doubt that any other man would have been running for the door, pleading for his life, scampering from the palpable threat which pulsed in the smoky air. But Erik took his time, his eyes making a slow circuit of the men in the room, drawing around to –

His gaze settled on hers, and Mary gasped as if an electric shock had coursed through her. For so long there had only been that one painting over the keep's fireplace, the eyes dead and stagnant. But this Erik was vibrantly alive, full of passionate energy, and the corners of his eyes creased with dawning understanding. She was not sure what he thought he knew, but she prayed to God that he would turn and leave before all Hell broke loose.

He nodded, and then he was taking Lynessa by the arm, stepping back toward the door, and ushering her through. He gave one last look to the room before closing the door behind them.

Mary leapt into the center of the room, shimmering her tambourine in triumph, raising her voice high. "Caradoc!" she cried out, hoping with all her heart to distract the men, to give Erik the cover he needed to safely get away. "Caradoc!"

The cries were taken up on all sides, tankards of ale were raised in toasts, and at long last Mary's breaths came in full, even draws.

Caradoc's eyes glazed in fury. "When I find him, I will kill him myself," he vowed. "I will break every bone in his body!"

"I know you will," encouraged Mary, taking the mug of mead that the barkeep pressed into her hand. "But make sure he is brought to you unharmed! You want to savor every moment of his punishment for yourself."

Flames of delight blossomed in Caradoc's eyes, and he climbed onto a nearby table. The surface groaned under his weight, but held steady.

"You men!" he cried out to the roiling masses. "Tomorrow we will go out to hunt down this Erik. But I want to make it clear – he is MINE. He is to be brought to me without one scratch on him. And then we shall have an arena!"

Cries of delight and anticipation thundered around her, ringing in her ears. She hoped by all that was Holy that she could get to Erik before Caradoc's clan put into motion their plans for revenge.